A VOW OF WRATH AND RUIN

K.W. FOSTER

aethonbooks.com

A VOW OF WRATH AND RUIN
©2025 K.W. FOSTER

This book is protected under the copyright laws of the United States of America. No part of this publication may be reproduced, stored in a retrieval system, or transmitted, in any form or by any means, without the prior permission in writing of the publisher, nor be otherwise circulated in any form of binding or cover other than that in which it is published and without a similar condition including this condition being imposed on the subsequent purchaser. Any reproduction or unauthorized use of the material or artwork contained herein is prohibited without the express written permission of the authors.

Aethon Books supports the right to free expression and the value of copyright. The purpose of copyright is to encourage writers and artists to produce the creative works that enrich our culture.

The scanning, uploading, and distribution of this book without permission is a theft of the author's intellectual property. If you would like to use material from the book (other than for review purposes), please contact editor@aethonbooks.com. Thank you for your support of the author's rights.

Aethon Books
www.aethonbooks.com

Cover design: Steve Beaulieu; Print and eBook formatting: Kevin G. Summers.

Published by Aethon Books LLC.

Aethon Books is not responsible for websites (or their content) that are not owned by the publisher.

This book is a work of fiction. Names, characters, places, and incidents are the product of the author's imagination or are used fictitiously. Any resemblance to actual events, locales, or persons, living or dead is coincidental.

All rights reserved.

ALSO IN SERIES

A Curse of Breath and Blood

A Vow of Wrath and Ruin

Want to discuss our books with other readers and even the authors?

JOIN THE AETHON DISCORD!

AUTHOR'S NOTE

This book features depictions of abuse, addiction, and violence that are not suitable for readers under the age of 18. If you or a loved one is trying to escape a domestic violence situation, please call **1-800-799-7233** or text **BEGIN** to **88788**.

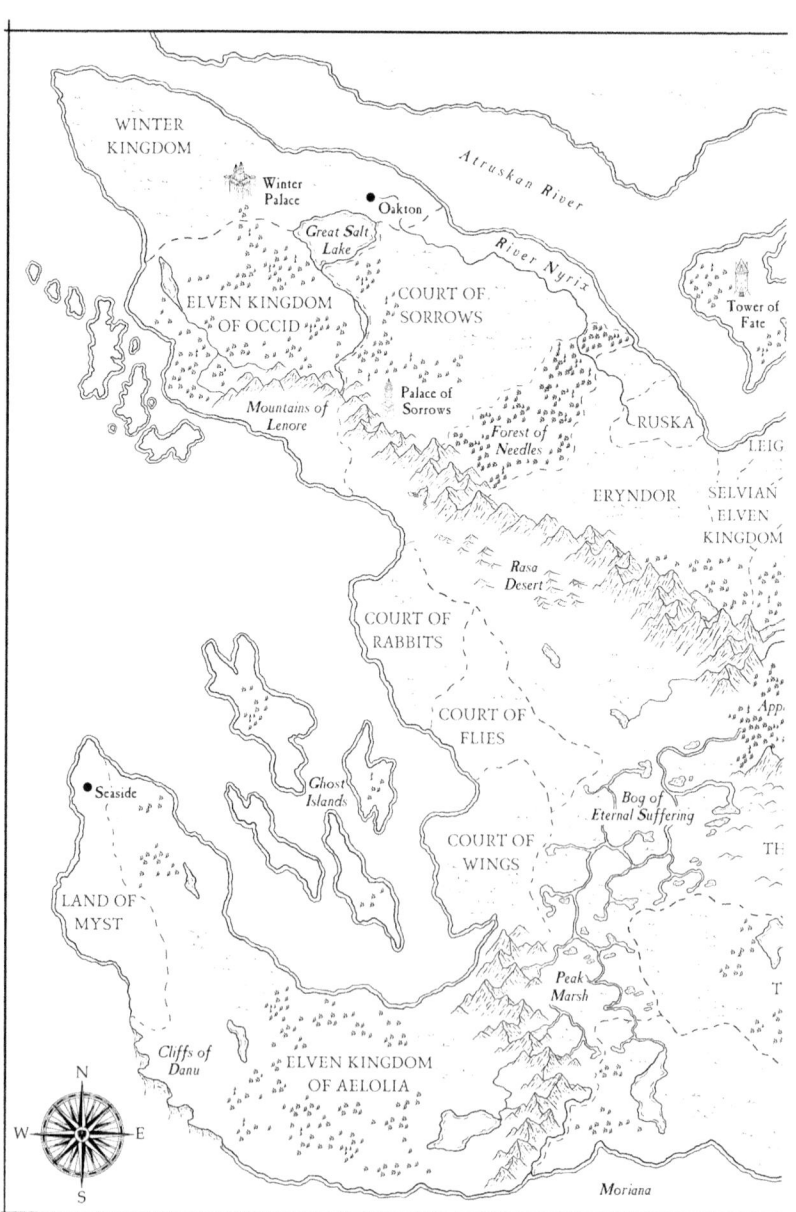

DEDICATION

To my son, James, who I wrote most of this book with, but who will never get to read it. Rest in peace, sweet angel.

A History of Moriana and the World of the Mind Breaker Series

Moriana is a diverse continent, home to many different races and cultures.

The Beginning

Before the Trinity culled the land and tamed the magic, the Gods of Old roamed freely, wreaking havoc. It was a brutal and bloody time. The people of Moriana called out for a hero, and they received three. Upon hearing their cries, the Trinity ascended from the heavens, smiting the Gods of Old and creating the three major races—the Elves, to which **Eris** gave her Breath and, with it, eternal life. They were meant to be the keepers of knowledge so that evil could not slink back into the world. **Illya** created the **Sylph** from her blood, instilling each of the founding families with a magical gift. The Sylph were created to protect the continent in case the evil ever arose again. With her golden apple, the goddess **Ammena** created the **Humans** to cultivate and care for the earth. She instilled in them a deep understanding of the importance of balance in nature and hoped that by making them mortal, they would value the time given to them.

War of Three Faces

Peace reigned over the land, but in secret, an orphan-turned-God was building a cult that would eventually consume the continent. His name was Crom Cruach. A half-elf, half-sylph magus (magic wielder) raised in a primitive sect of humans who feared magic. Once his magic was discovered, he was an outcast from the only family he'd ever known. Angry and alone, he made his way to the Rasa desert, where he unknowingly fulfilled an ancient prophecy of the Rasa Tribe. Made a living god, he used the Rasa to spread his influence by both diplomatic and violent means. When his powers had grown, as well as his influence, he left the desert, returning to his home in the mountains, where he took control of his old tribe and their fierce warriors. Crom used these warriors, combined with his political influence, to conquer the continent, wiping out all those who crossed him. Humans, Sylph, and Elves band together to fight Crom's influence, resulting in a brutal war that lasted a hundred years. In the end, Crom was defeated, and his followers fled the continent. Crom's body was burned and placed in an unmarked tomb. Only the Elven King, Arendir knows where he is entombed to this day.

Peace reigned once again, but many of the cities of the continent had been destroyed.

To celebrate their victory over Crom Cruach, the Elves invited the sylph and humans to a month-long victory celebration in the elven capital of Elohim. Jealous of the sylph's gifts and inherent strength, they hatched a plan to take their powers for their own. After the sylph leaders had been thoroughly plied with enchanted wine, the elves slipped into the sylph leaders' chambers, slit their wrists, and drank their blood, gaining the gifts Illya had instilled in them. But the effects were only temporary. Now that the elves had gotten a taste for The Blood, their lust for power was insatiable. Using these new gifts and gaining allies across the continent, the elves enslaved the sylph for nearly five hundred years.

The Sylph and Elven War

What started as a small rebellion grew into a full-blown war, raging for nearly fifty years and tearing the continent apart again. Most humans allied with the sylph, but some allied with the elves. Eventually, the Treaty of Three Kings was signed, freeing the sylph from their bondage. Torn between the old and new, the sylph split into two sets of Courts: The Wild, which upheld the old traditions, and the Council Courts, who considered themselves more civilized.

An uneasy peace has existed on the continent since.

RECAP
A CURSE OF BREATH AND BLOOD

AELIA SPRINGBORN IS A QUEEN ON THE RUN. HIDING FROM HER abusive husband, King Gideon, she uses her telepathic powers as a mercenary for hire. While in hiding, her ex-lover and Sylph lord, Caiden Stormweaver, tracks her down to tell her that Gideon has kidnapped her sister, Baylis, intending to trade her to the Alder King for the use of his legendary army.

Caiden and Aelia are bound together by more than just a shared history. Years ago, Caiden made a promise sealed in blood to her mother: He would protect the Springborn sisters at all costs. Now, he must fulfill that oath. But in order to proceed with their mission, he makes a deal with Aelia: Once his oath is fulfilled, she will erase all the memories of their past from his mind.

They journey to the Court of Sorrows, where they plan to have Aelia plant an idea in Tharan Greenblade's mind—the charming bastard son of the Alder King. The plan goes smoothly until goblins attack the Court to steal the Scepter of the Dead and, with it, the power of the Morrigan and her army. Luckily, Caiden takes the scepter first, but Gideon saves the day and becomes a hero.

After they escape, Tharan invites them to the revelry in gratitude. Upon reaching the camp, Aelia discovers that Baylis has been working with Gideon all along. Heartbroken, Aelia believes Baylis has been brainwashed. Aelia and Caiden hatch a plan to intercept her at the revelry. Despite the ticking clock on their time together, Caiden and Aelia rekindle their love.

Meanwhile, Aelia finds the Scepter of the Dead. The Morrigan shows herself to Aelia and states only she who has been to the other side can control the Morrigan's troops. Aelia denies the Morrigan's request, as the inscription on the scepter states that to call on the dead, the user will have to forfeit their life force.

Gideon's army lays siege to the Woodland Realm at the Yule revelry. A battle ensues between Gideon and the attending kingdoms.

As the battle rages, Baylis kills the Alder King, who declares Tharan, his successor with his dying breath. Aelia knocks Baylis unconscious, but Gideon escapes.

When the dust settles, Aelia learns Baylis' soul is trapped in Erissa's amulet. To free her, they must spill her blood on the amulet. Forced to complete their agreement, Aelia erases Caiden's memory of their relationship. Aelia is heartbroken. Seeing Aelia's pain, Tharan offers to accompany her to the Highlands to save her sister and gather information on Gideon. It is here that Tharan confesses his feelings for Aelia. Although she, too, has feelings for Tharan---Aelia wants to take things slow and be friends for the time being.

Meanwhile, Caiden returns to the Sylph lands to beg the Sylph High Council to retaliate against the Highlands. The court elders do not believe him and instead send him on a fact-finding mission to the Highlands.

Tharan and Aelia sneak into Gideon's palace. Meanwhile, Caiden and his spymaster are on their own mission to collect evidence against Gideon for the Sylph Council.

While Aelia, Tharan, and Caiden are all separately looking for information, Erissa captures them and brings them to her laboratory, where it is revealed that she is the mastermind behind everything.

A fight ensues, and the gang barely makes it out alive, only to find them surrounded by the Highland army. In a last-ditch attempt to save herself and her friends, Aelia pricks her finger and releases the Army of the Dead upon Gideon's forces. However, Erissa and Gideon escape.

The gang goes their separate ways but agrees to meet up in the Woodland Realm afterward. Tharan helps Aelia heal from her battle wounds, only furthering her feelings for him.

When they return to the Woodland Realm, Caiden and his spymaster await them. Aelia laments the fact that she did not get the amulet needed to free her sister from the spell. It is then that Caiden reveals he grabbed the amulet during the battle.

Aelia rushes to her sister's bedside, drawing a drop of her blood and placing it on the amulet. At first, nothing happens, and Baylis remains asleep. Aelia begins to cry, fearing all is lost. When her tears touch the amulet, the spell is broken. Baylis wakes with no recollection of her time with Gideon and Erissa.

As the gang gathers around Baylis, Aelia takes stock of how her life has changed since Tharan came into it. Seeing the improvements, she decides to throw caution to the wind and give Tharan her heart.

The epilogue hints at a bigger plan between Baylis and Gideon.

PROLOGUE

Two figures cloaked in shadow stood in front of a roaring fire. Across the flames, a band of mercenaries waited for their assignment, arms folded across their chests, feet tapping the frozen snow impatiently.

Erissa paced back and forth; her silk robes dragged behind her. A hood covered her mangled face.

"You've been called here because you are the best at what you do—oathbreakers."

The mercenaries grumbled under their breath. Once fearsome warriors, they killed for their kings—won them vast territories only to turn against their masters. Now, they lived in the shadows, hunting those who needed to disappear.

"Get on with it, witch," one of the men grumbled, his dark hair knotted with thick pieces of fat—tall and broad-shouldered, with pale skin, piercing blue eyes, and fangs marking him as vampyr.

"I'm not a witch," Erissa snapped, pulling back her hood to reveal her half-melted face. Where once porcelain skin grew, now only bone and mangled flesh remained. The light of the fire caught on the bumpy skin, revealing her for the monster she was. "I'm a mage—a priestess of the highest order of Eris."

An audible gasp rippled through the mercs. Half beauty, half monster, they could not look away.

Replacing her hood, she crossed the gap between her and the vampyr. Summoning her power, her eyes turned a glowing white, and a mysterious wind swirled around the two. She lifted the massive man off the ground, clenching her fingers yet not touching him. The mercenary grasped at his neck, eyes going wide as the air slowly drained from his lungs.

"Speak to me that way again, and I will cut off your manhood and use it for my spells."

The man nodded frantically, and she lowered him back to the ground.

Rubbing his neck, he fell to his knees, chest heaving.

"Oh, don't act like you need air to breathe, vampyr. You'll be fine." Erissa wiped her slender hands on her wool cloak. "Now." She cleared her throat. "Here's the job. Whoever brings me one or all of these three originals, I will pay you their weight in gold."

The mercs' eyes glimmered with the thrill of the hunt.

Erissa passed around rough sketches of three figures. The mercs examined the parchment.

"And where will we find them?" one asked.

"One is the Alder King, the other is his lover, and the third is a prince of the Stormlands."

Half the mercs threw the sketches into the fire.

"The Alder King? You tryin' ta get us killed?" a slender woman with eyes like sapphires and skin the color of moonlit snow asked. "The Wild Hunt will string our teeth to make new breastplates. Nah, I love the thrill of the chase, but this is suicide." She turned and headed into the darkness. Many of the others followed until only two remained. One male, brawny with dark wavy hair and tanned skin. The other a woman with deep tan skin, a hooked nose, and bloodred hair.

Erissa clicked her tongue. "Of course, it would be a Barbarian and a Rasa to be the only two up to the challenge."

The mercenaries eyed one another, sizing up their competition.

The man growled.

"Kita. I should have known you'd be here."

"Always a pleasure, Alwin." She folded the parchment, placing it in the fire.

Alwin shook his head. "I can't wait to see the look on your face when I bring these bastards in."

"Alive," Erissa interrupted.

Both mercenaries nodded.

"You'll use this talisman to alert me when you have secured one or all of the targets." She handed each mercenary a silver talisman inscribed with ancient runes. "Do not alert me if you do not have the target secured. Is that clear?" Her words bit like the cold.

The mercs nodded again.

"Good. And be warned. These are not your average targets. They are cunning and powerful. More powerful than either of you could comprehend."

Gideon stepped out of the shadows. A glamour covering his charred skin.

"And there will be another woman with them. Fair of skin and hair—she is not to be harmed."

The mercenaries rolled their eyes but agreed.

"Go, and do not disappoint me," Erissa said, taking Gideon's hand and disappearing into a swirl of snow.

Silence fell over the secluded wood.

"What did we just get ourselves into, Kita?" Alwin asked, but Kita had already disappeared into the night.

1 AELIA

The winter sun shone off Tharan's wine-red hair, his eyes darted beneath closed lids. I studied the contours of his angular face, scar, and lush lips, letting my eyes trail down his neck to his bare chest, committing the sight to memory. How many mornings like this would we have? We returned from Ryft's Edge weeks ago, hanging by a thread. Gideon and Erissa were in the wind, and my sister was safe. I should be happy. I had the love of a good man, my family and friends were safe, and I had a home once more. My heart was full, and yet, could I trust this happiness?

The smell of coffee and baking bread wafted up from the kitchens below. Despite Tharan being crowned the Alder King, he still preferred his chambers to the king's. I pulled the blanket tight around myself and snuggled close to him, breathing in the scent of pine lingering on his skin—a muscled arm wrapped around my waist.

"You're up early," he said sleepily.

"I haven't slept since I was fifteen. No amount of valerian root is going to change that."

He ran a hand down my back, making my skin tingle.

Inching closer, I kissed his neck, pulling a quiet moan from his lips.

"Don't start something you can't finish, King Killer."

A smile tugged at the corners of my lips.

"I haven't killed any kings… yet."

He pushed himself on top of me, and I sucked in a breath. Spreading my legs, I let him fill the space between us.

"I won't let this go too far," he murmured, every word shivering hot in the shell of my ear. "I promised I'd show you I wasn't the playboy, but that doesn't mean we can't have some fun."

I let out a laugh.

"Well, it's not like we're virgins."

I ran a hand down his bare chest, feeling the hard muscle beneath his skin. I hadn't seen Tharan's golden tattoo since the night at the inn. Chalking it up to my medicated delusion, I didn't bring it up.

"I know, but I want it to be special."

I cupped his face in my hand.

"Every day is special with you."

For a moment, Tharan just stared at me, lips parted, cheeks glowing. His eyes did not leave mine.

I studied the flecks of gold in his one green eye.

"What?" I asked.

Pushing a piece of hair behind my ear, he dipped his head and ran his tongue up my neck before nibbling my lobe playfully. "Sometimes you just like to stare at a piece of art."

"Tharan…" I said, trying to hide my blush.

"I won't apologize for thinking you're beautiful." He leaned in and planted a kiss on my waiting lips.

Like two pieces of a puzzle, Tharan and I fit together. Our mouths were made for the other's. Soft and supple, he anticipated my needs before I did, slipping his tongue between my lips. A heat grew between us, a yearning begging to be released.

I sucked in a breath at the weight of his growing erection at the juncture of my thighs.

"I've dreamed of this," his sultry voice purred in my ear, making me wet.

His hand roamed to the fasteners of my nightgown. Gently undoing the buttons, he released my breasts. The cool morning air pricked my nipples. Since coming to the Alder Palace, I'd regained my womanly figure.

Tharan leaned down, taking one of my nipples into his mouth.

I let out a groan of pleasure as his tongue teased me.

His hand wandered over my stomach.

I arched my back at his touch.

Slipping his fingers through the loops in my panties, he yanked them off in one fluid motion before turning me onto my stomach.

I lifted my ass into the air. The anticipation of what was to come made me wet with need.

Tharan's fingers traced their way up my legs to where my needy cunt waited for him.

A knock at the door interrupted us.

Tharan growled, "We're busy."

"Your Majesty, I wouldn't normally interrupt, but…"

He sighed, rolling off the bed and wrapping a fur-lined robe around his chiseled body. Running a hand through his hair, he did his best to collect himself.

I pulled the blanket over my exposed body. Being born royal myself, I was accustomed to attendants seeing me in various states of undress, but it didn't mean I wanted them to see me in such a compromising position.

"Yes?" Tharan said, opening the door.

"The Phantom sent word this morning." The satyr slipped a piece of parchment through the crack before shutting the door tightly.

Tharan unfolded the beige note, knitting his brows in concern.

"What is it?" I asked, slipping on a robe of my own, reveling in the feeling of the soft fur against my naked skin.

Tharan slumped into the carved chair at his desk. "Gideon and Erissa have seemingly disappeared."

"Maybe they fled across the sea?" I cinched the belt around my waist before sliding into Tharan's lap.

"They want the Trinity Wells. Erissa is power-hungry. Gideon is her mouthpiece. They wouldn't leave the continent. They'll look for other original blood."

"We have to warn the others… Are there others?"

"I have been thinking I need to pay my grandfather a visit…" He rubbed his chin nervously. "And you should probably visit your mother."

My heart wrenched in my chest. "I know you're right, but I'm not sure I'm ready to face her. It has been so long."

Snuggling his head into my breasts, he said, "You're stronger than you ever were."

"Because I have you." I kissed his head, taking in his distinct scent of pine and clove.

He squeezed me tight. "And you always will."

A breeze blew in through the open window, pebbling my skin with goosebumps. Spring would not come for ages. Snow still covered the burnt remains where the fire tore through the forest. Despite the cold, I loved winter—loved the snow, the solace, the feel of the frigid air burning in my lungs when outdoors. Summer meant sweat and bugs, but winter—things healed in winter. Maybe I would heal, too.

"Let's have breakfast and then discuss our plan of action with others."

"Fine," he huffed. "But first, let's finish what we started."

He lifted me off his lap and got to his feet, then set me back in the chair. Kneeling, he slid down between my legs, his lips gently caressing the inside of my thighs.

A fire roared through my veins. I lay back, gripping the chair's arm with one hand and softly playing with my nipple with the other.

"Are you ready, my darling?" he purred. Just the sound of his voice made me slick with need.

I bit my lip, trying to keep my lust at bay.

A coy smile brightened his face as he stared up at me.

"Are you sure?" He thumbed my clit, bringing a moan to the back of my throat.

"Yes," I whimpered.

"Good." Tharan dug his teeth hard into my clit, stealing the breath from my chest. A groan grew deep in my core, begging to be released.

He slid his fingers inside me, first one, then two, thrusting back and forth while his mouth on my little bead sent shock waves through my body.

I cried out with pleasure, fingers fisting his silken hair.

Wrapping his arm around my bottom, he pulled me in closer. My nipples pricked, and wetness flooded the chair. I couldn't get away. I was his captive, and my body yearned for more.

Bucking my hips, I moved with the rhythm of his fingers.

Tharan pulled away, giving me a devilish smile. "You're so close. Are you going to come for me?"

I nodded, my breath heavy with the whimper of desire. My orgasm clawed at my senses. I stared down at Tharan, my eyes catching on my perked nipples. I hadn't felt this good in a long time. No guilt accompanied this pleasure. It was all mine and all his. I couldn't help but let out a moan, watching his fingers slip in and out of me. My wetness glistened on his stubbled chin, marking him as mine.

The sound of my slickness grew louder, and I groaned with

pleasure as his tongue replaced his fingers, driving deep into my core. I was a goddess, and he was my acolyte, worshiping me with every stroke of his tongue. My body quaked harder and harder. My toes curled, and my hand spasmed. An orgasm built inside of me, and I cried out, "Oh, Trinity!"

Tharan paused, kissing my thighs. "Not yet, my darling. You can't come yet."

"Tease," I gasped through ragged breaths.

Tharan rose to his feet. His erection protruded through his robe, throbbing with need.

"I want us to come together. I want to see you as you orgasm." Spitting on his hand, he stroked his girthy cock. "Touch yourself like you want me to touch you."

I gently rubbed my aching clit—soft at first, then harder and harder until the need became unbearable.

Tharan stroked himself feverishly. His eyes burned with passion.

I tried to focus on him, but my climax demanded to be released, ripping through me like lightning. I cried out loud and hot.

"Yes. Oh, Trinity, yes, Aelia." Tharan's orgasm shook the room. Magic filled the air, and the taste of metal fizzled on my tongue. He was the master of this land, and the land responded to his emotions. Teacups shattered on the floor as he spilled his seed onto my stomach, hot and sticky.

I stared at the ceiling, trying to collect myself. "Trinity. You're going to be the death of me."

"I thought you wanted to take it slow," he said, gasping for air.

"You're making it hard for me to do that, Tharan." I ran my hand through my hair, thankful for the cool breeze.

Tharan chuckled as he leaned forward, touching our foreheads together, skin flushed with heat.

"I love the way you say my name," he purred, pulling me for another kiss. "And I'll love it even more the day I hear you scream it."

I bathed in eucalyptus and spearmint, washing the scent of the morning's activities away with their fragrant leaves. Since showing Tharan my scars, I had not replaced the earring, preferring to wear them as a badge of honor rather than hide behind a glamour.

Pulse still racing, I sunk low in the tub. Tharan was everything I dreamed of and more, but still, my heart ached a little thinking of how we met. I could never tell him about the night I dipped into his mind and planted the seed, leading us here. Truth be told, part of me wondered if he only loved me because I fiddled around in his mind. Then again, he was the Alder King; he knew of my powers and hadn't questioned my affection.

The sting of losing Caiden still bit at my heart. Seeing him in Ryft's Edge and then again in the palace when we returned ripped my healing wounds anew. I thought I'd have more time to forget him, and frankly, I hoped never to see him again—another test from the Trinity.

The water chilled, and my stomach grumbled with hunger, reminding me I now had duties beyond lounging about all day. Being the Hand of the King meant an onslaught of daily meetings on everything from military restocking to rebuilding what the fire took to foreign alliances.

Pulling myself from the water, my skin glistened in the bright morning light reflecting off the fresh snow. Despite recently using my life force to call upon the Morrigan's army, I felt normal, invigorated even. I braided my hair into loose pleats, donned a simple wool gown, and headed to the morning room, where Tharan and his advisors took their breakfast.

Pale light streamed in through stained-glass windows, filling the room with colorful designs. Vines crept up the wood walls, reminding us we were in a living tree. A small fire burned in the hearth, heating the room. Tharan sat at the head of a long table; hair pulled back with a leather tie. He thumbed through the daily reports. A cup of coffee steamed beside him. He smiled at me, and my heart skipped a beat. "Good morning, Aelia," he said as if we hadn't spent the morning wrapped around one another.

"Good morning, your Highness." I took a seat to his right. The smell of fresh coffee and crispy bacon filled the room.

Across from me, Sumac, Tharan's best friend and leader of the Wild Hunt sat, feasting on porridge and looking through her own morning reports. She wore a high-necked sweater the color of the forest after a rain, complementing her verdant eyes. Next to her sat Hopper, a green-skinned sylph with high cheekbones and gaunt features. His shoulder-length hair was tied back behind his ears. Hopper, Sumac, and Tharan grew up together, and when Tharan became king, they became heads of their respective units—Hopper, the diplomat, and Sumac, the head of the Wild Hunt.

Around the table sat the Master of Coin, Master of Forestry, and Master of Culture. I had no idea where the other advisors were, but it was nice to be in a small group. Savoring the momentary respite from sharing Tharan with his entire kingdom, I ran the tip of my slipper up his leg.

Beneath the table, Tharan's hand found my knee, and with a little squeeze, he let me know he was thinking of me.

"Where is everyone this morning?" he asked, taking a sip of his coffee.

A satyr set a pile of parchment in front of me. I huffed, reaching around it to fill my plate with bacon and eggs. Once satiated, I glanced at the stack while munching on a piece of bacon.

"It looks like half of your advisors are busy running your kingdom."

"I guess that's a good thing," Tharan said, turning to Wren, the Master of Forestry. "How is the forest healing?"

The sylph woman who smelled of lilac and elderberry and whose hair matched, lifted her head from her work, purple eyes sparkling in the soft light. Her pale skin reminded me of Lucius's. "Healing takes a long time, my King, but it is mending at a tremendous rate. Thanks to the renewed magic that comes with crowning a new Alder King."

"Very good." He turned to the Master of Coin. An elderly sylph with a long black beard and a shaved head. "And how about our finances?"

The man cleared his throat, and the teacup in his hand shook uncontrollably, an unfortunate side effect of extended life. Even Illya's gift could not stop the body from fraying. "We have enough coin to fund a war, should we need to."

"Let's hope we do not, but try to fill our coffers as much as possible. With the way things are going, we never know when we might need it." The elder nodded, and Tharan leaned back in his chair, muscles pushing through the thin linen of his shirt, and I wished the room was empty so I could throw my legs over him and finish what we'd started this morning. My pussy yearned to feel the girth of his cock inside me. Even now, my muscles clenched as I imagined him thrusting deeper and deeper.

"Any word from my sister, Hopper?" Tharan asked.

Hopper's mouth flattened into a straight line.

"No. We have not heard from her. I suspect she went to live with her mother's people in the ghost isles."

"I will send word to the Ghost Lord."

Seeing Tharan rule over his kingdom, with his power shown through his relaxed shoulders radiating casual confidence, filled me with want. My thoughts drifted to the vision of him between my legs, and my mouth went dry with desire.

"There's something else." Hopper patted his mouth with a napkin. "The Court of Sorrows needs a new ruler. Nysemia had no heir, and with most of her court dead, it is up to you to choose who will rule."

Tharan rubbed his jaw in thought, and I couldn't help but think of earlier when he smiled at me from between my legs, face covered in my wetness.

"Who do you suggest? I would give it to my sister if I can find her."

Hopper nodded.

"That would be wise, but she will need a husband."

A sigh escaped Tharan's lips.

"I suppose I'll have to make that match as well."

"Indeed, my King."

"Alright. Let's find my sister, and then we'll find her a worthy suitor."

"Very good, my Lord. I will work on finding her right away. In the meantime, I suggest sending one of your diplomats to run the Court of Sorrows. Perhaps my second, Mythra?"

"Very well," Tharan sighed.

Hopper nodded before grabbing a doughnut from the assortment of sweet treats adorning the table.

Tharan turned to me, a gleam in his eyes. "And what about my Hand? Do you have anything to report?"

His fingers mindlessly flipped through the papers in front of him, and I couldn't help but imagine the way they slid in and out of me earlier in the morning, glistening with my arousal. A quake ran through my core, and I crossed my legs to keep from feeling anything else.

"Aelia?" Tharan asked.

I snapped out of my fantasy, sitting up straight in my chair. "Um, yes."

Tharan gave me a devilish wink.

I shuffled through the papers in front of me, hiding my flaming blush. I couldn't read a word on them—too busy shoving the image of Tharan's head between my legs out of my mind—but they bought me time to gather my thoughts.

"It seems there's been some cases of root rot in the south. They're requesting a healer."

"Send one. Send two. What else?"

I shuffled through the correspondence. My heart leapt into my throat at the sight of an indigo-hued letter adorned with the silver seal of the Court of Storms: Lightning striking a tree.

"You have a letter from the Court of Storms." I slid my fingernail under the seal, cracking it in two. Scanning the contents, I let out a sigh of relief. "It's a letter of thanks for your support."

Hopper swallowed his mouthful of food.

"Ha! Looks as though we've got ourselves an ally."

Tharan's hand found mine underneath the table. The feeling of his soft skin on mine sent shock waves through my veins.

"It is all thanks to Aelia."

"Yes." Hopper excused himself as did the Masters of Coin and Culture.

"Our ranks are not what they need to be to handle a full-scale war. I'll need your help to make more Hunters," Sumac said.

I knitted my brow, my chest tightening.

"What does that entail?"

Tharan squeezed my hand.

"It is a ceremony. I will have to pull them from a sacred tree deep in the forest. It has not been done for an age."

My eyes flitted between Sumac and Tharan.

"But isn't Sumac part of the Hunt?"

"She is. Sumac is one of the very few Hunters who were born naturally. It's rare, but it does happen. Sylph mature around the age of fifty. That's when her abilities became visible. She had a natural talent for battle that only a member of the Hunt could possess."

Sumac's cheeks flushed.

"It is an honor to serve alongside such fearsome warriors."

Tharan sighed, leaning back in his chair.

"Have the priestesses prepare for the ceremony and make sure Elrida is able to travel."

Sumac nodded, pushing herself away from the table.

The room quieted.

Tharan leaned in close, whispering in my ear, "Finally. I've been thinking about you since we parted ways this morning."

I pushed a stray hair behind my ear. "I thought we were going to be professional while in public."

Hooking his hand under my chair, he pulled me close. The sound of wood scraping against wood screeched through the room.

"It's just us now," he said, kissing my neck, sending my pulse racing.

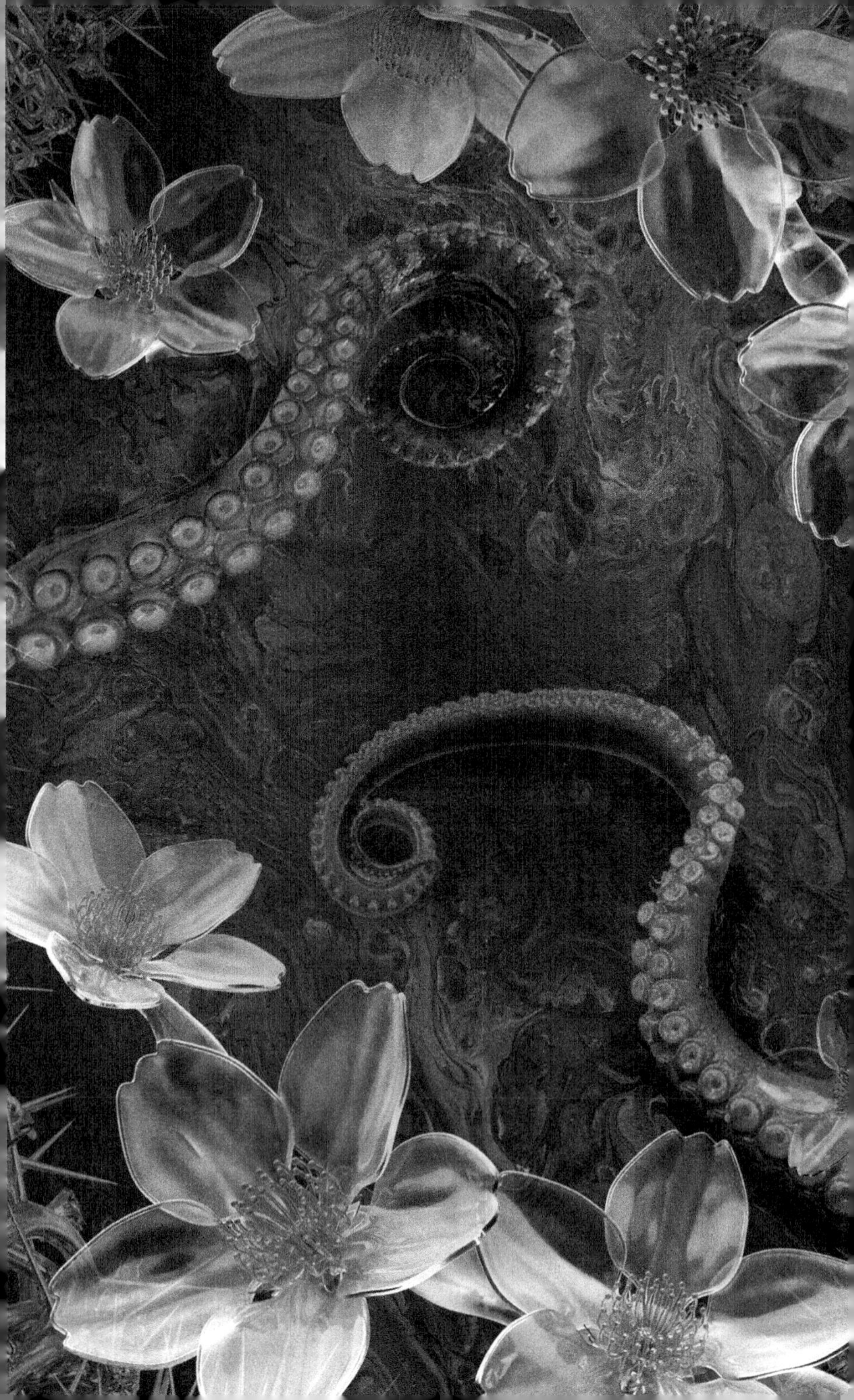

2 AELIA

AFTER BREAKFAST, I WENT TO FIND MY SISTER. BAYLIS HAD BEEN working with the Alder Palace healers to remember her time with Gideon. So far, they'd been unsuccessful in retrieving any of her memories.

Pushing the door to her room open, I found her and Amolie reading in front of a roaring fire. A plate of baked goods and steaming coffee sat on the table in front of them.

"Aelia!" Shutting her book, my sister crossed the room, embracing me in a hug. I squeezed her tight, treasuring the moment. We'd both been through so much in the past five years. Where do you even begin to heal with that kind of distance between two people?

"How are you feeling?" I examined her thoroughly; sure I'd find some mark from Gideon I'd missed. My eyes raked over her slender frame, and I gently turned her palms up, anticipating the discovery of some missed brand or healing bruise. What was her dress hiding? Surely there must be something. There can't be *nothing*, because if Gideon was good to her… actually good to her when he couldn't muster a morsel of affection for me—then all my self-doubt would be true. I am the unlovable one. I am the problem, and all those degrading things he said about me were true.

"I'm fine." She waved me off with a little chuckle, but I didn't trust it. How could she be fine when I knew what Gideon did to women? When I experienced first-hand the cruelty lingering under his handsome facade? I bit the inside of my lip to keep from saying something. I wanted Baylis to trust me enough to confide in me. We were starting from scratch.

"Never better, actually." She brushed her hands on her skirt nervously. "Just enjoying a morning with Amolie."

I wanted to dip into her mind to see if she was hiding anything in there, but that could set off alarms I wasn't ready to face. I needed her to trust me enough to let me in.

"Yes, won't you join us?" Amolie said, motioning for me to sit next to her on the little leather sofa.

"We have a meeting with the king. I just came to check on Baylis before heading up."

"Can I come?" Baylis asked, her delicate face bright with hope.

I didn't want to tell her that she was still being watched closely. As much as I loved my sister, there was no telling what kind of tracking spell Erissa and Gideon put on her. I couldn't risk the safety of an entire kingdom for her comfort. So, I dined with her in the evenings and made sure she had company at all times. I waited so long to find my sister, and now that I had her back, it was bittersweet. I wanted to ask her a million questions about Gideon, but I was afraid of the answers. Why had he been good to her but not me? A sour taste filled my mouth.

I swallowed my resentment.

"Sorry, not today. Official business. We can go riding later."

"Fine," she huffed, returning to her book.

Once a safe distance away, Amolie said, "You're going to

have to go into her mind and see if you can find any helpful memories."

I bit the inside of my cheek again.

"I don't want to do that. I don't want to ever dig into someone's mind ever again unless I have to. And I definitely don't want to have to go into my own sister's. The guilt I carry for all those years of mercenary work weighs heavily on me."

"I know, Aelia, but I'm not getting anywhere with her. The healers say she screams in her sleep." Amolie scanned the corridor for prying eyes. "Either she's hiding something, or it's buried so deep inside her mind we may never find it."

"I know. I want to believe her. I want to believe my sister is just a victim of circumstance, but I know Gideon and Erissa. Either they kept her in the dark of their plans…" My words caught in my throat.

"Or she *was* their plan?" Amolie said.

I sighed. "Right. I don't want to dig around in her mind yet. I'm not prepared for what I might find." Even just thinking about it made my skin prickle with disgust.

"We may not have a choice, Aelia."

"I know." I pushed the door open to Tharan's study, where Caiden, Lucius, Hopper, and Sumac waited.

Tharan took a drag off a cigarette, extinguishing it in an ashtray.

Frost and Winter ran to greet us, whining with excitement, claws scraping against the hardwood floor.

I bent down, rubbing each behind the ears. "Good girls."

"It's about time. We don't have all day," Lucius said, annoyed.

I stole a cigarette from the ornate box on Tharan's desk and lit it, letting the smoke fill my lungs. "We're here now. Let's get to it."

Lucius rolled his eyes. Some things never changed.

The room smelled of tobacco and clove. A fire roared in the massive hearth. Above it, the head of an elk guarded the study.

I propped myself on his massive desk while the others took seats around the room. I tried my best not to look at Caiden. I couldn't bear to see the man I'd loved for a decade.

Tharan lit another cigarette.

"The people in this room are the only ones on the continent who know what really happened in Ryft's Edge." He exhaled a plume of smoke into the air. "Gideon and Erissa are likely licking their wounds, biding their time until they come back to hit us harder. I have my best spy out looking for them, but they haven't turned up any leads yet. I think our best bet is to find the Trinity Wells before they do."

"And what exactly are we supposed to do when we find them?" Caiden asked, fiddling with the ring on his finger.

Tharan took another drag.

"Extract the magic and spread it throughout the land evenly. That way, no one can control it all."

"That's actually… a decent proposal," Lucius said, leaning against a bookshelf and looking out the window.

"I thought so." Tharan gave a little chuckle, pleased with himself. "So, here's what I'm proposing. I will go and see my grandfather in Elohim. Aelia and Baylis will go and speak with their mother in the Tower of Fate, and Caiden, if you wouldn't mind searching the library of Vantris."

Caiden nodded. His golden hair catching the light of the fire reminded me of the nights we spent together in the secluded atrium of the River House. I pushed away the memory, throat going dry, heart aching.

"We need to talk to the Morrigan. She knew Erissa back when the world was young," Tharan said.

Reluctantly, I pulled the scepter from its mahogany box on his desk. Running my fingers over the carved ruins, power radiated through my veins, up from my belly, and into my throat.

"Morrigan, show yourself."

White smoke poured from the bird's mouth, taking the shape of the warrior maiden. It slowly turned from translucent to opaque until the woman came into view.

"Hello, Master, how can I be of service?" She bowed to me.

"I told you not to call me that."

"What else should I call you? You *are* my master."

I crossed my arms over my chest. "You may call me Commander. I command your army."

"*Your* army now."

"We have some questions for you, Morrigan," Tharan interrupted.

The Morrigan batted her long lashes at him. "Yes, your Highness?"

I clenched my jaw, trying to keep my composure.

Tharan laid a reassuring hand on mine.

"What can you tell us about the Trinity Wells?"

She scoffed, stalking around the room, taking in the sights. Her periwinkle eyes widened when they fell upon Caiden.

"Trinity Wells?" She laughed, taking a seat next to him. "Those are a myth—an old wives' tale. Crom Cruach was obsessed with finding them, convinced he could harness the power within and call the deities down from their heavenly sanctuaries—to smite them for what they did to the land."

"You mean when they culled the old gods?" I asked through gritted teeth.

The Morrigan twisted her finger through one of Caiden's golden curls, ignoring my question. "Aren't you delicious? I haven't seen someone like you in an age."

"Stay on topic, Morrigan, and leave my guest alone," Tharan warned.

She pouted her bottom lip.

"I have been cooped up for thousands of years. Just the scent of a man is enough to drive me wild." She inhaled the secondhand smoke in the room then blew smoke rings shaped like hearts at Caiden.

He stiffened and waved the smoke out of his face, giving the Morrigan an uncomfortable, half-hearted smile.

I tightened my grip on the desk.

She continued, "When the Trinity came and culled the land, they were brutal in their retribution. Old gods like me either bent the knee, were banished to another realm, or killed—as much as a god can be. Those who chose the latter built resentment toward the Trinity and those they created. For thousands of years, they have bided their time, hiding deep in the underworld, plotting their revenge.

"That mage, Erissa? She was one of Crom's first followers. A zealot of the highest order. That was why the elven mages kicked her from their ranks. But elves, like gods, cannot die. So, she, too, has been biding her time, I suspect. Acting like a good little mage to the Ironhearts, rebuilding her power, waiting for the world to weaken again. Crom hated the Trinity and wanted to use their power against them. That's why he was looking for the Wells. I assume Erissa has been searching for them since he died. She loved him and likely thinks she can bring him back with the Wells power." She shuddered at the thought.

Caiden placed a reassuring hand on hers.

"Did Crom find any of the Trinty Wells?"

I gritted my teeth trying not to focus on their hands touching.

"We're all sitting here, aren't we?" A smug little grin tugged at the corners of her lips.

Caiden nodded.

The Morrigan's eyes flitted around the room. "No—you're not thinking about going after the Wells…"

"That's exactly what we're thinking of doing, unless you have a better idea." Tharan straightened to his full height, all of his power on display for the room to see.

"It's suicide. Even if you find them and somehow unlock them, the Wells will kill you. They don't want to be found."

"So, they *do* exist?" Caiden asked.

Crossing her arms over her chest, she sunk into the couch.

"I said, I don't know. And I don't. But if they did exist, it'd be suicide to try and find them. The Trinity designed them never to be found."

"Okay, thank you. It's time for you to go back into your scepter," I said, picking up the bone.

She winced, holding up her hands.

Caiden swiftly tucked his hands into his pockets, and I caught his eyes darting to mine before falling to the floor.

"No, I can help. Please don't send me back there yet."

"Oh?"

"Let me go between this world and the one beyond. I can help you and report back what the spirits are saying."

I took a puff of my cigarette, letting the smoke calm the jealousy pooling in my gut at the memory of her hand on Caiden's.

"How do I know you're not going to snitch to the other side?"

She rose and crossed the room in an instant. Our faces nearly touched. I could count the faint freckles on her pale skin. Fire danced in her pale blue eyes, then quickly dulled.

"I am bound to serve you." She fell to her knees, bowing her head low at my feet. "I have waited for a millennium to be freed. The Trinity Wells could be my ticket to freedom."

I tapped my foot on the floor.

"And a way for me to survive using the scepter," I said, my words dripping with condescension.

Even now, I could feel the magic tugging at the very fabric of my being.

"Rise, Morrigan. I will keep you around for now."

"Thank you." Grabbing my free hand, she laid a kiss onto my ring finger, as if I were a king of old.

Stunned, I yanked my hand back. Her ghostly lips sent a chill up my spine. I didn't trust the Morrigan. She was out for herself, and no amount of ring kissing could convince me otherwise.

"Well, now that we have that settled." Tharan took a drag from his cigarette. "I propose we all meet back here for Ostara to go over what we have found."

"And hopefully have a true spring celebration," Sumac said, flipping her dark hair to one side.

"And maybe something more," Tharan whispered into my ear as he ran a finger down my back, sending my heart into my throat.

I swallowed hard, unsure if I was ready for what came next in our relationship. Was he proposing a binding ceremony? That would be a huge commitment on my part.

I loved Tharan… at least I thought I did, more than I'd ever loved anyone before. When we were together, I could breathe easier. My nightmares ceased. But something held me back from fully giving myself to him—past wounds bubbled to the surface. If I were being honest with myself, I wasn't sure I deserved Tharan.

My eyes fell upon Caiden, who gave me a coy smile and cracked my heart a little more. We shared so much together. A history of happiness buried beneath a mountain of pain and hurt. Was it worth digging up? No—it needed to stay buried. I couldn't go back to the person I was before. Caiden and Gideon were intrinsically linked in my mind. I couldn't heal with Caiden in my life. As much as it pained me, I had to cut the cord between us. I swallowed a sob growing in my throat. Gideon hadn't just erased who I was, he'd taken everyone I'd ever loved from me. My mother, my sister, and Caiden.

I turned to Tharan who gave me a wink. Pressure built behind my eyes. How could I even think about Caiden when I had the perfect man standing in front of me? What was wrong with me? I deserved this. I deserved to be happy.

Reaching out my power, I tapped on Tharan's mind.

'Yes?'

I sent an image of him in between my legs early in the morning and promptly turned my gaze elsewhere.

'Naughty girl. You'll be punished for thinking such things during an official meeting.'

Promise?

'Get back to work.'

I didn't have to look at him to know he was fighting a grin. The guilt weighing on my conscience eased a little bit. I wanted Tharan to know how I felt about him. He was my priority now… my everything.

Caiden stood, clicking his heels together like the soldier he was. "I will get to work on my part. Lucius, have your shadows see what they can find out about the whereabouts of Gideon and Erissa."

Lucius nodded, pushing himself from where he leaned on the bookshelf, long white hair draped over his left shoulder, high cheekbones shadowed gaunt cheeks. "As if I didn't have them searching already."

"Very well, then, we will see you on Ostara." Caiden crossed the gap between us.

I straightened as he moved closer. I was a royal Hand now, not some lovesick teenager. I snuffed out the cigarette, swallowing hard.

Caiden reached for my right hand, and I found myself instinctively raising it to him. His lips gently grazed the thin skin on my hand. The contrast between his warm lips and the Morrigan's cold ghostly ones was a welcome relief.

A memory flashed through my mind: all the times we played coy when we were younger, hiding our affection for one another in plain sight. How many times had he kissed my hand before? I tapped the side of my nose like we used to when we were younger—A signal one of us needed saving. Not a hint of recognition flickered in his blue eyes. My heart sank a little. It was stupid of me to carry an ounce of hope.

"Thank you for saving us," he said, sapphire eyes locked on mine. "The Court of Storms owes you a great debt."

"It was nothing," I whispered.

He smirked. His dimples peeking through his cheeks. "It was much more than that."

I couldn't help my drying throat at the memory of what we used to be.

My eyes flitted to Tharan who stood stoically behind me, arms crossed over his chest. A muscle ticked in his jaw as he watched us.

I sheepishly tucked my hand into my pocket. I didn't want Tharan to see where another man's lips touched my skin.

"We leave in the morning," Lucius said. A warning lingered in his voice.

I turned to Amolie and asked, "Are you going with them?"

"I am. But I'll meet you at the Townhome in Ruska as soon as I can."

My heart ached at the thought of saying goodbye to my friends. These last few months, we'd grown closer than I could have imagined, and it pained me to see them go.

They filed out of the study, leaving just Tharan and me.

The winter sunset streaked the sky in dull pinks and oranges, gilding the room. Tharan leaned back in his chair, taking a long drag off his cigarette.

"I am not looking forward to seeing my grandfather," he admitted to the now empty room, closing his eyes as if he could avoid it by looking away. "The man who killed my mother for daring to love someone she shouldn't."

Smoke billowed into the air.

I moved closer, sliding into his lap, and gently stealing the cigarette from between his long fingers.

"I know what you mean. I haven't seen my mother in five years." A phantom pain radiated through my collarbone at the thought of coming face-to-face with the woman who kept her true identity a secret my whole life. I took a drag off the cigarette, savoring the taste of clove.

Tharan pulled me closer. His warm breath set my skin on fire.

"You know I would go with you if you wanted me to," he whispered into my ear.

I nuzzled my face into his neck.

"I know, but we do not have the luxury of time on our side."

"When this is all over, I am going to make you mine in front of the goddess so that our souls can bond for all eternity." His chest puffed as he held his breath.

"Tharan…" I said, voice trembling.

He cupped my face in his hands. "Yes?"

"I'm scared."

"Of what?"

"Of a million things. I'm afraid we'll be separated, and something will happen to one or both of us. I'm afraid I'll fail at being your queen. I'm afraid our marriage will ruffle feathers in the other courts and beyond. But mostly, I'm afraid I'm not good enough for you."

His gaze softened. "Oh, Aelia, how could you think that?"

How could I not?

A memory bubbled to the surface. *The first time I confronted Gideon about his infidelities.*

In my memories I imagined myself smaller than I was and Gideon as a massive figure towering over me. He held my wrists tight against a wall, the cold stone sent a chill down my spine. His brown eyes fixed on mine so I could not look away. He hated it when I looked away. He wanted me to feel his wrath and he wanted to see my pain.

"What would make you think you were worthy of someone like me?"

I winced, closing my eyes.

Releasing one of my arms, he gripped my chin.

A different version of me would've clocked him, but I was so broken, it wasn't worth the swift retribution that would ensue.

"Look at me."

Hesitantly, I opened my eyes.

"Don't forget I can get to you even when your eyes are closed. You are my pet now."

"Why?" I eked out. "Why can't you be good to me? I have been nothing but loyal to you."

A chuckle rippled through his shoulders. "The fact that you thought you'd ever be worthy of me is laughable."

I clenched my jaw, burying the hurt deep down. He wanted to see me cry. Each tear was a trophy to him.

"You are nothing, Aelia. I never loved you and I never will. I only married you because your kingdom is fertile… unlike you."

An invisible knife seared through my heart. It couldn't be true. He loved me once. I know he did. If only there was a way to make myself more lovable. I would be the perfect queen for him. Then he'd love me. I know he would.

"You're not even trying to love me."

Another condescending chuckle. "It's not like you make it easy."

My eyes drifted to the floor.

"Gideon burned it into me."

Tharan wiped away the tears I hadn't noticed rolling down my cheeks.

"You are everything I could have imagined in a partner. Every lover I took before was just a placeholder for you. I can't explain it... but when I'm with you... I just feel whole."

My chest tightened and then relaxed. Those were the words I'd always wanted to hear, yet there was still a part of me that didn't believe them. *Let yourself be loved, Aelia.*

"I feel the same way, and it scares me."

"We are not normal people, Aelia. We are the children of gods. Before I met you, my life was empty. I drifted from party to party, taking my fill of whatever lover presented themselves before me. But when I met you... I came alive."

I couldn't hide the smile tugging at the corners of my mouth. "I haven't had a single nightmare since we returned."

He stroked my hair gently, calming my racing heart.

"And I haven't either."

"Perhaps we are healing each other."

"I like to think so." He kissed my forehead, flooding my chest with warmth.

For a moment, I allowed myself to hope this is what our future would be. Heartache and violence replaced with soft caresses and mornings spent wrapped around each other in a bed I didn't have to rent. No fear, no weight pressing down on my chest, no more running, no darkened corridors filled with anguish. No, ours would be a simpler, kinder, life. One filled with sweet kisses in rooms warmed by stained-glass sunlight and scented with clove cigarettes and coffee.

A breath of relief slipped between my lips. For the first time in five years, I could imagine a future beyond the next mercenary contract. And maybe, someday, beyond Gideon.

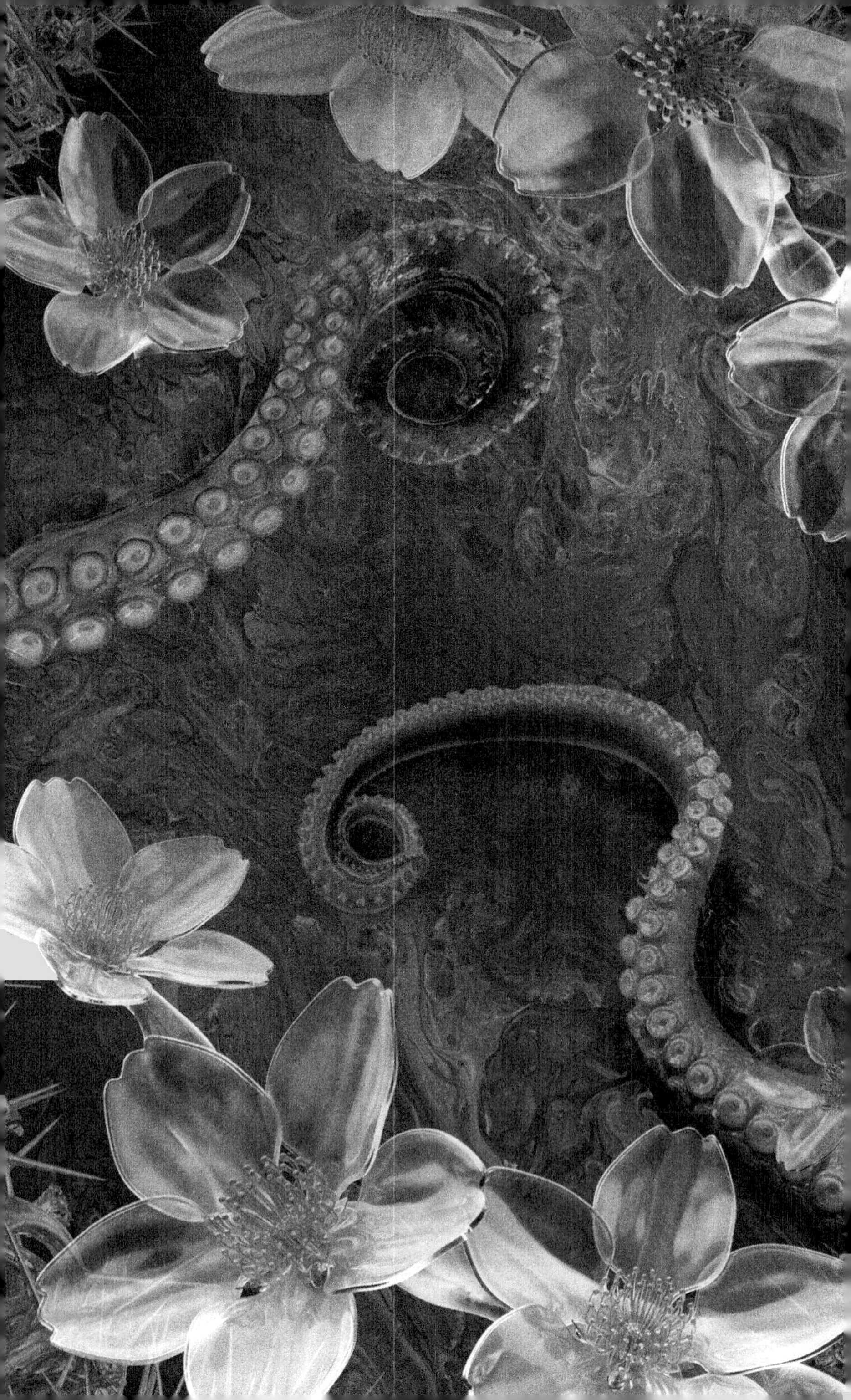

3 AELIA

I stood in the courtyard, letting the frigid winter wind whip my hair into knots. Gripping Amolie's hand, we waited for the sleigh to arrive to take my friends back to the Stormlands. Despite the cold, I chose not to wear gloves, preferring to feel the warmth of my friend's hand one last time.

"Be strong, Aelia. This is only the beginning of our quest. Your mother will be happy to see you."

A bitter taste filled my mouth. I kicked the gravel aimlessly. "Only time will tell what she is."

"No one has seen a Fate in hundreds of years. They are but a distant memory to most people." Amolie sighed. "I don't even know how we'll get to the tower. The Ferry hasn't run in a century."

"I'm going to do some research before we step foot anywhere near their island."

"Good idea."

The sound of sleigh bells echoed through the still morning air, followed by hoofbeats. Eight massive dapple-gray horses trotted over to us. The diamonds braided into their manes sparkled in the pale winter sun.

Amolie squeezed my hand then embraced me tightly.

"Be safe. I will see you soon," she said.

I breathed her in, committing the moment to memory.

"I'm going to miss you," I said.

"I'll miss you too."

The sleigh stopped, and the halfling driver jumped down to take Amolie's things. Caiden and Lucius appeared from behind us with Tharan in tow.

Lucius held out his hand.

Stunned, I shook it.

"You did good, Springborn."

I smirked.

"Dare I say you're warming up to me?"

"I wouldn't go that far. But I don't hate you the way I once did."

"I'll take it."

Lucius and Amolie hugged Baylis before saying their goodbyes to Tharan.

"I'm sorry we didn't get to spend more time together. I'd like to get to know you more," Caiden said, genuinely. His gloved hands wrapped tightly around one another. Hope flickered in his blue eyes.

The wind whipped an unruly piece of golden hair free from its binding, reminding me of the young emissary I met on balconies and kissed in alcoves.

You once knew everything about me.

"Perhaps at the Ostara festival," I replied.

Caiden's eyes flicked between me and Tharan. Clearing his throat, he said, "Yes, perhaps." He shook my hand, letting our fingers linger together for a moment before pulling away and hugging Baylis goodbye.

I couldn't look away from him, my traitor mind transfixed in place, memorizing every motion as he climbed into the sleigh.

Heart tearing in two directions, I fumbled behind me, clasping Tharan's waiting hand.

The coachman clicked his tongue, and with a flick of the wrist, the horses trotted on. A light snow began to fall. Snowflakes flitted aimlessly through the air. The sleigh disappeared into the forest.

My heart ached at the sight.

"You'll see them again." Tharan rubbed my arm reassuringly.

"I hope so." I leaned on him for support.

"I'm going to miss them," Baylis said. "Amolie is so sweet."

"Why don't we take a walk through the greenhouses, Baylis? You always loved gardening," I suggested, remembering her penchant for helping the farmers develop more hearty crops.

"Oh, that would be lovely," she said, pulling her fur-lined hood up over her ash-blonde hair, pale cheeks red from the cold.

I kissed Tharan on the cheek.

"I'll see you later."

He nodded and headed back inside. His wolves followed behind him, happily wagging their tails.

Baylis and I crossed the courtyard to where the greenhouses sat. Large glass structures filled with all manner of magical plants. Despite the chilly temperatures outside, a steady summer heat remained inside, thanks to the Alder magic. A sweet floral scent filled the air. The herbologists tended to the flora, barely noticing our presence. Plants of all shapes reached into the heavens. Vibrant colors splashed across massive leaves while sharp thorns clenched like jaws on others. Birds cawed from the rafters, and bees buzzed, spreading pollen throughout the atrium.

Baylis's eyes went wide.

"I thought you'd like it," I said, pleased I still knew my sister.

"I love it." She bent down to smell a bloodred rose. "Remember the garden I had at the River House?"

"I do."

"I loved that garden… and my dogs…" She swallowed a sob. "Oh, Trinity, Aelia. They're gone. It's all gone."

I helped her to a bench.

"Shhh, it's okay."

She buried her face in her hands.

"No, it's not. I'm missing so many memories. Caiden and you are my only tether to who I used to be." She lifted her head to face me, and a tear trickled down her cheek. "I don't know who I am or what I did while I was with Gideon."

My heart ached for my sister.

"I know everything you're going through right now. I was there once, too. But I promise it will get better. I will help you. I *can* help you…" It occurred to me Baylis had no idea of my powers or her own. So much needed to be explained. Caiden's indifference to me, my scars, her powers, our mother, but where to begin?

I breathed deeply, racking my brain for a way to tell her all the things I needed to say without overwhelming her more than she already was.

"How much do you remember from before you were with Gideon?"

Her gray eyes squinted, trying to pull the memories from her mind. "I remember you leaving—Father's death. The siege on Elyria, Caiden putting me on a horse and sending me into the wilds…"

"Do you remember how you came to be in Gideon's… company?"

Her expression darkened. She stared off into the distance, looking but not seeing.

"I was riding fast through the fog-filled lands to the south. Blood riders caught me." She winced. "I was their captive, but they had strict instructions not to harm me."

"And they took you to Gideon?"

"Yes, he was waiting for me in front of the castle in Ryft's Edge."

My throat thickened at the thought. Once, Gideon had waited for me in front of the castle with his endearing crooked smile plastered across his handsome face. I remember the way he took my hand, so confident and reassuring. The same hand that would be plastered across my mouth later as he whispered disgusting things into my ear. I shuddered at the thought, half embarrassed of how young and naive I had been, and half terrified of what torments he inflicted on Baylis. "And then what happened?"

Baylis stared into the distance, avoiding eye contact with me. Her legs crossed over one another. She picked a leaf from a nearby rosebush, gently pulling it through her fingers. Its jagged edge pierced her skin, drawing blood.

"Ouch." She sucked on her thumb for a moment. "They treated me to dinner, and then the next thing I remember, I was here... five years later."

"So, you really have no memory of your time with them at all?"

"No. It's as if I closed my eyes, and the next time I opened them, five years had passed."

My stomach dropped and I bit the inside of my cheek, dreading what I knew I had to do. "So you don't know about my —*gift*?"

She shook her head.

A sigh slipped between my lips.

"I have the power of telepathy. Gideon and I—we share the gift—an unbreakable bond, for we drank the same sylph's blood. It connected us... forever."

Her pale face contorted in shock, and her mouth fell open as her eyes raked over me, searching for a hint of the monster lurking within.

"Don't worry, I can only read your mind if you let me… or if I break in… and I don't plan on doing that."

She ran her thumb over her lower lip. Her brows knitted with concern as if she were putting puzzle pieces together in her mind.

"So, can you two communicate all the time?"

"No, only when we're close. Then there are no secrets between us. We can enter each other's minds freely unless one of us puts up a mental barrier."

"Why would you agree to do that? To bond yourself to someone like that?"

I swore I could hear a touch of disgust in her voice. The same disgust I'd heard in Gideon's voice a thousand times. Was it real or was I giving my sister attributes she didn't deserve. How would I feel if I were in her shoes? Was she judging me or just in shock? The sister I remember would not be so cruel.

I pinched the bridge of my nose.

"I didn't really have a choice. The blood was fed secretly to me at first, and then when I refused it…" I swallowed the lump growing in my throat. "It was forced upon me. That's also how I got these." I raised my upper lip, revealing a sharp incisor.

Baylis leaned in, examining me—looking for the invisible tether linking Gideon and me.

"Did it hurt?"

"It was torture—every minute of it. My powers were wild. I could hear every thought of every person in the palace. I thought I was going mad until Erissa told me of her little experiment." Bile rose in the back of my throat. Memories long buried bubbled to the surface. I breathed deeply, letting the specters of my past pass through me.

"I'm sorry, Aelia. I didn't—know. Once you left for Ryft's Edge… you were so distant. I thought you wanted to forget us. And I wouldn't have faulted you for that."

Pressure built behind my eyes.

"Forget you? You were—are my best friend. I risked my life to free you. And I'd do it again."

"Those were dark times, Aelia. We were all lost."

She moved closer, putting an arm around me like she had when we were children. That was the Baylis I knew. The caring one. Not the one who looked upon me with disgust just moments earlier.

I swallowed the sob growing in my chest.

"I know. I hoped they were over."

"Fate is a cruel master."

I let out a little chuckle. "Speaking of. Do you remember that mother is a Fate?"

"I do. I was there when they carted her off in front of me."

"Well, you share her gift."

She fiddled with the thin golden chain around her neck. Was that a gift from Gideon or a remnant of our old life? My memories were too blurry to remember something so simple.

"Me? A seer? I've never had a vision in my life."

"You have. I've seen you do it."

"No," she whispered, the word barely escaping her lips.

"I've seen you kill a god, Baylis."

"Me?" She clutched her chest.

"Yes, you. Do you remember this?" Pulling Little Death from its sheath, I presented it to Baylis. Its iridescent blade sparkled in the pale winter light.

Cautiously, Baylis reached for the dagger, turning it in her hand.

"I… I recognize its feel." She closed her eyes, focusing on the weapon.

I waited with bated breath.

Her eyes sprung open, and her gray irises turned white.

"Blood, so much blood. Running down my hand." She traced

the path of the blood down her delicate wrist. "A face... older than time. I... I..." She dropped the knife to the ground, burying her face in her hands. "I'm a monster."

"Shh... you're not a monster. Gideon is the monster." I couldn't tell her she'd killed Tharan's father and, in doing so, made Tharan the Alder King. Truths would have to come slowly. The mind could only take so much.

Sobs shook her body violently. She turned, gripping me tightly. Fingers digging into my arms. "I don't know who I am anymore, Aelia."

"I will help you find out. We have time now." I inhaled the scent of elderberry on her hair as she cried on my shoulder. "It's okay."

I would have to ask her to infiltrate her mind, there was no other choice. As Hand to the king I had a duty to protect the realm. But I was also her sister, and she was still so fragile. Pulling the memories could traumatize her more than she already was. Now was not the right time. But would there ever be a good time to go in? My heart twisted in my chest.

"I want to go back to the River House." Her words choked in her throat.

"Me too," I whispered. "There's something else I need to tell you."

She wiped her tears on her sleeve. "I don't know how much more I can take."

I stared at my toes, unable to look at her.

"That bad, huh?"

I nodded, trying to figure out where to start.

"It's about Caiden and me."

She arched her brow.

"The fact that you two act like strangers? I noticed."

"Yes... There's an explanation for that." I rubbed my palm

with my thumb, trying to calm my churning stomach. "We struck a bargain. To him, I am a stranger."

"Aelia, no," she gasped, covering her mouth with her hand, eyes widening.

"Once you were safe, I would erase the memories of our relationship from his mind." Thorns grew in my throat. "You are safe, and I am a stranger to him now."

"But you two were so—in love." Her gaze softened and her shoulders relaxed.

I clenched my jaw, holding back the ache splitting my heart in two.

"Our love died in Ryft's Edge, and that's all I'm going to say about it for now. We both hurt each other in ways we could never repair. It was for the best. At least one of us can move on."

"I'd say you're moving on just fine," she said through sniffles.

"Yes. Everything worked out the way it was supposed to." I tried to bury the pain, but the ache of losing Caiden still resonated deep within me.

"Tharan is good *to you* and *for you*. I've never seen anyone look at someone the way he looks at you."

Heat flushed my cheeks. "I am afraid of the feelings I have for him. We fit so perfectly together that I'm scared to get my hopes up. So many things could go wrong."

She squeezed my hand. "But so many things could go right, too. You deserve someone who loves you, who burns for you. And I can tell he does."

"I haven't allowed myself to hope in a very long time."

"Perhaps now is a good time to start." Her face brightened.

A sigh escaped my lips. "Maybe after we finish visiting Mother."

"And when will that be?"

"Soon. I don't know exactly when. Once we get to Ruska,

we'll have to find someone crazy enough to take us to the Island of Fate."

Baylis nervously bunched up the fabric of her dress. "This is a lot to take in. So much so fast."

"We don't have the luxury of time. Burning Ryft's Edge to the ground will only embolden Gideon, Erissa, and their allies."

"Then I guess I better get ready."

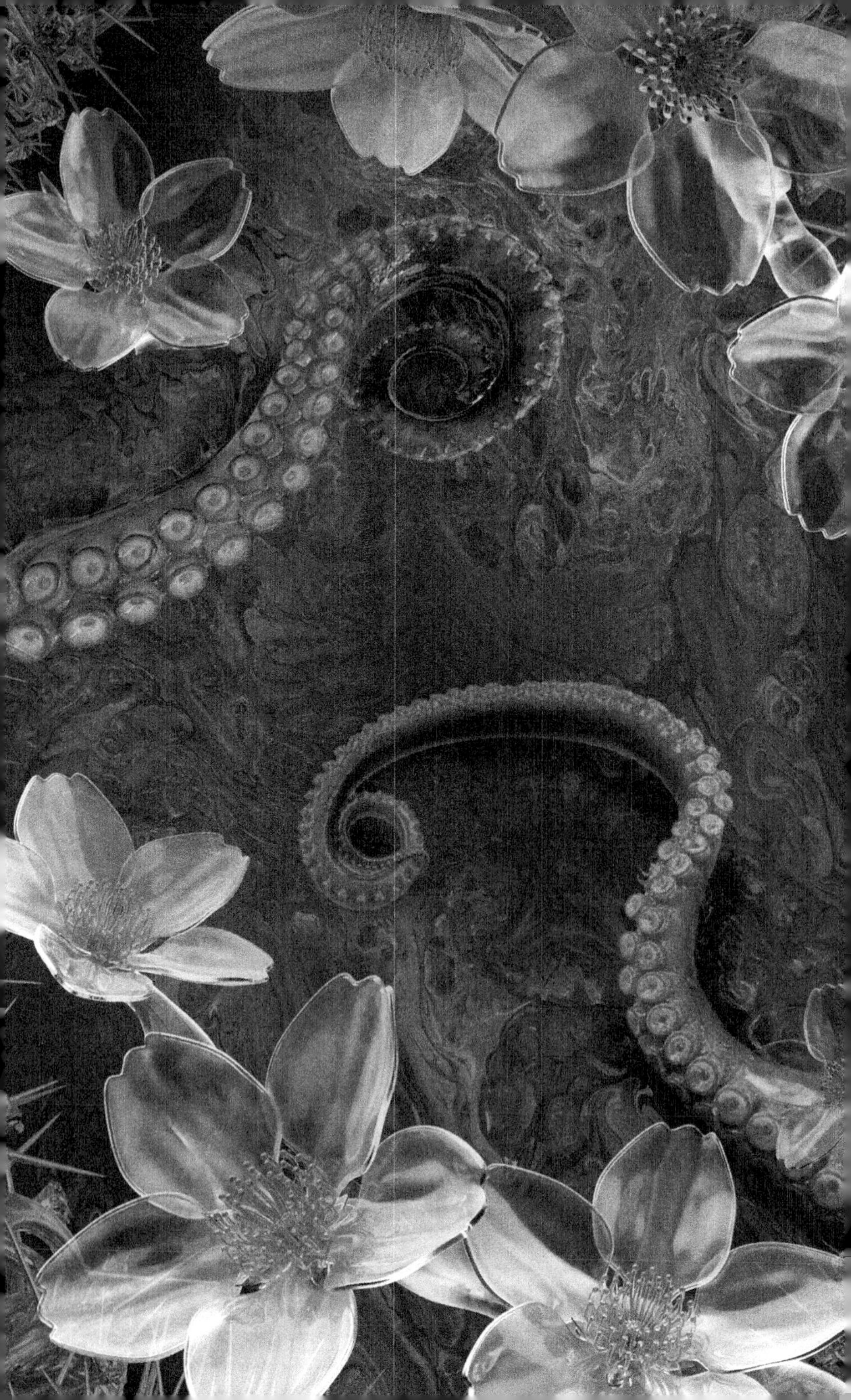

4 THARAN

Tharan stared out the window, glass of brandy in one hand, cigarette in the other, contemplating the journey ahead. Foot resting on the edge of his mahogany desk, he leaned back in his chair, taking a sip, reveling in the burn as it slid down his throat.

The door to his study creaked open, and Aelia appeared. He couldn't help but be in awe every time he laid his eyes on her. The curves of her body called to him, and he yearned to answer.

"Hello, my darling," he said, taking a drag of his cigarette.

"What a day."

She crossed the room, sliding onto his lap, stealing the cigarette from between his lips and placing it to her own.

The thought of her plush lips wrapped around his cock instead of a cigarette sent a quiver through him. He nuzzled his face into the crook of her neck, inhaling the scent of jasmine lingering on her skin. A reminder of the royalty she'd once been. Jasmine was expensive.

Her pulse quickened and she leaned into him.

"Drink?" he said, running kisses up her neck.

She took another drag off the cigarette.

"Yes, please."

Tharan gently lifted her from his lap, before pouring her a glass of whiskey.

Taking the glass, she crossed the room and plopped down on the couch, extinguishing the cigarette in a bronze ashtray on the marble coffee table.

"What's bothering you?"

Taking a seat next to her, he watched the bob of her throat as she drank the amber liquid, wondering what it would be like to sink his teeth into that pretty neck as he pushed inside her. His fingers itched to touch her. To claim her.

"I'm worried about traveling with Baylis. I'm worried she's not ready."

"She's not. She may never be, but the world doesn't wait for us to be ready."

"She had a vision today. Just a glimpse, and it scared her." She exhaled sharply. "I'm going to have to go into her mind… I just don't know if I'm strong enough to see what I may find there."

"Are you worried she was in love with Gideon, and he was good to her? Or are you worried he treated her worse than you?"

Aelia nodded.

"If he was good to her, I'm worried I will resent her for it. But if I found the latter, I wouldn't be surprised."

Tharan's heart ached for the woman he loved so much. Her pain was his pain. "Your feelings are valid, Aelia, but that was five years ago. You've moved on."

Her gaze softened upon him as she cupped his face in her hand.

"You're right. I shouldn't let old feelings get the better of me. The pain is duller now, more a memory of a wound than the wound itself."

He laid a kiss on her forehead.

"I hope I can help you to heal those wounds."

She leaned into his kiss, her body relaxing beneath his lips.

"But there is something I want to discuss," he said.

"Oh?" She took another swig of whiskey.

"Well, two things…"

"Go on."

"First, I think you should have Elrida lay hands on you. She is ancient and can sense spells. If your mother bound your power, she may be able to tell."

Aelia inhaled deeply.

"I suppose that is a reasonable ask. What's the other?"

Tharan pulled her onto his lap, so she was straddling him.

"I have seen the way you look at Caiden. I know you still harbor feelings for him. It's only natural."

She bit her lip, and her eyes flitted to the floor. Tharan could feel her body tense on top of his.

He pushed a stray hair behind her ear.

"I want to make you mine. I want us to bind our hands in the sacred ceremony so that our souls may find one another in the next life, but I want to make sure you are ready for such a commitment. So, if you want to be with Caiden, I will not stop you. But once I claim you, once we consummate our binding, you will be marked as mine, and I will defend what is mine at all costs."

Aelia swallowed hard; indecision plastered across her face. "I've never heard you speak like this before."

Tharan's eyes stared over her shoulder.

"It is part of the way of the Alder King. We have a primal nature. Our power comes with a price."

Aelia stroked his chin lovingly, forcing their eyes to meet.

"Caiden is my past. You are my future. But it may take some time for me to let go of him fully."

His gaze softened upon her, drinking her in. The ache of love grew in his chest. Even her scars were beautiful.

"I have nothing but time. Take as long as you need. After we are bound, I will not share you, but if you wanted to, I would share you with him for one last night. Together."

Her cheeks reddened.

"He doesn't even know who I am."

"It does not mean his heart does not remember." It pained Tharan to say those words, to think about losing Aelia to Caiden, but it was her choice.

She nuzzled her face in the crook of his neck, letting the full weight of her body rest on him.

"You are too good to me."

"It is easy to be good to you, my darling, my King Killer."

"You forgot Traitor." A smirk resonated in her voice.

Tharan stroked his long fingers through her thick hair.

"You are no longer a traitor, and I am no longer the Lord of Nothing."

"I am glad to be rid of that title."

"I will give you a title you are worthy of," he said.

"How about Queen of the Damned? I still have an army bound to my blood."

"We will find a way to remedy that. I am hoping my grandfather can help."

"My mother has to know something about the Trinity Wells and the Army of the Dead," she said. "Hopefully, she'll give us some answers as well.

"Her sisters will be tricky. They will want your power, Aelia. They have been trying to find a way back into the public's good graces for hundreds of years. Their greed cost them their acolytes."

"Did you know her—my mother—before?" she murmured.

Her head bobbed with the rising and falling of his chest.

Tharan couldn't remember the last time he felt so content. The love of his life resting her head on his chest, his wolves sleeping contently at his feet, a fire crackling while a winter storm raged outside. A bittersweet taste filled his mouth at the thought of having to part ways with them in such a short time. It wasn't fair. They just found each other, and now they'd have to leave again.

"Yes, I met her once. When I was young, it was a tradition to have our fates read at the time we came of age. Around fifty in human years."

"Oh?" She lifted her head, ebony hair falling over her freckled face.

"She was kind to me."

"What did the Fates say? If you don't mind me asking."

He reached for his glass of brandy and took a swig. "They told me I would be a great general. That I would lead an army to victory, but that my heart would get the better of me if I weren't careful."

Her mouth straightened into a tight line.

"I guess she was right."

"I was too young to understand what she meant then, too brash to think fate had any control over my life." He ground his teeth at the memory. "And then, one hundred years later, I met Lyra, and my fate was sealed."

"We are never ready to accept our fate, no matter what it is. We always think we can change what has been written into the fabric of time." She kissed his cheek, bringing a heat to his chest.

He cupped her face in his hands and whispered, "I am glad fate brought us together."

She smiled, bringing her lips to his for a kiss, their mouths said what words could not. His lips parted, and she slipped her tongue inside. A moan rose in his core. His fingers gripped her hips, and she instinctively began to grind her hips against his. The sensation sent lust running through his veins and his erection pressed against the ties of his pants, needing to be released.

"Let me repay you for the other morning," she whispered in his ear.

He arched his brow.

"What do you have in mind?"

"We can't consummate our bond yet, but I can still make you come." With a coy smile, she slid down his muscled torso. Her hazel eyes locked on his. She undid the laces of his trousers, pulling them to his knees, releasing his girthy cock.

"I've been thinking about this all day," she said, planting gentle kisses along the insides of his thighs.

His breath hitched in his throat, balls clenching at the touch of her lips. Taking him in one hand, she slowly glided her tongue up his hard shaft. Tharan leaned back on the couch.

"Trinity, I want you so bad," he whispered, his breaths coming faster as Aelia encircled the tip of his cock with her tongue, teasing him, making his erection bulge with need.

"I'm going to enjoy watching you," she said, slipping his thick member in her mouth, pressing her tongue against the sensitive tip.

Heat ran through Tharan's veins. His breath came faster and faster. Fisting her hair in his hands, he set her pace. Aelia thrust his massive cock in and out of her mouth. Taking him deeper with each motion until he hit the back of her throat.

"Oh, that's a good girl."

She moaned with pleasure, sucking harder.

Tightening his grip on her hair, his hips moved with the rhythm of her mouth, back and forth, until the fire running through his veins reached a fever pitch. He stared at the ceiling, focusing on the pleasure writhing in his veins.

"Aelia, I need you." He gripped her hair, forcing her face up so that their eyes met.

Reading his expression, she quickly undressed. Her curvaceous body on display for him. Only him. The sight of her plump breasts and pricked nipples made the want in his core steam with need.

"Trinity, you're gorgeous," he said through ragged breaths.

A smirk lit her face.

Kneeling beside him, so her feet were on the floor, she ran her tongue up and down his cock, dark hair falling in waves around her face. The jagged scars on her back were a reminder of the cruelty she'd endured. He would make Gideon suffer for that. Suffer so greatly his screams would echo through time itself. He traced the outline of one with his fingers.

Aelia lifted her hips so he could reach her cunt.

"Yes," she whispered as he slid his fingers inside her.

"You're so wet for me."

She nodded, stroking his cock.

Placing another finger inside her, he thrust in and out, loving the way her muscles clenched around him, longing for the day they would join as one.

"Oh, Tharan."

He increased his pace, making sure to scrape the soft place where he knew her orgasm would grow. "Don't stop sucking me, darling. I want to come in your mouth while you come on my fingers."

A blinding need coursed through his veins as she took him deeper and deeper. Balls clenching, his orgasm clawed at his senses, demanding to be released. But not until she came. Everything was for her.

The sound of her pleasure filled the room with heady moans and soft whimpers.

"That's it, you're so close, darling."

"I… ohhh…"

Wetness dripped down his fingers as she clenched tighter around him, making his cock pearl with the beginning of his orgasm.

She pulled her head away, crying out as she drenched him

with her pleasure. The feeling of her orgasm spurred his own. Tingles ran through every nerve of his body.

"Now, baby," he said, pushing her head down and spilling his seed into her perfect mouth. Muscles spasming, he held her down until he'd emptied every last drop into her.

She gripped his thighs tightly, swallowing his cum. Again, his pleasure shook the room, and the power of the Alder King coursed through his veins. He wanted to pick her up and ravage her right there on the couch. Fuck her until neither of them knew their names, but he couldn't.

He pulled on his pants. She dressed and climbed next to him on the couch, nuzzling her face into his neck once more. Sweat dampened both their brows.

Wiping the hair from her eyes, she said, "I want you, Tharan. I want you so badly. I think I'll die if I don't have you inside me soon."

Chests heaving, their breaths mixed. Words escaped him, so instead, he tilted her head, planting a passionate kiss on her lips, savoring the taste of his seed on her tongue.

A whimper echoed in her throat.

He ran a hand over her collarbone and down her breast to her perked nipple, thumbing it gently.

"I don't want to leave you."

"I don't either," she said through heavy breaths.

"I'm going to have our finest weapon makers work with our spell weavers to make it so we never have to be apart for long."

She lifted her head, brows knitted in confusion.

"A spell of sorts. So we can communicate over long distances."

"As long as I'm not drinking any more blood."

"No, my darling. Never again."

"Good." She laid her head on his chest, eyes heavy with exhaustion.

Combing his fingers through her hair, he watched as she drifted off to sleep in his arms. A glimpse of their fleeting future should they fail to stop Gideon and Erissa. Tharan pulled a wool blanket from the back of the couch, covering them both. Snapping his fingers, he extinguished the candles. Only the light of the crackling fire remained, casting a warm glow over them. He counted the freckles on Aelia's cheeks before drifting to sleep.

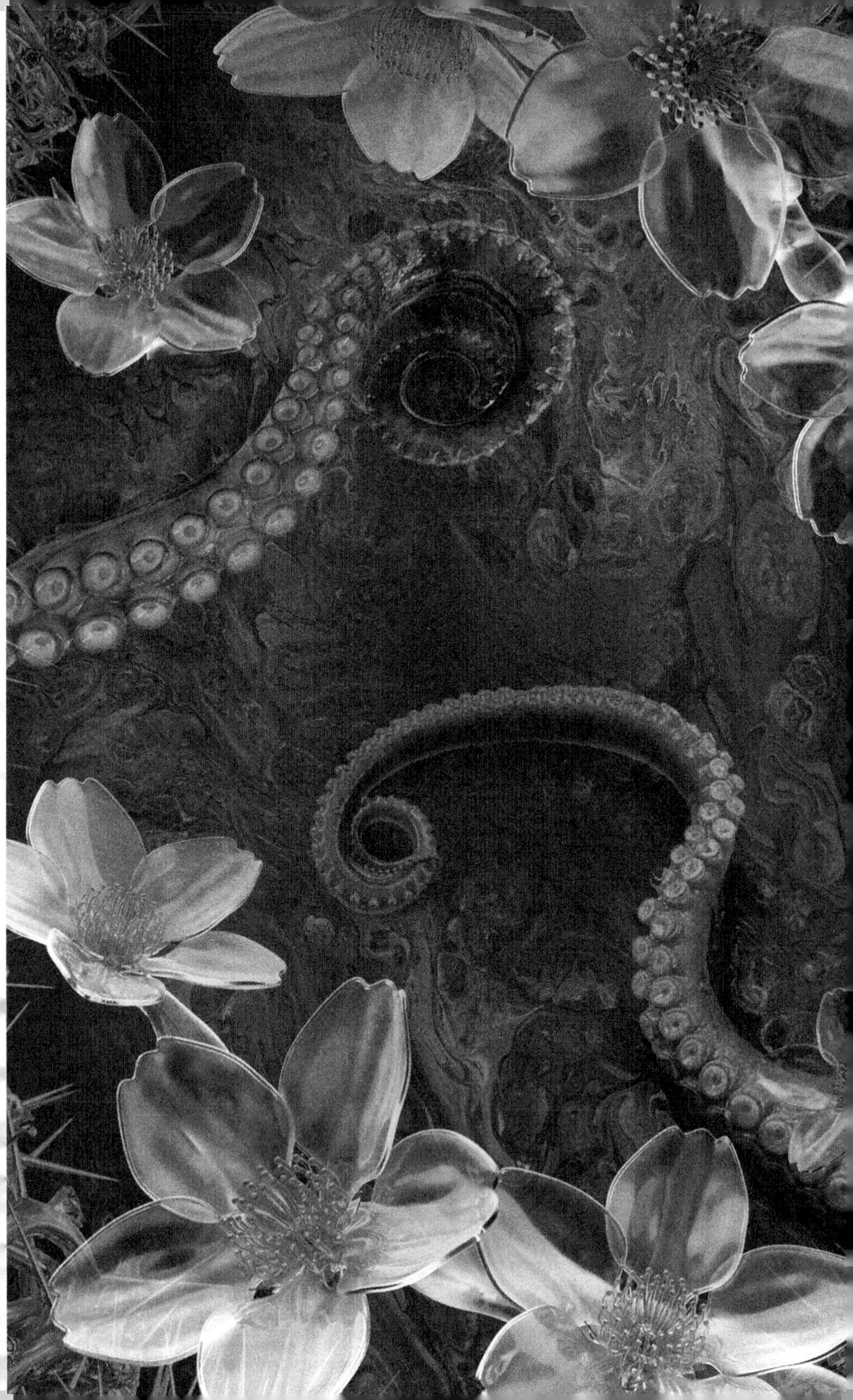

5 AELIA

"Come child, lay down, and let me take a look at you."

Elrida straightened a pair of thick glasses on her crooked nose as she ushered me toward a cot. Deep inside an oak tree, her workshop smelled of fresh-cut wood. Herbs hung from the rafters, lending their scents of sage, barley, and others I could not name. Low-burning candles cast a golden hue upon the workshop.

I laid down on the stiff cot next to a suspicious-looking jar of tentacles, still sucking on the glass.

Elrida cracked her ancient knuckles.

"Alright, lay still, this won't hurt."

I sucked a breath into my lungs, trying to still my racing heart. Tharan stood beside me; hand entwined with mine.

"I'm not going anywhere," he said, placing a kiss on my forehead.

"I'm afraid of what she'll find."

His gaze softened. "Whatever she finds, we'll face it together."

Elrida chuckled.

"What?" Tharan asked.

"I knew you two would fall in love. I've never been wrong about a match."

Tharan smirked, making a heat light in my chest.

"I shouldn't have doubted you, Elrida."

"I'm older than you. Almost older than your father. I think I know a thing or two about love."

Just how old was Elrida? Could she also be an original? Or was she something else entirely? Her short stature and signs of aging marked her as something other than a sylph, exactly what, I did not know.

"Alright, I'm going to start. You may feel some heat coming from my hands, but that's just the magic searching for a matching signal in your body."

She spread her long, spindled fingers wide over my abdomen.

A subtle heat radiated through me. I gripped Tharan's hand tighter.

Elrida's cracked face twisted with concern.

"Something is stuck, here, in her chest."

My eyes flicked to Tharan's.

"What does that mean?" he asked, trying to keep his voice steady for my sake.

The heat between my breasts increased as she tried to unravel the knot. Tongue between her teeth, she radiated more magic upon me.

"This is ancient magic, my King. I have no doubt there is power within her." Elrida strained her words as she focused her magic. "But it is more complex than I've ever seen before. This is no ordinary binding spell. This is something so intricate it could only have been done by one of the Zylrith."

Tharan arched a brow.

"Who?"

"The Zylrith Weavers. Legendary Magus with the power to shape raw magic. I wouldn't expect you to know who they are.

Their name has long since disappeared from the continent, but there are some of us who came before the Trinity, who still remember."

"What happened to them?" I asked.

Elrida shrugged. "What happened to anyone who did not bend to the Trinity's will? They were wiped out." Her mouth flattened into a straight line. "But this… this is spell-work I have not seen for an age."

"Could one of them have survived?" Tharan asked.

"Perhaps. Stranger things have happened," Elrida said.

"What can we do?" My chest tightened. What was inside of me? Had it been there my whole life and I never noticed? Was it something I was born with or had someone put it there?

My eyes flitted between Tharan and Elrida who exchanged worried looks.

She clicked her tongue.

"There is nothing to do. I cannot undo this spell, and part of me wonders if I want to. Whoever locked your magic away did so because it would be too great for you to handle, making me wonder if we should attempt to undo it."

I swallowed the dread creeping up my throat. Just what I needed, another thing to worry about. I thought Gideon had turned me into a monster, but perhaps I was a monster all along.

"But her father was mortal," Tharan said, rubbing his jaw while he searched for answers in his mind.

"The father she *knew* was mortal. It does not mean he was her real father."

"What are you saying?" I asked, a heaviness expanding from my core. My eyes locked on Elrida's.

"I'm saying whatever you are, it's certainly not human. Perhaps both your parents were hiding something."

"There's no way—I…" I paused, and the world went dark.

"Aelia?" Tharan said. Panic filled his voice.

"It's the knot containing her magic." Elrida's ancient voice echoed through the room. "It doesn't want to be undone. It will protect itself at all costs."

The world spun around me, and acid lapped at the back of my throat. I didn't want to think about my father or whoever my *real* father was. I didn't want to unravel the power within me. I wanted to marry Tharan and start a new life with him. I wanted my sister to get her memories back. I wanted to never break another mind again.

"Take me home," I commanded Tharan. It was rude to leave so suddenly, but I didn't care. The hut suffocated me. I needed to get out of there. I needed fresh air and time to process what I'd just been told.

Tharan swooped me up in his powerful arms and carried me back to the Alder Palace. Elrida followed close behind.

"Are you alright, my darling?" He laid me on the soft bed.

"I feel weak." Something burned in my chest, like a trap had been triggered. A fire lit in my chest, burning my lungs. I gasped for air. "It burns."

"Quickly, a cold compress," Tharan ordered one of the servants. A satyr returned a moment later with a damp cloth. Tharan placed it gently on my sweat-beaten forehead. "Is there anything you can do, Elrida?"

She mixed milk of the poppy with some thistle and handed it to Tharan. "This is the best I can do right now. The pain should fade. We must not disturb it again."

I drank the cool liquid, letting my body go slack. My brain remembered this feeling. Similar to dust, but less potent. I'd have to be careful.

Tharan patted the cold compress on my forehead. "Sleep now, my darling. I'll be right here."

With heavy eyes, I drifted off into a dreamless sleep.

I awoke to the sound of the wind rattling a shutter. Tharan was gone, but being the gentleman he was, he left a note.

Had to do kingly things. Be back soon. Meet me for dinner in the dining room.

I rubbed my chest where the knot had burned. No wound marked my skin. Sliding my feet into satin slippers, I padded down the hallway to Baylis's room.

She greeted me with a smile. "Oh, hello." Setting down the book she was reading on herbs and medical plants, "I was just honing up on my herbology. I was wondering… When we return, could I have a bit of earth in the greenhouses? I'd love to get back to cultivating my own species of plants."

"Of course," I said, my head still buzzing from the milk of the poppy. "Would you like to go to dinner with me?"

"Oh, yes, that would be lovely."

We made our way down to the great dining hall. I grappled with whether or not to tell my sister about what Elrida had found. On one hand if our father wasn't our real father, it could inhibit her healing. On the other hand, I had a duty to tell her. Weight settled itself over me. How much could I tell her? How much could Baylis take? I pushed it aside. I could tell her later.

Chandeliers made of elk antlers hung over a table laden with delicacies from far and wide—succulent fruits and berries, nuts and cheeses, along with roasted elk, and sauteed root vegetables.

My stomach grumbled at the aroma of herbs and roasted meats. Tharan stood at the end of the table, red hair shining in the flames. He wore a tunic of green and gold. My mouth went dry at the sight of him.

"Let me help you, my darling." He rushed to my side, wrapping an arm around my waist, and pulling the chair out for me.

"I'm fine. I feel much better after my rest."

I took my seat between Tharan and Sumac, who was running a cloth over her dagger. Her dark hair tied back in a neat knot, the way all military women wore their hair.

Tharan cleared his throat.

"I think we should leave before the next full moon. No doubt our enemies are already on the move. Plotting against us. We can't waste time, and we all have long journeys ahead of us. I suspect it will take the better part of a month to get to the elven capitol."

I sighed, shoveling a forkful of elk meat into my mouth.

"Who is going with you?" Hopper asked, not bothering to look up from the pile of papers stacked next to his plate.

Tharan thrummed his fingers on the oak table.

"You and Sumac, obviously, and I supposed at least eight of the Hunt. We don't want to seem too threatening."

Sumac and Hopper nodded.

"Very well, I shall see it done. And will the Hunt accompany Aelia and Baylis?"

"Yes, they are to escort them to Ruska, where they will stay in my townhome. But they are not to step foot on the Isle of Fate. Do you understand me?"

Sumac nodded. "Yes, my King."

Tharan turned to Baylis.

"Before we leave, you will let your sister take a look inside your mind. I can't have you putting anyone at risk."

I barely held back a pained gasp. I knew I'd have to do it. I just hoped I'd have more time.

Baylis swallowed hard. Her eyes cast downward to where her hands fiddled with the emerald napkin in her lap.

"Do you think she can bring back my memories?"

"She can certainly try." He laid a loving hand on mine and my cheeks flushed a rosy hue.

"Tharan is being too kind. I've never actually brought memories back; I've only erased or altered them."

"Have you ever gotten into someone's mind only to find their memories had already been altered?"

"As far as I know, there are only two remaining telepaths on this continent—myself and Gideon. I would be able to see his mark, and I have never seen another's."

Baylis nodded as if she understood, as if she could comprehend what it's like to be inside someone's mind.

"But I will look in yours if you want me to."

She played with the food on her plate, her eyes sliding away from mine.

"That's okay. I don't think I want to know."

I leaned in, taking her hand in mine.

"How about this, I will search through your mind, and if I find anything you can't handle, I will keep it my little secret. Alright?"

She bit her lip and nodded. "When?"

"We could do it tonight if you wanted."

"No, I'm not ready." Again, her eyes darted away from mine.

Tharan cleared his throat. "You may never be ready, but we do not have the luxury of time on our side."

"Fine. Tonight," she said more to herself than to anyone at the table.

I breathed deeply. Neither of us was prepared for what we might find inside her mind. My fingers itched after drinking the milk of the poppy. The remains of my need for dust still lingered in the back of my mind like another voice—always there, always watching, whispering in my ear. I pushed it away. Pulling a cigarette from my pouch, I lit it on one of the candles at the table, letting the smoke burn away the need scratching at my brain.

Tharan shot me a disapproving look.

I gave him a coy smile.

"Sorry, I need this."

"You need to eat." Tharan slid a plate of powdered confections my way. The sylph's love for sugar extended to dinner as well.

Reluctantly, I placed one on my plate, signaling to one of the servants to bring the coffee. There was nothing better than a sweet treat with a bitter cup of coffee.

"I'm nervous," Baylis said, shifting her seat. Her hands wrapped white around the seat of her chair.

"There's nothing to be nervous about. But we can have a healer bring some valerian root if you want," I said.

She nodded.

Hopper cleared his throat, shuffling the papers in front of him, so they stacked neatly. "There's something else we need to discuss."

"Oh?" Tharan asked.

Hopper's eyes flitted between Baylis and Tharan.

"In private."

Tharan nodded knowingly.

"Ah, yes, we can do this before Aelia enters Baylis's mind. Very well. Everyone meets in my study after dinner. Baylis, we'll meet you after in the healer's chambers."

After dinner, we climbed the great staircase to Tharan's study. Below us, the forest lights flickered like fireflies, and a fresh layer of powder covered the calm forest.

"Alright, Hopper, what is it?"

The green sylph ran a hand through his silken locks.

"The Highlands, sir. They have no leader."

"And why is that our problem?"

"I think we should install a leader there who can stabilize the region," Hopper said.

Tharan ran a hand over his jaw nervously. "But the optics of that. A sylph leader in a human realm."

"From my intel, to most of the continent, it's still a mystery how it all happened. Rumors are running wild of an army of the dead, but no one has seen that for an age so very few believe it. Some think it was a coup by Gideon's advisors. Without intervention, I believe the captain of the guard, Brutus, will try to take control of the Highlands, and he will have an ally in the Midlands to help him build a blockade. And then I have no doubt they will move on to conquer the Southlands and expand from there."

"So, we created a Hydra? Cutting off one head got us two more."

"Essentially, yes. Let me send emissaries to the Southlands to offer aid. That will at least win us goodwill."

"You're right."

I took a drink of whiskey.

"Is there a chance we could free the Midlands?"

Hopper and Tharan exchanged knowing glances.

"That will have to be sorted later. If we can clear your sister, do you think she would be able to run your old kingdom?"

"The Baylis I left in the Midlands five years ago could have… I have no idea if this one could."

"We will find out shortly."

I took a drag off my cigarette. The smoke crackled in my lungs.

"We will."

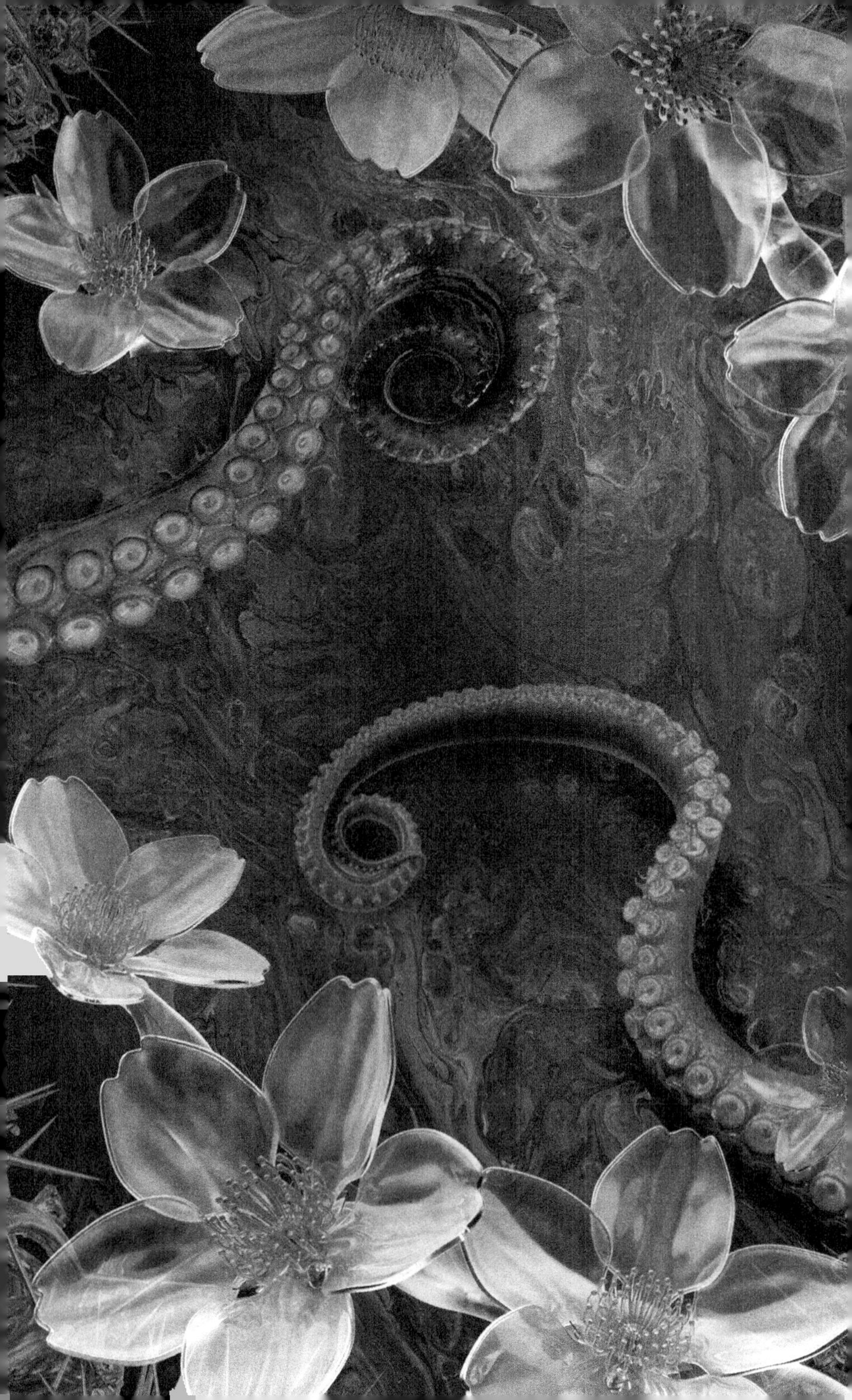

6 AELIA

TORCHES FLICKERED AROUND THE HEALER'S LABORATORY, AND the smell of sage and eucalyptus filled the air. A tall, slender, sylph woman with mousy brown hair and sharp features welcomed us.

"My King, what can I do for you this evening?" She bowed her head.

"We need you to sedate young Baylis here." He gestured to Baylis, who stood with her hand clasped in front of her. A blue silk gown hung from her lithe body. When had she gotten so thin?

I took her hand in mine, and she gave me a brave smile.

"It'll be alright," I whispered, squeezing tight.

"Come here, child. Lay on this bed, and I'll administer the valerian root."

Baylis did as she was told and lay on the bed. I pulled a chair next to her as the healer dabbed the sedative on her lips.

"Not too much," I said, throat going dry with anticipation. "I need her sedated, not asleep."

The woman nodded. Her hair glinted in the firelight.

Baylis's eyes flickered and relaxed.

I took a deep breath, calming my body. I needed a clear head if I was going to be successful. Tharan ran a loving hand over my back before kissing my cheek softly.

"I'll be right here the whole time."

At his words, a calm settled over me. Tharan was the partner I'd longed for but never had.

"Thank you."

He took a seat behind me.

A breath escaped my lips. I reached out with all my might, knocking at the door of Baylis's mind, noticing it was the same door as the one we had at the River House in the Midlands. Red with silver numbers. I pushed the sentimental feelings bubbling in my chest down. *This is a job, Aelia. Stay focused.*

The door unlocked, and a cheerful Baylis greeted me, "That was quick."

"It is easy to enter the mind of someone you love. The psyche recognizes it as *safe*." I stepped inside. The foyer of the River House greeted me with a curling staircase and dark wallpaper decorated with lush greenery and exotic birds from far away kingdoms. It was warm and inviting, just as I remembered it, with dark wood and plush leather sofas. The smell of cinnamon and oranges wafted through the air.

"Yule," I said under my breath.

"It was always our happiest time."

I took my sister's hand, and she led me up the stairs to a door I didn't recognize, carved with intricate flourishes and eagles.

"I think this is where we need to go, but it's locked, and I have no key," she said, pointing to the intricate brass knob.

I held my ear to the carved wood, but only silence echoed from beyond. The hair on the back of my neck stood on end.

"I think you're right." Slowly, I reached for the handle. Within the confines of a person's mind, I could manipulate anything I wanted—even locked doors. I focused my power on the knob, slowly turning it until I heard a *click*. Pushing the door open, we entered a storm of memories.

The wind whipped, and paper flew around us violently—the contents of Baylis's memories torn apart in perpetual chaos. Thunder rolled, and lightning cracked, but no rain fell.

The raging wind gnarled my hair, obstructing my vision. I took a deep breath. Calming this storm would take all my power and more.

"What's going on?" Baylis shouted over the wailing wind.

"Someone has set a trap in your mind. I triggered it when I opened the door. They knew I could do it. This trap was set specifically for me, so I wouldn't be able to piece your mind back together." The gusts carried my voice far away.

Narrowing my eyes, I focused my power, trying to tame the storm, but it would not yield. Erissa was a powerful wielder, and my powers were no match for hers.

While I tried to contain the storm, Baylis grabbed random papers as they flew past her. Good. At least we could put some of her back together.

Lightning cracked, illuminating the chaotic library. The spell fought against my magic, intensifying its attack and pushing me toward the door. I grit my teeth, grabbing onto the nearest table for support as I focused my power on quieting the raging wind. Power surged through my bones like fire.

A foreboding growl echoed from deep within the library of her mind.

I swallowed the sense of dread rising in my gut.

"Grab what you can, Baylis! We need to get out of here!"

Baylis nodded and feverishly grabbed at the parchments. I did the same, hoping to find something useful.

The growl grew louder.

Through the darkness, two glowing eyes appeared at the end of one of the rows of books. The creature stalked toward us.

I barely had a handful of papers, but that would have to do.

"Baylis, back toward the door, slowly."

She did as I commanded.

The creature inched closer. Lightning flashed and two giant fangs came into view. The enormous jungle cat lowered itself into a striking position. My heart raced. We couldn't die in her mind. If we did our bodies would linger on without consciousness. I had to time everything just right and get Baylis out before her own mind devoured her.

Every hair stood on end.

The creature's claws clicked on the wood. We were so close to the door. All we had to do was shut it before the creature lunged.

"Baylis, run!"

She bolted for the door, her blonde hair nothing but a streak of gold in my periphery. The cat's eyes fell upon Baylis, and it moved to strike. Back arched, it leapt toward my sister, claws reaching for her, but I had a few tricks up my sleeve.

Balling my power in one hand, an eerie glow lit the room, swirling like a storm within the orb.

Just as the cat was about to reach my sister, I flung the orb at it, hitting it in the abdomen and knocking it backward. The creature's mighty body slid across the floor before crashing into a massive wooden bookshelf, which tipped over onto the animal.

I had enough time to slip back through the door and lock it.

I let out the breath I had been holding in, resting my back against the door.

"That was close."

The creature's claws pierced through the door next to my head. I squeezed my eyes tight. A bone-chilling roar echoed from beyond, vibrating my entire body.

"Too close," Baylis said, running a hand through her hair.

The creature dislodged its claws from the door and returned to guard Baylis's memories.

"How many pages did you grab?"

"Just a handful." She held up a stack of parchment.

"Let's go into the dining room and see what we grabbed."

We headed down the creaky stairs to the large dining room, where our mother's beloved crystal chandelier hung, a reminder of the family we used to be—of Yuletide feasts surrounded by friends and intimate dinners with just the three of us.

We spread the papers out on the table. Each page was a fraction of a memory—like putting together a puzzle without a reference picture.

"Let's see what we have here." I picked up the first page, gripped Baylis's hand, and focused my power on the memory. We were transported to the night of the attack on Elyria. Fires blazed around us. My beloved home, burning to ash. The smell of charred flesh and the sound of desperate screams filled the air. My chest tightened.

A horse with no rider ran past us, saddle riddled with flaming arrows.

I had never seen this before—the result of my weakness. I sank to my knees, the weight of my actions pressing into my flesh, heavy and leaden. Baylis touched my shoulder just as the memory faded away.

Back in the dining room, I wiped the tears from my eyes and took gasping breaths. "I knew it was bad, but I…"

Baylis rubbed my back. "It's not your fault, Aelia. There was nothing you could have done."

The blood turned to ice in my veins. She didn't know. How could she? Gideon wouldn't have told her—or perhaps he had.

"Gideon didn't tell you?"

Her brows knitted with concern.

"Tell me what?"

I wasn't sure how much I should tell her. Gideon wouldn't have passed up the chance to disparage me in an attempt to turn my sister against me. Perhaps those memories were lost in the storm. "I gave him the information he needed to infiltrate Elyria."

Baylis's expression went blank as she mulled that over.

"I want to be mad at you, Aelia, but I know the Highlands would've found a way in whether you gave them a tip or not. They are, and always have been, a warring kingdom. They wanted the Midlands. I suspected as much when Gideon agreed to marry you."

"You did?" I rubbed my eyes in disbelief.

"Yes. Why would the Ironhearts marry a lesser kingdom when they could have married into an elven bloodline and secured their reign for thousands of years? Instead, they chose to ally with a poorer kingdom. A kingdom that just happened to be rich in the one thing they didn't have—fertile soil and enough cattle to feed the continent. They wanted Moriana's breadbasket, and they were going to take it one way or another."

A calmness washed over me. For five years, I had carried the weight of my guilt like a yolk around my neck. My breaths came easier now, and my burden lightened just a bit. "Thank you," I said.

Baylis gave me a reassuring smile; her gray eyes sparkled in the dazzling light of the chandelier.

"Alright, let's see what else we have here." I ran my hands over the parchment, trying to sense what lay within. Some were from our early years, and others were too private for me to explore—nothing from her time with Gideon. *Shit.*

"Anything?" Baylis bit her thumbnail nervously.

"Not that I can see." I scanned the parchments, hoping something would catch my eye. At the end of the table sat two torn strips of paper. Reluctantly, I picked one up, focusing my power on the words. It was a memory of Baylis playing with her dogs. I let out a sigh of relief before grabbing the next one. The paper fizzled with heat. I scanned it with my mind—a lover's touch.

I had never known Baylis to take a lover, but that didn't mean she didn't do so in secret. While my sister gazed at the papers, I focused my mind, diving into the snippet of a memory.

A room full of dark wood with bloodred curtains. This was not Elyria, or at least no place I had ever been in Elyria. The smell of leather and mahogany swirled in the air. The sound of wine being poured drew my attention. Gideon drank red wine. He loved it. It was the only alcohol he'd put into his body. I tried to expand the memory, but it fought against me. The edges of my vision blurred, but I needed to see who poured the wine. A cold hand traced my jaw before running down my collarbone and over my shoulder. I didn't have to see the source of the touch to know it was Gideon. My guts twisted inside me, but Baylis's didn't.

She… she felt attraction, possibly even love.

The memory spit me out before I could investigate further. Was this a trap set by Gideon and Erissa to turn me against my sister, or was this affection she felt real?

Baylis stared at an old memory of us at a Yule celebration, utterly calm as if we hadn't just been attacked by a giant cat lurking in her mind. Was she a part of this? I shook the thought from my mind. *No, don't be stupid, Aelia. Baylis is not your enemy. She's your sister. She'd never intentionally hurt you.*

I tucked the sheet of paper into my pocket. The memory belonged to me now; if she hadn't remembered it before, she wouldn't miss it now.

"I loved this Yule," she whispered, running her hands over the inscription on the parchment, trying to absorb the memory.

"Do you want to go in?" I asked.

Baylis held the paper to her chest.

"Yes."

"It's your memory. You don't need me to enter it. Just focus on it."

"Will you come with me?"

"Of course." Despite what I had just witnessed in Baylis's memory, when I looked at her, all I could see was my innocent sister.

Taking her hand, I closed my eyes and focused my waning power one last time. When I opened my eyes, we were sitting around a roaring fire in the parlor. Typically, when I entered a mind, I took the place of the memory holder, but with Baylis here, I took my own body.

The smell of cinnamon, nutmeg, and pine filled the air. My heart stopped at the sight of Caiden slouched in a plush armchair, Baylis's dogs asleep at his feet. His golden hair was tied behind his ears—a crown of holly around his head.

I sat next to him—my cheeks round with youth. This was the first Yule Caiden spent with us. The jitters I'd felt then reverberated through my body. We had been friends for years prior, and this was the first time he'd come to visit for the holiday. I swallowed hard.

Caiden passed me a gift wrapped in delicate tissue adorned with silver birds.

"You shouldn't have," I said, cheeks flushed.

"My mother wouldn't have let me come empty-handed." He gave me a dimpled smile, melting my heart.

I gently unfolded the wrapping, taking great care not to rip it. Inside, a wooden box with a golden lock sat.

"You'll need this." Caiden handed me a tiny gold key.

Nervously, I inserted it into the lock. The box cracked open, revealing a silver necklace like cracking lightning. A note perched on top of the jewelry. *May this spark courage whenever you need it. Caiden.*

My heart lurched into my throat. The memory was bittersweet. Before I left for the Highlands, I buried the necklace, along with everything Caiden had ever given me, in the garden of the

River House. I wanted to forget Caiden, just as he would eventually want to forget me.

"It's too much," I said, hiding the scarf I'd knitted for him.

"No, it's not."

I bit my lip, pushing back the tears welling behind my eyes. "I, uh, made this for you." I handed him the scarf wrapped in tawny parchment.

His eyes brightened. "You shouldn't have."

"Yes, she should," my sister said, shooting me a coy smile.

I stared daggers into her.

Caiden unwrapped the heavy scarf made of thick wool—blue with the crest of the Stormlands woven into it.

"It's wonderful," he said.

I searched his eyes for a hint of a lie, but only genuine happiness stared back at me as he wrapped it around his neck.

"Thank you," he said.

Butterflies flitted in my stomach.

The memory cut out.

"Well, that hurt." I piled the papers together, ignoring the pressure behind my eyes.

"You were so happy," Baylis said, reaching for me. Her voice filled with concern. "I don't understand. I thought you'd want to relive that moment."

I stared at her for a moment. Her once disheveled hair now perfectly pinned back like she wore it when we were younger. When had she done that? Even I couldn't manipulate two realities at once.

Exhaustion tugged at the corners of my senses. "I know you thought you were helping, but I need to let him go."

"Sorry. I just wanted to remember something good." Her eyes flitted to the floor, and she crumpled a piece of paper in her hand.

"It's okay." I leaned in, kissing her on the forehead.

We exited the way we came in.

When I opened my eyes, I was back in the healer's chambers with Tharan at my side. The grit of sand filled my mouth—an unfortunate side effect of reading minds. I wanted to tell him what I saw in her mind, but that would come with many more questions, including some I wasn't ready to face yet.

Baylis slept silently in the healer's bed. Her eyes danced beneath closed lids.

"She'll be safe here," the healer said. "Why don't you get some rest? It's nearly half past two in the morning."

I went to stand, but my legs collapsed underneath me.

"I've got you," Tharan said, scoping me up and carrying me to his chamber.

7 AELIA

Tharan brought me a glass of water, and I drank it greedily.

"What happened in there? I saw your hands grip the side of the chair."

I swallowed hard. "That's never happened before. Or at least I don't think it has." My chest tightened. Should I tell Tharan about what happened in Baylis's mind? I didn't want him to become even more suspicious of my sister when all I had was a fragment of a memory to work from. Furthermore, I didn't want to draw attention to my past with Caiden.

"What's going on in that head of yours, Aelia? I see the wheels turning." His verdant gaze made me melt. I could not keep a secret from him.

"I saw something. Something I think was meant to be hidden." I sat up on the bed, pulling my knees into my chest.

Tharan sat down on the bed next to me.

"Oh?" His brows knitted with concern.

"Gideon set a trap for us in her memories. I triggered it when I entered. We almost didn't make it out. Her memories… the ones I need are guarded by a creature I have not encountered before." I ran my hand through my hair nervously. "It was foolish of me to go in without even thinking about a trap."

Tharan rubbed my back lovingly. "Do not underestimate Gideon's prowess. He may not be as cunning as Erissa, but he's no fool. He led armies into battle and ran secret missions for his father for years."

"That's true."

I fiddled with the invisible ring on my finger.

"Don't be too hard on yourself. Even if it weren't a blatant trap, he would've found a way to make it so you couldn't get her memories. Made them disintegrate when you touch them or something like that."

"You're right." A sigh escaped my lips.

"Did you get anything useful?"

"I, uh, saw something I don't think I was supposed to see."

"Like what?" He scooted closer to me on the bed.

I rubbed my tired eyes, smearing the kohl I placed earlier.

"I don't know. It was just a flash of a memory. But I recognized it because…" I hesitated.

"Because you *recognized* it?"

A sob formed in my throat. "Yes," I eked out.

"Oh, Aelia. What was it? Did he hurt her?"

I leaned my head on his shoulder. "I think they were in love. Or at least at one point, she was attracted to him."

Tharan was silent for a moment.

"What?" I asked, looking up with a frown.

Tharan chewed the inside of his lip, eyes uneasy. His shoulders folded in.

"Don't take this the wrong way, Aelia… but weren't you at one time attracted him?"

My mouth fell agape. He was right. I could be overreacting. Gideon loved to shower you affectionately before pulling the rug out from beneath you. "Yes, that's possible."

"You saw a snapshot in time. It could have been anything. She could've loved him, but if her memories were as jumbled as you say, she might not remember. Or that could be planted to fuck with your head."

"You're right. I don't know what I saw. Gideon knows how to get to me. My sister is a weapon to him." I let my body relax.

Tharan ran a loving hand down my chin.

"I know you know this, but love your sister, be there for her, but always keep an eye out. Gideon and Erissa know how to play the game. You're right; she might be a weapon. Who is wielding her is still up for debate."

"My mother will know. Although where *her* loyalties lie is murky, too."

"The Fates will show you what they want you to see. Don't forget that. They were supposed to be impartial, but somewhere along the way, they forgot that and became something more like future makers instead of future seers."

"I like to think that's why my mother left. Like she wanted a better life."

"There were always rumors of squabbles between the sisters, but people love to gossip."

I nuzzled my face into Tharan's neck. "When are we leaving?"

"Two days." He brushed a strand of hair behind my ear, and I buried my face deeper, savoring the scent of pine and sweat on his skin.

"So soon?"

"We can't wait any longer." He kissed my forehead, and lust roiled in my veins.

I wanted him—wanted him so badly I would tear myself apart if I didn't have him inside me soon, but that would all have to wait until we returned. I needed to have a clear head. Committing myself to Tharan was more than just saying vows. To commit myself to a god meant binding ourselves together for an eternity. Before the Trinity culled the land, women presented themselves to gods, hoping to be chosen as their mate. They would inherit some of the god's power when their souls were bound. What would that mean for me?

Tharan hooked a finger under my chin. "Hey, come back to me."

"Sorry," I said, cheeks flushed. "My mind is heavy."

"I know, my King Killer." He pressed his lips to mine, lighting a fire in my core.

I breathed him in. I wanted him to consume me. To forget our troubles and disappear into one another. Tharan's teeth grazed the soft flesh of my neck, making me suck in a breath. "Yes," I whispered.

Slowly, Tharan undid the ties of my tunic before slipping it off. My nipples pricked at the cool night air. Kissing his way down my neck, igniting a fire under my skin, Tharan took my nipple into his mouth. A moan escaped my lips, and I arched my back as his tongue teased me—tension building in my core.

I quickly untied my pants, but Tharan's hand caught mine before I could tend to the need quaking between my legs.

"Not yet. You need your rest, but I wanted to give you something to think about while you recover."

"Tease."

He dragged his teeth over my nipple. The delicious sensation of pain and pleasure mixed, making my core thrum with need. "Tharan," I gasped out.

A devious smile split his face in two. His fangs glinted in the firelight. "Trinity, I can't hold myself together when you say my name like that."

I smiled, pulling him in for another passionate kiss. Slipping my tongue between his lips, I savored the taste of spiced cider on his tongue. It reminded me of the night we'd spent together in the little elven town, where we'd shared our shame and ignited sparks of love. My heart warmed at the memory. I fisted my hands in his lush locks, and he let out a moan of pleasure before pulling away.

"Aelia, I can't. We can't."

"I know, but I can't help it. You are my light, my life, Tharan." The words spilled out of me—words I had never shared before. Words I had never thought of before.

He nuzzled my nose with his. "There are things I want to tell you, Aelia. Things I haven't uttered for half a century."

My heart leapt into my throat.

"I know what you mean."

Brushing my hair behind my ear, he leaned in and whispered, "I want to save them for our binding day. I want the gods to know our truths."

"Oh, Tharan." I bit my lip. My fingers shook with a mix of apprehension and excitement.

He kissed my cheek. "Sleep now, my King Killer, my Queen of the Dead."

A smile tugged at the corners of my lips as I drifted off to sleep in his arms.

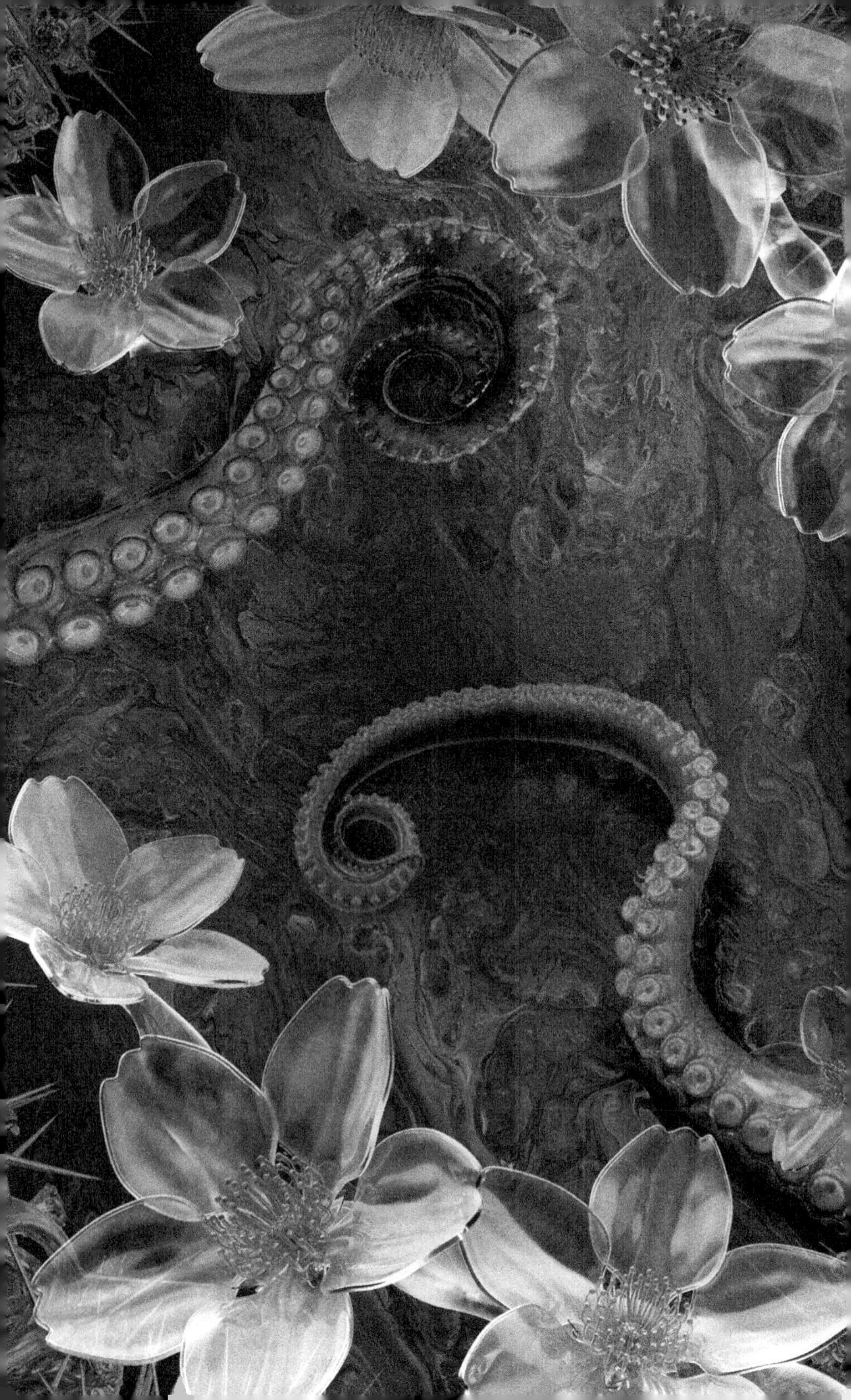

8 AELIA

I HURRIED AROUND THE PALACE, GATHERING THINGS FOR OUR TRIP. A weight settled on me as the reality of seeing my mother after so many years set in.

You're nervous, the Morrigan's voice echoed in my head.

"You'd be nervous too if you hadn't seen your mother in five years, and she sent you to your own personal hell." I held the scepter, releasing the Morrigan.

The curvaceous warrior goddess materialized; her ashen hair braided in spirals around her head.

"Ah, that's better." She stretched out her arms. "As for my mother—she tried to kill me at least six times."

"Lovely," I said, folding a dress into a suitcase.

The Morrigan let out a sigh.

"It is. It is an honor to kill your parent in battle."

I cringed. "Gods."

"We don't stay dead," she chuckled.

I arched a brow.

"I know you're immortal."

"We go into the land beyond."

"And what does that look like?"

"Similar to this plane of existence, but there are harsher parts and calmer parts depending on what lessons you learned or didn't learn while here, and how you died. I was young for a god when Crum Cruach trapped me and my army in the scepter. I've never been resurrected like the gods of old. Inside the scepter, I wander the Veiled Lands."

"And are there any grumblings from beyond the veil?" I laid a bandolier of daggers on top of the fine dresses.

"I have my scouts scouring the inner reaches of the beyond where I dare not tread for information." She picked at her nails carelessly.

I tried to decipher whether she was telling the truth, but Morrigan had been playing the game far longer than I had and she hid her true intentions well.

"So, you're not allowed in certain places?"

She sighed. "The world beyond has laws just like this one."

"Sounds awful."

"It is."

"Is Crom there?"

She shivered, and her eyes shut tight. "I've heard whispers. If he is there, he would be deep in the lower levels of the world beyond. Whoever buried him made sure his soul wouldn't escape. My scouts don't go down that far, but I know there are grumblings of an uprising."

Was she telling me the truth or just what I wanted to hear? My eyes raked over her ghostly body, but hers stayed locked on mine. She had no *tell* or at least not one I could discern.

"Was he as bad as they say?"

Her lush lips straightened into a thin line. "He was worse than you could even imagine. He would drink the blood of infants." She winced. "To his followers, it was considered an honor to sacrifice your firstborn to him by smashing their skull on his throne."

My stomach turned, and acid crept up the back of my throat. "Vile."

"They thought it would bring them a prosperous harvest. Not unlike your Ostara celebrations."

"During Ostara, we celebrate fertility and pray to Ammena that she makes our lands fertile. No one dies. People enjoy each other."

She covered her mouth, squeezing her eyes tight. A tiny tremble shook her ghostly body. If I hadn't been looking for it, I wouldn't have even noticed.

"If Crom is allowed back into this world, you will never know joy again. You will only know pain. Babies will be born to be sacrificed. He will blot out the sun and make it rain brimstone. Nothing will grow. Everything will die."

"Why does he hate this world so much?"

"Crom was an orphan—shunned from his village due to his magic. People thought differently back then about magic. It was seen as a curse rather than a blessing among some humans or whatever they were called back then. They sent Crom into the wild. Into the desert, where he earned a following in the fighting Rasa pits. Eventually, he became their king. The only king they'd ever have. Crom used them to spread his influence, conquering other tribes until he made his way out of the desert back to his homeland."

"I thought he was half elf and half sylph?"

She shrugged. "He could have been. His history has turned to myth in the millennium since his reign. Even my memory is cloudy."

I swallowed the dread pooling in my stomach.

"So, these kingdoms he won favor with... he slaughtered them, didn't he?"

"That was the first time I heard a whisper of his name. He gave the desert back to the Rasa and took his place on the Skull

Throne of his home tribe. By then, no one recognized him, and he became a god to the people who once shunned him."

The hair on my arms pricked at her words.

"And then?"

She picked up one of my cigarettes and held it to her pale lips, lighting it on the nearest candle.

"And then it went as most things go. They start small, like a pebble in a hoof that festers and lames the horse." Smoke billowed from her mouth. "He was smart about it, banding together those the gods left behind. People with nothing to lose make the best zealots. Gods like Eoghan—the Alder King and I didn't think much of it. The desert had been returned to the Rasa. What did we care if a few rogue clans banded together?"

"But it wasn't just a few rogue clans, was it?" A question I already knew the answer to.

She shook her head. "No, he spread his roots deep, turning the mages to his cause. Things went downhill quickly once he got his claws in them. He used them to glamour his armies to feel no fear or pain."

"Sounds familiar," I said, lighting a cigarette of my own and letting the smoke fizzle in my lungs. "When did he become obsessed with the origins of magic?"

She gave me a coy look. "That is the natural order of things, isn't it? Once you get a taste of power, it'll never be enough. Crom thought if he could find the Trinity's rumored Wells, he could become them. And he almost succeeded. Until the sylph, humans, and elves banded together to take him on."

"So now Erissa's got a new plaything in Gideon."

"He does seem to fit the bill. Handsome, arrogant, brutal."

I ashed my cigarette on the glass tray. "What I can't figure out, is her end game. Is she trying to resurrect Crom or recreate him?"

The Morrigan nodded. "Could be either. Could be neither.

Erissa is a deep thinker. She's been planning this for centuries. She won't go down easily. And if I were you, I'd watch my back. I have no doubt she's hired someone to take you out."

"Let her try," I said, putting out my cigarette.

Baylis was still asleep when I entered the healer's chambers.

"I don't think she's slept this soundly since we returned," I said to the woman mixing tonics.

"I barely gave her any valerian root. She should've woken by now."

I touched my sister's shoulder, gently rattling her. Eyes dashed beneath veined lids. I tried shaking her a bit harder.

"Baylis, it's time to get up."

She thrashed violently like she had when Erissa controlled her mind.

"Baylis, Baylis!" I tried to hold her down.

The healer rushed to my side. "Try to hold her as still as possible." She took a vial of green liquid from her pocket, lifted Baylis's chin, and poured it down her throat. Almost instantly, her gray eyes fluttered open.

"What's going on?"

"You wouldn't wake. I was worried, so the healer gave you a tonic."

"I… I was having a nightmare about the night our kingdom burned." She ran her hand down her face. "So much terror. So much destruction."

Guilt tugged at my heart. "I'm sorry those came to the surface when we entered your mind."

"I wish you could take them like you took Caiden's."

I must have blanched, because she forced a smile.

"I didn't *actually* mean it." She gave a half-hearted chuckle.

"We'd have to tame the storm in your mind and fight whatever creature lurks there before I could, and I haven't quite figured out what to do about that yet."

"No. This is something I need to face."

The healer brought her a glass of water, and Baylis drank it down in one breath.

"Will she be able to travel tomorrow?"

The healer nodded. "I assume so. She is physically healthy. It's her mind that is tearing her up."

I let out a breath as I helped my sister out of the bed. "Thank you," I said to the healer.

"I'm alright, Aelia. I can walk on my own. I just had a nightmare. That's it." Baylis pulled away from me, bracing herself on the stone railing. "I just need to collect myself, and I'll be fine."

"I'm just worried about you."

"I know, but I'm not some delicate flower. I can handle a nightmare."

I backed off. "I know. I'm worried we did more harm than good when we went into your mind."

We reached the foyer of the palace, where a large chandelier of elk antlers hung. Baylis straightened her blue gown. "I think I'll take a walk through the botanical gardens to clear my head."

My muscles stiffened. Was Baylis well enough to be on her own? Was I being too overbearing? I want to protect her—to help her heal, but everyone heals at their own pace, and perhaps Baylis needed time on her own to sort things out for herself.

"Alright. We're leaving tomorrow, Baylis. I'm having the servants prepare your things."

"I'll be ready." She brushed her ashen hair behind her ears. "Need to get some fresh air before we depart."

"Don't forget a cloak. It is terribly cold out there." I waved down a nearby servant. "Please bring my sister a cloak and some boots. We can't have her catching a cold."

The young halfling with rosy cheeks and curly hair nodded and went to fetch her things.

"Oh, and one more thing!" I shouted after the man. "A cinnamon roll too."

He nodded and continued on his way.

Baylis shook her head. "Always the big sister."

"Hard habit to break."

The servant returned moments later with a cloak, boots, and a cinnamon roll wrapped in parchment.

Donning the cloak and slipping the confection into her pocket, she bid me farewell.

I waved her goodbye. The memory of Gideon's touch replayed in my head. The feeling of Gideon's light touch on her collarbone—how her heart spiked. My head swirled with possibilities. Maybe Tharan was right. Maybe this was all a carefully laid plan to ensnare me and tear my sister and me apart. Maybe she had loved him, and he'd done the same thing to her he'd done to me. The lack of scars on Baylis's body gave me pause. Either Gideon changed his tactics, learned to hide them better, or… he'd never hurt Baylis.

I let out a breath. *Get it together, Aelia. He'd want her pristine to use as a bargaining chip.*

I couldn't shake the feeling something was off. I summoned the nearest server to fetch a cloak and headed into the snow after my sister.

Baylis's delicate footsteps headed straight for the botanical garden but suddenly disappeared.

I bit the inside of my cheek. Where could she have gone?

A wisp of blue fabric caught in the corner of my eye. I turned to see Baylis heading into the forest. Creeping behind a snow-covered bush, I watched as she stared at something high in the trees. I focused my vision, but the winter sun impaired my line of sight.

"What are you after?" I whispered to myself.

She continued to tramp through the forest until she came to a large oak with a hole in it.

My heart stopped and then relaxed as she pulled a tiny bird out of the tree.

Get it together, Aelia. Your sister isn't a spy. She's just taking care of an injured bird.

The bluebird tweeted happily as Baylis fed it pieces of her roll.

If I were going on this journey with my sister, I would have to trust her more. Feeling foolish, I headed back to the palace to prepare for dinner. Tharan wanted to make our last night together special. My heart raced at the thought of seeing him. Even now, my fingers itched to run through his silken locks.

9 AELIA

A GOWN OF OLIVE-GREEN SATIN WITH GOLDEN LAURELS WOVEN into it lay on my dressing table. Next to it, a crown of matching golden laurels sat on a velvet pillow. I had worn many fine gowns in my time as queen, but there was something special about being given such a gorgeous gown by your suitor.

I picked up the note with *King Killer* inscribed in golden letters.

> *To My King Killer,*
> *May this dress be worthy of your beauty. Meet me downstairs and bring a cloak.*
> *All My Love,*
> *Tharan*

I held the note to my chest and closed my eyes, fighting back the tears threatening to stain my cheeks. Tharan was good to me in ways I couldn't imagine. Wiping the moisture from my face, I applied a stain to my lips before outlining my eyes in a brown kohl. An attendant braided my hair in a crown around my head while letting the back fall in long waves.

"And now for the finishing touch," the attendant said, placing the tiara atop my head.

"I thought it would be heavier," I said, adjusting the headpiece.

"It is made of the finest gold mined from far in the north across the Atruskan River. The king had it made for you."

"But I've only been here for a few weeks."

"He can be very persuasive, as I'm sure you know." A coy smile tugged at the corners of her mouth.

I chuckled.

"There's one more thing." She hurried out of the room.

"Oh?"

Before I could follow her, she popped back in, holding a beautiful cloak, the same color as my dress, lined with wolf fur.

I ran my hands over the soft pelt.

"Is this what I think it is?"

She nodded curtly.

"It is a dire wolf pelt. When a wolf dies, the pelt is given to its rider. This one's rider fell in battle alongside their wolf. So the king had it fashioned into this cloak for you." She fastened the heavy garment around my neck before taking a step back. "You look like a queen."

My breath caught in my throat at those words. I hadn't been a queen in a long time and hadn't been very good at it. Could I be the kind of queen Tharan needed me to be? Could I bear the weight of ruling again?

Pushing my thoughts to the side, I headed out. As I walked down the magnificent spiral staircase, Tharan came into view. Back to me, his burgundy hair shone in the flames of the chandelier. He wore a green vest and white undershirt. With his hands behind his back, I could see the laurel cufflinks on his wrists. Atop his head sat the Alder Crown of Antlers.

I couldn't help but smile.

He turned to face me, and his verdant eyes brightened. A blinding smile cut his handsome face in two.

Heat flushed my cheeks at the sight of him. Pure power radiated from him like an overflowing fountain. He reached out a hand to guide me down the last few steps. Electricity roiled through my veins at his touch.

"You look stunning," he said, kissing my cheek.

"And you look very handsome as well." I entwined my arms around my neck.

"I've been known to clean up from time to time."

"A humble king."

"I try." He leaned in and planted a kiss on my lips. His mouth tasted of blackberries and bourbon. The scent of clove cigarettes clung to his skin.

"Trinity, I love your scent," I whispered in his ear.

"I love you," he growled in my ear.

Goosebumps pricked my skin. I hadn't told anyone I loved them since Caiden. And if I was being honest with myself, I wasn't sure I'd truly loved anyone. Looking back, I doubted my love for Caiden. Was I just young and infatuated? No. *Who am I kidding?* I loved him. Loved him enough to set him free. The love Caiden and I shared was forbidden and exciting, while the feelings I had for Tharan were warm and stable, like a steady thrum underneath my skin.

"I… I…" I couldn't say the words—I wasn't ready, and I hated to disappoint him. Tharan was safety. Tharan was stability and a home—something I hadn't even known I'd been missing.

His fingers laced with mine.

"It's alright. You don't have to say it. I know you're not ready."

My eyes flitted to the floor.

"I'm sorry."

He lifted my chin so that our eyes met.

"Don't be. I don't want you to lie to me. I want you to tell me when you're ready."

Pressure built behind my eyes.

"Thank you."

A smile tugged at the corners of his lips.

"Of course." He patted my hand. "Now, I've got something to show you."

Tharan led me out of the palace to a waiting sleigh pulled by two snow-white horses with bells, and holly braided into their manes. Lanterns gilded the carriage in a golden light.

"After you."

I climbed into the sleigh and settled into the plush seats. Tharan covered us in a thick wool blanket.

"Are you warm enough?"

I nodded and snuggled into the crook of his arm.

"Let's go."

The driver clicked his tongue, and the horses trotted on.

"Care to tell me where we're going?"

"That would ruin the surprise."

"Tease." I slapped his chest playfully.

We glided through the forest. The snow glistened like diamonds in the moon's light, and the bells braided into the horses chimed in a calming melody. I tried to savor each moment with Tharan, noting every detail—the feeling of his hand on mine, the outline of his face in the golden light. This would be the last night we would spend together for a long time, and I wanted to make it count.

We stopped in front of the entrance to a cave just as the snow began falling harder.

Tharan whispered something to the driver, but all I could focus on was the gaping hole in the rock, jagged and dark.

"What is this place?" I asked, staring at the ominous mouth of the cave.

Grabbing a lantern, Tharan said, "It's a special place only a few people know exists."

"No kraken, hopefully."

He chuckled.

"Not this time."

Entwining our hands, he led me deep into the cave. The lantern did little to warn off the ever-encroaching darkness.

An intoxicating scent wafted through the air—part floral, part sweet. I couldn't quite place it.

"We're getting close," Tharan said.

"How can you tell?"

"The smell is getting stronger."

"What exactly am I smelling?"

"You'll see soon."

The sound of our footsteps through the silence as we crossed over caverns filled with stalagmites growing from the floor.

The cave continued to twist and turn with no end in sight. When I suspected we were thoroughly lost, Tharan stopped in front of a seemingly innocuous boulder.

"We're here."

I looked around, but only darkness met my gaze.

"You had me get dressed up to take me to a dead end in a cave?"

"Oh, my sweet, you have no idea what lies behind this boulder."

He pressed his hand to the stone, and an ancient rune inscription appeared at his fingertips, illuminating the darkness around us in a pale blue.

"I've never seen that script before."

He looked at me over his shoulder.

"You wouldn't have. This language was dead before the Trinity culled the land."

I swallowed hard. What was this place?

At Tharan's touch, the boulder rolled out of the way, revealing yet another corridor, but instead of hard black stone, it was made of polished white marble.

Tharan snapped his fingers, and torches lining the wall lit instantaneously.

My pulse quickened. Magic swirled around us, leaving a coppery taste on my tongue.

"Ready?"

"Yes."

He took my hand and led me down the pristine hall.

"What is this place?"

"It is an ancient temple where the forest birthed my father eons ago. It contains the source of our magic."

"Oh." Words evaded me. Tharan trusted me completely without asking for anything in return. Goosebumps flushed my skin. How did I end up this lucky?

Before we entered the next room, he turned to face me. "What I'm about to show you has not been seen for an age. And you must not tell anyone what you saw here."

"Of course."

He stepped to the side, revealing an oasis of bioluminescent plants of every shape and color radiating light in the darkness. Above, an opening revealed the night sky dotted with stars. A canopy of sparkling leaves cast a golden glow on the setting. Not a flake of snow dotted the ground, as if it couldn't touch this place. The air felt like the first day of summer.

"Oh, Tharan. This is too much." I untied my cloak and draped it over my arm.

He kissed my hand. "Nothing is too much for you."

My heart skipped a beat as his eyes locked on mine. The tension pulled taut between us. Neither of us uttered a word. We didn't have to.

"There's more."

Tharan escorted me to a table low to the ground, adorned with various fruits, roasted hens, and delicately crafted desserts. Fireflies flickered in the air like twinkling stars.

Taking our seats, he poured us each a glass of sparkling wine.

"A toast to us," he said, giving me a smile that made my knees go weak. "May this not be our last night but the first of many."

"To us," I said, clinking my glass with his. The bubbles fizzed in my head, making my chest warm.

"There's something else I need to give you." He pulled a small velvet box from behind his back.

I sucked in a breath. In the human lands, these were usually filled with an engagement ring. Oh Trinity, I wasn't ready for this. I didn't want to hurt Tharan's feelings, but I didn't know if I could commit to something so big. The last time I married someone was Gideon, and that day still haunts me.

Reading the look on my face, Tharan said, "It's not what you're thinking, but if you want it to be, that could be arranged."

I cracked open the box to find a single diamond earring. "Oh, it's lovely, Tharan, but shouldn't there be two?"

He gave me a coy smile, pushing his hair behind his right ear to show its sister earring. "They are no ordinary jewels. They are whisper stones. Specially designed so only you and I can speak to one another across vast distances. So even when we're apart, we can still communicate."

A weight lifted from my chest.

"Oh, Tharan." I said, piercing the earring through the hole in my lobe where the glamoured stud used to rest. "How do I use it?"

"Just turn it gently to the right, and it will ping me."

I did as he said, and Tharan jolted a bit. "It works!"

"Probably shouldn't have done it so close to one another," I laughed.

"Just wasn't expecting it, that's all." He took another drink of champagne. "Let's eat. We don't want this going to waste."

The flavor of the enchanted foods danced on my tongue. I ate until my stomach begged me to stop.

"Everything is so wonderful," I said, staring up at the stars.

"There's one more thing." Tharan stood, offering me his hand.

"Oh?" I clasped my hand around his, wondering what could make this night better.

Slipping an arm around my waist, he pulled me in close. "One last dance before we part."

"But there's no music."

He snapped his fingers, and a string quartet of only instruments appeared through the entrance.

"You've really thought of everything."

"I wanted everything to be perfect for you. And I didn't know the next time we'd get the chance to dance together."

My heart overflowed with love, and words emptied out of my head.

"I don't know what to say, Tharan."

He smiled as we danced around the meadow, illuminated by the golden leaves above and the luminescent flowers below. Color danced across our faces.

"I told you I'd show you just what kind of man I am."

"And you haven't disappointed."

"I try not to disappoint the ones I love anymore."

I nuzzled my nose against his, and he pulled me in closer.

"If I die tomorrow, I would die a happy man. This time with you has been the happiest I've been… well, possibly ever," he whispered, as if saying it too loud would jinx it.

A pressure built behind my eyes. "I don't want to think about you dying. Not on a night this perfect."

"You're right, my love. Let's just enjoy the evening." He rested his head on me as we swayed to the cheerful music.

We danced until late in the evening, neither wanting to let the other go.

"Aelia, we need our rest."

I nodded into his chest.

Tharan snapped his fingers, and the instruments disappeared. Only the sound of crickets filled the night air.

"What now?" I asked. "Are we going back?"

Tharan gave me a coy smile.

"I thought we'd spend our last night together under the stars." He snapped his fingers. Vines climbed from the earth, twisting themselves into a bedframe. Cotton sprouted and rolled itself into the shape of a mattress. Bioluminescent flowers sprouted from the vines, casting the oasis in a delicate pink light.

"Oh, Tharan."

"Not bad. I'll admit—one of my cleverer ideas." He laid a fur-lined blanket on top of the bed and two down pillows. "I can't make everything."

Everything was so perfect—the stars twinkling overhead, the carpet of luminescent flowers below us, and the man I loved by my side. How did I end up here after everything I went through? I wanted to freeze this moment in time.

A feeling of dread threatened to poison my happiness. I pushed it away. There would be time to worry tomorrow. Tonight was for us.

"Is everything alright?" Tharan asked. He made a line of kisses down my neck and over my bare shoulders, each touch lighting a fire beneath my skin.

"Everything's fine," I said, facing him, tears welling in my eyes. "I can't remember the last time I was this happy, and it's overwhelming."

"Oh, my darling." His gaze softened, and he wiped the tears from my eyes.

"And if I am being honest... I'm afraid to be happy. I'm afraid the universe will pull the rug out from under me, and this will all disappear."

Tharan pulled me in tight to his chest. His distinct scent of pine and clove calmed my senses.

"The world will always try to tear us apart, Aelia, but I promise you this. I will always come back to you. I will find you in the darkness and in the light. I will walk through fire to get back to you, and I will conquer death if it means I can spend just one more night in your arms."

Overwhelmed with love, words refused to formulate. "Tharan... I..."

"Shh... you don't have to say anything."

Slowly, he unbuttoned my dress, my heart rate increasing with each snap. We did not take our eyes off each other, and the tension pulled tighter between us with each passing second.

I undid the buttons on his vest. The silk slipped between my shaking fingers.

When every button had been undone, he leaned in and whispered in my ear, "I love you, Aelia Springborn, King Killer, Queen of the Damned, and Ruler of my Heart."

My heart burst in my chest, but I couldn't get the words out. I had told other men I loved them and, in turn they'd hurt me. I wouldn't give my love away so easily this time.

I stepped out of my dress and Tharan slipped a thin silk nightgown over my head. The fabric was so light it barely felt like anything at all against my skin.

"I'll just hold you tonight. I promise," he said, pulling the crown from my head and helping me into bed.

My body sunk into the plush mattress, reminding me of how tired I was.

Tharan took off his crown before pulling off his shirt. My mouth went dry at the sight of his toned body glistening in the pale light of the luminescent flowers.

"Tharan?" I eked out.

"Yes?" he said, sliding into bed next to me.

"Can I ask you something?"

"Anything," he said, pulling the blankets tight around us.

"That night at the Inn in Mineralia, when you gave me the bath. I noticed a golden tattoo. Brand? Snaking its way up your arm, but I haven't seen it since."

He arched a brow. "You could see that?"

I nodded.

"It's an old army tattoo infused with magic. It's supposed to only be visible to certain people. So they could identify your body should you fall in battle." His eyes left mine. "But I had mine removed when I was…" His words caught in his throat.

"It's okay. We don't have to talk about it anymore," I said, running a loving hand down his chin.

"No, it's fine. I just… thought they took that from me. Forever." His brows knitted with concern. "It's not just a way to identify my body should I fall. It's a way for those of us who fought together to identify each other. A kind of brotherhood for those of us who remember the Sylph and Elven War." He leaned his forehead against mine. "But let's talk about that some other time. I see the sleep clawing at your eyes, and I don't want to keep you up too late when we both have to travel tomorrow."

"I think it's a little late for that." A smile tugged at the corner of my lips.

He pressed his lips to mine, and my whole body responded as though every nerve had been waiting for his touch.

I spread my legs, and he filled the space between them. His

hard body pressed against mine—tongues entwining in a sanguine dance. A fire lit in my core, making me wet. Wet for him. I quickly slid my underwear off.

"I want you, Aelia, but this is as far as we go tonight." Tharan nuzzled his nose against mine.

"No," I pleaded, "I want you. I want to feel you inside me, coursing through my veins. I want to feel your teeth on my neck and my name on your breath as you groan into my ear."

"Trinity, Aelia." His hips rocked rhythmically against mine. Only a thin layer of fabric separated us. The temptation built each time his erection slid over my aching clit.

A moan escaped my lips, and his pace increased.

"Fuck, Aelia… I…" His words were breathy and full of need, but his eyes stayed locked on mine.

"Touch me, Tharan." I guided his hand between my legs where my slick cunt waited for him.

He slipped his fingers inside me.

"Trinity, you're so wet for me. Is this how wet you get when you touch yourself when I'm not around?"

I arched my back as his fingers found the soft spot beneath my mound.

"Yes," I hissed out between ragged breaths.

"Good girl," he whispered into my ear while his fingers pulsed in and out of me slowly, deliberately, coaxing my orgasm. Tharan's thumb found a home on my clit, and lightning shot through every nerve in my body.

Trinity, this man made me feel things I hadn't felt in ages. Like I would shrivel up and die without his touch.

"Aelia, I'd like to try something if you're alright with it."

My mind went blank, and I blurted out, "Anything."

He paused, snapping his fingers. A vine curled onto the bed, unraveling a consolateur—blown glass with three orbs for varying pleasure.

My eyes went wide at the sight of it. Anticipation pricked the hairs on my arms. "I've never used anything like that before. You'll have to guide me."

A mischievous gleam lit in his eyes. "I want you to pretend it's me fucking you. Do you understand?"

"Yes," I said, laying back on the bed and spreading my legs again.

Tharan rubbed my clit, sending a thousand shock waves through me. I moaned with pleasure, fisting my hands in his hair, pulling him closer to me.

"Are you ready, my darling?"

I nodded, fighting the growing orgasm inside me.

Tharan guided the consolateur into my cunt. My breath hitched as it stretched me. "Oh, Trinity."

"Are you alright?" His brows knitted with concern.

"Yes," I said through ragged breaths. "Don't stop."

He moved the glass orbs in and out of me—pleasure built with each stroke. "You're doing so good, my darling, taking this as if you were taking me."

I arched my back, whimpering as he increased his pace.

"Such a good girl," Tharan whispered as he ran his tongue up my neck.

My breath hitched in my throat, my throbbing core on the edge of climax. Each thrust brought me closer.

"Trinity, don't stop," I exclaimed, digging my fingernails into the hard flesh of Tharan's back. I wanted to brand myself on to him so everyone would know I belonged to him and him to me. Two broken pieces of a puzzle that only fit with one another.

"Aelia, I'm so fucking hard for you. The sounds of your moans are like music to my ears."

I let out a groan of pleasure. "I'm so close."

"Yes, my love, say my name." He thrust the consolateur into me harder and harder so that I felt every ridge against my soft insides. My body responded with a jot of lightning through my nerves, and I bucked my hips with his thrusts.

My hands trembled as I gripped the blanket. Lifting my head to the sky, I let my orgasm rip through me.

"Tharan, oh fuck, Tharan!"

He sunk his fangs into my neck, not hard enough to break the skin but enough to send my pulse racing. I let out a guttural cry into the silent night. The pain mixed with pleasure, creating a euphoria inside me, unlike anything I had felt before. Tears built behind my eyes, but I pushed them away, focusing on the grooves in Tharan's back. He pulled the toy from me and replaced it with his fingers.

"You did such a good job. Such a good girl, coming on my fingers."

Ragged gasps ripped through me as my climax reverberated through every muscle. I imagined him coming inside me.

Tharan removed his fingers, and the cool night air licked my slick core. Using my wetness to pleasure himself, he worked his throbbing cock.

Trinty, he was gorgeous. Every muscle gleamed in the light of the flowers. Watching him touch himself while my cunt still throbbed made a fire light inside me all over again.

With one hand squeezing my breast, he worked himself with quick, short strokes, favoring his crown.

I lifted his chin so that our eyes met. "I want you to look at me when you come."

"Yes, my queen," he said, increasing his pace.

"I want you to imagine spilling yourself inside me."

"Oh, Trinity." The muscles on his abdomen tightened, but his eyes did not leave mine.

"I want you to imagine how wet my cunt is for you. Only for you." He pumped himself feverishly.

"Say it. Fucking say my name. Tell me what I want to hear."

"Tharan. I love you." The words left my lips so effortlessly, the truth unable to be kept at bay any longer.

A look of relief washed over his face as he came hard onto my stomach. Here, the earth would not shake at his orgasm, for this is where he was created, where the magic outweighed his. He collapsed on top of me, muscles still twitching.

I ran my fingers down his back. The sweat glistened the soft pink light of the flowers. "That was…"

He laid a passionate kiss on my lips before rolling onto his back, and gasping out, "Amazing? Life changing? The best sex of your life?"

"Fine," I said, unable to hide the smirk tugging at the corners of my lips.

"I'll take it. There's always room for improvement." Chest heaving, his breaths were ragged and strained.

I snuggled myself into the crook of his arm, and we gazed up at the stars.

"Aelia?" Tharan asked, his chest still heaving.

"Yes?"

"I don't know how to say this, so I'm just going to say it."

My stomach tightened.

"I'm going to miss you. I don't want to be separated, but I know we must."

"I'm going to miss you too."

"My heart already aches just thinking of not waking up next to you." He kissed my head. A simple act, but deeply intimate.

"At least we'll always be looking at the same sky. No matter where we are."

Tharan didn't respond, and when I lifted my head, he was fast asleep. I lay awake, listening to the sound of his content breathing. If I stayed awake all night, perhaps tomorrow would never come.

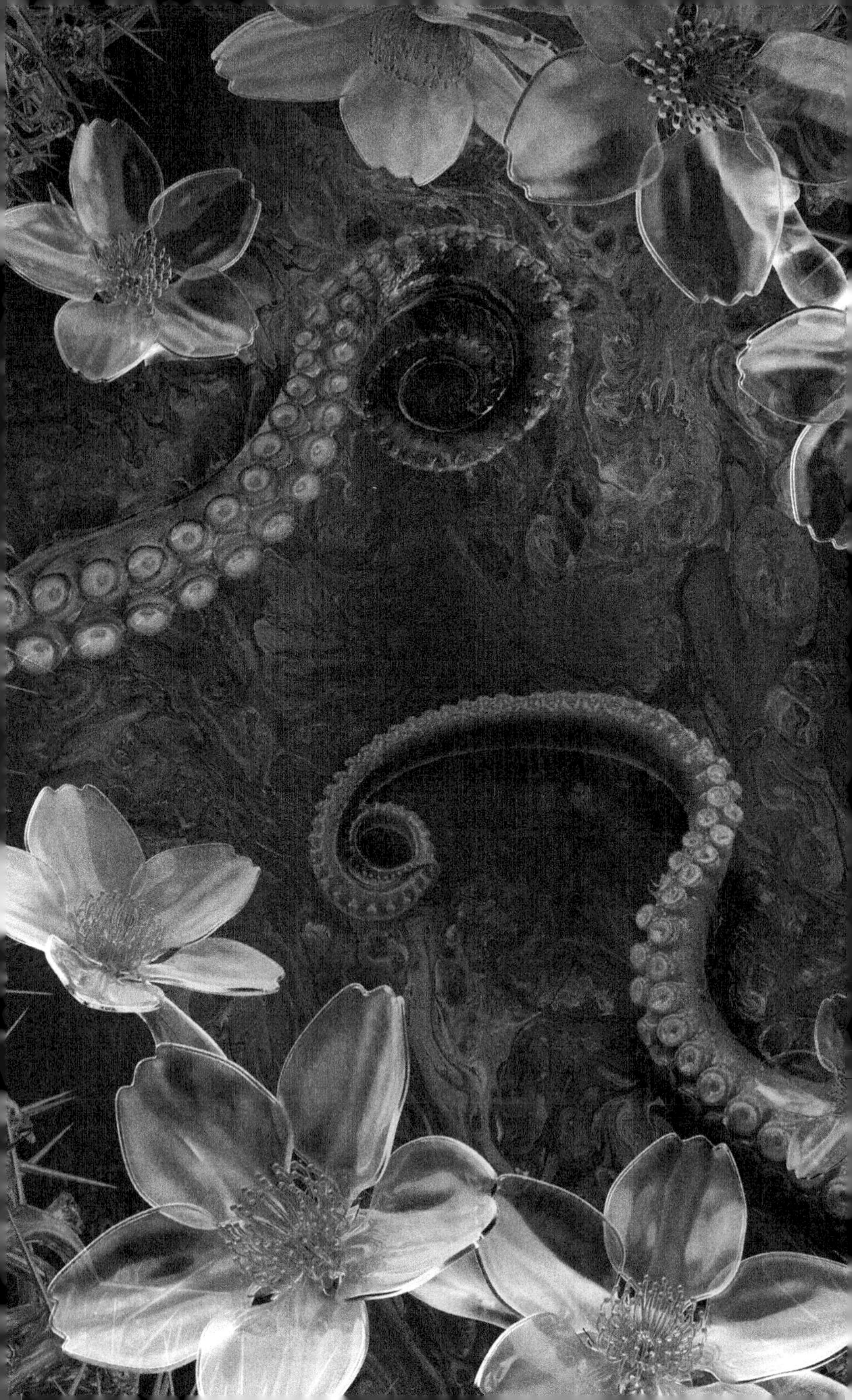

10 AELIA

The sound of birds chirping woke me early the next morning. The winter sun cast everything in a pale light. Tharan lay asleep next to me. I wanted to wake him, but I also wanted to freeze this picture of him in my mind: his wine-colored hair, the way his lips looked so lush and kissable even when he was asleep. His chest rose and fell with deep breaths, the way you sleep when you know you're perfectly safe.

My eyes fell to his bare chest, and I traced his toned muscles down to where a deep v cut his hips. I bit my lip. My core quaked at the thought of him inside me. I could already imagine the beautiful feeling of my breath catching in my throat, as his sensual mouth claimed mine while our bodies became one. The delicious ache between my legs—a reminder of the passion we'd shared last night.

His eyes flickered open. "Enjoying the view?"

"Always," I said, giving him a wink. "Thank you for last night. This place is amazing."

"You're welcome." He pulled me in for a kiss. His mouth still tasted of the champagne we'd had the night before. "I wanted to make it a night to remember."

"I'd say you succeeded." A smile tugged at the corners of my lips.

Our foreheads touched, and Tharan let out a sigh. "Let's just stay here and let the world melt away."

"Both of us have too much of a conscience for that."

He clicked his tongue. "Don't I know it?"

"It's still early, though."

"Time is irrelevant when you're a king. There are always things that need tending to, and with our impending travel, we must get back. A sleigh should arrive shortly, and we will be on our way."

I lay back in the bed, dramatically draping my forearm over my eyes. "I don't want to."

Tharan trailed kisses down my arm, playfully nipping at my neck. I tried to steel my face, but I couldn't help but smile when I was around him.

"The sleigh will be here shortly, and I'm sure you'll want a hot cup of cocoa for the ride home."

"Well, I guess I could be persuaded."

"That's what I thought." He kissed my cheek before rolling out of bed.

I pulled the fur-lined cloak over my nightgown and slipped my feet into a pair of satin slippers while Tharan donned his white shirt and cloak. Taking my hand in his, he led me out of the sanctuary, back down the marble corridor, and into the chilly winter morning, where a sleigh pulled by two dappled draft horses waited for us. Tharan helped me to my seat.

We sped through the forest. I sipped hot cocoa while the trees sped by. As we approached the Alder Palace, a pit grew ever larger in my stomach. I didn't want to leave this place—the first place I'd known true peace in fifteen years, but like most good things in my life, it was not meant to last.

Tharan pulled me close, and I reveled in his warmth. Neither of us said anything, not wanting words to spoil our remaining hours together.

Frost and Winter sprinted up to the sleigh when we arrived at the palace, whining and wagging their tails. Tharan helped me out before kneeling to let his wolves lick his face. Winter trotted over to me, nuzzling my hand with her nose.

"I've missed you too, girl," I said, giving her a scratch on the neck.

She wagged her tail happily.

Hopper and Sumac appeared in the doorway. Each dressed in their respective traveling attire. Sumac in a light armor made of silver leaves and Hopper in a brass buttoned jacket. The morning sun caught in his amber eyes, illuminating the deep golden hues within. He stood the way only someone with military experience could: feet shoulder-width apart, eyes straight ahead, stoic expression on his handsome face. I imagined all the trouble Tharan and Hopper got into in their youth. Both handsome cadets—lovers would have fallen at their feet. An old version of myself would have felt jealous at that thought, but I knew Tharan only had eyes for me.

I hadn't forgotten his proposition from the other night. I'd never been with two men at once. The idea was intriguing, but I didn't want to hurt either of them, and these sorts of things usually ended badly.

"The servants have prepared your things, my Lord," Hopper said, not breaking his gaze.

"Ah, very well then," he took my hand. "We will ready ourselves to leave. Is Baylis awake?"

"Yes, she's awake, and she is also ready to depart."

"Good," Tharan said, leading me into the palace. "Have everything packed and ready in an hour."

My stomach tightened. "So soon?"

"There's no sense in putting it off." He squeezed my hand.

"You're right." I was going to have to face my fears sometime, so I might as well get it over with.

I stared at the bedchamber we shared for the last few weeks. It had become my home. I hadn't felt comfortable in anyone's bed but my own in a very long time, and Tharan made me feel like this was ours, not just some place where his lover slept. I ran my hand over the intricately patterned quilt, tracing the delicate designs made of fine thread.

"Aelia, it's time." Tharan stood in the doorway to his dressing room. His hair was tied back in an olive ribbon, and he wore his royal doublet, complete with the seal of the Alder King on the breast. I sucked in a breath and the sight of him. Power seemed to radiate from every pore. His skin glowed with vitality… with magic.

"What about the crown?" I asked.

"I am not that audacious. I'll put it on when I get to Elohim."

"I wish I could see you walk into the Great Hall. I'm sure your grandfather will be shocked to see you."

"More like annoyed. But he did agree to see me, so I guess that's something."

"I've heard stories of Elohim. How the streets are paved with gold."

Tharan chuckled. "Not quite. White marble or granite, but yes, it is very lavish."

I quickly changed into my traveling outfit: leather boots and a white tunic with a burgundy sweater over it.

"Are we meeting back here, or should I meet you in Elohim?"

"Back here. I doubt they'd let you through the gates."

"That's very true." I strapped my dagger to my thigh.

"Ready?" he asked with a smile.

"I guess. There's one last thing I need to do."

I grabbed the Scepter of the Dead from where it sat on a plush pillow. "Take this, and I'll meet you out front shortly."

Tharan nodded, taking the scepter from me.

Can I come out for the trip? the Morrigan's voice whined in my ear.

I rolled my eyes. "You can come out when we get to Ruska."

Fine.

I kissed Tharan on the cheek and quickly ran to the stables, where Arion waited for me. He greeted me with a snort, and his breath turned to vapor in the cool air.

I snagged an apple from a barrel and laid it flat in my hand before offering it to Arion. He nibbled it delicately. I ran a loving hand over his velvet fur.

"I'm sorry I can't take you on this adventure, boy." I leaned in one last time to take in his scent before planting a kiss on his mane. We'd been through so much together, and it felt wrong to leave him. But he'd be safe here.

"Be good." I gave him one last pat before returning to the castle.

Tharan entwined his hand with mine. Two carriages sat, ready to depart in opposite directions. Royal advisors and the palace staff lined the walkway, waving to us as we passed. Before we parted ways, Tharan turned to face them. "I appreciate everything you do for this kingdom and the Wild Courts. I will be gone for a long while. While I am away, Fionn, Master of Coin, and Wren, Master of Forestry, will be in charge. Please give them the same respect you would give me."

The servants bowed their heads in respect. Some wiped tears from their eyes. In the short time Tharan had been the Alder King, his people had come to love him. A far cry from the iron fist Gideon ruled with.

Hopper and Sumac stood in front of Tharan's carriage while

Baylis waited for me in front of ours. I didn't want to let go of Tharan's hand. I wasn't ready to say goodbye.

"You must be strong, my love. We will see each other again. And we have these." He tapped his ear.

I mustered the best smile I could. "This isn't goodbye."

"No. We'll see each other soon." His hands cupped my face, and he leaned in for one last kiss.

The crowd cheered, and my cheeks reddened. Taking one last look at Tharan, I held a fist to my heart.

"I love you," he whispered in my ear before escorting me into the black, lacquered carriage.

My heart twisted in my chest. In the heat of passion, I told Tharan I loved him, but now in the clear light of day, my hesitations returned in full.

Baylis took a seat across from me, and I fought the tears welling behind my eyes. A horrible feeling of dread swept over me, chilling me to the bone. I may not be a seer like my sister, but I knew enough to read the signs.

"It will be alright, Aelia. We'll be back here in no time," Baylis said, patting my knee.

I blew Tharan one last kiss. He caught it and put it in his pocket before disappearing into his carriage.

Fingers shaking, I lit a cigarette, hoping the smoke would calm my nerves.

"I know, I have to keep telling myself that. But I can't shake this feeling that something is going to go terribly wrong."

"Things have been going wrong for fifteen years, Aelia." She took the cigarette from me and held it to her lips, inhaled, and blew the smoke out the little window of the carriage. "You'd think we'd be used to it by now."

"Part of me thinks it's good we haven't yet. My humanity isn't fully gone."

The carriages pulled away, and I sunk into the plush seat,

taking another drag off my cigarette. I wanted to turn my whisper stone to check if it worked, but I wasn't ready to show Baylis yet.

We glided through the burned forest into the lush area unaffected by the battle that threatened to ruin an entire faction of sylph. A smooth ride, the elegant carriage was a far cry from the rattling boxes I'd traveled in as a mercenary. The trees reached into the heavens; their trunks so wide they carved tunnels through them. Snow trickled through the thick canopy as the horses trotted along. With each passing step, the knots in my chest tightened a little bit more.

With the dense snow and cold temperatures, it would take us weeks to get to Ruska, but luckily, there was a portal to the Alder Embassy a few days' ride away—a precaution in case any adversaries ever got through.

Tharan would not be so lucky. Elohim would never allow a sylph court to portal into their territory. He'd have to go through countless checkpoints, and even then, he would be watched like a hawk. It would take at least a month, if not more, for him to get to Elohim, unless they allowed him to portal once he entered their territory.

I leaned back, cigarette to my lips. "What do you think Mother looks like now?" I inhaled the smoke into my lungs.

"Probably the same. She never aged in the years I knew her. They say all three need to be together for their powers to work—past, present, and future." She stared out the window. The reflection of light off the snow made her pale complexion sparkle. Her hands twisted a handkerchief nervously.

"All these years, I've resented her for seeing my future and knowingly sending me to my doom. Now, I wonder if she could see anything at all," I said.

Baylis bit her nail, shaving off little bits of herself. "I wonder why I can suddenly see things too. What did I see for Gideon? Is what I'm seeing correct or only the possibility of things to come?"

"Maybe Mother will have the answers. You saw the past before—Or… was that a memory?"

Baylis didn't answer.

I stared out at the forest. A red cardinal flitted between the branches—a sign of good fortune. Perhaps my fears were unfounded.

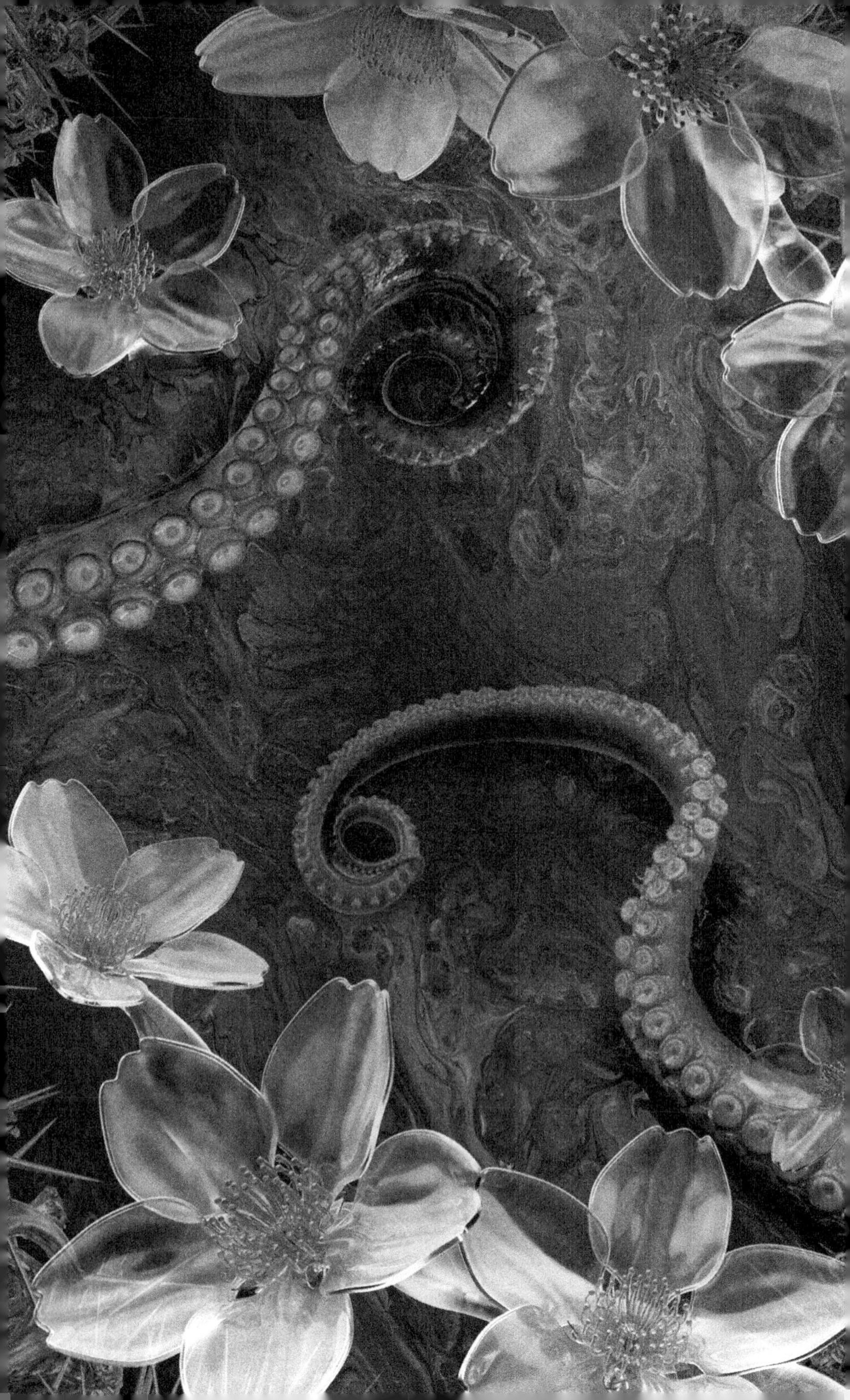

11 CAIDEN

Caiden's fingers drummed on the old oak table deep beneath Vantris. The smell of ancient parchment mixed with the dampness of the basement made him shiver as he thumbed through the ancient texts.

"Find anything?" a deep voice asked.

Caiden looked up to see Roderick standing over the desk. "Not yet," he replied. "I can barely read this ancient script."

"Let me look at it." Roderick pulled a pair of round spectacles from his breast pocket and placed them over his aquiline nose.

Caiden handed him the book. "You can read ancient sylph?"

"A little. Some of the most revered writings on war were written before the Trinity. So, I had to learn," Roderick replied.

"Huh, you learn something new every day, I guess."

"It's not something I've shared before. I don't think it's ever come up." Roderick dragged a finger over the script. "This is an old remedy for watery bowels. I don't think we will find anything about the Trinity Wells in this one."

Caiden ran a hand down his chiseled face. "I've been reading about watery bowels for hours?"

"Perhaps you need a break, my friend. These scrolls will be

here tomorrow, I assure you. Come to dinner at our place. Amolie has prepared a lovely pasta, and you look like you could use a glass of wine."

Caiden rubbed the weariness from his eyes.

"I guess I have been down here a long time."

"C'mon, it'll be nice."

Caiden looked at the stacks of tomes surrounding him. There was so much to dig through and not enough hours in the day to do so. Guilt pulled at his heart.

"Fine."

"Wonderful, Amolie will be so happy to see you."

Caiden's stomach grumbled. "I guess I am hungry."

"Let's go." Roderick ushered him out of the cold basement of the library.

As they walked through the rows of ancient books, a question gnawed at Caiden. "Roderick?"

"Yes?"

"What do you know about Aelia?"

His friend shot him a questioning look, not halting his stride. "What do you want to know?"

"I feel like we've met somewhere before, but I can't put my finger on it."

"You were the emissary to all the human lands, you probably met on one of your visits."

Caiden's mouth twisted as he wracked his brain, trying to remember their meeting. "That has to be it."

"She's trouble, Caiden, and she's taken. You're better off forgetting her."

Caiden sighed. "I know, but I see her face every time I close my eyes. I can't help but be attracted to her."

Roderick stopped dead in his tracks. The flames of the torches danced across his fearsome face. His eyes narrowed on his friend. "Forget. Her."

Caiden swallowed hard. "How can I?"

"Find someone else, anyone else, but not Aelia. She is taken, and the Alder King would have every right to kill you if he knew you were attracted to his lover."

Caiden ran a hand through his golden locks. "You're right. I know. I need to find someone new." Even as the words left his mouth, he knew they were lies. He wanted to know Aelia in a way he hadn't wanted to know any woman since his wife. Tharan was a known flirt who broke every heart he encountered. It would only be a matter of time before he broke Aelia's. Being the Alder King, he'd be expected to marry for an alliance, and as far as he knew, Aelia had no land, magic, or money to her name. Unless controlling the army of the dead counted. Now that he thought about it, it was a very good thing to have in one's back pocket.

"You are a Lord of the Stormlands. You can have any woman you want. Cassandra would want that for you," Roderick said.

"After we find these Trinity Wells. There's no use in starting something if there's a war going on."

Roderick nodded in agreement, and they continued on their way through the ancient library. The smell of old parchment and incense filled the air. Scholars studied at long wooden tables littered with low-burning candles.

"Have you asked any of the scholars for help?" Roderick asked, smiling at the intellects as they passed—some of the younger ones hid coy smiles.

"You're popular here."

Roderick smiled incredulously. "They only know me for my love of poetry and history and as the captain of the Stormland armies. They have no idea who I am beyond that. Now, let's find Ora. She can help us."

They wandered to the reference desk, where a scholar dressed in heavy brown robes sat, her head covered with a hood. Three silver bars clipped to the hood indicated that she had been training for thirty years.

Roderick cleared his throat, and the woman looked up from the book she was reading. Caiden's heart skipped a beat when her brown eyes met his.

"Oh, Roderick, I didn't see you there," she said in a high-pitched whisper, smiling wide.

"Master Ora, we could use your help locating something." He leaned against the desk in the way only Roderick could, naturally sensual and sending hearts racing.

"Of course, what is it you are looking for?" Her eyes flitted to Caiden's momentarily and then back to Roderick's.

Roderick craned his neck, noting every person, both seen and unseen. "It's a delicate matter. Perhaps there's somewhere more private we could go?"

She nodded and closed her book.

"Follow me."

The pair followed the woman through the hallowed halls of the Great Library, up twisted staircases, and through secret passageways until they reached the inner sanctum, where the scholars kept their private residences. Ora led them through a simple wooden door to a suite with modest accommodations: a single bed, desk, fireplace, and washroom—the only things a scholar needed when the university provided the rest.

Taking a seat on the bed, Ora removed her hood, dark curls spilled over her shoulders. In the dim light, her brown eyes glowed against her tanned skin. Her striking features left Caiden speechless. Deep-set eyes complimented her Roman nose and Cupid's bow lips. Too beautiful to be a scholar—too beautiful to be untouchable. "This should do for privacy. Now, what is it I am looking for?"

Caiden cleared his throat. "What do you know of the Trinity Wells?"

She arched a brow. "I know they are nothing but a myth as far as most are concerned. A tale used to put restless minds at ease."

"What if they were real?" Roderick asked.

"If they were real, everyone and their mother would be out looking for them. Did you come here to waste my time?"

Caiden cleared his throat again, narrowing his eyes on the scholar. "Hypothetically speaking, we may or may not have found evidence to suggest they're not just real, but capable of releasing an ancient evil in the very immediate future."

She placed her hands on her hips, studying the two men before her. Her angular face contorted as she tried to decipher whether they were lying.

"I assume you've heard of Crom Cruach?" Caiden asked.

She nodded.

"Well, we have reason to believe two individuals plan to use the Wells to bring him back," Caiden said.

The color drained from her face. "No one knows where he's buried. I think you need a body to resurrect it," she said.

"There's no telling what raw magic can do."

Caiden gazed into the embers of the fire.

Ora's mouth scrunched to the side as she considered everything Caiden had just told her.

"Then I guess it is serious." The words rolled off her tongue in an accent Caiden didn't recognize.

"We'd be grateful for the help, Ora," Roderick said.

"Meet me tomorrow in the archives, and we will search together. I can't promise anything. Much of our collection was destroyed during the Sylph and Elven War."

"Thank you," Caiden said.

"I live to serve, my Lord." She bowed her head in reverence to him, and his mouth went dry at the sight of her.

"I'll meet you tomorrow afternoon in the archives then."

"See you tomorrow." She escorted them out of her chambers,

back down the twisting staircases, and through the various studies. The smell of old books and leather made Caiden feel at ease.

A breath slipped between his lips as he and Roderick entered the crowded square.

"Somebody has a crush," Roderick said, elbowing his friend in the ribs.

"She's very pretty, but I meant what I said. We need to focus on the Wells, and then I can think about romance."

Roderick clicked his tongue. "There is always time for romance. Even in battle."

"Not all of us are honey tongues."

"I don't even need that gift. I'm attractive without it." He puffed out his buff chest.

"Yeah, yeah, we all know you're the most handsome of the group." Caiden rolled his eyes at his friend. It was true, though. Anywhere they went, lustful eyes fell on Roderick. Between his height, masculine jaw, and piercing green eyes, it was hard to look away from him.

The capital city buzzed with energy as citizens went about their day, working and caring for children, oblivious to the evil lurking outside their doors.

"I'm scared, Roderick," Caiden said as they turned down a cobblestone street lined with brightly colored townhomes.

Roderick let out an audible sigh. "I know what you mean. I am afraid, too. Afraid I'll never get to marry Amolie. Afraid there will be no home for our children. Or no children at all if we can't stop what's coming."

"Let's hope Ora finds something. Let's hope Aelia and Tharan can find something as well."

They stopped in front of a townhome painted a bright shade of pink with blue shutters. Roderick bought this place long ago when he was a bachelor. It was where he and Amolie met in secret before they came out as a couple.

"Ah, home sweet home," Roderick said, turning the key in the lock.

"Like you don't have another house in the Stormlands."

"Well, you know what I mean." He pushed open the door, and the smell of butter and roasted garlic filled their senses.

"Trinity, that smells good," Caiden said, unhooking his cloak and handing it to Roderick.

"Caiden!" Amolie came bounding from the kitchen, wooden spoon in hand, curls spilling over a hastily tied handkerchief. "I'm so happy you could join us. Lucius has been regaling me with tales of his secret missions while we waited for you." She gave him a warm smile and pulled him in for a hug. The smell of sage was still detectable on her skin under a medley of savory scents.

Roderick and Caiden exchanged knowing glances. Lucius never regaled. He only stated the facts and the facts alone. But sure enough, as they entered the kitchen, they found the wraith, wine in hand, leaning against the butcher's block, his normally quaffed hair disheveled.

"Someone is having a good time," Caiden said, pouring himself a glass.

"The world will end soon, and I can't stop it. My shadows can't stop it. So why not drink?"

"I don't think I've ever seen you drink before, Lucius. How many have you had?" Roderick asked, chopping up a carrot for Amolie.

"This is my first time. Can you believe it?" He held up his glass.

"He's only had the one," Amolie whispered to Roderick.

Caiden rolled his eyes. "Why don't you sit down? We're about to eat."

Lucius sipped his drink and slumped into a chair at the nearby table.

"I have to go on a mission tomorrow. I got a lead on Gideon

and Erissa and want to check it out myself. My men do not know them like I do," he hiccupped.

In all his years, Caiden had never seen Lucius drink; especially not before he went on a hunt. "Is everything alright?"

"The mission in the Land of Myst—far on the other side of the continent. It will take me ages to get there. And… it's where I got my curse from." He leaned his head back and extended his long legs out in front of him, practically laying in the chair.

Caiden, Roderick, and Amolie all paused to stare at their friend. He'd never talked about the source of his curse before, only that his mother gave it to him and then abandoned him.

"Is that where your mother is from?" Caiden asked.

He stared at the ceiling, his hands intertwined, resting on his chest.

"I do not know where my mother is, but my father is… alive and well there. He is the reason wraiths exist at all. The master of their power. The keeper of the souls, the one who created the curse."

Everyone blinked at him.

"Wow, everyone is just coming out of the woodwork with secrets today. First, Roderick and his ability to read ancient sylph, and now you with your weird father… er, maker?"

Lucius pulled his lithe body forward as though it was made of lead. Reaching for his glass, he drank deeply, until it was empty.

"He does not know of my existence. But if he did, I assume he would try to pull my strings and make me a servant like turned wraiths. But I am… as far as I know… the only born wraith on this continent." Lucius wiped his mouth with his sleeve.

Caiden downed his wine.

"Are you going to see him? Can he reverse it? How did it happen in the first place?"

Lucius shook his head.

"I've been asking those questions to myself my whole life."

He drummed his long fingers on the table. "I was looking through some old books to see if I had anything on the Trinity Wells, and I came across the packet the orphanage sent with me to the military academy. And they had what is akin to a birth certificate, where my mother's name was, and next to Father, she wrote *The Master of the Myst.* So that's how I found out."

"That's brutal," Roderick said. "No wonder you're drinking. I would be, too."

Lucius pushed a stray piece of white hair out of his face. "Sorry, I didn't mean to ruin the special occasion."

"What special occasion?" Amolie asked, tossing noodles in a hefty amount of butter and thyme.

Roderick shot his friend a look that said, *I will kill you later.* "Well, I guess there's no time better than the present." He gently took the bowl from Amolie's dainty fingers and placed it on the counter before falling to one knee.

Amolie's freckled cheeks flushed. "Oh, uh. Is this what I think it is?"

"If you want it to be." He pulled a ring on a silver chain from his back pocket. "It's an emerald, your favorite."

Amolie gasped at the ring. "I don't know what to say."

A bright smile cut his face in two. "Say you'll be mine. Forever. Say you'll have children with me. Say you'll sleep next to me every night until we take our last breaths."

"Yes. Of course, yes!" She wrapped her arms around Roderick, and he lifted her. Their mouths met in a passionate kiss.

Caiden and Lucius could only smile at their friends. They'd loved secretly for so long and would now start a family together. Caiden couldn't help the ache in his heart. He'd once asked the love of his life to marry him on a beach in the Court of Scales in early spring. It had been unusually cold that day, and Cassandra hadn't wanted to go to begin with, but Caiden begged her for a walk. He had it all planned out. He'd propose where they first met. It seemed only fitting. He could still remember the look on Cassandra's jovial face when he'd gotten down on one knee and asked her to be his for an eternity. His heart swelled and shrank all at once. He doubted he'd ever feel that way again.

Setting Amolie down, Roderick fastened the necklace around her neck, as was customary, until the couple's hands were bound.

Lucius and Caiden cheered, hearts full for their friends.

"Do you think your father would perform the ceremony tomorrow? Just us," Amolie asked.

"I'll send a messenger over first thing after dinner. Now… about dinner…"

"Of course," Amolie said, passing him a bowl of chopped tomatoes in olive oil. "Let's eat!"

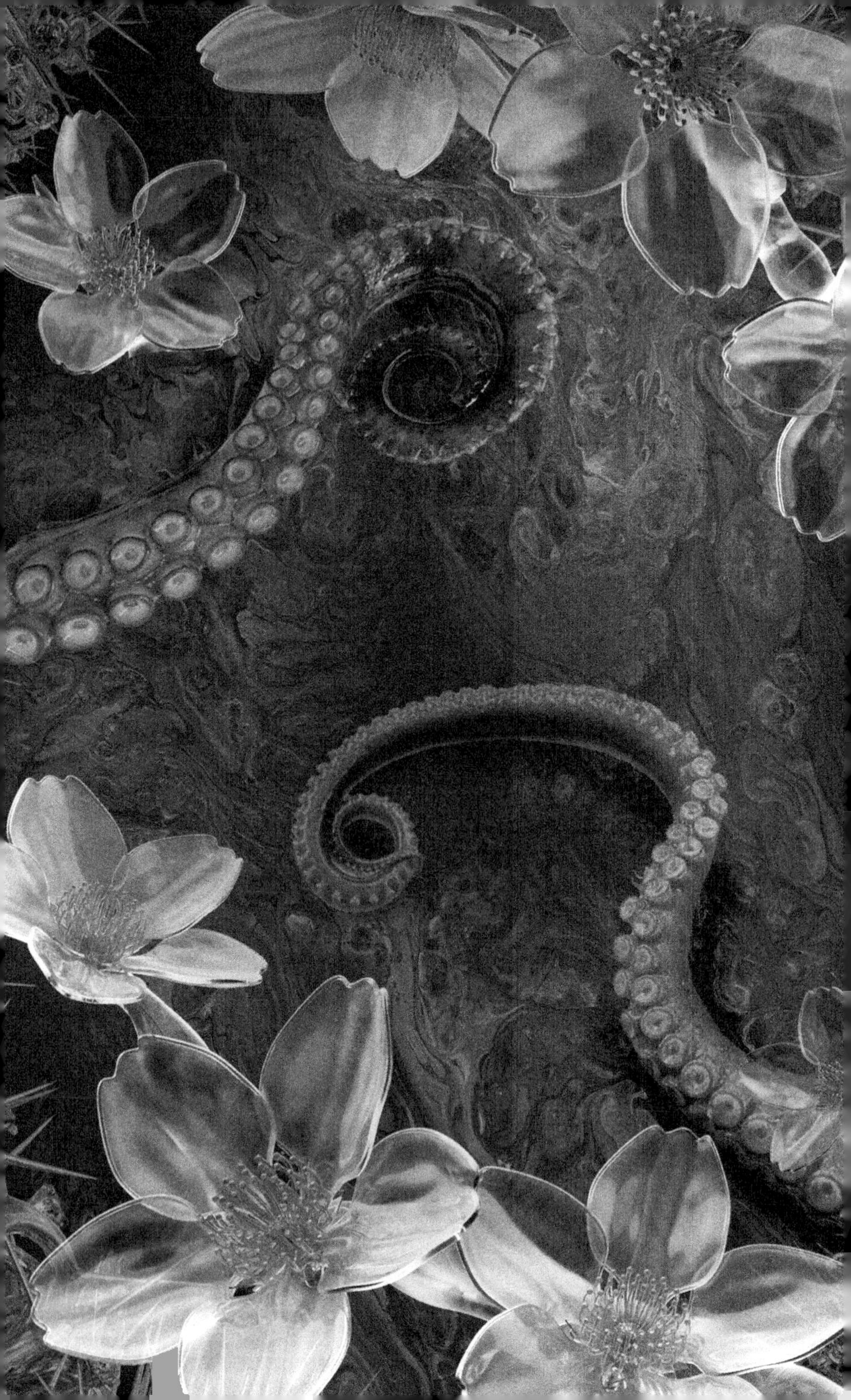

12 CAIDEN

Caiden walked through the snowy streets of Vantris, chewing on a piece of willow bark to ease his throbbing head as he went. His stomach fluttered thinking about seeing Ora again, but he still hadn't shaken the way his heart leapt when he thought of Aelia. Her inviting eyes, the way her hips rounded, the smile that lit up her face. He wanted to make her laugh, and he didn't know why.

The library was quieter in the afternoons when most classes at the university took place. Paintings of the War of Three Kings scaled the walls. The dancing flames of the torches made them come alive.

"Beautiful, isn't it?" Ora's soft voice echoed from behind him. He turned to see the brown-eyed beauty staring up at the intricate painting of the famous Alder King Eoghan smiting a demon with the horns of a goat and the fangs of a wolf.

"It's certainly something," he said, wiping his palms on his pants. "I dreamed of being a fierce warrior, but a poison arrow cut my dreams short."

"Not all warriors kill with swords," Ora said.

"I guess that's true."

"Come, my Lord, I think I have found something you may be interested in."

Caiden followed Ora down into the depths of the archives, where stacks of manuscripts piled high. She pulled a massive leather-bound tome from one of the shelves and heaved it onto a nearby desk. Blowing the dust off it, she cracked it open to a page depicting the three goddesses Amenna, Eris, and Illya. All three pointed skyward to a constellation of stars known as the Huntress.

"What does the Huntress have to do with this?"

"Nothing, I thought at first, then I read the inscription: *In the darkest nights when hope hangs askew, look to the stars to guide you through.*"

"So?" Caiden still didn't understand how this connected to the Wells. "That's just an old saying for children who get lost in the woods."

"Look at her, the tip of her arrow. They are all pointing to it. I think it has something to do with it."

"Why do you think that?"

"This book is old. It was written when the Trinity still walked the earth, yet look at the colors. They're vibrant. This book should be faded and disintegrated into pieces, but no, it's pristine as though it was printed yesterday. It is brimming with magic. I can feel it radiating through me. As far as I know, the Trinity created the Wells as a kind of fail-safe should the world need saving or the magic ran out… or something terrible like that, but they couldn't just put them out in plain sight."

"Okay, and?"

"And look at the stars!" Her eyes widened, and her nostrils flared. "They are off. They aren't correct. Only the tip of the arrow is correct. The Trinity is standing on the highest peak of the Cheyne Mountains, looking north. They shouldn't even be able to see the Huntress from that view."

"This was made over ten thousand years ago. Maybe the skies were different then?"

She pinched the bridge of her nose. "It's a puzzle. I think we need to take this book somewhere and align it with the north star."

"Oh," Caiden said, swallowing his fear of heights. "You mean the mountains?"

"Maybe? I need to take this to my elders. Maybe they know more."

"No." He touched her arm. "No, we have to keep this between us. Whatever is hidden in this book, we can figure it out."

Her eyes flitted between him and the book.

"You're really serious about this, aren't you? Someone *is* after the Trinity Wells."

"Yes," Caiden said. "It's like I said before. Crom's followers will stop at nothing to bring him back."

Her eyes fell to the book. "It has been so long since he walked this plane. I thought his name would be forgotten to time."

"Evil is never truly dead."

Ora bit her plump lower lip, and Caiden recognized the fear in her eyes. It had been a long time since such a threat knocked on Vantris's door. People forgot what evil looked like. But that's what evil wanted. It waited for you to forget its monstrous ways, to become comfortable in your life, and then it struck.

The bells of the temple chimed, and Caiden knew he had to get to his parents' for Amolie and Roderick's binding ceremony. "I have to go, but I'll be back tomorrow. Keep looking." His voice trailed off as he climbed the ancient stairs.

Walking through the great halls of the library, Caiden stared up at the ceiling where the night sky was painted in silver and gold. He stopped and stared at the Huntress. The same star at the tip of her arrow shone brighter than the others.

"That's odd," he said to himself. Scanning the rest of the ceiling, he noticed each of the other constellations had one prominent star. Could they be related, or was this just a feature of the paintings at the time? He should get to his parents' house, but something tugged at him. Turning on his heel, he raced down to the archives where Ora still studied the book, spectacle over one eye.

"I think it has something to do with the painting upstairs," he said, trying to catch his breath.

Ora arched a brow. "Which one? You're going to have to be more specific. This is a gallery as well as a library."

"The one on the ceiling. All the constellations have one illuminated star."

"Hmmm... Okay, grab the book, and let's go look."

Caiden lifted the massive tome from the desk and carried it up the stairs after Ora.

She gazed at the ceiling, and Caiden's pulse quickened as her silken hair fell over one shoulder, revealing her long, delicate neck.

"These must have been done by the same artist. Or at least someone who studied under him," she said, pointing to the arrow of the Huntress.

Caiden sat the book on the table, and she hurriedly flipped through the pages.

"Ah-ha!" she proclaimed to the sound of multiple shushes.

Caiden moved in closer to get a better look. The smell of honeysuckle on her hair made him think of summer days lying in the grass in his youth. "What is it?"

"See here, the artist left his signature." She pointed to what looked like a scribble at the corner of the painting.

Caiden spread a piece of tracing paper over it and traced the symbol. It looked awfully familiar. Had he seen it before or were his eyes playing tricks on him? He wracked his brain trying to remember where he'd seen the twisted symbol before. Was it at his parents' house? He'd have to look.

"Have you seen this before?" he asked.

"No, but art history is not my specialty. Let's see if we can find something similar on the ceiling. If we can match the signatures, perhaps they're connected."

The two spread out. Heads to the sky, looking for the infamous mark. Caiden squinted and nearly ran into an elderly scholar with a long white beard.

"Watch where you're going," he mumbled under his breath and pushed past Caiden.

Another bell chimed. "Shit," Caiden whispered. He couldn't stay much longer, or he'd be late for Amolie and Roderick's ceremony. His eyes frantically searched the night sky for anything resembling the signature. Eventually, Caiden and Ora's paths led them back together.

"Find anything?" Caiden asked.

"No. It's too high up. I'll have to find an art historian to help us." She closed the book on the desk. "I'll let you know when I have more information."

The two parted ways, and Caiden headed for his parent's house across the city. As he walked, he replayed the image of the map in his mind over and over again. There had to be something more to it. What was he missing?

Before he realized it, he was on his parents' doorstep, red ribbons tangled in the breeze—a blessing of fertility for the couple.

The music of a small string band floated through the house. Caiden made his way to the conservatory, where Lucius waited in his finest doublet adorned with golden accents.

"Glad to see you delayed your mission to be here."

"How could I miss my best friend's binding ceremony? I'm cold, not heartless."

Caiden shot his friend a knowing glance. "I always knew you were a romantic at heart."

"Let's not go that far." He smoothed his perfectly quaffed long hair before tugging at his doublet. Caiden wondered whether Lucius kept lovers in secret. With his striking features and toned body, he would be attractive to anyone, man or woman. But Caiden also knew not to ask him about it. What Lucius did on his own time was his business.

"Are you going to change before the ceremony?" he asked, looking Caiden up and down.

"What's wrong with this?" Caiden examined his simple vest and breeches.

"Well, it's your friend's binding ceremony. I hope you'd want to celebrate the occasion."

Caiden sighed and headed to his room, where he quickly changed into a navy velvet doublet with lightning embroidered on it. As he glanced at himself in the mirror, he caught a glimpse of a bookshelf behind him. Inscribed on one of the book's spines was none other than the same signature he'd seen at the library. Grabbing the book, he raced down to meet his father. Tonin looked ever the king with his short, clipped beard and crown of silver lightning.

"Father, do you know what this symbol is? Who made it?"

Tonin glanced at the book. "This is the ancient symbol for the Trinity. The Trinity or one of their advisors wrote this. Why are you asking me about this old book?"

"I found a similar marking in a book in the library. But we couldn't decipher the artists' names. We think it may have something to do with the Trinity Wells."

His father's blue eyes grew wide. "*A History of Moriana*. I can't even remember where we got this. It must have been in our family for generations."

"I'm going to take it to the library and see if I can learn anything about it tomorrow."

"Just bring it back."

Caiden tucked the book away just as his mother came into the conservatory.

"It's time," she said, clasping her hands together in excitement. Her tight ringlets bounced as she took her place next to Tonin.

The band began to play, and Amolie appeared in the doorway dressed head to toe in red satin. Her hair was immaculately braided into a crown around her head, and her eyes sparkled in a way only a bride's could. She held a bouquet of bloodred roses to complement her dress. Caiden's eyes flitted to Roderick, whose normally stoic demeanor was now one of awe. He'd known his friend for sixty years and never once seen him look at anyone the way he was looking at Amolie now.

Caiden's heart swelled, remembering his own binding ceremony with his wife, Cassandra. They were married at her family's palace in the Court of Scales. She glowed just like Amolie did. He wiped a tear from his eye at the memory. Some days, he missed her terribly. On other days, the pain was easier to bear.

Lucius patted him on the shoulder. "It's okay. We all miss her."

Caiden nodded, putting his best smile forward for Amolie and Roderick.

Roderick extended a hand to his bride, and together they knelt before Tonin.

"Today, we are here to witness the binding of Amolie Hazelwood and Roderick Bonecleaver. Just a few decades ago, it would've been illegal for such a marriage to take place, but I am happy to see us moving forward and away from our prejudices. I have known Roderick since his days at the Academy. I will say I never thought he'd settle down, but then I met Amolie, and I knew she was the one who would tame him."

A chuckle from the crowd.

Tonin turned his piercing gaze to Amolie, who knelt with her head bowed. "Amolie, you are one of the strongest women I have ever met. Save for my wife, of course." He winked at Tempestia, who blushed. "A binding is not to be taken lightly. I know both of you know this."

Amolie and Roderick nodded. "We do."

"And you promise to care for one another until the end of your days?"

"We do."

Tonin pulled the ceremonial dagger from behind his back, the sigil of the Stormlands engraved into its hilt. "Let your blood flow through this dagger the way Illya intended." He handed the blade to Roderick, who made a slit across his palm, letting the blood fill the engraving before handing it to Amolie, who did the same.

"Your blood has mixed on the sacred dagger. You are known to our goddess. Let your bodies and blood become one."

Amolie and Roderick pressed their palms together, and Tonin wrapped them in the sacred cloth.

"Rise, my children, and be known as bonded."

They rose to their feet, facing their friends, who clapped and cheered. Roderick beamed a white smile. Amolie's cheeks flushed pink.

After the ceremony, they gathered in the formal dining room of the townhome. Delicate pastries lined the table, including several rose cakes, which were Caiden and Lucius's favorite.

Amolie and Roderick stared at each other lovingly while the rest ate their dinner.

Caiden sipped his champagne, trying to fight the bittersweet feeling in his gut. He was happy for his friends, but the loss of his wife loomed large at the table. He stood, clinking his fork against his champagne glass.

"A toast to the happy couple. May your days be long, your fights be short, and your womb be fertile. Amolie, you tamed the untamable. Roderick, you won the lottery with this one. Treasure each other, for you never know what day will be your last." He mustered the best smile he could.

"Hear, hear!" the others said, clinking their glasses together and sipping their bubbly. Their eyes glittered with delight in the light of the chandelier.

Caiden took his seat next to Amolie.

"I know this is hard for you," she said, placing a hand over his. "Thank you for everything."

"That's what you do for friends." Caiden pushed away the pressure building in his eyes.

"Today has been perfect, but I'm sad Aelia couldn't be here." Her eyes lowered, and she fiddled with the napkin in her lap.

"You'll see her soon, though, right? You're going to Ruska in the morning?"

She nodded, and looped her arm around Roderick's bicep, gripping it tightly. He placed a reassuring hand over hers as he continued to joke with Lucius.

"Yes, such a bittersweet binding." She swallowed as she glanced around the room, clearly fighting tears. "It seems I may never have my family and friends in the same room again."

Caiden's heart ached for the witch. She was right. There would be no peace until they wiped Erissa and Gideon from the continent, and even then, certain factions had been hungry for war for a long time.

"C'mon, let's dance," Roderick chimed in, leading Amolie to the dance floor where once-grand balls had been held. Now, just two solo dancers swayed in the twinkling light of burning fairy lamps, holding each other tightly, knowing this could be the last night they ever spend together. Amolie laid her head on Roderick's broad chest. Shutting her eyes to savor the moment. Roderick rested his chin on his bride's head and together they swayed back and forth to the sound of the music as if there was no one else in the room but them.

Tonin escorted Tempestia to the floor, and together, the two danced looking lovingly at one another. Tempestia's diamond earrings sparkled in the light—a gift from Tonin on their binding day. Still in love after centuries, they shared the love Caiden longed for. The kind he'd thought he'd found with Cassandra.

He sighed, finishing his drink.

"I think I'm going to head up for the night. I've got an early morning tomorrow. I think Ora... er, one of the scholars at the library, has found something pertaining to the Trinity Wells."

"Well, that's something at least," Lucius said. He gazed out the window at the starless night. "Seems like a perfect time for me to slip away as well. I will meet you in the Woodland Realm for the Ostara celebration."

Caiden nodded, and the friends slipped out of the ballroom.

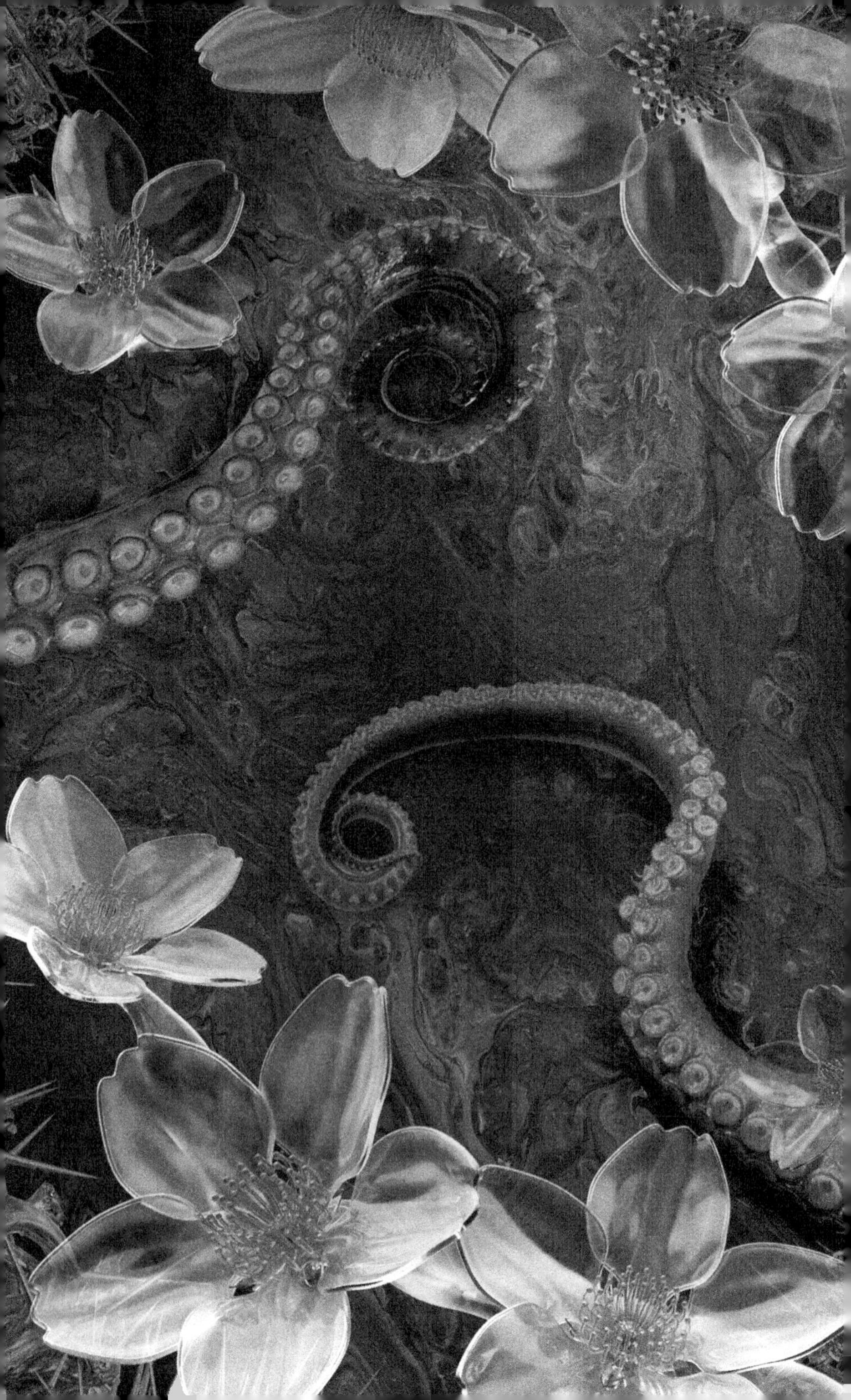

13 CAIDEN

Caiden's head ached from the champagne as he pulled himself out of bed the next morning. The house was still asleep when he tucked the book into the back of his trousers and donned his cloak. A thick layer of snow fell overnight, making the street slick. He did his best to hurry to the library.

The massive stone building stood high on a hill overlooking the city of Vantris. Built after the War of Three Kings, the library and university housed some of Moriana's greatest antiquities. Many of which were hidden during the Sylph and Elven War.

The enormous wood doors creaked open as Caiden entered. Rows of scholars and students lined the massive reading room where the starry night flickered overhead.

Ora sat hunched over a book. Her hair was tied back in a neat bun, save for two unruly pieces framing her face.

Caiden set the book he'd found on the table next to her. "I thought you might find this interesting."

Her brown eyes flitted to the book.

"Look at the marking on the spine…" Caiden said.

She ran her finger over the symbol. "*A History of Moriana.*

Hmm… could be useful. Let's see." Opening the book, she scanned the pages until she found something. "Ah-ha! Look!"

She held up a page just like the one they'd found the day before, but the consolation was different. This time, the Trinity pointed to the constellation of the Warrior.

"The star on the tip of his spear…" Caiden said, more to himself than to anyone else.

"You're right. It's glowing." Ora looked up to see the Warrior overhead. It wasn't simply glowing, a beam of light stretched from the spear's tip to the book's star.

"It *is* part of a puzzle!" Caiden exclaimed, followed by the inevitable shush from the scholars.

"Should we take this to a Grand Master?" Ora asked.

"No," Caiden whispered.

Ora scowled and signaled for an assistant, who came eagerly.

"We need Grand Master Quail to come here as quickly as possible."

The assistant bowed and rushed away.

Caiden clicked his tongue in disapproval.

"We need his help," she defended. "He can keep a secret."

"Can he? Because I've heard of his penchant for drinking and gambling."

"He's not like that anymore."

"Fine. If you say he's trustworthy."

The two waited silently for Grand Master Quail while other scholars shot them questioning looks. Ora shut the book, cutting off the beam. "Best not to draw attention."

A few moments later, a fumbling man in black robes with a tuft of white hair on his head appeared, sweat glistening on his brow. "Ah, Master Ora, I heard you found something interesting."

Ora cleared her throat. "Yes, Grand Master. What do you know of this symbol?" She pointed to the mark on the spine of the book.

Master Quail took out a pair of spectacles and placed them on the bridge of his button nose. "Ah yes, this is the mark of the Zylrith Weavers. It's a knot of magic being woven together. Some scholars think the Trinity tricked the Weavers into doing their bidding, stole their magic, and then eradicated them from the continent. Others believe a certain disease wiped them out. Who can say? They were immensely powerful magus, and now their name is but a whisper in history."

"Master, did the Weavers build this library?"

"I believe they did, yes." Master Quail picked up Caiden's book and examined it. "Where did you get this?"

"My father's library. Lord Tonin Stormweaver," Caiden said, leaning back on the desk, arms crossed over his chest.

Grand Master Quail straightened his glasses. "Well, that would make sense."

"Why is that?" Caiden's curiosity was piqued.

"An original family would have gotten something like this from the Lady Illya as a sign of gratitude." The man's shaking finger grazed over the ancient pages of the book.

"A book?" Caiden asked, cocking his head in confusion.

The Grand Master clicked his tongue. "Not just a book, my child. A history of the land. Of how we came to be."

"Sounds like a shit gift," Caiden huffed, crossing his legs over one another.

The old man scowled at him.

"They were numbered. Many are kept here for safety reasons. But some families kept them."

"So, the Weavers built this library, wrote these books, and then just disappeared?" Ora asked, looking up at the Grand Master like he was a god.

"In a manner of speaking, yes," Grand Master Quail said with a little chuckle.

Ora tapped her lips with one slim finger, contemplating whether to show her mentor the books or not.

"What is it, my child? Is something on your mind?"

Ora's eye flicked from Quail's to Caiden and back again.

"Just show him," Caiden said with a huff.

Cautiously, Ora opened the book, and light beamed out, connecting the two stars.

Grand Master Quail stared up at the ceiling in wonder. "Yes, a nifty little trick, isn't it?"

"You mean you knew about this?" Ora's mouth fell agape.

"Yes, the stars of the book connect to their respective stars on the ceiling."

"But why? There must be a reason."

"That, my dear, has been lost to time. If you'll excuse me, I have a class to teach on ancient sylph calligraphy."

Grand Master Quail shuffled away, muttering to himself under his breath.

"Well, that wasn't helpful," Ora said, shoulders slumping with disappointment.

"Yes, it was," Caiden said. "He said most of the other books are here. I think if we line all of them up, we'll get some answers, but we'll have to do it later when everyone is asleep."

"How will we get the other books if they're locked away? I don't have the clearance to check out books in the restricted section without a Grand Master."

"Would a letter from a High Council Member be helpful?"

"That could work." Her green eyes lit with excitement.

"I'll get a letter from my father and meet you back here as soon as I have it."

Caiden raced to his father's office in the capitol, where aids hurried from one meeting to another. The sounds of their heels clicking on the marble floors echoed through the hallways. Tonin sat at his desk, hunched over some papers, his gray hair shining in the sunlight. Caiden wondered when his father started to age. Despite being nearly a millennium old, he looked to be around the age of a human in their fifties. He wasn't frail, but he certainly wasn't the fearsome commander he'd once been.

"Caiden! How goes it today?" His face brightened at the sight of his youngest son. Creases appeared around his pale blue eyes. Tonin was as close to an original as the sylph could get. Born from one of the original families, he escaped elven slavery and worked to free others.

A rebellion leader, he led the forces into battle in the Sylph and Elven Wars, only to become their captive again. He nearly died in a prison camp, but he wouldn't give them the satisfaction of killing him. Every sylph born after the treaty was signed knew who Tonin Stormweaver was. A legend among his people, Caiden hoped his signature would carry enough weight to get them into the library's restricted section.

"It goes well. I trust Amolie took the portal to Ruska safely."

"She did." Tonin nodded. "Terrible that she had to leave so soon after her wedding."

"Life does not wait for us, Father. You should know that by now."

"True." He sighed and poured himself a glass of amber liquor. "Want one?"

Caiden waved him off. "I'm here for a favor."

"Oho, and what is it for?"

"I need a note to get into the restricted section of the Great Library."

"And why would you need that?"

"We... er, I may have found something to help us locate the

Trinity Wells. That book you let me borrow is part of a set—a gift from the goddess Illya to the original sylph families."

Tonin scribbled something down—signing it with big, swooped lettering. "Say no more." Dripping wax onto the letter, he stamped it with the seal of the Stormlands and handed it to Caiden.

"Thanks, Dad," he said with a sheepish smile as if he were receiving a note to miss his tutoring lessons.

"Of course." He smiled back at his son. "Now, go save the world."

Caiden turned to leave, but his father called after him, "One more thing."

"Yes?"

"I'm proud of you."

Caiden's chest warmed. "I try my best to make you proud."

Tonin nodded at his son. "I'll see you back at the townhouse tonight. Your mother is making a hearty stew."

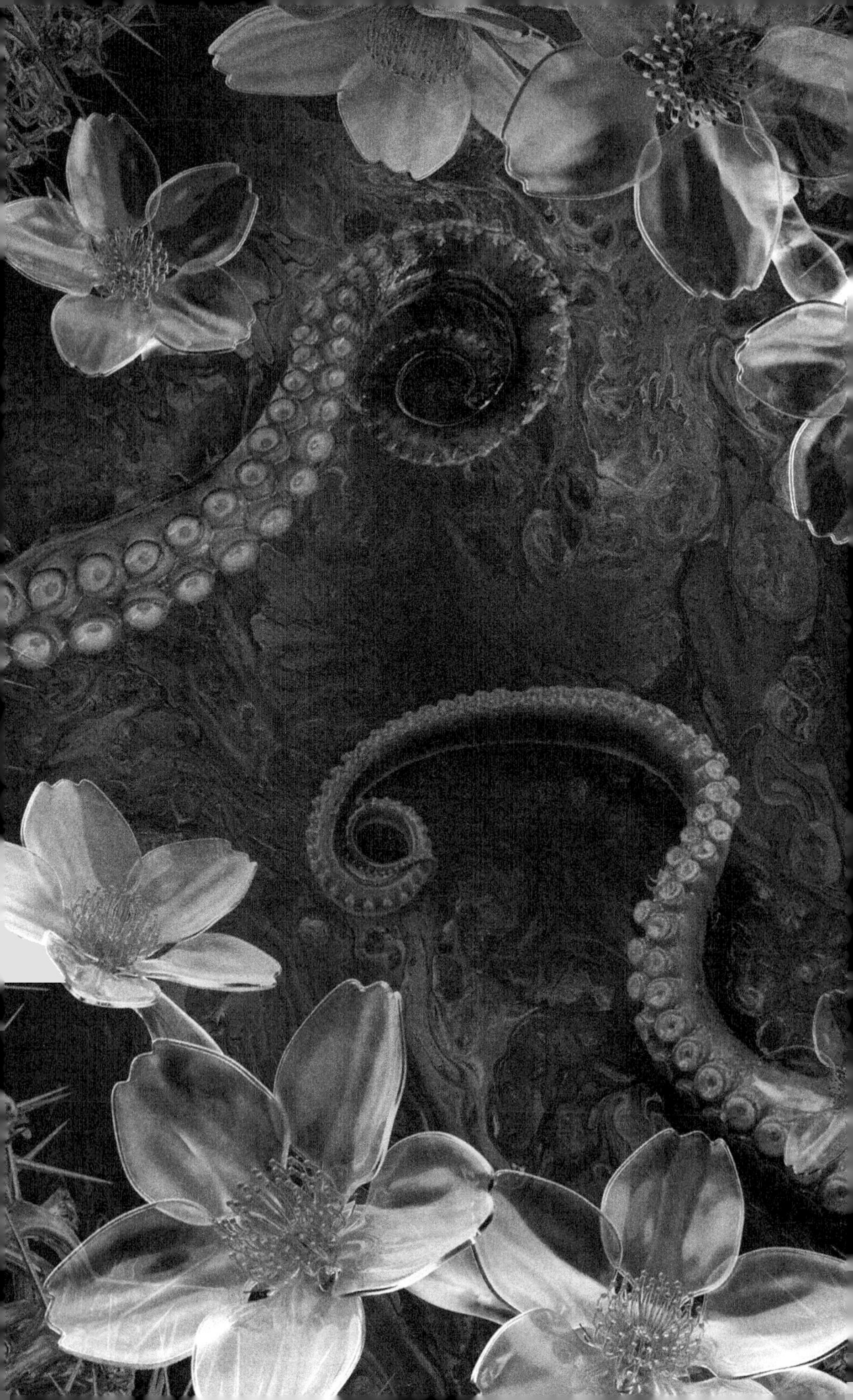

14 CAIDEN

"Did Amolie get to Ruska alright?" Caiden asked as he and Roderick walked through the snowy streets. Lights twinkled above their heads, making the snow sparkle like diamonds. He loved the city at night, when everyone was tucked into their beds, fast asleep.

"She did. I had our binding bands enchanted to tell each other if we're safe or in trouble."

"Smart."

"I hope they make it to the Isle of Fate."

"I'm sure someone still knows a way to get there. The Fates are surely getting supplies," Caiden said. "And I'm sure there are still some who worship them."

"Probably," Roderick said, heaving open the heavy doors of the library.

Only a few candles lit the rows of books, casting eerie glows around the ancient library. They walked on padded feet toward the restricted section, trying to keep their pulses at bay.

"Wish Lucius was here to help," Roderick whispered. "He'd be in and out of here in no time. Wouldn't even break a sweat."

"Yeah, and he'd be smug about it too," Caiden said.

Ora waited outside the restricted section where two iron gates held the sylph's most prized possessions. On either side of the gates stood a Stone Soldier, the city's most fierce warrior. Whatever was behind these bars was precious and dangerous to have such an elite set of warriors guarding it.

The men nodded to Ora, who bowed her head, her hood slipping back to reveal her dark hair. Caiden unfolded the letter his father signed and handed it to the soldier, who nodded.

Tapping his spear on the floor three times, the iron gates creaked open.

Caiden swallowed hard before taking a step forward. The smell of old parchment mixed with sage and myrrh wafted from beyond.

The soldier stopped him before he entered.

"Be careful. There are things inside that don't want to be disturbed."

Caiden nodded and proceeded forward. The gates closed behind them with an ominous thud.

"Well, I guess there's no going back now," Caiden said, rolling his shoulders in preparation for what awaited them.

"This way." Ora led them down the torch-lined steps into the library's depths.

A chill wafted up from the rock below.

"This part of the library was built before the sylph existed. It's where the founders met long before they built the library above and where many hid during the elven occupation," Ora said.

Magic rippled through the air, tingling Caiden's tongue with the metallic taste of copper. Deeper and deeper, they descended into the bowels of the library. Doors marked with a language Caiden did not recognize lined the wall.

"Can you read what these say?" he asked.

"They are markers of life and death," Roderick chimed in.

"Yes, that's correct. Each of the original sylph families has a vault. And then others are marked by topic," Ora said. "We want to be at the very bottom, in the room with the most wards.

"So, we can't just grab the books and go?" Caiden asked, exchanging knowing glances with Roderick who smirked.

"Of course not. You don't think they'd let anyone waltz in and take the original family's books?"

"Well, kind of, yeah."

They came to a set of doors engraved with the picture of Illya slitting her wrists for the sylph to feed from. Caiden's stomach turned. Pulling keys from her pocket, Ora undid the lock.

Caiden arched a brow.

"Before you say anything, I swiped them from Grand Master Quail while he slept. I will return them before he wakes up."

"Perhaps we don't need Lucius after all," Roderick said, elbowing Caiden in the ribs.

Caiden rolled his eyes.

Ora pushed open the heavy doors. Inside, a set of books sat behind a locked cage in the center of the room. Bookcases surrounded the cage in a circle. The ceiling reached into the heavens, and moonlight illuminated the caged books.

"Do you have a key to this?" Caiden asked Ora, who was staring in amazement at the shelves of ancient texts.

"Look at this? Look at all of this," she exclaimed, rushing to the first shelf.

"Don't!" Caiden cried, staying her hand before she touched anything.

"What?" She knitted her brows.

"You said wards protect this place. Anything could be a trap."

She snapped her hand back.

"You're right. How foolish of me. I lost myself for a moment."

"Let's just get the books and get out of here," Caiden said. He carefully walked down the steps to where the cage sat, bathed in moonlight. A plaque on the front read, "*For those whose blood runs true.*"

"What does that mean?" Ora asked, examining the inscription.

Caiden pulled the dagger from his back pocket.

"It means I must prove my blood is that of an original if we want to gain access to the books." He sighed before pricking his finger. "Here goes nothing." He pressed his thumb to the space shaped like a fingerprint.

The lock quietly unlatched.

All three let out relieved breaths.

"That was easy, Roderick said.

"Don't speak so soon. We still have to leave here with the books, and two soldiers are standing guard outside."

"I'll take care of them." Rodrick smiled coyly.

The books corresponded to each original family—seven books for seven families: Stormweavers, Sweetwords, Shadowalkers, Lightbringers, Firebreathers, Deathwards, and Greenblades. Each text carried the family's insignia and the Zylrinth's Weaver's mark. These seven held the reins of the sylph long before the courts divided. As far as Caiden knew, only he and Tharan remained.

"So many lost during the war," Roderick whispered to himself, shaking his head.

"Let us hope we do not lose anymore." Caiden grabbed the first book and handed it to Roderick. Suspicious that this was all too easy, he looked around the room for any sort of ward, but there was nothing—no creature released or poison dart, only silence. "Ora, what protection spells are down here?"

"I am not a Grand Master. I do not know what lurks down here."

"Then we better get out quickly." He piled the rest of the books into Roderick's arms. "Let's go."

Roderick turned to leave, but as his feet hit the stairs, a fiery ring sprung up around them. "Okay, well, this is a setback."

"Shit," Caiden cursed under his breath. The flames grew higher, and the three stepped back toward the cage. "Any ideas?"

"Hold these." Roderick shifted the books to Caiden and Ora. He pulled the chain earring from his ear, and with a flick of the wrist, a whip of pure light appeared.

"Here goes nothing." Climbing on top of the cage, he snapped his whip, looping it around one of the railings above before heaving himself over the fire and onto the other side, banging into a bookshelf and knocking countless artifacts to the ground. "It worked!" he exclaimed.

"Great, but what about us?" Caiden yelled.

"Are you not a son of the Stormlands?" Roderick yelled over the flames.

"I'm the lightning kind, not the rain kind. Ora, what is your gift?"

"I, uh, I'm not very good at it." She wrung her hands together nervously. "That's why I'm a scholar."

The flames moved closer.

"Well, now would be a good time to try," Caiden said, taking a step backward clutching the remaining books. Fear sank like a rock in his stomach.

Ora took a deep breath, and the flames died a bit.

"You're a wind wailer?" Caiden asked.

Ora nodded sheepishly. "But I've never produced a gale."

Caiden wracked his brain, trying to remember what he knew of the Court of Wailing Winds. Some had gales, some were wailers, and others were extinguishers. "Try breathing in deep like you're sucking in smoke from a cigarette."

"I've never smoked a cigarette," she protested. Sweat glistened on her brow.

The two climbed on top of the cage. Sylph were vengeful in

their retribution. They would destroy the books before they fell into the wrong hands.

"Well, you'll have to try, or else we'll die."

She sucked in a deep breath, and the fire slowly began to diminish, but not enough.

"Can you blow it out?"

Her eyes said she would try. She slowly let the air out, but it did little to quell the flames. "I'm sorry, I'm not good at this."

"It's okay," Caiden said, trying not to sound panicked. "Try again. Really focus on letting the air out. Let it build in your chest. That's what I do with my lightning. I let it build in my fingertips and then release it." The flames licked at the soles of their shoes. "No pressure."

Closing her eyes, she sucked in another breath, magic swirled in the air. Her chest buffed, and then she let go of what Caiden could only describe as a gale-force wind, extinguishing the flames enough for them to jump through with the remainder of the books.

Roderick met them on the other side. "Give them to me. I can run faster with them."

"Why do we need to run?" Caiden asked, not daring to turn around.

Roderick pointed to the ceiling where a swarm of angry bees loomed overhead.

"Well, I assume they're about to dive on us."

As soon as the words left his lips, the bees shot toward them like an arrow being released.

"Run!" Caiden yelled. They headed for the door, but their hopes of escape were quickly dashed.

"It's locked!" Ora shouted, glancing back at the fasting approaching bees.

Caiden twisted the lightning between his fingers into the best net he could make in seconds, creating a shield. Thousands of insects buzzed as they hit the net and fell to their deaths.

"Hold these," Roderick said, handing the books to Ora, who could barely carry them. With a kick, he knocked one of the doors off its hinges. "Go!" he yelled at Ora, who handed off the books and ran up the stairs.

"I can't hold them much longer. Go, Roderick. I'll follow behind."

Roderick nodded and followed Ora up the stairs.

Caiden waited as long as he could before dropping the net and following his friends. The remaining bees swarmed around him, stinging every piece of flesh they could, even through his thick wool sweater. Poison seeped into his blood at such a rate even Illya's gift could not protect him. He fell to his knees, grabbing at each step as the onslaught of stings continued. His throat swelled, and each breath became a struggle. His fingernails scraped against the stone, but he couldn't stop, not when they were so close. He shut his eyes just for a moment, just to collect himself. His throat thickened and his breathing strained—the world went dark, and then a bright light shone upon him.

He blinked repeatedly, trying to focus on what he thought must be the veil, but instead, a man wearing white robes with a thick head of white hair stared back at him.

"Caiden Stormweaver, someone on the other side has struck a bargain for your life. You will not die today." He pressed a ball of light into Caiden's chest, and energy shot through him like lightning in his veins. He gasped for air, filling his lungs. Was the venom poisoning his brain? Was he hallucinating? He didn't know whether to be confused or grateful. Darkness closed in around him.

When he opened his eyes, Roderick stared back at him.

"Thought I lost you."

He shook his head.

"I'm not easy to kill."

"Yeah, yeah, yeah…" He pulled Caiden to his feet.

Caiden examined the welts covering his body. "I guess it could be worse." He looked around. They were in the Great Hall with the stars overhead. "How did you get out of the Restricted Section? Did you use your honey tongue, Roderick?"

A coy smile split Roderick's face in two. "You could say I used another form of persuasion."

"He cracked their heads together," Ora said, nose deep in one of the books.

"Well, that's one way of getting something done." Caiden shook his head at his friend.

Ora ignored the men, laying out the books open on the table to the corresponding pages. "Help me match these," she said, taking the nearest book and aligning it with the constellation of the Hive. A beam of light connected the book and the star at the tip of the beehive. "Only four more."

The men hurried around and connected the rest: the Lion, the Specter, the Scorpion, and the one of the Goddess Illya herself. Beams of light danced across the room. The three met in the middle and gazed at the sight.

"What now?" Caiden asked, his heart in his throat. Either this was going to reveal something amazing, or it was a nice trick to show children.

"Just wait a minute. This is old magic," Ora said.

The three held their breaths for a moment longer. The bells of the clock tower in the center of Vantris chimed their midnight tune.

"Nothing? Really?" Roderick said, clicking his tongue in annoyance.

"Look!" Ora said, pointing to a space in the night sky. The last bell of midnight chimed, and from behind a set of clouds, a moon appeared, casting a blinding light onto a long center table.

"What is it?" Caiden said, rushing to the table, looking for something, anything of significance.

Roderick climbed onto the nearest table. "It's something. I can't tell what, though."

Snapping her fingers, Ora ran to the second-floor balcony. "Oh, Trinity! It's a map! A map to what I can only think is a Trinity Well. The Well of the sylph of the Goddess Illya. Quick, help me sketch it!"

The two men sprinted to the top of the staircase. Adrenaline coursed through Caiden's veins, but his excitement soured when he laid eyes on the location.

"Of course, it's in the Court of Screams."

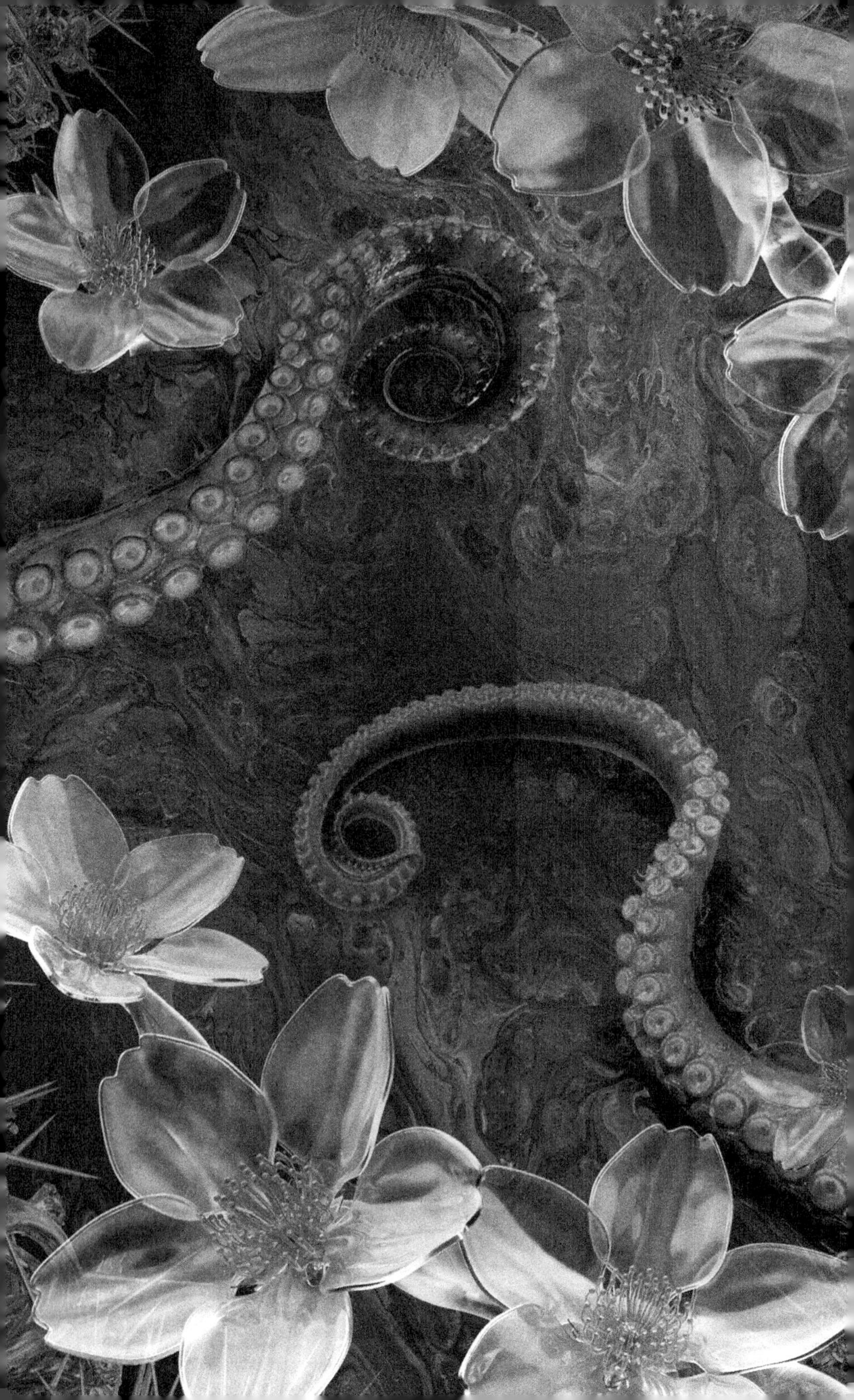

15 AELIA

A BREATH SLIPPED BETWEEN MY LIPS AS I STARED AT THE ALDER Townhome. Like its palace, the house resembled a living tree with vines wrapped around branches and birds cawing at one another. It was located in the oldest part of the city, where the ancient families of Moriana built their sanctuaries, where they could meet privately. In times long past, they would throw balls to celebrate the Fates in hopes of winning their favor, but now, with tensions among kingdoms at an all-time high, they were used to plot against one another.

A satyr with curly brown hair and bright blue horns answered the door with a bow. "Greetings, Lady Aelia. I am Finneas, head satyr. We have prepared the master suite for you."

I mustered my best smile, but my heart ached to think about sleeping alone.

"Great. Please have my things taken up."

He signaled for the other servants to take our things upstairs.

"Would you like anything to eat, my Lady? The chef has prepared a lovely roast goose for dinner."

"Famished," I said.

He escorted us to the ballroom, where a chandelier of bioluminescent flowers hung from the ceiling.

"You should have seen this place before the war," the satyr said, catching me staring. "The parties would last for days. Creatures from all over the continent and across the sea would come to stand in the presence of our Alder King." His round face beamed with pride before darkening. "But that was a long time ago. This place has been quiet for centuries except for the occasional overnight. It's good to have some life back here."

"What about Tharan? Briar? They never stayed here?"

"Occasionally, but they were born after the good times."

I eyed the satyr, wondering how old he was. His plump cheeks and rosy demeanor camouflaged his actual age.

"Trinity," Baylis gasped as she entered the ballroom. "This looks like an enchanted forest."

I hadn't noticed the night sky adorning the ceiling and trees lining the walls until now.

"It's modeled after the Alder Forest in the Woodland Realm." The satyr ushered us to the table where two place settings sat.

"A lot of fuss for only two guests," I said. "You really don't have to do this."

"Nonsense. As I said, we haven't had guests in ages, and it's nice for the staff to feel useful."

We took our seats at the massive oak table stretching the length of the room. What must it have been like to experience this place full of music and laughter? Taking out the Scepter of the Dead, I called on the Morrigan.

She yawned, stretching her arms high into the sky.

"Hello, Commander." Recognizing where she was, her blue eyes went wide. "I haven't been here in an age." She walked around the room, running her hands over the painted walls. "Oh, this takes me back."

"So, you attended parties here?"

"Oh yes, Eoghan always threw the most amazing balls. This place was really something then. *I* was really something then. A goddess to be worshiped." She ran her fingers through her hair. "It was here I came to love Eoghan, although he never had eyes for me." She took a shaky breath, and her eyes fell to the floor. "I was always his war partner. He never even kissed me."

Baylis and I exchanged knowing glances, and she urged me to comfort the goddess.

"I'm sorry, Morrigan."

She waved me away, plopping down into the chair opposite Baylis.

"There is nothing to be sorry about. You can't make someone love you."

I swallowed the memory of the embarrassment I'd brought upon myself, trying to make Gideon love me.

"You have no idea how right you are."

A line of satyrs set steaming plates of goose and roasted vegetables on the table.

The Morrigan poured herself a glass of wine and downed it, pouring another.

"Anyways… enough about my shit love life. Are you girls ready to see your mother tomorrow?"

"As ready as we can be," I said, gritting my jaw.

"Well, that will be lovely. Tell the Fates I say *hi*."

"You don't want to come?"

She shook her head. "No. I never want to go back there again. I never want to kneel in front of those women and offer up my soul."

An awkward silence fell over the table, and Baylis and I picked at our food.

"Your mother wasn't bad. But the other two… will be difficult. They hate that they can't see the future. Decuma sees the past, and Clotho sees the present. Few want their opinion. They are and were jealous of your mother… or at least that's what the rumors said."

Knots tied themselves in my stomach, souring my dinner. I gave her a half-hearted smile.

"Morrigan, did you live when dragons roamed the continent?" Baylis chimed in.

"Yes, I saw the first egg hatch and the last dragon fall from the sky—tragedy. Their wings blotted out the sun, and their fire scorched entire battlefields."

"Did you ride one?"

She stared off into space.

"I did. I had a dragon named Bruxa. Her beautiful iridescent scales sparkled in the sunlight, and her silver flame turned men to stone." She wiped a tear from her eye. "I tried to hide her as best I could, but the hunters came for her and…"

She bit her bottom lip.

Baylis placed a reassuring hand over hers.

"It's alright. I didn't mean to…"

"It's fine. I should be over it by now. Death is a part of life. Even dragons die."

"I heard across the Black Sea they still have dragons," I chimed in.

Morrigan shrugged.

"It is inevitable some survived. Some say they went underground to wait until the world was ripe for them to emerge again."

"Sounds like a perfect war machine for Gideon to harness. Let's hope they stay gone for a while longer," I said, taking a drink of wine.

"If Erissa and Gideon get ahold of the power in the alleged Wells, there's no telling what monsters they could pull from the depths of hell."

"Speaking of… Any news from beyond?" I eyed the Morrigan with suspicion.

"It takes time to travel through the realms beyond the veil," she snapped at me. "I will report something as soon as I hear it."

"Very well, I believe you."

"Thank you." She downed her wine. "Now, if I can ask you something…"

"Sure."

"How are you planning on getting to the Island of Fate? The waters are treacherous, and the island has been sealed off for ages. I don't know how they got your mother back."

I leaned back in my chair, exuding confidence. "I lived in the shadows for half a decade. I know how to find people who will do impossible jobs."

"Is it the water that is dangerous or something lurking within?" Baylis asked.

"Both. The water is choppy and never settles, and giant river serpents lurk in the depths surrounding the island. If you manage to make it onto land, the Fates will be protected by the Eternal Guard, fierce warriors whose sole purpose is to keep them safe both from themselves and others."

I took a deep breath. I didn't even want to see my mother, and now I was going to have to fight to do so. My sister laid a reassuring hand over mine. "We'll find a way, I know it."

"We have no other choice."

Amolie arrived the following day from Vantris. Bright and full of energy, she bounded into the breakfast nook.

"Good morning, Springborns," she said, kissing my cheek.

"Good morning… What's gotten into you?" I asked as I fought the sleep still clinging to my eyes.

"Oh, nothing. Just this." She dangled her fingers in front of my face. On her fourth sat a large emerald sparkling in the morning light.

Grabbing her hand, I examined the stone.

"Amolie… you and Roderick? Bound?"

"You're not mad? I wanted you to be there, but we didn't know if we'd have more time…"

"Of course, I'm not mad." I pulled my friend in for a hug, heart bursting with love. "I'm so happy for you. You two deserve each other."

"Let me see!" Baylis squealed with delight.

"This calls for champagne!" I rang for one of the servants, who quickly brought over a fresh bottle and poured us three glasses. "To Amolie and Roderick!" We clinked our glasses together and sipped the bubbly.

"Well, now that that's out of the way. We can get down to business." Amolie sat beside me and piled her plate high with sausage, eggs, and fresh biscuits. "The portals always make me famished."

"It's the magic. It speeds up your metabolism. Magus is unaffected, but as humans, it takes a lot of energy to access the portal." As I was now a magus, the portal didn't affect me as much, but it would make me ravenous when I was fully human. I'd send a note ahead to have a meal prepared for me on the other side.

"So what's the plan?" Amolie spread a thick layer of butter onto a flakey biscuit.

"We need to find someone to take us to the Isle of Fate. The journey is treacherous and filled with monsters, and that's not even including the things that will undoubtedly try to kill us once we're on the island."

"Ha! Well, what else is new? Everything is always trying to kill us."

"I think we all know who can help us with the monsters."

Amolie arched a brow. "Ursula?"

"The one and only," I said, finishing my champagne. The bubbles buzzed through my brain and down to the ends of my fingertips. "She likes to hang out at the Rusted Bucket near the docks." I looked at the clock on the wall that read 10 A.M. "We should go soon."

"What about a boat? You can do a lot of things, Aelia, but I've never seen you captain a boat."

"We'll cross that bridge when we come to it," I said. I finished my coffee and got to my feet.

While I waited for the others to get ready, I turned the whisper stone and lit a cigarette. "Tharan? Can you hear me?"

"I can hear you, my love."

My whole body relaxed at the sound of his voice. "I miss you so much. I could barely sleep last night without you."

"I know, my darling. My heart aches every second I am away from you."

My pulse quickened at his words. "How far are you away from elven territory?"

"We're close, just a few more days."

"You're making great time." I let smoke plume into the air. "You wouldn't happen to know a sailor crazy enough to brave sea monsters."

"Hmm…"

I pictured him staring out the window of an elegant carriage, the winter sun illuminating his glowing skin. His hair was tied back behind his ears, and he had a cigarette between his perfect lips.

"An old war buddy of mine resides in Ruska, but he's *eccentric*. He might take you."

"Where can we find him?"

"He lives down by the docks. Last I heard from him, he was

the captain of a ship. His name is Conrad Teeling. Ask the Harbor Master about him."

"You're too good to be true. You know that?"

"You won't say that after you meet Conrad," he chuckled.

I pictured the corners of his eyes creasing when he was pleased with himself.

Footsteps shuffled down the hallway.

"I have to go. Stay safe, and don't do anything stupid," I whispered.

"I love you too, Aelia."

Baylis entered the parlor dressed in a wool cloak in the color of Robin's egg and with gray fur trim.

"Ready?"

"Just waiting on—"

"Me?" Amolie appeared behind Baylis, her curls pinned neatly on the top of her head.

"Yes, let's go."

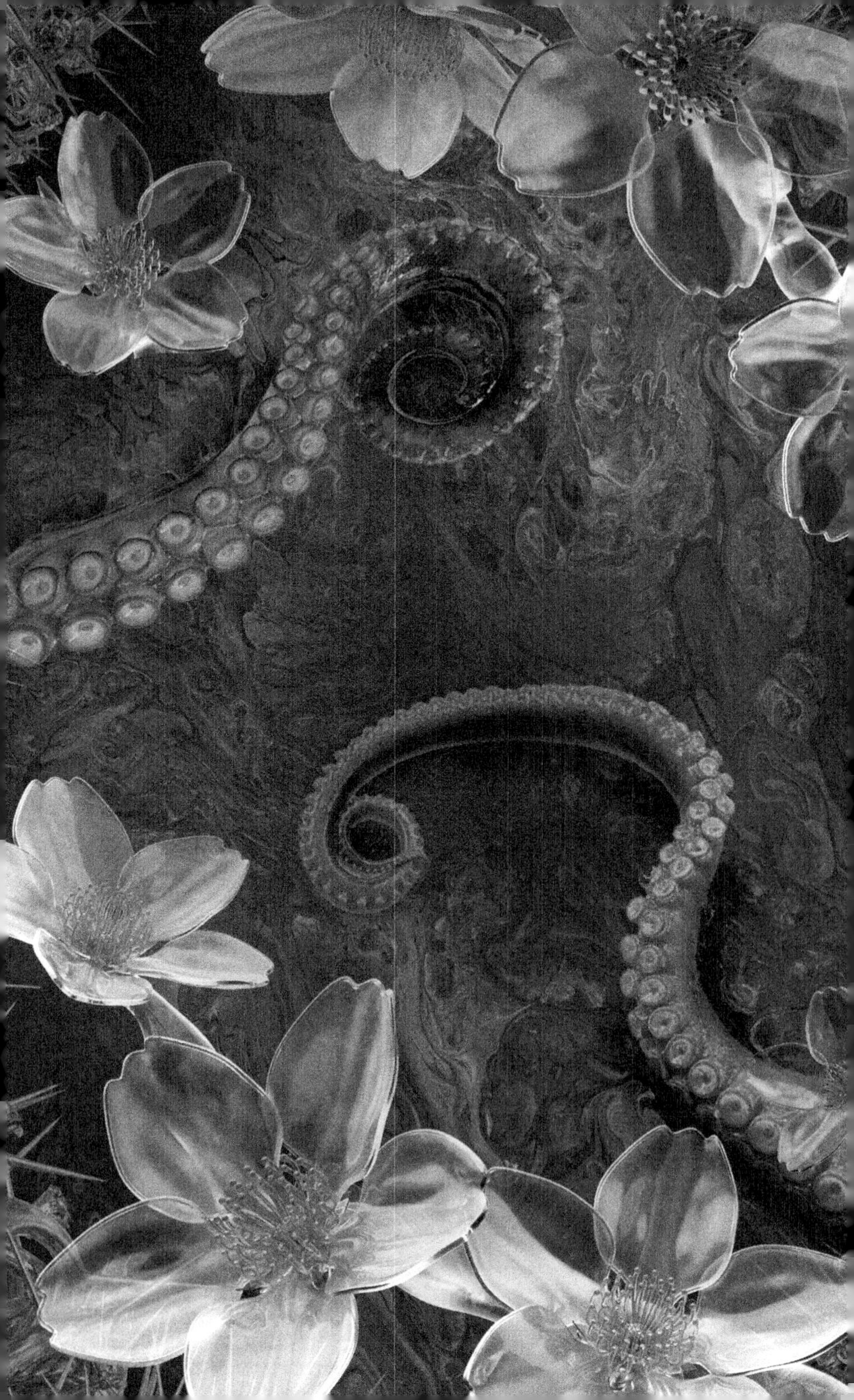

16 AELIA

Fishermen and sailors alike hurried around the docks, unloading cargo and passengers. The wind swept up from the Atruskan River, bringing with it a fishy musk. Massive ships carrying goods from all over the continent lined the docks. Crewmen spilled from their hulls. Some kissed the filthy cobblestone street, thanking their respective Goddess or God for a safe trip. Many seamen paid homage to both Manannán and a goddess of the Trinity.

The Island of Fate loomed large in the distance, dark and ominous. Ruska was built to serve the Fates. Before their fall from grace, the passage between Ruska and the Island was easy, but now a dark ring, filled with monsters, kept the public at a distance and the Fates imprisoned. So much work to go such a short distance.

I dug my fingers into my palms as we neared the inn.

"Here we are—the Rusty Bucket," I said, stopping in front of a precarious-looking establishment where two men sat slumped over in front.

"Lovely," Baylis said, stepping over the men.

"Let me do the talking." I pushed the door open to find more men and women bent over the dark wood bar. The stench of stale air made my stomach turn. Some hissed at the sensation of the light hitting their pale faces.

I sauntered up to the bar, where a nymph with pearlescent skin and black hair cleaned pints from the night before. She raked her serpent eyes over our pristine skin.

"I don't want any trouble. If your husband is here, go find him yourself."

"I'm here for someone else." I slid a piece of gold onto the bar.

"Go on…" she said, eying the coin.

"Mermaid, white pearlescent skin, blue hair. Sharp teeth."

The nymph chuckled. "You'll have to pay me more than one gold piece for me to sell out, Ursula."

"So, she's here?"

The nymph didn't look up from her polishing.

"I didn't say that."

"You didn't have to." I flipped the coin between my fingers. "Now, is she upstairs or in the back?"

"She's not here. I told you."

"Tell her Aelia is here to see her."

The bartender scoffed before whispering into one of the guard's ears. "He'll tell her you're here."

I gave her a shit-eating grin. "Great, and we'll take three pints of cider while we wait."

The nymph mumbled some half-breed slur under her breath as she poured us three pints.

"This is a side of you I've never seen before," Baylis said, taking a swig of her drink.

"This is what five years of living in the shadows will do to you." I drank deeply, savoring the shitty cider.

The man returned, whispering something in the nymph's ear.

"She'll see you. Up the stairs to the left. Last door on the right."

"Thank you." I returned the gold coin to the bar and signaled Baylis and Amolie to follow me.

The water-warped stairs creaked under our feet.

"Maybe I should have asked this earlier, but who is Ursula?" Baylis asked.

"She's the queen of the Undersea's favorite assassin," I said, wiping my moist palms on my cloak.

"And your former paramour," Amolie chimed in.

"Yes, we have a history."

"Ah, I see." Baylis didn't ask any further questions.

We stopped in front of the master suite. How predictable of Ursula to stay in the best room in the shittiest dive.

I knocked. "Ursula? It's Aelia. Can I come in?"

A faint, "Yes," answered me.

I opened the door to find Ursula in the center of a plush bed, flanked by a nymph and a merman. Feathers and broken glass littered the room. Clothes lay strewn about, and the smell of incense and myrrh hung heavy in the air. A single candle burned low on a desk covered with a half-eaten roast chicken and lines of half-snorted dust.

Anxiety clenched my stomach tight at the sight. I hesitated in the doorway, knuckles white on the knob, bracing myself for the familiar craving. This looked like too many of my rooms in the past. A different version of myself would've leapt at the chance to join in on the debauchery. But now, the sight of the dust didn't make my brain light up like a firecracker. Instead, I felt... numb. Sad. If I was being honest with myself, a little ashamed of the person I had been—so much time wasted drowning in self-pity. And for what? Terrible things happen to people every day. What made me think I was special? My own ego?

Releasing my grip on the door, I strode across the room.

I pulled open the curtains, and light came streaming in. Ursula hissed, shielding her eyes. Her companions groaned with displeasure, pulling the nearest pillow over their faces.

"Ugh. What do you want, Springborn?"

"I need something from your queen."

She let out a hearty laugh. "Oh yeah? You think the queen of the Undersea just does favors for mercenaries?"

"No, but she would do something for the Alder King who technically is her superior."

Ursula rubbed the sleep from her eyes.

"Eh, maybe. But she *would* have use for a telepath."

"I'm not in the mercenary business anymore, Ursula."

Sitting up in the bed, she picked at her nails lazily.

"What is the favor anyway?"

"I need her to call off the creatures protecting the Isle of Fate so we can enter."

"Going home to see Mommy?"

"That's not our home. That is a prison where our mother is kept."

She huffed, pulling herself from the bed, her naked body on display for all of us to see. "I guess I could speak to my queen." She poured herself a glass of wine, the morning sun illuminated her curves.

"Thank you, Ursula," I said, crossing my arms over my chest. "You can find us at the Alder Townhome when you have an answer."

Her eyes brightened. "Aren't you going to invite me over for a drink? Dinner perhaps? I am doing you a favor, and I'd love to see what the Alder Townhome is like."

"As soon as you have information for me, you are welcome to dine at my table."

She clicked her tongue and moved closer before pulling my

hands to her hips. "Remember how much fun we had at the Yule Revelry? We could have more."

I couldn't deny my quickening pulse at her touch. A hazy memory of our time together at the Yule Revelry streaked through my mind. The taste of salt and brine fizzled on my tongue and goosebumps rose on my arms at the memory of Caiden and Ursula's lips on my skin.

I swallowed hard.

"I can't. I'm with Tharan now."

"I don't think he would mind," she whispered in my ear.

"I'm trying to turn over a new leaf, Ursula." I let my arms fall slack.

She pouted her lower lip in protest. "You were so fun before you settled down and, you know, became important. However, your curves look delicious. What's Alder King feeding you?"

"Stability. You should try it."

"Ha! I am stable as can be. I have my little nest here." She pointed at her two lovers hiding beneath the thick blankets. "And a bank vault full of gold at the Free Cities Trust. What more could I need?"

I shook my head, trying to conceal my smile. "Nothing."

She downed her glass of wine. "Exactly."

"I'll see you in a few days, Ursula. Don't dally. I know where to find you, and I have ways of getting the information I need," I huffed. The memories of my past indiscretions unnerved me.

"Is that a threat?" She narrowed her sea green eyes at me.

"Consider it motivation." I turned and motioned for Amolie and Baylis to follow. "Come on, we have other matters to attend to."

We headed out into the cold, briny streets once more.

"Well, that went as about as well as could be expected," Amolie said.

"She can be prickly, but she'll come through. She owes me for Oakton."

Amolie touched my wrist. "Are you okay?"

"I'm fine." I shrugged then straightened my cloak.

"Well, you just threatened an emissary of a friendly court—"

I interrupted her, "Ursula knows how to conduct herself accordingly."

Amolie backed away.

Baylis picked at her nails aimlessly.

"What's your backup plan?"

"Get her drunk, have her take me to bed, and plant the idea in her head," I said.

"Couldn't we have just done that from the get-go?" Baylis asked. Her voice dripped with a condescension I'd not heard before. Was this a development from her time with Gideon?

I eyed my sister suspiciously. The Baylis I knew would have never wanted me to invade someone's private thoughts, or perhaps she would have. My memories were just as cloudy as hers. Guilt and shame bit at my heart like two dogs pulling on a rope.

"Four years ago, I would have done it and not thought twice about it, but I am not that person anymore."

She nodded with indifference.

"Now, we need to find someone named Conrad Teeling. Tharan said the Harbor Master would know where to find him."

We headed to a large brick building where a massive gold clock kept time. Our boots clacked on black and white marble floors as we entered.

"Hello," I said to a human woman wearing reading spectacles with her silver hair tied neatly in a tight bun.

"Hello, how may I help you?"

"I need to speak to the Harbor Master. I'm looking for a man named Conrad Teeling."

"Oh, I'm sorry, my dear. The Harbor Master has left for a meeting at the governor's residence. He won't be back until tomorrow."

I sighed, my shoulders slumping. "Can we make an appointment for tomorrow?"

She gave a little chuckle. "Oh no, the Harbor Master is booked for the next month. But I can pencil you in for the spring."

"Ah, no, thank you. We need something a little sooner than that."

"Suit yourself." She returned to her work.

I resisted groaning. Could one thing, just one thing, go the way I had hoped?

"But…" the woman piped up.

"Yes?"

"If you want to find Conrad, I'd look at the Kissing Guppy."

I stared blankly at her.

"Down the path to the left after you exit."

"Thanks."

We headed down the steep path where the water lapped against an old wooden shack. Seaweed snaked its way around a rickety dock, and algae floated aimlessly in the water. A sign twisting on rusted hooks read *The Kissing Guppy*.

"And I thought the Rusted Bucket was bad," Amolie said.

The inside was just as bleak as the outside. Light trickled in through green glass windows, casting everything in a verdant hue. The smell of sour ale and vomit wafted through the air. Men sat slumped over water-logged tables and in benches engraved with slurs of every kind.

A merman with long white hair, a pointed nose, and tattoos covering his bare chest nodded to us as we entered. For the second time in one day, I felt the pull of my past. It was in places like this I learned how to read people—how to manipulate them without breaking their mind.

"Can I help you ladies?" the barman asked, raking his eyes over us.

"We're looking for Conrad Teeling."

He leaned over the bar, narrowing his blue eyes at me. "And wha' would you be wantin' with Conrad?"

"The Alder King has need of his services."

"And yet, he sent three ladies to do his job…"

"He sent one better… his Hand."

His fishlike eyes widened. "He's in the back."

Two sailors watched us with guarded gazes as we made our way through a dust-covered velvet curtain into the back room. Three sylph men sat with courtesans on their laps, breasts bare and cheeks rosy. Piles of gold sat on the table between them, and each man held a hand of cards. Cigarettes rested in brass ashtrays. Smoke billowed into the air, filling the room with the distinct scent of clove and tobacco.

"Who rang for more women?" one of the men said, tossing his hand down. "These ones look expensive." He tossed the woman on his lap to the side and sauntered up to Baylis.

His dirty fingers reached for her pristine hair. I stepped between them, holding my dagger to his throat.

"I will not hesitate to slit your throat if you come any closer."

The mercenary I'd once been rattled the bars of the cage I trapped her in. Maybe it was seeing the dust, maybe it was seeing Ursula living the life I'd come accustomed to, but I couldn't help but slip back into the mask I'd worn for so long. Was this who I really was? The thought sent a chill down my spine. I pushed it away and focused on the task at hand.

The man's eyes widened—red from lack of sleep. Ale hung heavy on his breath. I could take him if I needed to. He was in no state to fight me. A bar brawler would be no match for Little Death.

"And who do you think you are, little missy?"

The men at the table laughed as though I was some trollop on the street who'd never held a knife before.

"I am Aelia Springborn, Hand of the Alder King, but in these circles, they call me the Traitorous Queen."

The man's Adam's apple bobbed as he swallowed hard. "Mind Breaker."

I pushed the dagger into his skin, drawing blood. I'd played this part for years, and I'd be lying if there wasn't a part of me who missed it.

"Yes, that is what I am. Would you like me to show you what I can do?"

He raised his hands and took a step backward.

"What do you want?"

"I'm looking for Conrad Teeling."

He pointed to a curved door at the back of the room.

"Thank you." I sheathed my dagger before knocking on the door.

"No!" a voice sounded from the other side.

"Conrad! Tharan Greenblade sent me to find you."

"Oh, in that case, come in!" The tone lightened.

The rusty hinges creaked as I pushed open the door to find a sylph man, shirtless, hanging upside down from his ankles. Tattoos of sea creatures covered his muscled body. Long black hair pooled on the floor.

"I can come back if this isn't a good time." I couldn't hide the shock on my face.

"Nonsense," Conrad said.

He untied his ankles and swung to his feet. It was then I noticed his missing eye.

"Conrad, I presume?"

"The one and only." He took a drink of some green concoction.

I grimaced, watching him down the potion.

"Helps with the sea sickness," he said, wiping the excess from his mouth.

"I'm not here to judge." Although, I wasn't sure if the potion or the hanging upside down helped with the sea sickness.

"And what are you here for, Lady…" He brushed his long hair to one side, revealing slightly sloped ears full of hooped earrings and a shaved side of his head. He placed an eye patch over the hole where his eye had once been.

"Aelia Springborn. Tharan said you might be able to help us get to the Isle of Fate."

Conrad lit a cigarette, holding it between his lips while slipping on a button-up shirt over his toned torso.

"And what would the three of you need from the Isle of Fate?" He let smoke billow into the air. I followed its trail over the peeling wallpaper to the single porthole window.

"That's our business and our business alone. I just need to know if you can get us there."

"Oh, I can get you there, alright, but it'll cost you." He plopped onto the sagging bed.

"I have gold. Name your price."

A smirk crossed his handsome face. Two dimples marked his cheeks. "What I want can't be bought with gold. Only someone with your talent, Mind Breaker, can get it for me."

"And what's that?"

"The siren's song."

My mouth fell open. "You want me to steal a song from the temptresses of the sea? How exactly am I supposed to do that?"

He reached for an apple on the side of the bed. "The sirens have a queen who lives in the caves just south of Ruska. Without her, their songs are useless against seamen. They all harmonize to her tune. Use your abilities to convince her to give it to you. It shouldn't be hard if you're as good as they say."

I took a deep breath, contemplating my options.

"It's suicide to enter the siren's lair," Amolie chimed in. "You're sending us to our deaths."

Conrad got to his feet, straightening himself to his full height. His blue eye locked on Amolie's. "I am the only one who can get you to the Isle of Fate, and even then, the odds of dying are high. If I get you there and back, I want a reward and I need the song... for personal reasons. The exchange only seems fair. One suicidal mission for another."

"What if I could guarantee our safe passage?" I asked.

"Ha! Only the queen of the Undersea could do that, and I wouldn't make a deal with her." He sliced his apple, lifting a piece to his lips.

"She will make one with me. And she will honor it."

He shrugged. "Whatever you say, Mind Breaker. Just get me the song." He leaned back on the bed and shut his eyes. "You're lucky Tharan saved my life. I wouldn't do this for anyone but him."

I went to speak, but he waved us away.

"Come back when you have the song, or don't come back at all."

The Tower of Fate loomed ominously across the bay, perched upon its unapproachable island. Did my mother know Baylis and I were so close? I pushed the thought out of my mind. This would all be for naught if I couldn't get the siren song and if Ursula couldn't make a deal with her queen.

I lit a cigarette, letting it burn in my lungs. Fucking sirens, why did it have to be sirens of all people? My fingers itched to turn the whisper stone in my ear and tell Tharan about what a ridiculous ask his friend posed. Had Tharan sent word ahead of me? Had he promised him things I couldn't deliver? Was I being paranoid? Tharan hadn't shown me any indication he was manipulating me. I shook my head. I'd only been sober for a few months. My mind was still healing from years of abuse. Was I putting too much faith in Tharan?

Amolie touched my arm, bringing me back to reality.

"What are you going to do?"

I exhaled smoke into the cool afternoon air.

"I guess I'm going to have to break the siren queen's mind. The very thing I didn't want to do anymore. I should have known it wouldn't be that easy."

"I thought you weren't going to do that anymore," Baylis chimed in.

I eyed my sister sharply. She was fine with me breaking Ursula's mind but now that I needed to go into the siren queen's, she had an issue with it? What was going on here? I took another drag off my cigarette. I needed to calm down. Surely Baylis only wanted what was best for me. I was letting the ghost of my past control me and I needed to put them in the grave once and for all.

"We all have to do things we don't want to do," I said firmly.

She nodded before taking my hand in hers. "I know, I just don't want you to fall into your old ways."

How would she know about my old ways?

I shook my head. Stop looking for reasons to suspect Baylis—that would be falling back into your old ways.

"Well, if anyone can do it, you can," Amolie said, breaking the tension growing between and my sister.

I took another drag off my cigarette. "Yeah, well, I was hoping not to make any more enemies on this trip, but here we are."

"Can someone fill me in on sirens? I mean, I've heard the stories," Baylis asked.

"They're sea creatures who lure sailors to their lairs and… well, I suppose eat them. I'm not really sure. All I know is the men never come back."

"So you can see why Aelia would be nervous," Amolie said.

"Maybe I can help," Baylis chimed in. "Maybe I can try to use my gift to see the outcome?"

My chest tightened at the thought of making Baylis use her powers, but I was willing to try anything if it could help me with the siren queen.

"I don't think that will be necessary yet. But thank you."

As we walked back to the townhome, the sky darkened—clouds heavy with snow. Would I be so lucky as to be snowed in for a few days? To stave off my visit to the sirens? Only the Trinity knew.

17 AELIA

I paced around my room, emotions swirling in my head. Between my suspicion of Baylis and Tharan, I didn't know who to trust. I didn't want to think either of them would betray me, but then again, I had been tricked before.

I let out a long breath. I needed to talk to Tharan.

Twisting the stone in my ear, Tharan's jovial voice came through, "Hello, my darling."

"Your friend wants me to steal the siren's song, Tharan. Did you know about this?" I tried my best to keep my voice calm.

"I knew he would ask you something far-fetched. I just wasn't sure what exactly he wanted. He was very cagey about it in his letter." From the defensiveness in his voice, he knew I suspected something.

"Oh, so he knew I was coming? Why didn't you just tell me before I left?"

"I'm sorry, Aelia, I wasn't sure if he'd even agree to see you. As you know, he's quite eccentric." He paused. "Is everything alright?"

I shut my eyes. Was I being too hard on him? He had only ever shown me love, affection, and acceptance. I couldn't let my old relationships influence this one. Tharan loved me and I loved him. I didn't need to be afraid, but old habits are hard to shake.

"I'm fine. Just tell me next time. I can handle it."

"You know you can tell me if you're not fine."

Guilt struck at my heart, and a familiar loneliness washed over me. I shouldn't have been so harsh with Tharan. I should've trusted him.

"I know. I'm sorry."

"So, are you going to the siren's lair?"

"I don't think I really have another choice. We asked around the docks, and everyone else laughed in our faces when we asked if they'd take us to the Isle of Fate."

"Well, you knew that going in. No one has stepped foot on that island for at least two hundred years. There's no telling how wild it has become."

I blew out a breath. "Lovely. Can't wait to face certain death to see my own mother."

There were so many things I wanted to say to her. Did you know where you were sending me when you signed my marriage contract? Was it a part of some grand plan? If so, why? Why was I a pawn in their game? What was this thing in my chest and who is my father? I did also want to know if she was alright. Our lives had been nothing but turmoil for so long, part of me couldn't blame her for the things she'd done.

"I wish I was there with you, Aelia. I wish I could help more."

"I wish you were here too. But you've got an important mission of your own."

Only silence answered. I twisted the whisper stone, and my heart clenched in my chest. There were certain places magic could not penetrate, and some towns put up wards to disrupt the magic. Had I lost Tharan?

"Aelia?" His voice sent a warming sensation through my body.

"Yes?"

"I miss you. That's all. I miss everything about you. The way your skin feels against mine. The sparkle in your eyes when you laugh. The whimpers you make in your sleep."

"I miss you too, Tharan. It's funny. I've only known you a few months, but I feel as though we've known each other for ages."

"I know, I feel the same way."

A knock at the door tore me from my thoughts of Tharan.

"I've got to go. There's someone here." I wanted to tell him I loved him, but the words stuck in my throat like flies in molasses.

"I love you, Aelia."

I twisted the whisper stone, and the connection was severed.

"Come in!"

The head servant entered, bowing his head low.

"My Lady, Miss Ursula is here. She said she's here for dinner."

"Wonderful. Set a place for her, and I'll get ready."

The servant bowed and shut the door behind him. I quickly changed into a low-cut satin gown, letting my hair fall in loose waves. Ursula had a penchant for long hair, and I knew how to tempt her. Pulling a soft wool shawl over my shoulders, I took one last look at myself in the mirror. Tonight, I would be the queen I was, and the mercenary would be put away... at least for now.

I stopped at Amolie's room and knocked.

A sleepy-eyed Amolie answered the door.

"Ursula is here."

She yawned. "I didn't expect her to have an answer from her queen so quickly. It's only been two days."

"The queen of the Undersea never misses an opportunity to gain power. She's likely been waiting for an opportunity to present itself."

"Then we better not keep Ursula waiting. I won't be long changing. Come on in. I have news."

Amolie shut the door behind me, and I sat on the bed.

"What is it? Did Caiden and Roderick find something?"

She nodded excitedly, her brown curls bouncing. "Yes, well, kind of. They found a map to where they think a Well is."

My pulse quickened. We were one step closer to finding at least one Well. "That's fantastic. Did he say where?"

"No. It's all very hush-hush. We're sending messages in code via raven. Just in case they get intercepted; our rings will glow if the other one is in danger."

That made my load a little lighter. "Smart."

Amolie changed into a black satin gown that cinched at the waist, making her breasts look particularly ample. "Ready."

We pulled Baylis from the library, where she was studying a book on poisonous mushrooms, and headed down to greet Ursula.

Thanks to the blue fire sprites I hired to light the chandelier, the ballroom glowed an elegant aqua.

Ursula marveled at the intricate murals on the walls depicting ancient battles of the Alder King riding his famed white stag. Her spider silk dress of woven fishnets left little to the imagination, and she wore her blue hair in pleats around her head. She was a clever girl. She knew we'd be playing games tonight, and she came prepared.

"Beautiful, aren't they?" I asked, summoning the diplomat I'd been in another life.

She raked her sea glass eyes over my curves, lingering where my hair brushed my collarbones.

"Quite exquisite."

Baylis and Amolie took their seats at the long table.

"Come, sit. I hope you have good news for me, my friend."

She took the open seat next to the head of the table.

I ran my hands over my dress, collecting myself. *Do not let the merc out no matter how she may tempt you. You are not that person anymore.*

I snapped my fingers, and satyrs streamed from the kitchens into the grand ballroom, silver trays stretched high over their horns.

Finneas, the head satyr, poured us a glass of red wine each.

I held my glass in the air. "A toast. To friendship."

"To friendship!" We clinked our glasses together.

The satyrs pulled the lids off the plates, revealing an array of suckling meats and roasted vegetables, complete with an assortment of pastries for dessert.

"Did you speak to your queen, Ursula?"

She clicked her tongue. "In the court of the Undersea, we wait until after dinner to discuss business. But yes, I did."

"And?"

She sighed, toying with her food.

"She said she'll make a deal with you."

My chest tightened, but I dared not show it on my face.

"That's good. What does she want?"

"We can discuss that after dinner. I'd like to finish my meal first. Then we can talk about a bargain."

I shut my eyes. Should have known a magical bargain would've been involved. At least Conrad had the decency to spare me that.

"Wait, she's not here. I'd have to shake her hand to make a bargain with her."

"Who said anything about the bargain being with her?" A wicked smile cut across Ursula's delicate yet terrifying face.

"I should have known better." I downed the rest of my drink. "The deal will be with you on behalf of your queen."

"Everything I do is for my queen. My life is hers to do with as she commands."

"Ursula," Baylis chimed in. "How did you become the queen's assassin? I bet there's a story there."

Blue flame flicked across Ursula's face. Her eyes lowered as she dredged up a memory.

"My mother was her favorite handmaiden. I grew up in the halls of the Undersea Court, which, as you may or may not know, is half above water and half below so we could entertain those courts who did not have gills. My mother and father, a soldier, accompanied the queen on a diplomatic trip. They were attacked by a band of barbarians—no doubt hired by another court. Both my mother and father died defending the queen, and in return, she promised to care for me as her own. I wanted to ensure no one would ever hurt her or me again, so I became an assassin."

"Blood is always thicker than water," Baylis said, laying a hand on mine.

Ursula nodded. "It is easy to be thrown into the depths of the Undersea. Many orphans are taken to the underwater mines to work for room and board. The queen spared me that fate, and I am forever in her debt."

Amolie and I exchanged knowing glances.

"Your queen is just."

"As any good ruler should be. She does what she feels is best for her people. And I hope I am a part of that."

At that, we finished dinner, the conversation much lighter.

Finneas and the other satyrs cleared the plates sometime later.

Turning to Ursula, I leaned in and whispered, "Why don't you and I have a drink in the study? Just the two of us?"

A flirtatious smile full of sharp teeth brightened her face.

"I'll see you two ladies in the morning. Ursula and I have business to discuss." Taking Ursula's hand in mine, I led her into the study, where rows of books lined the walls. The room smelled of leather and parchment. I poured her and I a glass of brandy, and we took seats on the couch.

She swirled it around the finely cut crystal.

"The Alder King knows how to stock a bar."

"Nothing but the best for our guests."

"Oh, I'm just a guest now? A few weeks ago, you were nearly in my bed. And now we are just friends?" She leaned into me—the smell of brandy heavy on her breath.

"A lot has changed since the Yule Revelry, Ursula. I was a mercenary out for revenge, trying to save my sister. Now, I am the Hand to the Alder King, trying to save the continent. Perhaps the world."

Her bright expression darkened.

"Oh, you mean Gideon and Erissa? I heard their kingdom burned to the ground." She moved closer. Her breath made the hair on the back of my neck stand on end. "They had to flee. What a pity. You land dwellers love to burn each other. The sea folk know the order of things."

I tightened my jaw, the weight of our actions pressing down on me, the realization of the destruction we had caused. "Tell me what your queen wants, Ursula."

A smile tugged at the corner of her lips.

"It's really a very simple ask. She wants the siren's song."

Fuck. I downed my glass of brandy, letting it burn away everything I wanted to say.

"Can't the queen of the Undersea get that herself? Are the sirens not her subjects?"

Ursula twiddled her webbed fingers.

"It's complicated. Calypso, the queen of the sirens, is my queen's sister. And she can't very well go and just take it from her. They struck a bargain long ago. Calypso would rule the sirens while Calliope ruled everything else. But my queen has grown tired of her sister's antics and wants the song for herself. She would pull back the monsters guarding the Isle of Fate so a boat could dock to get it." Her sea glass eyes narrowed on me.

I swallowed hard.

"What is your queen planning?"

"She just wants to be prepared." Ursula twirled a piece of my hair around her finger. "You know how monarchs are... Always scheming."

I bit my lip. I *did* know how monarchs were. There was more to this than she was letting on, but what choice did I have? I needed those monsters cleared.

"Do we have a deal?" Her eyes sparkled with the delight of trapping me.

"Fine." I held out my hand. "I will secure the song, and in exchange, your queen will remove the monsters from the Isle of Fate so we may dock and hold them off until we are safely back on shore."

Ursula scrunched her mouth to one side as she contemplated the bargain.

"That seems right." She moved closer, running her tongue up the side of my neck before grabbing my hand. "Although in the Undersea, we seal our bargains with a kiss, too."

My pulse raced as her lips met mine, wet with brandy. Magic swirled around us, binding us to our words. Either Ursula hadn't noticed my specific wording, or she didn't care that I had given myself an out.

She pulled me in closer and my hand naturally went to her hips, grasping the soft flesh. She fisted her hands in my hair while slipping her tongue past my lips. A heat rose inside me.

I let my lips linger on hers for a moment before pulling away. I didn't want to upset her.

"The bargain is sealed. I will get the song, Ursula." I combed my fingers through my hair.

Ursula pouted.

"Oh? The night's over? But we were having so much fun. Don't you want to play like we used to?"

I took a deep breath averting my eyes.

"I am loyal to Tharan." I scooted away from her. Part of me wanted to see if she would fill the space between us, but when she didn't, a weight lifted itself from me.

Ursula flipped her aqua-blue hair to one side, framing her long face. A diamond not unlike my own whisper stone glinted in her ear. Had the queen been listening in this whole time or was it just a normal gem?

She started to slide her hand toward mine but stopped herself. "Fine."

Ursula smoothed out the wrinkles in her dress.

"Let me show you out," I said, and reached for her hand, but she pulled it away.

"I can see myself out." Without looking at me, she rose abruptly and floated to the door.

"Don't be like this, Ursula. You have two lovers waiting for you. You said you wanted to be my friend… so be my friend," I pleaded.

Pausing, she did not look back at me, but from where I was sitting, I could see her wipe a tear from her eye.

"I know," she said. Her voice was barely a whisper. "I was just…" Her words faded into nothingness—a dagger to my heart. I never meant to hurt her.

Ursula straightened and adjusted her dress.

"Goodnight, Aelia. I will see you in two days." She peered over her shoulder. "The sirens will require all of your strength, so be ready."

18 AELIA

I stood on the balcony of the Alder Townhome, cigarette in hand, watching the lights of the city twinkle around me. My stomach twisted. I hadn't intended to hurt Ursula, but our relationship started as a job and needed to stay that way. She was bound to her queen in a way I never could be. It had taken me a long time to realize that not all relationships were meant to be forever, but everyone taught me something new. Ursula taught me how to embrace myself. I meant what I said—I wanted to be friends with Ursula. I never meant to hurt her, but things are never cut and dry when it comes to matters of the heart.

Besides, that part of me needed to die. I was not the merciless mercenary anymore. I was not the "Mind Breaker," or the "Traitorous Queen." Taking a drag of my cigarette, I let smoke billow into the cold night air. To be honest, I didn't know what I was—stuck somewhere in the middle of becoming someone new while carrying the weight of who I used to be.

Footsteps behind me caught my attention.

"You don't have to sneak around. I know it's you two."

"You're no fun," Amolie said, joining me on the balcony, followed by Baylis.

"Fun is a privilege I haven't been afforded in a very long time." I took another drag.

"Well? What did Ursula want?" She tapped her toe on the cold stone.

I blew out a breath.

"She wanted what Conrad wanted. The siren's song."

Baylis and Amolie just blinked at me.

"That's peculiar," Baylis said, wrapping her wool shawl tighter around herself.

"Nothing surprises me anymore," I said. "I am the only person immune to their song. I can block it out. Queen Calliope has been waiting for me to need a favor. I may have stolen her pearl, but the song is worth more than my weight in pearls."

"So, what are you going to do?" Amolie swallowed nervously.

"I made a bargain with Ursula and intend to keep it."

"But what about Conrad?"

"Don't worry about it. I've got it under control. Let's just focus on getting the song. Then we can deal with who to give it to." I shot Amolie a look that said *don't push it*. I was still wary of Baylis's allegiance and didn't want to give out too much information in front of her.

"When are you going?" Amolie asked.

"In two days. And apparently, Ursula will be there to chaperone. How lovely."

"Well, at least you'll have company." Amolie grabbed a piece of willow bark from her satchel and placed it between her teeth.

"Since when do you chew willow bark?"

"Since we started saving the world." She giggled.

"Fair enough. Speaking of... could you mix up a little of that valerian root? You never know when you're going to have to sedate someone."

"Of course." She yawned. "I'll get started on it in the morning. Do you want me to stay with you tonight, or are you alright to sleep alone? I heard Ursula leave in a huff."

A breath slipped between my lips.

"I'm fine, but the bed is big enough for all three of us." My chest twisted a little. With Baylis and Amolie in my bed, I couldn't use my whisper stone. I hoped Tharan would understand. I sent a silent prayer up to Ammena to watch over him and keep him safe. I had to find time tomorrow to slip away and speak with him.

We all climbed into the plush bed and stared at the star-covered ceiling.

"Just like when we were kids," Baylis whispered softly.

"Yep. Only this time, no one can get us here." I threaded my fingers through hers. "This is the safest I've felt in a long time."

"Me too." She rested her head against my arm, and Amolie did the same on the other.

I thought of Tharan—his warm smile, the way he always twisted his feet with mine when we slept. If I had to sleep without him, at least it was between my sister and my best friend. Amolie was no doubt missing Roderick.

"Amolie?"

"Yes?"

"Tell me about your wedding."

"Caiden's father, Tonin, married us in the afternoon at their townhome in Vantris. The sunset, just as we said our vows, forged the unbreakable bond."

"What did it feel like?" Baylis asked.

"It felt like losing and gaining part of your soul." She gave a little chuckle. "I don't know any other way of describing it beyond that."

Baylis let out a sigh, and I swore I heard her say, "I know what you mean," under her breath. Was she talking about Gideon? The scene I'd witnessed in her mind flashed before my eyes. My chest tightened. Had they truly been in love? Were they *still* in love now?

I pushed the thoughts away. I needed to focus on the sirens. Ursula was right. It would take everything in me to face them. I had to conserve my energy. I'd need to take food with me; focusing on keeping the siren song out would take a massive amount of mental fortitude.

Amolie continued, "I wish you could have been there, Aelia. You would have loved it."

"I wish I could have been there too." I choked back tears. "I bet you looked so beautiful. I bet Roderick cried."

She squeezed my hand. "He did. He's really a big softy. And then we had a wonderful dinner and danced the night away."

"Did Caiden dance?"

"I… I don't think he did. I couldn't really tell. The world just kind of faded away when Roderick and I were dancing." She fiddled with the ring around her finger. "But even now, I can feel the bond pulled tight between us. I know he's thinking of me, just as I am thinking of him. I can't wait to see him when we return to the Alder Palace."

I sighed.

"Amolie. I don't want you to wait. I want you to go back to Vantris. To Roderick and have a lovely little honeymoon."

She waved me off.

"Don't be silly, Aelia. I love Roderick, but I want to be here to support you when you go to the Isle of Fate. Who knows what will happen? You need someone here who can get help if you don't come back."

"Alright, alright. You're right. Though you're being very presumptuous in assuming we'll even make it to the island."

"Like you've ever failed at anything you've set out to do." She clicked her tongue at me, and Baylis laughed in agreement.

A small streak of light in an otherwise bleak situation. We all knew the risks of what we were here to do. Death waited for us around every corner. I was grateful for this time with my best friend, and even my sister—despite being suspicious of her. I just hoped she proved me wrong.

"I've failed at lots of things. I failed at being a wife, a queen, a—"

Amolie interrupted me, "Don't finish that sentence. Some of those things were out of your control."

"And some were only controlled by me. But that is in the past now. All I can do is move on." That familiar heaviness weighed on my heart.

"That's right," Amolie agreed.

"Amolie, while we're gone, can you do a little more research into necromancy? Particularly the kind Erissa would use?"

Amolie yawned.

"Of course, but tomorrow." Her words faded off into nothing. I looked to see if Baylis was still awake but found her breathing softly beside me.

I shut my eyes and drifted off into a deep and dreamless sleep.

I awoke to the whisper stone vibrating in my ear. Pulling myself from between the two sleeping women, I slid into the changing room. "Tharan?"

"Oh, thank the Trinity, you're alright. I got worried when you didn't buzz me earlier." The concern in his voice made my heart beat a little faster.

"It's been a long night, to say the least."

"Well, we made it to Elohim. I haven't seen my grandfather yet. This place is so cold. So empty."

"What does it look like? I've heard Elohim is the most beautiful city in all of Moriana."

I could hear him light his cigarette and take a drag. "The elegance is tainted by the fact it was built on the backs of my people. This could be a sylph city. It was built with sylph hands." He let out a sigh. "But I must admit it is beautiful. All white marble and granite, like the city we stayed in the first night we met. Only there's a castle that rises into the sky with spindled spires. You can see all the way to the Atruskan River from my balcony. And there's a huge river that cuts the city in two. Boats from across the continent come and go all day long. It is like Ruska in that way."

"I wish I were there to see it," I said, trying to hide the sadness in my voice.

"Me too, Aelia. I can't sleep without you."

My heart twisted at those words. I had felt this way before, first with Caiden and then with Gideon, but this tug was different. It wasn't a need, more like an urge. I wasn't whole without him.

"Come back to me as soon as you can."

"I should say the same to you. You're the one who has to convince a siren to give you her song and see your mother."

I chuckled. "At least you will avoid an awkward reunion."

"Oh, it'll still be awkward."

I could hear Tharan's smile through the whisper stone.

I let out a yawn.

"I'll let you get your rest," he said.

"Not yet. Don't go yet. I…" I slumped down on the plush couch in his study. Even without him there I could feel him all around me. His energy, his scent—I wanted him.

"Yes?" He asked. Hope radiated through his voice.

"I want you, Tharan. I miss your touch, your scent, the feeling of your lips on mine."

"Oh Trinity, Aelia. I want you too."

Sliding my silk nightgown down. I clasped my nipple in between my fingers. "Touch yourself Tharan and pretend it's me."

"Fuck, Aelia…I already am."

I envisioned him gripping his glistening cock, eyes shut as he pleasured himself.

"Are you imagining what it's like to feel my tight pussy around you?"

Tharan let out a heady breath. "Yes."

I reached down between my legs and began to rub my clit. "Tell me what you want to do to me."

"I want to fuck that tight little cunt of yours. I want to fill you, stretch you, make you moan my name."

"Yes, oh fuck, Tharan." I rubbed my clit harder, sending shocks of pleasure through my veins all the while twisting my nipple, delighting in the mixture of pain and pleasure.

"Put your fingers inside yourself."

I did as he commanded. Savoring the delightful feeling of my wetness. "I am."

"Slow, darling, we don't want you coming too soon."

I arched my back as I slid my fingers in and out, making sure to scrape the front of my mound. My breaths came faster as heat grew in my core.

"That's a good girl, Aelia. Just like that. Slow and steady, just like my cock would be."

"Tharan…"

"Shh... Just keep stroking. I love it when you touch yourself for me. It makes me so fucking hard, knowing you're getting off at just the thought of me inside you."

My breath caught in my throat. "Can I… go harder?"

"Just a bit. I want to make you work for it. Trinity I'm so hard right now."

"I want to wrap my lips around your throbbing cock and suck you until you come in my mouth."

"Shit, Aelia." I could hear his hand rapidly stroking his erection, and I increased my pace, tightening my pussy around my fingers, groaning with pleasure.

"Aelia, you better not come yet. Good girls only come when commanded."

"Yes. Are you close?"

"So close."

"I want you to think of me bent over the desk in your study. Gripping the edges, as you thrust deep inside of me."

Tharan let out a loud moan.

"I'm so wet, baby. Your cock is making me so wet."

"You're so tight. Fuck you're so tight. I'm going to come."

"Not yet. You made me wait." I thrust my fingers harder and harder imagining Tharan's body over top of mine. Filling me, stretching me, as I gripped the edge of his desk. My nipples hard against the cold, polished wood.

"I can't hold it back much longer."

"Do you feel me tightening around your cock?"

"Yes. Trinity yes." His breath caught in his throat.

"Come for me, Tharan."

"Oh…Oh…Trinity. Fuck"

His orgasm only made mine yearn to be released. The sound of my fingers penetrating my wet pussy radiated through the silent study. "I'm so close…"

"Yes, my darling. Come for me."

Working my clit harder and harder a swell of pleasure grew inside me. Electricity radiated through every limb of my body, begging for release.

"Say my name, Aelia. Say my name when you come."

Leaning back, I let my orgasm overtake me. My breath hitched in my throat and as I exhaled, I said, "I'm coming Tharan. For you. Only for you." My body went limp, and a beautiful ache bloomed between my legs. The need extinguished for now.

"Good girl."

The doorbell to the Alder Townhome rang bright and early on the second day.

Finneas escorted Ursula into the morning room, where bright blue wallpaper adorned with drawings of orange trees covered the walls.

"Good morning, Ursula. You're looking well," I said before biting into a piece of toast covered in orange jam. She wore her scaled armor. Its iridescent steel sparkled in the morning light, making her look like one of those exotic fish you find on the coasts.

"As are you, Aelia. Or should I call you Lady now?" She poured herself a cup of coffee, resting the cup between her slender fingers.

"Just Aelia is fine. Hungry?"

"I ate before I came. And I prefer the fresh fish of the markets to that of land dwellers." She pushed away a plate of small pies in disgust.

I shrugged and kept eating.

"Suit yourself."

Ursula waited patiently, sipping her coffee while I finished my breakfast.

When I was done, I got up and pushed my chair in.

"Does the siren queen know we're coming?"

She rolled her eyes. "No, of course not. Early in the morning, most of her clan will be gone hunting. Only the breeders will be left behind, and they can't do much to stop us."

"What about guards? She is a queen, after all."

"There should only be a few this early in the day. But we may have dispatched a few, if you know what I mean."

Now it was my turn for an eye roll.

"I don't want to hurt anyone."

"I miss the old Aelia, who wasn't afraid to kill anyone. That Aelia was a lot hotter."

I breathed deeply. "Let's try to keep the killing to a minimum. I'm sure your queen would appreciate that."

"Fine. If you say so." She finished her coffee, and I watched her eyes take in my new Woodland armor. Boiled leather embossed with golden leaves and braces with a hidden blade.

"The Alder King treats you well. I am almost jealous of your armor... almost."

"I'm happy to ask Tharan to provide you with a set if you're ever in the market for a new employer."

She scoffed. "And live on land full time? Never."

A smile tugged at the corner of my lips.

"Suit yourself."

We took a carriage to the edge of Ruska, where the elven lands touched the free city.

"What exactly are we going to say we're here for, Ursula?" I asked as the carriage bumped along the quiet morning streets.

"Official Undersea business."

She stared out the window, unable to meet my gaze.

By now, I knew what to expect from Ursula. She was loyal to a fault to her queen, which meant she would try to double-cross me at some point, but what choice did I have?

"So, we're just going to waltz in there and what? Demand the queen let me dig around in her mind?"

"The siren queen has angered Queen Calliope, and we are there to discuss diplomatic terms."

My stomach hardened at her words. I couldn't shake the feeling something bad was headed our way.

"Mmhmm," I said, knowing full well there was more to this than just procuring a simple song. "I'll let you lead."

She smirked. "I always do."

The carriage stopped just before the border, where a path led down to the riverbank. I pulled my cloak tighter around my neck, preparing for the icy chill of the breeze wafting off the river.

"It's just down here," Ursula said, whipping her blue hair behind her shoulder.

We followed the narrow path marked with footprints down to the river's edge, then along a narrow ledge to where the mouth of a massive cave opened. The smell of fish mixed with the salty scent of the cave made my stomach turn. Two male sirens kept guard, spears in hand. Seaweed crowns twisted over their heads. Their bare chests exposed to the elements. Waves crashed upon the jagged rocks, spraying us with frigid water.

"What business do you have with Queen Calypso, mer?" one of the guards said, disdain dripping from every word.

"That's for me to discuss with Queen Calypso and her alone. You may show her this if she insists." Ursula held out a piece of parchment embossed with the seal of the Undersea; a trident skewering a fish.

The guards eyed the letter before exchanging glances.

"Fine. But stick to the path."

Ursula pocketed the letter, and we continued into the cave. On one side of us were stalactites and an underground river on the other. I craned my neck to catch a glimpse of any sirens, but only the crystal-clear water stared back at me.

"I told you. It's empty here during the mornings," Ursula said, leading us farther into the cave. Light beamed in from cracks in the thick rock, illuminating our way.

"She'll be in the birthing wing." She took a hard left down a narrow corridor leading to a large opening where shallow pools of water housed pregnant sirens. Some were in human form, others in their more mer shape, but each one's belly swelled with a child.

The siren queen sat high above the pools, perched on a stone throne. She was unlike anything I expected. Eight purple tentacles wriggled beneath her human torso. Hair as black as night cascaded down ample breasts, where two sailors suckled greedily. Tentacles wrapped around their necks.

"Let my milk nourish you. So that you may, in turn, nourish our young," she said, tilting her head back in pleasure. Around her neck sat a large sapphire encrusted with diamonds.

I noted the guards positioned sporadically throughout the room. Ursula and I could easily take them down if necessary.

A low hum echoed through the air. I looked at Ursula, who quickly stuffed something into her ears. I raised my mental shields, focusing on keeping their song out.

We approached the throne. The siren queen lowered her intimidating gaze upon us.

"You dare to interrupt my feeding time? These sirens are nearly ready to birth."

I swallowed hard, trying to hide my growing fear that something terrible was going to happen.

Ursula clicked her tongue at the queen before bowing low. "Queen Calliope sends her regards and hopes you have a fertile and successful birthing season."

I bowed in unison with Ursula, and she gave me a look that said, "*Any time you want to jump into her mind would be great.*"

I widened my eyes at her, wishing she had planned this better.

The queen scoffed. "Now, I know that's a lie. My sister and I have been at each other's throats for centuries." She turned her fishlike gaze upon me. "And who, may I ask, are you?"

My mind screamed at me to lie, but my Woodland armor already gave me away.

"I am Aelia Springborn."

"Ah, the Traitorous Queen. Looking to burn down another kingdom? Or do you only do that to your own family?" She chuckled to herself.

I gritted my teeth; she was technically a member of my court. I needed to keep the wild part of me contained for as long as I could. She was trying to provoke me. I knew it, and she knew it. Still, it did not ease the sting of her words.

"I am here as an emissary from the Woodland Realm to send my king's well wishes."

The siren queen eyed me suspiciously.

"It's about time the Alder King took some interest in me. I had been trying to court his father for years. And now that his heir has taken over, it would be wise for him to make an alliance with me."

Jealousy pooled in my stomach, and I dug my nails into my palms to keep myself calm. Is this how Tharan felt when he saw me look at Caiden? I stilled myself before responding.

"What kind of alliance are you proposing?"

She let out a hearty laugh. "Why, marriage, of course. We could rule land and sea together. Calliope would have to bow before me. And our offspring would reign for a thousand years—sylph who walk on land and breathe in the sea."

"I'm happy to bring it up with my king." A lie, and one I hoped she would believe.

Calypso opened her mouth to speak, but a loud wail ripped through the room before she could, bringing Ursula and me to our knees.

"What's that noise?" Ursula said, covering her ears with her hands.

More wails came from below.

"It's the birthing. It's beginning early." Calypso motioned for her attendants to help the laboring mothers.

Below us, dozens of pregnant sirens lay on their back in pools of pristine water, legs spread, pushing with all their might.

"Yes! My children! Yes! You're bringing the next generation of sirens into the world."

With no guards nearby and the queen distracted, I launched into her mind.

19 AELIA

A THICK GROVE OF SEAWEED WRAPPED AROUND MY LIMBS, pulling me down into the darkness of the queen's mind. The smell of muck turned my stomach. I held my breath but remembered I didn't need air to survive here. Balling my fists, I pulled as hard as I could against the slippery tendrils. Breaking free, I floated to the surface, where water lapped at an entrance to a small cave. *Great, another fucking cave.*

I hauled myself onto the rocky shore. Darkness loomed before me. Trinity only knew what awaited me inside. Snapping my fingers, I dried myself before summoning a torch to my hand. If Calypso was Calliope's sister, then she was ancient. Likely as old as the Alder King had been. Possibly even an original. Her mind would be full of traps. However, I'd been surprised more than once at how few precautions those who perceived themselves as deities took when protecting their minds. To most, telepaths were a myth. Why would they need to protect themselves from a ghost?

Damp air seeped into my bones, sending a chill down my spine as I traversed the circuitous tunnel through the cave. Like warm coffee with cream, Calypso's deep voice echoed through the cavern's halls.

"Mind Breaker—why have you come?"

I swallowed hard. "I think you know why I am here."

"Ah, yes, the song—*my* song. Despite my sister's royal standing, she has always been jealous of my gift."

"It's nothing personal."

"It never is."

"I need Calliope to clear the monsters surrounding the Isle of Fate. The song was her price." And before I could stop myself, the words, "Make a deal with me," came out of my mouth.

"A deal? What could you possibly give me for my song?"

"Give me the song. Just long enough to complete my bargain with Ursula, er, Calliope. I have also promised it to a sailor who wishes to see his love. Let them each have their moment, and then I will return it. I will also bring back a vision from the Fates."

Calypso chuckled then stopped abruptly. "The Fates are useless gossip whores. They twist their visions to suit the highest bidder."

I entered a clearing where the lute sat on a pedestal bathed in sunlight. Vines snaked their way up the walls.

"You underestimate my power, Calypso. You can make this deal with me, and I can leave with the song, or I can take the song and crush your mind as I leave. You decide." I picked up the lute, and as my fingers touched it, the gold vines wrapped themselves around my legs.

"Oh, I don't think you'll be going anywhere with my song." An evil cackle echoed through the chamber.

Adrenaline coursed through my veins. The vines sprouted thorns, ripping through my flesh. *Breathe, Aelia. This isn't real.*

"You may be a god, but I am the master here." My fingernails turned to claws, and I ripped the vines from my body before running into the tunnels.

The sound of beating wings followed me. Bats. Giant fucking

bats. Their red eyes glowed through the darkness, fangs bared, ready to sink into me.

The mind was my domain, and I could bend it to my will. Calling a ball of fire to my hand, I sent one flying at the giant beasts, sending it hurtling to the ground. It did little to deter the others.

The path twisted and turned, confusing me. Which way had I come in? Was this maze part of the mind's protection?

The sharp sensation of teeth on flesh pulled me from my thoughts. A bat latched onto my neck, pulling a scream from deep within me. My chest tightened. I hadn't been afraid in a mind in a long time, but Calypso had been luring men to their deaths for millennia. Perhaps even my powers might not be enough to outwit her.

I slammed my body into the nearest wall, and the bat fell to the ground. Pain radiated through me. Hot blood spewed from the wound. I placed my hand over the gash and summoned the power to close it. My skin grew, knitting together the throbbing tear.

More bats flooded the corridor. It would take all my power to get out of here. I turned another corner. Light streamed in through a crack in the wall. What was going on in the real world? *Trinity, Ursula, what are you doing?*

The squeaking of bats and flapping wings echoed behind me. Without thinking, I wedged myself through the crack, but the lute wouldn't fit through. As hard as I tried it refused to leave Calypso's mind. Seemed the old god had a few tricks left up her sleeve.

A horrifying sight awaited me when I opened my eyes. Ursula perched atop the throne, knife to the queen's neck.

"Ursula, what are you doing? She will give us the song!" The words scraped against the dryness of my mouth.

"Saving our asses." She motioned to something behind me.

I turned to see dozens of freshly born siren guppies crawling toward us in their creature form. Half human, half fish, their razor-sharp teeth glinted in the sunlight, and their beady eyes were full of hunger.

I narrowed my eyes at Calypso, who smiled deviously at me. "Give me the song, Calypso, and I won't murder every last one of these infants."

"Here." She ripped the sapphire from her neck and tossed it to me. "You can have the song, but I can't guarantee you'll make it out of here alive. My children are hungry." She pulled the still-suckling men from her breasts and tossed them into the sea of guppies. The men's screams reverberated through the cavern as the infants ripped them apart. Blood stained the once-pristine water.

I latched the sapphire around my neck. Its power radiated through me.

A boisterous melody echoed through the chamber, making my limbs rubbery. *Focus, Aelia, block out the song.*

"They are singing for you. They need to harmonize with their queen, or else their vocal cords will be useless," the queen said, squirming beneath Ursula's blade.

"Good," I said. "Let's get out of here, Ursula."

Ursula nodded, sliding off the throne with ease.

The queen seized on the moment, "Attack, my children! Feed on the blood of your kind." Calypso called to the ravenous infants. Their claws dragged on the edge of the balcony where the throne perched.

I backed away, my boots slipping on the wet stone.

Two guards came running up the path. Ursula slit the first one's throat before he knew what was happening.

Chest heaving, I charged toward the other. His spear clashed with my dagger. Going into Calypso's mind left me exhausted. I didn't know how much strength I had left to fight off an angry horde of sirens.

Gritting my teeth, I pushed the soldier back, feet slipping on the wet rock.

"Not so fast, Mind Breaker," Calypso wrapped a tentacle around my ankle. "If my children get a taste of your blood, they'll inherit your gift. I can't let you walk out."

Yanking my feet out from under me, my head hit the wet stone, blurring my vision. Calypso tugged me toward her hungry children.

Ursula thrust her sword through the soldier's chest. Blood gushed from the wound. His lifeless body slumped to the ground.

"Help me, Ursula!" I reached out a desperate hand.

"Toss me the song!" she called.

"What?" I asked frantically.

Calypso wrapped another tentacle around my limbs and pulled me upright so that my eyes locked with Ursula's. I squirmed against the restraints.

"You stole from my queen, and now you'll pay for what you did." She cut the gem off my neck.

"Fuck you. I'll make you pay for this," I spat at her. I knew Ursula would betray me; I just didn't know she wanted me dead.

A sly smile cut across her face, sharp teeth gleamed in the eerie light revealing her for what she truly was—a monster.

"Doubtful," she said before diving into the water below. Her legs became an iridescent fin.

"Get her!" Calypso cried. Sirens dove into the water after Ursula, leaving only me, the queen, and dozens of starving hatchlings in the cavern.

My heart beat wildly. How was I going to get out of this? *Think, Aelia, think.*

The queen tightened her grip on me. Her tentacles sucked tightly to my skin. I gasped for air. There had to be something I could say to make her rethink this. My ending would not be written by this sea witch.

"Don't do this. My blood isn't powerful enough to feed all these children. It's not a gift. It's a curse. They will never know silence. Never know rest."

"Maybe so, but it's a chance I'm willing to take."

"Please, please, please, I beg you. Please don't do this."

She lifted me high in the air. Her children jumped, scratching at my feet with their little clawed hands.

"Feast, my children. Let her blood nourish you."

I focused on the nearest hatchling and called my dagger to my hand.

Calypso dropped me.

I buried my dagger in the guppie's skull. Blood splattered across my face.

The other children quickly moved to devour the dead siren.

"No… you monster!" Calypso cried.

"We are all monsters here." I launched myself at her distracted and dismayed form, burying my dagger in her neck. Blood poured down her naked body to the waiting mouths of the hatchlings. "Feast."

Calypso let out a guttural scream as I dragged Little Death through the thick flesh of her neck. Her tentacles clawed at me, sucking at my skin, but still I sawed through her flesh. Blood gurgled in her throat.

The life faded from her eyes and with her dying breath she said, "You'll pay for this Mind Breaker."

I set my jaw and with one final tear I severed her head from her neck. The body went limp beneath me.

Fisting her hair in my hand, I leapt from the throne onto the slick dais while the hungry hoard of hatchlings devoured the corpse of their queen. The sounds of their teeth ripping through flesh made my skin crawl. I didn't stay to witness the carnage. I had to get the song back from Ursula.

I fled, head in hand, as the cavern descended into madness.

Sirens fled the flesh-eating frenzied guppies. The sound of their bodies hitting the water mixed with the sounds of screams as the hatchlings devoured their mothers.

Blood stained the once-pristine water, snaking its way out of the cavern and into the river.

Guards ducked out of the way as I passed, holding their queen's head—her mouth still agape, frozen in fear for an eternity.

Once a safe distance away from the cave, I sank the head into the snow and fell to my knees in exhaustion. I had to tell Tharan. Word would spread of the queen's death at the hands of a Woodland emissary.

Twisting the whisper stone, I waited for the reassuring sound of Tharan's voice, but no answer came. He must be busy in the elven court.

I sighed, burying my face in my hands. I needed to find Ursula and get the song back. But first, I needed to get a bag to cover this head. I buried the monstrous thing in snow. Wiping the blood from my face, I headed toward the outskirts of Ruska.

The streets bustled with midday foot traffic while vendors sold their wares. Pulling my hood over my head, I approached the stall of a fishmonger. With a sleight of hand even Lucius would find impressive, I nabbed the nearest burlap sack, tucking it under my arm, before walking cooly out of the bazaar.

A rush of adrenaline dissipated any exhaustion I felt. I learned to be quick and quiet with my hands if I wanted to survive out in the world. Escaping Gideon meant leaving every possession behind. I sold the very dress off my back to put food in my belly. It was desperation that made me turn to mercenary work, and I didn't relish the memories that came with it, but I will say there was a thrill in stealing and not getting caught. Although the adrenaline from chopping off a queen's head was nothing to scoff at.

With the bag secured, I headed back to where I hid the head

and quickly concealed it. Now, I needed to find Ursula and get the song back.

Catching a ride on the back of a cart, I made my way to the docks. The bagged head shook as the cart rumbled over the cobblestones. I hoped Ursula would go back to her lair at the Rusty Bucket before making the arduous trip to the Undersea Palace.

I burst through the door to the dive. Blood seeped through the burlap sack, dripping on the grimy floor.

"Is she here?" I said to the bartender, whose eyes went wide at the sight of what remained of the blood still smeared across my face and the bag in my hand.

He nodded frantically and pointed up the stairs.

Flinging her door open. I found Ursula frantically trying to wake one of her paramours.

"Come on, get up. We have to go," she said, tugging at the man's limp body. I recognized the signs of overdose. This man had likely mixed too much alcohol with dust and choked on his own vomit. The other woman sat crumbled in the corner, hiding her face.

I didn't have time for empathy. In an instant I was on top of her, fist clenched around her delicate neck. Her eyes went wide.

"Is this how you saw your little plan going?" I squeezed tighter.

She gasped for air, clawing at my hand. A strength I had never experienced before radiated through me, fueled by my rage.

"Please, Aelia, it's just business."

I gritted my teeth, wondering if I should crush her windpipe and be done with it. I tried to be cordial—tried to be her friend. This was our end.

I shook my head. I was no longer the mercenary. I was the Hand to the Alder King. I couldn't just go around killing whoever. I'd already fucked up by beheading Calypso. Another dead body wouldn't do me any good.

I released Ursula.

She leaned against the bed, clutching her throat, gasping for air.

"What... the... fuck... Aelia?"

I laid my head on the table beside the bed, examining the body lying face down beside her.

"He's dead, Ursula."

"What?" She turned to the body. The sapphire necklace sparkled around her long neck. "No, he's... just asleep."

Pulling my dagger from its bandolier, I stabbed it into the man's back.

He didn't move—didn't even flinch.

"He's dead, Ursula."

I grabbed her shoulders, turning her face me before yanking the necklace from her collarbone.

"You're heartless. You know that?" She narrowed her seaglass eyes at me, and I felt nothing.

"Yeah, well, forgive me if I don't feel anything for a man I didn't know." I leaned in so close our noses nearly touched. "You left me for dead back there. You're lucky I don't break your mind right now."

There was a part of me that wanted to—wanted to see the consciousness slip from her eyes. A great assassin reduced to a vegetable. I could do it. Could wipe every memory she had. Her parents, her lovers, all gone.

A chill ran up my spine and I shook the urge away. I was not that person anymore.

"What about our bargain?"

"It was complete when you pulled the stone from my neck."

Her mouth fell agape. "How…"

"That's how magical bargains work, Ursula. I made the bargain *to secure the song* with you, not your queen. And the second your hand pulled the necklace from my neck, it was complete."

"That's not fair." She put her hands on her hips.

"Take it up with your queen. She's the one who had you make the bargain, so if something went wrong or neither of us fulfilled our end, you'd suffer the consequences and not her." I shrugged.

"She would never." Her nostrils flared.

"She would, and she did." I clasped the song around my neck. "You can take Calypso's head back to your queen. Tell her I will give her the song as soon as I return safely from the Isle of Fate."

For a brief moment, I again considered snapping Ursula's neck, to steal the whisper stone from her ear and communicate directly with her queen, but I stopped myself.

Ursula nodded; her eyes fixed on the corpse splayed out across the bed. "She will not be pleased."

"I don't really care as long as she clears the waters."

I left the room, leaving Ursula with her dead lover and the head of her queen's sister, a stark reminder that Aelia Springborn, Traitorous Queen, Mind Breaker, Commander of the Army of the Dead, and now Slayer of Sirens, was not to be trifled with.

I hailed a petty cab. Sinking into the seat, my body relaxed, and soreness set in. I knew getting the song wouldn't be easy, but I hadn't expected having to kill the queen. I closed my eyes and let the rhythm of the carriage lull me to sleep. When I awoke, the cab was parked out front of the Alder Townhome.

Finneas opened the door, and a rush of cold air swooped into the cab. I pulled my cloak tighter around my neck. The siren sapphire weighed heavy on my chest.

"Welcome back, my Lady," he said, extending a hand to me.

Out of the corner of my eye, I caught a swath of baby blue. Baylis strolled up the circle drive, two of the Hunt in tow.

"What are you doing?" I sounded like our mother, but I didn't care.

Her cheeks flushed.

"I just wanted to see the city. I haven't been here before, and you were gone. I took the Hunt with me."

Her face paled as she noticed the blood strewn across my face.

"Are you alright? What happened?"

I waved her off. "I'm fine. Now get inside"

Amolie greeted us when we walked in. "Hi—"

"I need you to look at my wounds," I said before she could finish.

Taking the hint, she set down her needle work.

"Of course, I'll meet you in your chambers. Just let me grab my things." She turned and headed up the stairs.

"Do you want me to help you to your room?" Baylis asked, gently touching my arm.

I sighed. "No, it's fine. I'm just exhausted." I motioned for Finneas. "Go with Finn and have the cooks make you something sweet. I just need to rest for a little bit."

Her gray eyes flicked between the satyr and me suspiciously, but she did not protest.

I quickly climbed the stairs to my room where Amolie waited for me. Jars of herbs and salves adorned the side table.

"Sit," she said, and I did as she commanded. "I assume this is more than just the usual mending."

She took a cloth and cleaned my face.

"Mmhmm. I don't know if I can trust Baylis, but I know I can trust you, Amolie."

"What happened?" She scooped salve onto her fingers, dabbing it into my cuts.

"Well, I killed the siren queen, for starters, but I also got this." I pulled the sapphire from my neck and dangled it from my fingers.

Her hazel eyes went wide.

"Is this… the song?"

"Yes."

She set down the salve, wiped her hands on a cloth, and took the jewel from me.

"It's stunning. I want to open it…"

"Don't. They say it only works at sea but who knows. Calliope thinks she can make it work on land."

Amolie clicked her tongue at me.

"I may have a penchant for shiny things, but I'm not dumb enough to open this."

A smile tugged at the corners of my lips.

"I know. I'm just tired and paranoid."

She handed me the necklace and I clasped it around my neck. It was the safest place I could think of to keep it.

A breath slipped between my lips.

"What am I going to tell Tharan? I killed a member of his court—a royal."

Amolie grimaced.

"I don't know, but you better do it soon. You know how magus love to gossip."

I leaned back on the bed, scrunching the pillow under my head.

"I'm too tired for this right now." My heavy-lidded eyes closed. "I'll deal with this later."

Amolie pulled the blankets over me before sneaking out of the room.

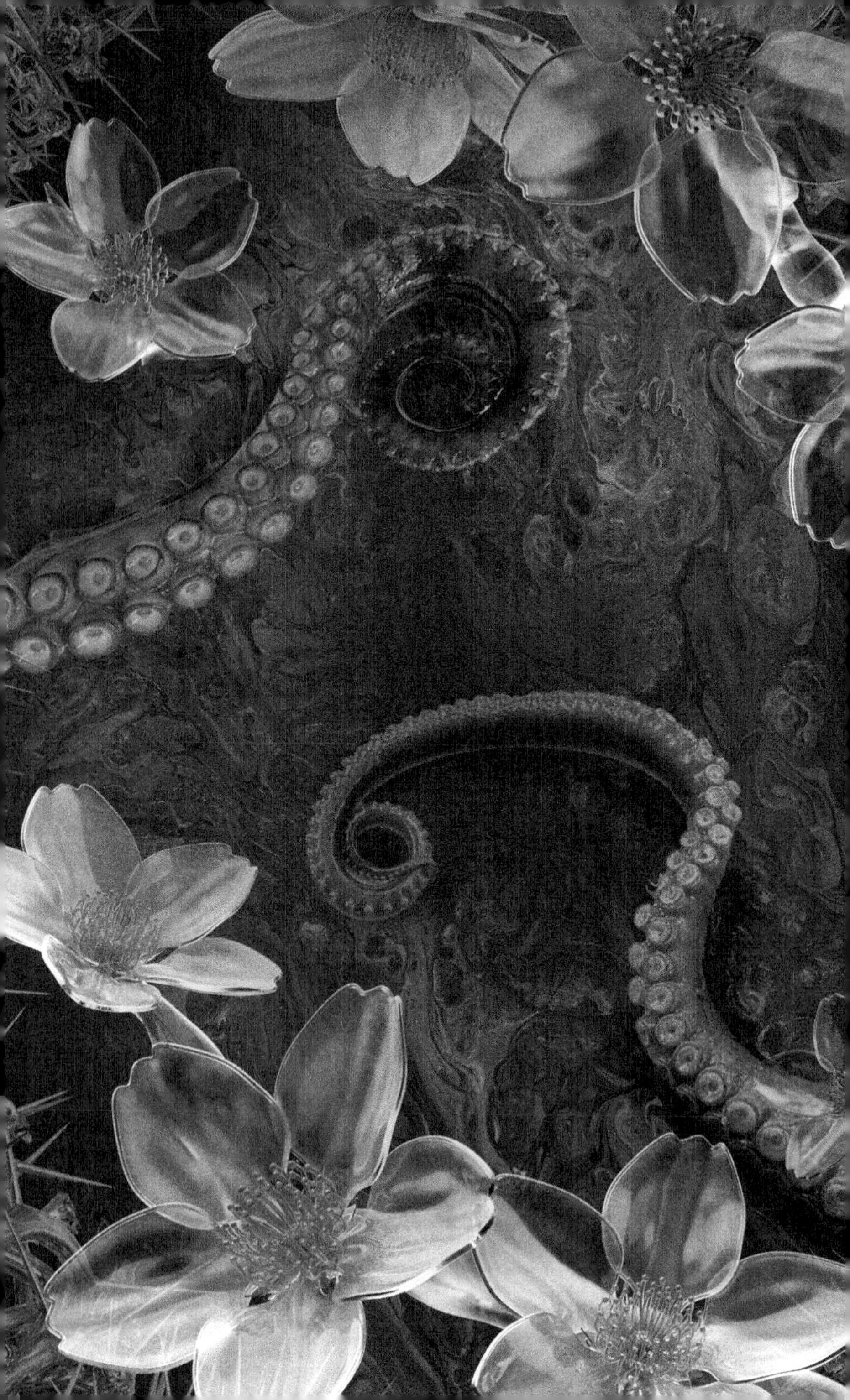

20 THARAN

Tharan stared out at the white city of Elohim. A triumph of architecture, spindled pillars of white marble rose high into the blue sky. Beneath him, the river Wayren carried elegant ships and passengers alike—all this beauty built on the backs of the sylph. Tales of the grandeur of Elohim had spread far and wide, but nothing could quite prepare him for this splendor—each building a work of art, with intricately carved designs displaying the nature of the work done inside. If only Aelia was here to see this.

He took a drag from his cigarette, leaning against one of the granite pillars of his balcony in the palace. Weeks of travel exhausted him, but the prospect of seeing his grandfather kept him up for most of the night. With morning on the horizon, he wished he had slept more. He would have slept if Aelia had been here.

A knock at the door pulled him from his thoughts.

"Yes, come in."

Hopper and Sumac entered, each wearing their finest attire. Hopper wore a black caftan embroidered with the seal of the Alder King in gold thread on his breast. His emerald, green hair was slicked back, and his ears were adorned with jeweled earrings. Sumac wore the armor of the Hunt—tungsten leaves woven together like chainmail. Her helmet was tucked under her arm.

"You're not even dressed," Hopper said, disapproval plastered across his face. "We are meant to be presented to the king this morning." He walked to the closet where Tharan's royal attire hung. "Where is your servant?"

"It's fine, Hopper. I can dress myself. I sent my servant away."

"It is not fine. I need you to look your best. We must present ourselves as a legitimate kingdom, not some Wild Court."

Tharan sighed.

"But we *are* a Wild Court. In fact, we oversee all the Wild Courts."

"Yes, well. We don't have to remind them of that." Hopper laid a houppelande of deep green and gold on the bed. "Now, go wash. I will call a servant to do something with your hair."

Tharan and Sumac exchanged knowing glances. Hopper had always kept them in line, even when they were children, but that didn't mean it didn't annoy them.

Tharan pulled himself from the balcony and quickly bathed before returning to his suite, where a team of satyrs waited to make him presentable. Weeks in a carriage had left his beard shaggy, and his fingernails needed a good trimming. The attendant made quick work of him, shaving his beard and plucking his eyebrows until the ethereal Alder King emerged once more.

"That's better," Hopper said, buttoning the high collar around Tharan's neck.

"I hate this." Tharan fidgeted under the stiffness of the fabric.

"I know, but it won't be for long." He twisted Tharan's burgundy hair back behind his ears, before placing the golden antler crown atop his head. "There. Now you look the part."

Tharan stared at himself in the mirror. A man he didn't recognize stared back—for the first time since donning the crown, he felt like the Alder King. Power flickered behind his verdant green eyes, and he practiced holding his head high like the elves.

"You look... magnificent," Sumac said in awe.

"Don't you start." Tharan crooked his head at her, brows knitted. "I don't want you two to treat me differently now that I'm king."

Hopper stepped forward, fanning out the skirt of Tharan's robe. "But that's just it. You *are our king* now. Not our friend. Not the playboy bastard son. *The* Alder King. It is only right we hold you in reverence."

"Fine. Let's get this over with so we can find the Well and return to the Woodland Realm."

"Very Well." Hopper bowed his head to his king. "I will lead. You will follow, and Sumac and the Hunt will take up the rear."

Light streamed through the massive windows of the throne room, casting everything in a white light. Tharan tried to keep his eyes on the back of Hopper's head, but the elegant paintings of the Trinity besting deities long dead pulled his eyes toward the ceiling. Strings of floral garlands hung from the rafters, and the sigil of the Woodland Realm hung prominently above the dais. He wished Aelia was by his side to give him courage and ward off any talk of potential suitors.

Trumpets played as they made their way down the aisle. Hundreds, maybe even thousands of eyes, bored into them. Sylph were rarely welcomed with such pomp and circumstance, but it wasn't every day the Alder King graced them with his presence.

Tharan wondered if this was where they dragged his mother when Arendir found her pregnant with a sylph's child. Is this where they killed her? Or did they do that in a more public place so the elven kingdom could see? His chest tightened with anger, but he did not let it show on his face. He would not give these petty elves something to whisper about.

Hopper stopped short, and Tharan nearly ran into him. Bowing low, he announced Tharan's arrival, "Your Highness, I present to you, Tharan Greenblade, the Alder King, Ruler of the Wild Courts, and keeper of the sacred magic of the Woodland Realm."

Tharan kneeled before the dais. It was customary to avert your eyes before being acknowledged by the king in an elven court.

"Rise," an ancient voice echoed through the marbled halls.

Tharan looked up to see a figure bathed in white staring down at him from atop the dais. Long white hair flowed over tanned skin with a face not unlike his own. Sharp features gave way to an elegant mouth and large green eyes—his eyes. A crown of woven silver with a ruby in the center sat atop his head. With the Original Breath still in his lungs, he looked no older than fifty despite being thousands of years old.

In his right hand, he held a staff of carved White Ash. Behind him, a dozen similar looking elves sat, their eyes lowered on Tharan. Were these the king's children? No. Everyone knew the elves had trouble conceiving. To have two children was considered a blessing from Eris. Arendir looked to have at least twenty sitting behind him. Where was their mother? Mothers?

"My grandson has finally come to visit me," he said to the chuckle of the crowd.

Tharan gritted his teeth and tried not to roll his eyes. "Greetings, mighty King Arendir. It is an honor to be in your presence."

"The honor is all mine. It's not every day your grandson becomes the Alder King."

You've known it was possible my whole life, yet you have refused to acknowledge me.

Tharan cleared his throat.

"It is time our great houses joined forces. I've brought you gifts from the Woodland Realm." He stepped to the side, and the Hunt placed chests of treasures in front of the dais for the entire court to see.

The king's eyes raked over the gold and jewels.

"An acceptable offering, if meager."

"There is one more thing." Tharan snapped his fingers, and the clacking of hooves echoed through the halls of the throne room. Two satyrs trotted astride two white unicorns.

An audible gasp rippled through the crowd.

Arendir's eyes widened, and he stepped toward the magnificent creatures, moving with the ethereal grace that only comes from millennia of life. "Now, this is a gift worthy of the original Elven King."

The horses stopped when they reached Tharan, pawing at the ancient tile and champing at their bits. He took their reins and gently ran his hands over their soft cheeks, settling the creatures. "A mating pair so that you may grow your herd."

The king approached the horses, stroking their muscular necks softly so as not to spook the flighty creatures. "Shh… It's alright," he cooed. The unicorns pawed at the marble floor.

"I hope you find this more acceptable," Tharan said, a smug smile tugging at the corners of his lips.

"How did you…" The king shook his head before clapping his hands together gleefully. "Come. We have much to discuss." Turning to his court, he dismissed them. Elves filed out of the Great Hall, whispering under their breath as they went.

The satyrs followed the crowd with the horses. In contrast, Tharan and his company followed Arendir and his advisors into an elegant marble meeting room with floor-to-ceiling windows overlooking the bay.

Plush velvet chairs surrounded a white granite meeting table, and a fire crackled in the mammoth fireplace at the edge of the room. Tharan noticed the distinct smell of bergamot and lavender in the air. He took his seat next to his grandfather. Hopper and Sumac took their respective seats next to him, and the Hunt took up residence at the door.

"Wine. Please." Arendir signaled to a servant who appeared to be human.

"Since when do the elves use human labor?" Tharan asked.

"They are cheaper and more obedient than the sylph," Arendir said, holding up a silver chalice for the servant. "Pity they only live a few dozen decades."

"Yes, that is the flaw of a mortal life," Tharan said, sniffing his wine.

"A toast," Arendir raised his chalice, and the rest of the table followed, "to my grandson, Tharan Greenblade, Lord of the Wild Courts and king of the Alders."

"Hear, hear!" the table proclaimed. Tharan gazed at the elves' long, elegant faces, all of them strangers. All of them possible enemies. Did they know his mother? Did they advise him on how best to punish her for the crime of loving someone she shouldn't?

"Thank you, King Arendir. You are a gracious host."

The ancient king nodded.

"It has been too long. I should have sought you out sooner. Perhaps old age is making me soft."

Or perhaps you want the power of the Alder King in your arsenal.

"Yes, well, I've come here to discuss a matter of great importance."

"Oh?" Arendir arched a brow. Servants laid silver platters of exotic fruits and cheeses on the table. The king reached for something green with black seeds. "Nothing in the continent happens that I don't know about. So, I can't imagine what it is."

"It's about the Trinity Wells."

The king's face paled, and his expression darkened.

"What could you possibly want with the Trinity Wells?"

"So, you're saying they exist?"

Arendir raked his eyes over his grandson. "Everyone out. I have much to discuss with my grandson."

His advisors grumbled but did as they were told. Sumac and Hopper gave Tharan questioning glances, but at his nod, they reluctantly exited with the rest of the advisors.

When they had all gone, Arendir turned to Tharan and said, "Come with me to a more private space so that we may speak freely. Even here, the walls have ears."

Tharan followed his grandfather up a winding staircase to the top of a spindled tower. The elven Kingdom of Eden stretched out before them. A gleaming white city led to snow-covered fields where grapes and barley would soon bloom. Past that, Tharan could make out the edge of the mighty Atruskan River—a blue sliver in the distance.

"This is quite a view."

"It is good to see one's kingdom now and again." He poured two glasses of amber liquor, handed one to Tharan, then sat in front of a roaring fire. "Now, what's this about the Trinity Wells?"

Tharan took a seat across from his grandfather.

"King Gideon of the Highland and his mage, Erissa, are looking for them. We don't know why, but it would be devastating for this kingdom if they fell into their hands. As you are well aware, they attacked my kingdom... and killed my father."

Arendir held up a hand.

"And in retaliation, you destroyed their kingdom, did you not?"

"Yes, well, that's very complicated."

"It is not. An eye for an eye, as the old saying goes." He gazed into the fire. "I am in a hard spot here. The Highlands have been our allies for hundreds of years—"

Tharan interrupted before he could go any further, "I know,

but with the power of just one Well, they could level this continent. Even you."

"What use would a human have with such power?" Arendir chuckled.

Tharan smiled to himself.

"What?" the king asked.

"You are foolish if you think humans do not yearn for power the way elves do. Or perhaps you have been locked in this tower for so long that you have forgotten how vicious the world can be?"

Arendir's nostrils flared.

"You come here to ask me a favor, and yet you end up insulting my intelligence. Just like a sylph."

Tharan gritted his teeth and tried not to become the savage beast his grandfather thought he was. "I came here because I thought you could help me save the continent. I see now that I was wrong. That you're just as fickle and foolish as they say you are." He stood and glanced out the window at the snow-covered city. "You elves think you can hide here in your lavish cities because you possess the Breath of Eris, but that breath will not save you when fire rains from the sky. It will not save you when Gideon and Erissa bring back the nightmares that haunt your dreams." He turned to look at his grandfather, who stared at him with great interest. "Tell me, Arendir, are you prepared to hear the screams of the children of Elohim as their bodies are consumed by the creatures of darkness? Are you prepared to flee the continent?"

"What are you talking about? This is madness. What does this have to do with the Trinity Wells?"

"Gideon and Erissa are looking for them. I think they plan to resurrect Crom Cruach."

"An elven mage would never do such a thing, and Crom has

been dead for thousands of years. Not even I know where his body lies."

Tharan wanted to shake the arrogant king.

"It does not matter where his body lies. If Erissa gets ahold of the magic of the Wells, she will be able to summon him back through the veil, and there's no telling what kind of army he has amassed on the other side."

Arendir shook his head.

"I have walked this earth since nearly its inception. Do you think I have not faced threats like this before?" He took a swig of his drink. "They rarely amount to anything. Besides, I cannot help you. I do not know where Lady Eris hid her Well. It is something only she knows."

"Can you not communicate with her?"

"I have not spoken to the goddess since the day she blessed me with her breath. Do I still pray to her? Yes, of course, but she has not answered me in an age."

"So, you can't help me?" Tharan shut his eyes. He should have known better.

"I didn't say that. Just because she didn't tell me where the Well was doesn't mean she didn't leave clues."

"Do not play with me, old man. The fate of this continent... of this world, hangs in the balance."

"Make a bargain with me, and I will help you."

Tharan scoffed. "I should have known. Elves never do anything out of the goodness of their heart."

"This is serious. As you may or may not know, our magic is dwindling. It would benefit me just as much as you to find Eris's Well and restore my people to their former glory."

"Judging by this palace, you look like you're doing just fine."

The king cocked his head. "There is more to this world than meets the eye, and you and I know that."

"True. What's your bargain?"

"I will help you find the Trinity Well if you marry a high-born elven woman."

Tharan's chest tightened, and he blurted out, "No."

A smile graced Arendir's lips. "I know you are in love with the Mind Breaker, but she has no land, no house, and no power. Think of your people, Tharan. Think of what an alliance between our kingdoms could afford them. They could come and go as they please across our borders. And our kingdom would come to your aid should the need arise."

Tharan bit the inside of his cheek. "You mean I could bond with an elven woman, give her part of my power, and she would pass it down to our offspring. An offspring that could control the Wild Hunt."

"That would be ideal, yes," Arendir said, finishing his drink before lighting a long pipe.

"No. I love Aelia."

The king rose slowly, laying a hand on Tharan's shoulder. "Love has always gotten you into trouble, boy. Sleep on it, and we will talk about it again in a few days. Besides, there is someone I would like you to meet."

"I'm not in the mood to be courted," Tharan hissed.

"It is no bride." He banged his staff on the floor, and a doorway opened, revealing an elven woman with long auburn hair and verdant green eyes—Tharan's eyes. She wore a beautiful white satin gown that cinched at the waist, and a diamond diadem sat atop her head.

Tharan's heart leapt into his throat, and he nearly lost the ability to speak. "Mother?"

21 THARAN

"Yes, child, it is me." With arms outstretched, his mother beckoned him forward.

Tharan's heart tore in two, half filled with anger and resentment; she had been alive all this time and never reached out to him, and half desperate to feel the warmth of a mother he'd never known.

"I… I don't know what to say. I thought you were dead."

Her expression darkened, and her shoulders drooped.

"In a way, I was."

"My father… " Tharan's words caught in his throat. He moved closer to the stranger claiming to be his mother. Elves were cunning. Could this be a trap? A way to manipulate him? The resemblance between the two was uncanny. Was this his mother or just a woman who looked like her? Shaking off his thoughts, he continued, "I'm sorry, I don't know what to call you. My father never spoke your name."

Her lids lowered.

"I had hoped you'd call me Mother, but I understand if you're not ready for that. My name is Elowen."

Tharan chuckled.

"My father *would* fall in love with someone named after a tree."

She moved closer, taking his face into the palm of her hand. "You look like him, you know? Your father was so handsome when we met. I'm sure he was just as handsome when he passed."

Tharan couldn't help but lean into her warmth. He wished to have a mother all his life. Only… now that she was here, the feeling was bittersweet. Had she tried to find him? Had his father known she was alive all this time? So many questions left unanswered. A tear trickled down his cheek for all the time lost between them.

"Do not cry, my child. I am here now."

He fell into her embrace, taking in the scent of pine and mulberry on her skin. Despite being a head taller than her, Elowen ran her fingers through his silken hair. "Shh, my child, we have much to discuss."

She led him out of the study.

"Think about my offer," Arendir called after him.

With their fingers linked, Elowen led him to her extravagant chambers, where six human servants dressed in fine linens waited for them. Each had their hair pleated in neat braids, and each wore a golden collar, not unlike the ones the Highland servants wore. Tharan couldn't help but wonder whether they were actually here of their own volition or if something more nefarious was at play.

His mother took a seat on a plush circle of satin pillows. "Sit."

Tharan did as she commanded. One of the servants poured them each a chalice of wine, and Tharan drank deeply, hoping to calm his nerves.

"We have so much to catch up on. Tell me what your life has been like. I heard some rumors while in exile… but… nothing until you were crowned Alder King." She stared longingly out the window. "I am sad I did not get to say goodbye to Eoghan. He was my first love, and I have never stopped loving him. Even when my father sent me to live in the Great White North."

"Is that where you have been all these years?"

She nodded, her eyes lowered in shame.

"I was foolish to think Arendir would allow me to keep you. But for a moment, I held out hope we could be a family." She took his hand in hers, and he couldn't help but share in her pain. "I wanted you; you know? I wanted to be your mother. I wanted to raise you in the Woodlands. Perhaps if I had been there…"

A storm of emotions raged inside Tharan. Why would she reveal herself now? She was likely a pawn in Arendir's game. A tool to distract him—to soften him. He'd yearned to have a mother his whole life. Looking at her now, he was transformed into that little boy who wished for a mother to hug before bed. He resisted falling into those emotions. If this was the game Arendir wanted to play… he would play it.

"Shh…" Tharan whispered. "It does neither of us good to dwell on what might have been when we both know our fates were sealed long before either of us took our first breath."

She nodded, her auburn hair falling in waves over her bare shoulders. He noticed the freckles dotting her skin, just like his when he was a boy.

"Can I ask you something?"

"Anything."

"Do you know of the Trinity Wells?"

Her eyes darted around the room, landing on each one of the servants, before she grabbed his wrist more tightly than he was expecting. Was this a warning or a threat?

"No. I do not. You would be wise to take your grandfather's offer of marriage if you want to learn more."

He patted her hand reassuringly, not wanting to raise any alarm bells.

"I said I would sleep on it, and I will, but I am in love with someone. I cannot just throw those feelings away."

"You're a king now, not just some bastard son," she said with a tone of warning in her voice. "You have to think about your kingdom. Think of the alliances you could make. Kings will brave the seas to bring their daughters to your bed. Besides, I was in love once. Look how it turned out for me."

Tharan tightened his jaw.

"Your fate does not have to be mine, *Mother*."

"It is a harsh world, Tharan. You are old enough to know that by now."

Tharan took another swig from his chalice, wishing he'd brought his cigarettes with him.

"I don't want to fight with you. We have so much lost time to make up for. Let's not spend it fighting."

She sighed, twisting the stem of her chalice in her hand. "You're right. We have much to discuss."

"Where would you like to start?"

"At the beginning. You were still a babe at my breast when they ripped you away from me."

Tharan examined his wine glass, focusing on the sloshing red liquid within. "We're going to need more wine then."

His mother's smile brightened, and she ushered her servants over.

The pair talked until late in the evening, when the stars speckled the night sky. Tharan told her of his time in the sylph military and his fall from grace, and his mother told him of her time in exile with the elven mages of the Great White North across the Atruskan River, where the snow never melts and night lasts for eternity. Tharan poured his heart out to her, yet, at the same time, only scratched the surface of his life.

"It seems you have become a good man despite my absence," his mother said, wiping a tear from her eye.

"My father did well in that regard. I think he softened in his later years."

"And what of this woman you are willing to risk your kingdom for?"

Tharan hesitated, unsure of how much to tell his mother about Aelia. "Her name is Aelia Springborn. She is a half-breed like me. She is smart, funny, and deadly, and I intend to make her mine in the binding ceremonies of old."

"Be careful who you bind yourself to, son."

"I am old enough to know what I want in a partner."

Elowen stared into her now empty chalice. "Your grandfather would make a good match for you."

Tharan wanted to protest, but a knock on the door interrupted their reunion.

"Enter," Elowen said, a bit slurred.

A servant girl with mousy brown hair and rosy cheeks entered head lowered. "Excuse me, my Lady, but dinner is being served in the dining room, and the king requests your attendance."

"Well, I better not keep him waiting then. Father does love our dinners." She rose and straightened her gown. "I, uh, I'd like to ask you for a hug, but I don't know if that would be appropriate given our distance these last seven hundred years."

Tharan didn't hesitate. He pulled his mother close, taking in her scent, squeezing her tightly, not wanting to let go.

She pulled him close, whispering in his ear, "All is not as it seems here."

The hairs on the back of Tharan's neck stood on end, but he played his part well.

"I love you too, Mother," he said loud enough for the servant girl to hear.

The two parted ways.

"Marta will show you back to your chambers," his mother said before slipping into her changing suite.

Tharan followed the servant through the elegant halls of the elven palace, past ancient carvings and beautiful paintings, through halls of sculptures, and vast greenhouses filled with plants Tharan couldn't have imagined in his wildest dreams. But the plants recognized him. All bowed in their own way. If the servant girl noticed, she did not say anything. In fact, she did not look back at him at all. None of the staff did.

Pillars of light illuminated their path. Tharan wanted to reach out and touch it, though thought better of it.

"Where is everyone?" Tharan asked when the silence became too much.

"They are either in the dining hall, or they have gone home for the evening," the girl said. "During the day, it is quite lively, with the king having nearly twenty children."

"Twenty?" Tharan spat out in surprise. "I thought it was difficult for an original to conceive. How many wives does he have?"

"None," the servant said matter-of-factly.

"Then how?" He knew the rumors. Sylph and elves used humans to keep their bloodlines going for a millennium. It was their dirty little secret, but he wanted the girl to admit it out loud.

They stopped in front of his chambers, where two members of the Hunt stood guard. "Here are your chambers. A meal will be brought to you shortly. I do hope you have a good night, Your Majesty." She bowed. "And if you need anything, please ring the bell in your room, and a servant will be right up." With a click of her heels, she turned and headed down the hallway.

Tharan lay on his bed. His heart ached for Aelia—to hear her laugh and run his fingers through her thick hair. Hoping he could still catch her; he twisted the stone in his ear.

"Tharan?" her perfectly high-pitched voice echoed through the void.

"Hello, my darling."

She let out a breath.

"Oh, Tharan, there is so much I have to tell you. I royally fucked things up. I tried to contact you earlier, but you didn't answer, and now I have the siren's song, but…" she hesitated.

"Well, that's good."

"Yes, well, I may have had to cut off the siren queen's head to get it. It's a long story. The Undersea queen and Ursula were involved, and she tricked me and left me for dead. So, I had to cut off the queen's head to escape a hoard of guppy baby sirens, and… DID YOU KNOW SHE IS—*ER*—WAS, QUEEN CALLIOPE'S SISTER?"

Tharan squeezed his eyes tight. "Shit."

"Yeah, deep fucking shit."

"I'm going to have to speak with Hopper about this. Calliope is not a forgiving woman."

"I didn't plan on killing her! Ursula tricked me! I swear!"

He rubbed his nose. Aelia and Ursula had a past. What had she said to Aelia to trick her again? His blood boiled, both at the deceit of the mermaid, and Aelia for allowing herself to fall back into her old ways.

"Aelia, what happened?" He tried to hide the anger in his voice.

"I…" she paused. "I needed her to get the song. I knew she would cross me, but I didn't know how far she would go. I didn't know she would try to *kill* me."

Tharan took a deep breath, trying to keep his temper at bay.

"She is an assassin, Aelia. Killing is her job."

Only silence answered him.

"I guess I just… I don't know. I wanted to see something good in her."

His temper simmered at the sound of the sadness in her voice.

"Not everyone deserves our empathy, and Ursula is one of those people."

She sighed.

"You're right."

Tharan changed the topic. This was a lesson Aelia needed to learn but he didn't want to push her away.

"Whatever happens, we will face it together."

Aelia let out a breath.

"Thank you, Tharan. That means a lot to me."

Tharan's mood lightened a bit, glad he hadn't upset her.

"Of course. What are you going to do with the song? Give it to Conrad?"

"That's my plan."

"But what about the monsters surrounding the island?"

"Well, Calliope still thinks I'm giving the song to her."

"So, you're going to kill her sister and double-cross her?"

"Yes."

"Okay, just as long as we're on the same page."

Aelia let out a chuckle, and Tharan imagined the way her eyes sparkled when she laughed. His heart swelled with love but then quickly soured. "Aelia, there's something I have to tell you."

"Oh?" He could feel the tension in her voice.

"My grandfather wants to make a bargain with me. He wants me to marry an elf of his choosing, and in return, he will give me information on the Wells."

Only silence met his words. Tharan's chest tightened all over again.

"Say something, Aelia."

"What is there to say? I knew this would happen. I told you as much." Her voice caught in her throat, and Tharan knew she was holding back tears. "You are the Alder King, and I am nothing. I should not have held out hope we would be together."

"I will find a way around this. Aelia, please, you must trust me." He tried to keep his voice steady for her sake.

"You need to do what is best for the Woodland Realm—what is best for this continent. The Wells are all that matters. Finding Gideon and Erissa is all that matters. I don't know if I could stay on as your Hand… I will not watch you love another woman. My heart couldn't take it."

He didn't have to see her to know she was crying. A weight settled itself over him. Were they foolish to think this could ever last? The Fates told him his heart would get him into trouble. Was this a part of their prophecy? Would ruling his kingdom mean losing the woman he loved? They'd both grown up as royalty—they understood the sacrifices required to run a kingdom. But didn't they deserve some happiness too?

"I would never ask that of you. Aelia, I love you." His words caught in his throat, and he choked back tears. Loving someone meant letting them go if need be.

"Love is not enough, Tharan. I have nothing to offer you. Do what is best for your kingdom—for this continent. Think with your head." Her words were muffled through her tears.

Tharan's heart ached.

"Aelia, please don't cry. We will figure this out. I will find a way."

She sniffled.

"I'm never going to hold you again, am I?"

"Don't say that." Yes, it was a real possibility, but one of them had to stay strong. Clutching a pillow close to his chest, he tried not to cry.

"How can I not? The man I love will marry someone else. This is the cadence of my life."

A dagger dug itself into his heart.

"Aelia…" He desperately wanted to portal to Ruska and take her into his arms.

"I have to go. We're meeting Conrad. There is nothing more to say. I care for you, Tharan, but I will not let you jeopardize your kingdom for me. I've already destroyed more than I ever planned to."

A knife twisted in his heart.

"Aelia…"

Only silence echoed his words.

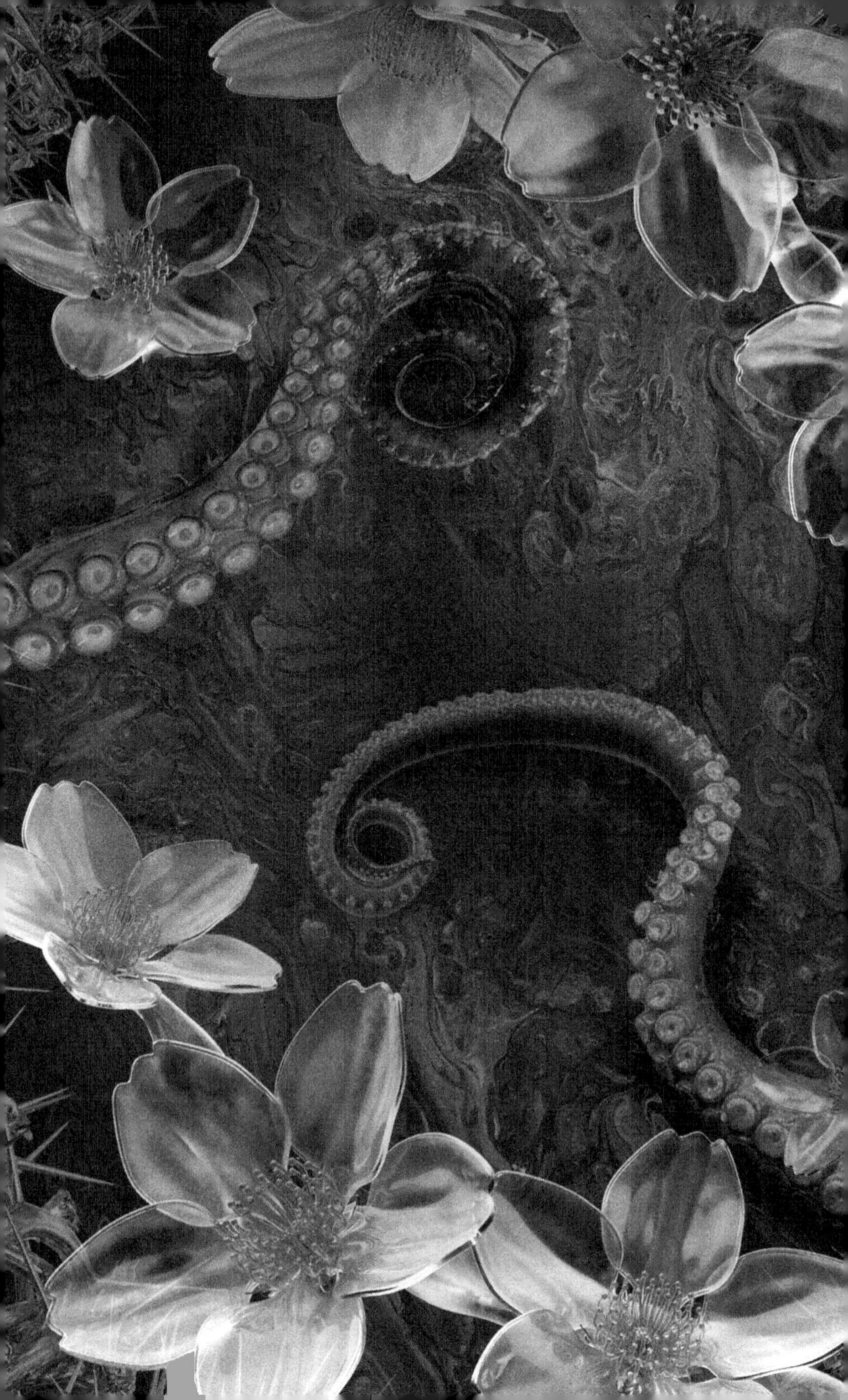

22 THARAN

Tharan tapped his fingers on the marble balcony of his room overlooking Elohim. He knew being the Alder King would mean making sacrifices. He just didn't know that meant giving up happiness. There had to be another way. He had to get his mother to help him. She'd already warned him this place was not as it seemed. There were pieces of the puzzle he didn't have yet, and he couldn't put them all together until he did.

A knock at the door echoed through his chamber.

"Enter," Tharan said, watching his breath turn to vapor and billow into the wintery night.

Hopper and Sumac entered, each wearing an elaborate satin dining outfit.

"The king didn't ask you to dine with him. This is an insult!" Hopper said, pounding his fist on the table.

"Dinner is the least of our concerns, Hopper." Tharan crossed his arms over his chest. "And I hate to say it, but it's going to fall on you to solve."

"Wonderful." Hopper popped an almond into his mouth. "So, what is it?"

"Arendir will only help me find the Wells if I agree to marry an elven woman."

Hopper shrugged.

"You should do it. Allying with the elves will strengthen us in the long run despite our history of aggression."

"But allying with Arendir means allying with the Highlands," Sumac said.

Hopper laughed.

"A kingdom that has no ruler? Wars will be fought over their lucrative mines. I have no doubt Arendir is marching a battalion to the Highlands as we speak. You likely did him a favor. He no longer has to ally with a race he hates."

"He hates everyone but himself," Tharan said, sitting at the long dining room table in his quarters. He rang a bell to alert the servants they were ready for dinner. Three human servants placed a silver platter in front of each.

"Smoked whitefish—an elven delicacy, on a bed of rice," one of the servants said, promptly pouring Tharan a glass of wine.

Tharan stared at the very bland-looking meal on his plate. Elves were known for their elaborate cuisine. Were they being punished, or was this how all sylph were treated here? He dismissed the servants and threw up a silencing shield so they could eat in peace.

"Now, where were we?"

"Your marriage."

Tharan's fork clinked on the porcelain plate.

"My *proposed* marriage."

"Yes, that."

"That you're going to find a way for me to get out of." Tharan pointed his fork at his emissary.

"Short of pulling the information from his mind, what do you expect me to do?" Hopper said with an exasperated huff.

"I expect you to handle the fallout when I don't marry the woman of his choosing."

Hopper rolled his eyes.

"Are you rolling your eyes at your king?" Tharan asked.

He set down his utensils, mouth still full of food. "No, I'm rolling my eyes at my friend, who is being foolish. If these were normal times and your father had passed down the crown to you, we would've had a festival to find you a wife. But these aren't normal times. We need the Trinity Wells, and we need allies. Think with your head instead of your heart, Tharan. Did you tell Aelia this? I'm sure that diamond in your ear is a whisper stone."

Tharan's mouth flattened into a straight line. His heart ached, and his blood boiled. His friend had a point, but his love for Aelia tugged at him like an invisible bond.

"She said she knew it would happen, and I need to do what's best for my kingdom."

"See? Smart woman. What do you think, Sumac?"

Sumac took a long drink from her goblet. "I think that Aelia controls an army of the undead and that, combined with the Hunt, would tackle any army that comes our way. So, no, I don't think she has nothing to offer."

"Exactly. Someone has some sense here," Tharan said.

"I'm not saying throw Arendir's offer out the window. I just think there's a lot to consider here," Sumac added.

"My mother said not to take the deal."

Hopper and Sumac's eyes went wide. "Your mother?" they both blurted out at the same time.

"She's alive?" Hopper gasped.

"Oh yes!" Tharan gave a little chuckle.

"Way to bury the lede!" Sumac laughed.

"Sorry, I was caught up on the marriage contract thing."

"Fair," Sumac said. "Where has she been? What has she been doing for all these hundreds of years?"

"Arendir sent her to the Great White North, where she lived with the mages in isolation. I don't know when he brought her back to the continent."

Hopper scoffed. "Arendir brought her back as soon as she became useful to him. The day he found out you'd been crowned the Alder King."

Tharan gasped, slamming his fist on the table. "Trinity, you're right." He buried his face in his hands. "I am so foolish."

Hopper rubbed his friend's back. "Don't beat yourself up. It must have been overwhelming to see her."

"She told me not to trust Arendir." Tharan's stomach clenched. The wine made his thoughts cloudy. What if he'd told her something he shouldn't have? He was so stupid. So foolish. So trusting.

"It is only normal that you would want to trust your mother," Hopper said, taking a bite of his fish.

"I should know better. I am a king now, not some orphan desperate for love."

"We are all children at heart."

Tharan nodded but couldn't shake the feeling of dread.

The three finished their dinner in silence before parting ways.

After dinner, Tharan returned to his place on his balcony overlooking the city. Lighting a cigarette, he wished Aelia was here with him. Although had he brought her, the whole court would've known of their relationship—a bitter taste filled his mouth. He had told his mother about Aelia, and she had likely told Arendir. And Arendir could use that against him. His stupid heart had gotten him in trouble. Again. At least the Fates were right about that.

Tharan's fingers itched to turn the whisper stone, hear her voice at the other end and tell her everything would be alright, but he thought it best to keep his distance for now. She needed time to clear her head, and he would give that to her as much as it pained him to.

Flicking the cigarette off his balcony, he turned to find a cloaked figure standing in his room.

Pulling back the hood, his mother's auburn hair sparkled in the moonlight.

"I will help you find the Well of Eris."

Tharan could only blink in response. What kind of trickery was this?

"What?"

She stepped closer. Moonlight danced on her ethereal face.

"The king plans to present you with a lineup of possible brides tomorrow. And if you do not choose one, he will not be pleased."

Tharan bit his lip. She was either telling the truth or this was some kind of game to trap him.

"You could be lying to me now for all I know."

Her eyes fell to the floor.

"You have no reason to trust me. I'm fully aware of that, but I want to help you. I failed at being your mother for so long. Please let me help you with this."

Tharan didn't dare to hope she was being sincere.

"Tell me what you know."

"The mages are tasked with guarding something. They would never tell me what it is, but it would make sense that they're guarding a Trinity Well."

"But Erissa was a mage. Wouldn't she know where to find at least one Well?"

His mother shook her head.

"She is older than me. I do not know which order she belonged to. Her order may have been tasked with something else. They each follow a different set of instructions. The mages of the Great White North *are* hiding something. Perhaps it is nothing. You must go there, but you'll need a pass from Arendir to enter. The mages are skeptical of outsiders, to say the least. They will not let you into their compound without the king's seal of approval."

Tharan stared at his mother, trying to decipher whether she was lying or not. He wanted to believe her, but Hopper's words resounded in his head. "I want to trust you… but I don't know if I can. Answer me this: How does the king have so many children when elven blood is so thin their numbers are dying off."

She hesitated.

"Tell me, Mother… what is going on here? You want me to travel to the Great White North… tell me how the king has so many children." He tried his best to keep his temper at bay.

She sank onto the bed. Her eyes were full of tears.

"They are mine."

Bile lapped at the back of Tharan's throat, and he found himself leaning over the railing, hurling into the night. How could she even entertain something like this, let alone go through with it multiple times?

"What?"

She kept her eyes glued to the floor.

"For the past hundred years, he has taken me to his bed in order to create a line of *purebloods*."

Tharan could not believe his ears.

"But that would make the blood even thinner."

She crossed her arms over her chest, making herself small.

"It does not always work. Sometimes, the children die before they have a chance to live." She ran her hand over her stomach. "Do not judge us. Our love is pure. It is an honor to serve as a mother to so many children. It is an honor to give Father a pureblood lineage. Especially after…" Her voice trailed off.

"After the mistake you made by having me." He practically spat the words at her.

She nodded. "I was desperate to leave the north. I was desperate to get back in his good graces. It was my idea. Not his. The magic *is* dwindling. This was the only thing I could think of…"

She fell to her knees in front of Tharan, wrapping her hands around his.

He pushed her away in disgust, and she crumpled into a ball on the floor.

"You're sick. You're all sick here. Is this going on throughout the elven kingdoms? Are you all interbreeding the strongest magus?"

Digging her nails into the stone she pulled herself up.

"I don't know, but I do know this: If you stay here and make a deal with him, he will find a way to use you as he uses his favorite stallions." She smoothed the pleats from her dress, avoiding eye contact with him. "You will be a stud, used to breed to whomever he chooses."

"But then, how do I get the seal from him?"

Her brows knitted in concern. "Let me handle that. Give me a day to forge something. I sleep in his bed. I should be able to get you something."

"Hopefully, before dinner tomorrow."

"I'll do my best."

Tharan wanted to say more, but words evaded him. He couldn't fully comprehend what his mother had just told him. For almost one hundred years, she had been procreating with her own father, his grandfather, in an attempt to strengthen the magic in their blood. And she was in love with him.

He swallowed the bile rising his throat.

"I have to go, my love. He will notice if I do not come to bed in a timely fashion."

"Of course," Tharan said, releasing her.

She disappeared into the darkness, leaving Tharan with more questions than answers.

23 THARAN

THARAN AWOKE THE NEXT MORNING, UNSURE IF THE MEETING with his mother had been real or imagined. Had the wine gone to his head? Or had she really told him she'd been reproducing with her father for nearly a century? Either way, he hoped she wasn't lying about getting him the letter with the seal.

Stealing himself from his bed, he found an elegantly addressed letter slipped beneath his door. He ran a nail under the silver wax seal of the elven king, which depicted Eris giving the breath to Arendir and the other original eleven kings, all of whom had perished since.

He read the invitation: *Dearest Grandson, you are cordially invited to join me for dinner at four o'clock in the afternoon for a night of dancing and entertainment.*

The elves were odd, to say the least. Tharan would never let a guest dine in their chambers on the first night and invite them to a party the next. Then again, eternity did funny things to the mind.

He sighed, setting the elegant dark blue invitation down on the desk in the entryway. Sleep still clawed at his eyes. He rang for a servant. A gaunt-looking man in his sixties appeared dressed in the same golden-collared garment as the others.

"How may I help you, Your Majesty?" He bowed low.

"That's not necessary. Just some coffee and sausages, please." Tharan slid into a plush chair. "And could you please call for my companions?"

The man nodded and disappeared through the servant's doors. Moments later, a young woman appeared with a silver platter. Placing it in front of Tharan, she revealed a plate of pork sausages and a silver coffee pot with a long, curved stem.

"Thank you," Tharan said. The woman nodded, pouring him a steaming cup of coffee.

He sat listening to the sounds of the river below. Gulls called to one another, and fishermen hailed orders. Despite the cold, Tharan liked having the windows open. It kept him connected to nature. The mammoth fireplace in each of his suite's rooms kept the quarters warm.

Elowen's words replayed over and over again in his mind. The mere thought of her lying with her father turned his stomach. He wanted to tell Aelia.

"Fuck it." He twisted the stone in his ear.

"Tharan?" a sleepy voice answered.

"Hi," he said timidly.

"Hi," she said, letting out a gasp of relief. "I've missed you. I'm sorry I was so cross last night."

He smiled softly. "It's alright. I think I've found a way out of our little predicament."

"How?" A guarded excitement filled her voice.

"Just let me worry about it. You worry about getting to the Isle of Fate."

"Tharan, do not get my hopes up."

"Nothing is ever guaranteed here, my love."

He could hear her lighting a cigarette, taking a long drag. Tharan pictured her standing on the balcony all those months ago, the wind whipping at her cheeks. Her lush lips begging to be kissed. His cock twitched with lust. He stilled himself. Now was not the time for pleasure.

"I don't know how long this trip to see the Fates will last or if we'll even make it back." Aelia's voice quivered with apprehension.

His chest tightened.

"Don't speak like that, my love. We will be together soon."

"I hope so."

A knock at the door interrupted them.

"I've got to go. I love you, Aelia."

He twisted the whisper stone and cut the connection. "Enter," he said, and Sumac and Hopper took seats at his table.

"What is so important you had to wake us this early?" Hopper said, rubbing his eyes.

Tharan rang the bell and motioned for the servant to bring more coffee. "I thought you'd like to take a walk."

"This early in the morning? You know I'm a night owl."

Sumac kicked Hopper under the table.

"Ow. What was that for?"

Sumac gave him a look that said, "It's not about the walk."

The servant girl returned with two more silver coffee carafes, pouring Sumac and Hopper a cup.

Taking a sip, Hopper straightened.

"Yes, I would."

They finished their coffees and headed into the wintery streets of the elven capitol. The granite sparkled in the gray light of morning. The elves ran hot water beneath their streets to clear them of any snow, leaving a clear path for them to walk. Elegant marble and granite homes rose along the water's edge. Tharan wondered how many of these were built by sylph hands with money made off the backs of sylph slaves.

They strolled through the town center where elven merchants sold their goods, not unlike the markets of the Woodland Realm.

A harpist strummed a magical tune very similar to one the sylph often played at their fairs. Throughout their centuries of enslavement, the sylph and the elves had picked up some of the other's culture. Even some of their baked goods were similar. But where sylph obsessed over sugar, the elves loved savory treats, adding vegetables and herbs to their baked goods.

"How utterly boring," Sumac said, gazing at the assortment of nut breads displayed at one of the vendor's shops.

"It's not that bad," Hopper said, smiling at the attractive elven man behind the stand.

Sumac rolled her eyes. "Now is not the time for you to be shopping for a date."

Hopper chuckled. "I don't date. I have brief affairs of the heart, and all parties leave satisfied."

"Just make sure you don't scorn any of them while we're here."

"I wouldn't dream of it." Hopper stole one last glance of the shopkeeper, who smiled, brushing a dark curl behind his sloped ear.

They slipped through alleyways and down long promenades of gilded mansions until they reached the edge of the city, where the terrain became flat farmland.

They huddled under a bare oak tree. The wind whipped at their already red cheeks.

"What was so important you had to drag us all the way out here instead of just throwing up a silencing charm?" Hopper asked, tightening his cape around his neck.

Tharan threw up a sound shield. "All the elves we saw on stage yesterday behind the king were his children."

"Well, that makes sense. He abides by the rules of old where kings would reproduce with as many women as possible." Hopper picked at his nails lazily.

"They're all by the same woman…"

Sumac and Hopper blinked unbelievingly at Tharan.

"Bullshit. Elves and sylphs have trouble conceiving one child, let alone twenty with one woman." Sumac arched a brow at her friend.

"It's true."

"How?" Hopper asked incredulously.

Taking a deep breath, Tharan pondered how to explain it best. "They are my mother's children."

"Uh, what?" Hopper and Sumac exchanged baffled looks.

"My mother and grandfather have shared a bed for over a hundred years and are seemingly in love." Just saying the words brought bile to the back of his throat. "And he plans to use me as his next breeding stud."

"Gross," Hopper said. "Well, we're certainly not going to let *that* happen."

"There's more."

"There always is," Hopper sighed.

"My mother thinks the mages of the Great White North know something about the Trinity Wells."

Sumac chuckled. "That sounds like a wild goose chase if I ever heard one. Have you travel to the Great White North while Arendir invades the Woodlands? I don't think so."

"I don't think she was lying." Tharan fiddled with the rings on his fingers nervously.

"And what gave you that impression? She's literally fucking her own father. All of those children are your siblings *and* your aunts and uncles." Sumac's nostrils flared as she waved her hands around.

"What other choice do we have? I'm not marrying one of the brides he puts before me. My mother said she would get a letter with the king's seal on it so that we may enter the mage's compound."

Hopper rubbed his bottom lip with his thumb, deep in thought.

"Here's what we're going to do. We will attend the king's dinner tonight. Tharan, you will let him parade the possible brides in front of you, but you will caveat that it is only fair that other kingdoms have the chance to do the same. He will be upset, but it is a reasonable request. That way, we don't look suspicious. We will leave promptly afterward. Letter or not."

Tharan sighed. "Fine. I trust you two. If you say this is the plan. This is the plan."

The three nodded and headed back to the palace.

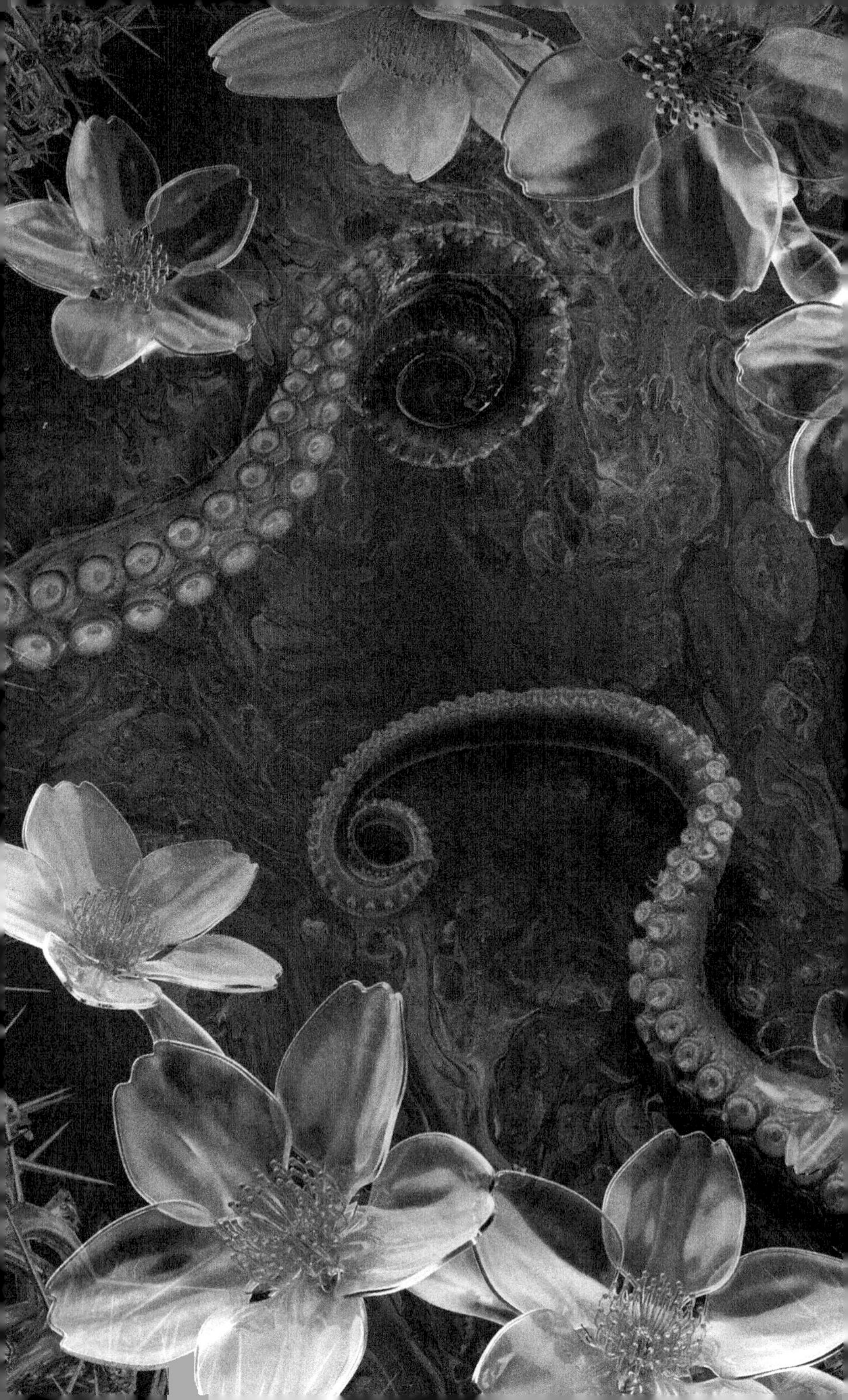

24 THARAN

The Great Elven Hall sparkled with the light of a thousand fire sprites dancing around giant crystal chandeliers. Elegant tapestries lined the walls. The smell of roasted meats and wine filled the air. Elves chatted with one another, flinging their heads back with laughter while holding golden chalices. All in attendance wore their finest attire---tailored jackets and low-cut dresses, donning glittering diadems. Tharan's crown of antlers sparkled in the gilded light. Elves danced and ate as a string band played a cheerful tune.

Arendir, Elowen, and their twenty children were waiting when Tharan arrived. Each wore an intricately designed tailed overcoat embroidered with the seal of the Alder King.

Arendir stood, offering Tharan a seat next to him on the dais.

"Come, my child. Sit next to me. I have prepared a wonderful selection of elven women for you to choose from."

Tharan swallowed hard but took his seat next to his grandfather, who was preparing a spread of assorted meats and stews on a long oak table.

Sumac and Hopper took their places at the far end of the table next to two of Arendir's younger children. Their hair was a fiery red and their faces were painted with freckles. They had the same green eyes as Tharan. He was drowning in a sea of eyes like his, and it made his skin crawl. Were these "wonderful women" going to be related to him somehow? Would he be expected to procreate with his half-sisters or nieces?

His mother put a loving hand over his, and he couldn't help but grimace. Part of him wondered if it would've been better if she *had* died. That way he wouldn't have to deal with the reality of who she truly was: a woman who reproduced with her own father.

"You look so handsome," she whispered in his ear. A necklace of black pearls dangled around her neck, leading to a dress of black satin. Her skin glowed with the Elven Breath like a light lit from within. "I have what we need. I will bring it to you tonight."

"You look beautiful as well," Tharan said, pouring himself a glass of wine. Shit. Now, he would have to stay in this Trinity-forsaken place another night.

Arendir clapped his long, spindled fingers, and the music promptly stopped.

"Tonight, we celebrate my grandson, Tharan Greenblade, Master of the Wild Courts and king of the Alders."

The crowd clapped, and Tharan bowed his head in reverence.

Arendir continued, "Now, please make way for the potential brides."

The crowd parted, and a carpet of red and gold unfurled itself. Six elven women paraded down the aisle. Each wore the same low-cut silver gown adorned with diamonds. Reaching the base of the dais, they kneeled so their bosom was presented to the royals above. A veil of delicate lace obscured their faces and hair. Were they concealed to hide faces like his?

An uneasiness settled over Tharan.

"These are the finest women my kingdom has to offer. Each one from a noble house. Each one a proven producer."

Tharan's stomach turned at the word, but he smiled at his grandfather convincingly. He needed to act interested if he wanted to get out of there alive.

"Number one," his grandfather said.

The woman rose and removed her veil, revealing golden-blonde hair and blue eyes with a button nose—attractive by any measurement. How old were these women? Elves lived for an eternity, but unlike the sylph, their age eventually showed on their skin. This woman did not have a wrinkle to be seen. Was she young, or had they figured out a way to stem the corruption of time?

The woman smiled.

"Vansyra from the Kingdom of Eden. Not far from your realm. She has already given birth to two children and would be honored to grace you with more," his grandfather said enthusiastically.

Tharan nodded. The woman gave him a hopeful smile and stepped back into line.

"Next," Arendir called, and the woman beside her stepped forward, pulling her veil as the previous woman had done, revealing dark umber skin and amber eyes with lips so lush any man would be tempted to kiss them. "Marise hails from Eryndor and carries her third child."

Tharan's eyes flitted to the woman's bulging stomach. "Whose children do they bear?" he asked louder than he intended to.

"It does not matter," Arendir said with a smile. "All that matters is they will be ready to give you a child once the bond is complete."

Tharan suspected their little *experiment* was happening in more than just the capitol.

The third woman stepped forward. Hair of copper cascaded

over her ample bosom. A single tear snaked its way down her cheek as her verdant eyes met Tharan's.

"Callini from Occid, who has given us four children already. Quite the match. Her father controls a fierce army."

Tharan swallowed the bitter taste in his mouth. "But what about their children? Who will care for them?"

"I forget you are a stranger here, Grandson. They will be cared for as all those of royal elven blood are by the nannies and teachers we assign to them. They will be shaped and molded into erudite scholars and fearsome warriors. Some may even be chosen to be mages. The highest honor a female elf can have. Besides being blessed as a mother, that is." He said the word as if it were a title and not a person.

How deep does their little test go? How long had they been perfecting it? Perfecting their bloodlines. And what did this mean for the future of their race? His eyes flitted toward Arendir's children. They did not appear inbred, but he had not heard one of them speak. Could the purity of magic and blood have warped their minds? He didn't want to stay and find out. He wanted to leave as soon as he could.

Tharan downed his wine and smiled politely as Arendir introduced the rest of the women. His head swirled. Elven wine was known to be strong, but he did not expect it to be *this* strong.

Arendir looped an arm around Tharan's and hauled him to his feet. With his vision blurred, he looked desperately for Hopper and Sumac but couldn't focus enough to find them in the spinning ballroom.

"Now, why don't you get to know these ladies more? We can discuss your choice in the morning." He led Tharan down the marble steps of the dais, where the women waited with open arms.

Tharan looked back at his mother in desperation, but she only smiled. Glee flickered in her green eyes. Had he been tricked again, or was this something he could easily get out of? The women did not seem particularly fierce, but you never knew with elves. They looked docile but could be deadly underneath.

The women led him up the twisting spiral staircase to another wing of the castle overlooking the city. Tharan tried to spot any exits, but his head felt heavy and light simultaneously. The women laid him on a bed of satin and poured him another goblet of wine.

Only the redheaded one did not join in.

"We're so happy to meet you," the blonde one said. Tharan couldn't remember her name. His pulse beat in his ears. He smiled politely at her.

"Water. Please, I need some water," he said, his voice harsh like gravel in his throat.

The redhead, Callini, rushed over with a carafe of water and handed him a glass.

"Drink. The wine is strong."

The other women hissed and shushed her.

"What's going on here?" Tharan asked after he chugged the entire glass and the redhead poured him another.

"We're here as a sampling," the blonde woman said, dropping her dress to reveal her naked body. "You are to have your pick of us."

"I… I can't," Tharan said, sitting up straight. "This isn't right."

The blonde knitted her brow. "You have to. I can't go back to fucking my relatives. I can't go back to that life." Her blue eyes were full of desperation.

Tharan shook his head, trying to get rid of the fog surrounding his mind.

The other girls chimed in, "Please, please, please pick me."

"Pick me, Lord Tharan. I will be good. I promise." Every

word dripped with desperation. Every word a plea for a bit of kindness.

Tharan threw up his hands.

"I can't do this with any of you. It's not right, and I'm not some stud to breed you."

"This is our only hope of escaping a life of bedding our relatives," the pregnant woman said, crawling toward him.

Tharan's heart broke for them. They just wanted to escape the nightmare they'd been forced into. Focusing, he tried to clear his head. "Stop, all of you."

The women stared at Tharan.

"I will not be bedding any of you tonight."

An echo of disappointment rippled through the women. Some started crying, others let out a sigh of relief, and the redhead said nothing.

Tharan forced his thoughts to straighten through the fog. He needed to get out of here, but he also couldn't leave them. They were desperate for a way out, just as he was. What other choice did he have but to take them with him? This would not bode well for his kingdom's relationship with the elves, but he'd rather die with a clean conscious than live knowing he could've helped them and didn't.

"We're going to get out of here—all of us. You can live in the Woodland Realm or wherever you choose, but we must be quick. Can any of you hold a sword?"

The redhead and the pregnant woman nodded *yes*, while the others shook their heads *no*.

Tharan let out a sigh. "Well, two is better than none."

Tharan rose, his head wobbled on his neck, but he fought past it. They needed to get out of here.

He cracked the door. Two guards stood watch outside. Quietly he shut the door again. Turning to the women, he whispered, "If you want to leave, now is your chance, otherwise, stay here."

The women nodded, putting on their clothes.

Tharan cracked the door again.

"Uh, excuse me. I've chosen, could one of you tell the king?"

The soldiers exchanged knowing glances and one left to tell the king. When he was out of sight, Tharan looped his arm around the other guard's neck, squeezing until the guard sank to his knees. He quickly picked up the soldier's sword and tucked it into his belt, signaling for the women to follow him.

They snuck down the stone stairs as quietly as they could, making sure to check around corners. It seemed everyone was in the throne room.

Tharan didn't know where he was going, but away from his grandfather was their best bet.

They trekked through the massive palace until they came to a hallway filled with windows. Tharan peered out only to see frantic guards below running through the crowd, searching for something... searching for them.

His chest tightened, clearing his head that bit more, and he signaled for the women to duck down as low as they could to avoid being seen through the windows. Footsteps came from around the corner. Tharan held his breath. He was a trained swordsman, but how many were there?

Laying himself flat against the stone wall, he signaled for the women to stay still.

The footsteps grew nearer.

Tharan sucked in a breath. There were at least two of them. Two he could take on.

He raised his sword into the air before darting around the corner to bring it down upon the unsuspecting guard. But when he went to strike, he was met with Sumac and Hopper.

"What in the Trinity is going on in here?" Sumac said, dodging Tharan's attack.

"I could ask you the same thing."

Hopper t'sked. "Well, obviously they know you've escaped." He tossed Tharan his curved sword. "They're looking everywhere for you."

Tharan twisted the smooth handle in his grip, remembering the feel of his weapon. Before signaling to the women to follow him. "We're taking them with us."

Sumac and Hopper rolled their eyes.

"You don't always have to be the hero," Hopper said. "We can leave people behind. We have no allegiance to these women."

"But they need our help," Tharan said, tossing his sword to Callini. "Follow us, protect the other women."

She nodded, adjusting the grip on her sword. Callini cut the long skirt from her dress and proceeded to do the same for all the women.

"We can run faster without them."

Tharan nodded.

"Sumac, you go first. Where is the rest of the Hunt?"

"They should be guarding our envoy. Others will still be guarding your chambers."

"Very well. You go ahead with Hopper and the women and get everything ready for our escape. I need to get something."

"Don't risk your life on something stupid."

"Trust me," Tharan said, giving Sumac a devilish grin.

"Let's go, ladies!" Sumac whisper-shouted as she ushered the women down the hallway.

"Seriously, don't do anything too risky," Hopper said before following the women.

"Go!" Tharan said.

Taking one last look behind him, he saw a hoard of elven soldiers approaching Sumac, Hopper, and the women. Sumac and Hopper could handle themselves; he needed to make it back to his chambers before they were raided.

Sumac's sword clashed against elven steel, but one by one,

she dispatched them. Her adamant weapon cut through each as if they were nothing but a training dummy. Chest heaving and face covered in blood, she fought her way down the staircase until none remained.

Tharan headed toward his guest suite. His mother may have betrayed him, but he had made a plan just in case. Of course, he hadn't factored in the harem of women he was supposed to bed, but that was only a minor inconvenience.

On padded feet, he snuck through the castle teaming with guards, setting traps for anyone following him. Trip wires from his vines and poisonous flowers made excellent deterrents.

The halls of the ancient palace twisted and turned in no discernible direction. Tharan hoped he was going the right way. None of the cold corridors looked familiar. He tried to remember how the servant had taken him the previous night, but everything was foreign. He continued to run until he came to the room with the statue of Eris. He could find his way to his quarters from here.

Elven soldiers entered the room from the opposite entryway. Their legendary armor, light as air but as hard as dragon scales, glimmered in the firelight of the torches lining the room.

An arrow whizzed at him. Tharan called upon his power, and his skin fizzled with electricity. He caught the arrow midair just before it collided with his face.

"Idiot!" one of the guards called. "We need him alive."

Tharan made a run for it, releasing a cloud of poisonous gas. The elves choked, falling to their knees. He let out a breath of relief before disappearing down the stairs toward the guest wing.

Rounding a corner, he met his Hunt clashing with elven soldiers, their sabers rattling through the stone corridor. Ducking low, he snuck into the servant's entrance. Two servants huddled in the corner of the kitchen, holding one another.

"It's okay," Tharan said, looking toward his chambers. "Is anyone in there waiting to ambush me?"

With wide eyes, they shook their heads frantically.

Tharan gritted his teeth.

"Are you lying to me?" He held the point of his sword under the chin of the woman who had served him breakfast earlier that morning.

"No," she whispered.

Tharan lowered his blade.

"Get out of here."

The two scrambled away while Tharan positioned himself to enter the chambers, aware an ambush could be waiting for him, despite the maid's assurance.

Bursting through the door with his sword raised, fully prepared to land a skull-crushing blow on his nearest foe, all he was met with was an empty room.

"Huh," he said, lowering his sword, slightly disappointed he wouldn't be splitting the head of an elven soldier. Blades clashed outside the doors. Tharan moved through the suite until he reached the entryway. "Ah-ha," he said, swiping the invitation with Arendir's seal still intact.

"Don't do this, my son," his mother's soothing voice said from across the room.

Stunned, Tharan looked up to see his mother's silhouette standing in the light from the balcony. The kohl around her eyes smeared from tears.

"Is anything you told me true?" Tharan yelled over the sounds of battle growing closer to the doorway.

She moved closer, falling to her knees.

"Please, my darling boy. Whatever you are planning. It is not worth it. Stay here with me. In time, Arendir will trust you and let you leave."

Tharan's eyes widened at the woman he knew as Mother in title only.

"You're all mad here."

"Desperation makes madmen of us all. You don't know what it was like in the north. Mountains of ice. White as far as you can see." She stared out into the distance, looking but not seeing.

"Get off me," Tharan said, pushing his mother away.

"Nothing good will come of this. Some things do not want to be found, my child. Remember that."

Soldiers broke through the door. Tharan turned, raising his sword just as an elven guard lowered his. The sound of steel on adamant clanged through the chamber. Tharan gritted his teeth, kicking the soldier as hard as he could. The man stumbled backward. Thinking quickly, Tharan pulled a dagger from his bandolier and buried it in the sliver of exposed skin on the man's neck.

A look of shock crossed the man's face, and blood gushed from the wound. Falling to his knees, he collapsed into a heap on the floor, staining the white marble red.

Tharan looked back where his mother had been but only an empty balcony met his gaze.

"My King, we must go," one of the Hunt said, pulling her bloody sword from a still twitching elf.

Tharan chuckled, thinking about Aelia's debacle with the Undersea queen as he stepped over dead elves.

"Sir?" The soldier cocked her head at him.

"It's all so fucking hilarious, isn't it?"

"My Lord? Did you hit your head? Do you need a healer?"

Stilling himself, Tharan said, "No. Let's get out of here. Sumac and Hopper should have a carriage waiting for us."

Tharan and the two guards fled down the nearest stairwell toward the carriage house. He prayed to Illya that Hopper, Sumac, and the brides had made it out. Knowing the skill of Sumac alone, he had no doubt they left a trail of slaughtered elves in their wake.

Tharan and his guards cut through the onslaught of elven

soldiers until they reached the grand entrance of the palace, where banners displaying the king's seal hung from the rafters.

Not a soul stirred. Something was off. Arendir wouldn't let him walk out of here without one last fight. He signaled for his soldiers to flank him. He scanned the room for a hint of a ward or charm set to detonate if they crossed it, but he didn't see anything.

Cautiously, he stepped forward, taking each step as if it could be his last. The hairs on the back of his neck pricked. Something was off.

Out of the corner of his eye, something shimmered. He turned to look but saw nothing. His heart leapt into his throat when he turned again to see Arendir standing in front of him. His long white hair was braided in battle fashion down his back. His white robes were replaced with light silver armor.

"You didn't think I'd let you go that easily, did you?" His evil cackle echoed through the hall. A row of soldiers wearing the bronze helmets of the Breathless Guard, the elves' most fearsome warriors, assembled behind him. Each one carried a long tungsten spear.

"You can't be serious. I am the Alder King. Let me go, or my kingdom will have no choice but to attack. And judging by what I have seen here today. Your army is not up to the task." Tharan readied his sword.

"I do not need to attack you to get what I want," Arendir said, motioning for a soldier to bring something… someone, forward.

He threw his mother on the ground in front of Tharan. Her lip was bloodied, the makings of a black eye already purpling. "Tharan, do as he says, please!" She fought against the man's iron grip.

"What is this?"

"A bargain. Stay here, father children. I only need a few. Then you may go back to your beloved forest."

Tharan's stomach twisted. "And if I don't?"

The ancient king narrowed his eyes. "Then I'll kill your mother and force what I need out of you."

Tharan's power twitched under his skin. The sound of growing thorns echoed through the hall as feral plants wrapped themselves around the men, sending thick thorns into their soft flesh.

The soldiers cried out in pain, but it was too late for them. Arendir could bring them back with his breath, but would he give up his youthful glow for these warriors, or were they expendable like everything else?

The vines twisted and constricted like the snakes of the desert. The sound of crushing bone brought bile to the back of Tharan's throat, but he couldn't stop now. There was no room for mercy here.

"Enough," Arendir said. Motioning for the man threatening Elowen's life to release her.

She scrambled to her feet and ran to Tharan.

"Thank you," she said.

Tharan pushed her away.

"You are both vile beings who deserve each other. I came here seeking an ally to help me save this continent we call home, but you can't look past your selfish desires for purity and power."

Tharan took a step toward Arendir, who stood stoically at the grand entrance. The light of the fresh snow illuminated him like the gods of old. He grabbed Tharan's arm as he passed. "You will regret crossing me, boy."

Pain seared into Tharan's bicep, but he did not wince. He would not show these people an ounce of weakness. "I am no boy. I am the Alder King, and if you do not remove your hand, I will send you to meet your goddess sooner than you expected." A green flame flickered in Tharan's eyes.

Arendir flinched and released him.

Tharan walked out of the palace. Adrenaline coursed through

his veins. Part of him wanted to look back. Part of him wanted to forget this place forever. At least they had a lead on the Well of Eris... if his mother could be trusted.

Tharan and his guards met Hopper and their envoy by the stables.

"Thank the Trinity, you made it. We were starting to worry," Sumac said, opening the carriage door.

Tharan climbed inside, where the six women sat holding one another. Worry etched across their faces.

"Take us to the nearest portal. Let's get out of this nightmare."

The carriage sped off into the snowy night.

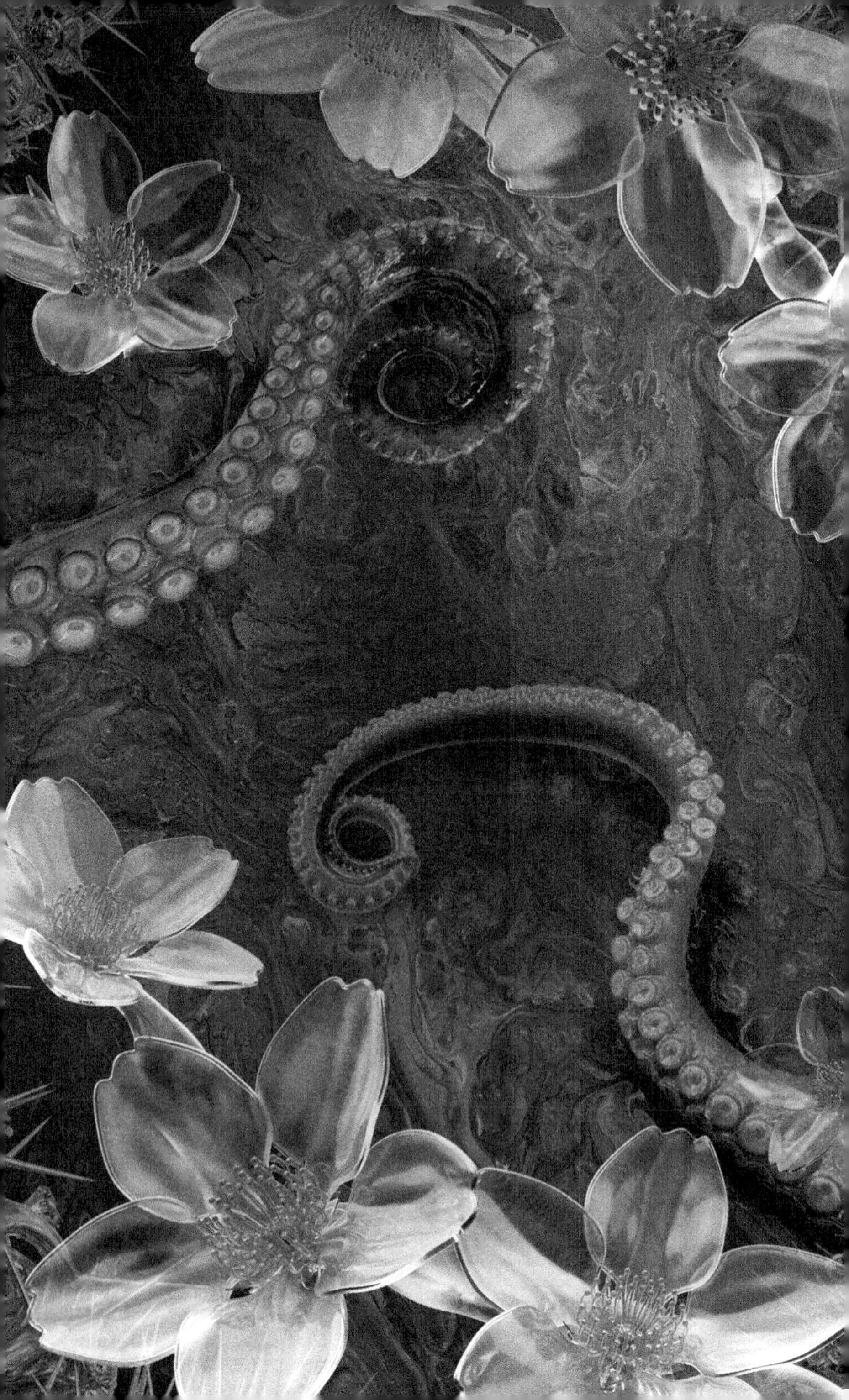

25 AELIA

Knots twisted in my chest as Baylis and I walked to Conrad's sinking dive. Why couldn't I tell Tharan I loved him? I wanted to, but the words stuck in my throat. What if we died and I never got the chance to say it?

The smell of rotted wood and ale stung my nostrils as we entered the bar.

I concealed the sapphire containing the song hanging around my neck. This was not the place to flaunt wealth. Although, after my show of strength the other day, I doubted anyone would be stupid enough to trifle with me.

"Ladies," the bartender said with a nod.

Conrad sat in his room, sharpening a dagger, a toothpick between his teeth, while two longswords lay on his bed.

"That was fast," he said, not bothering to look up from his task.

"I always deliver on time," I said, pulling the sapphire from around my neck and dangling it in front of Conrad's crooked nose.

A glimmer of excitement flashed in his brown eyes.

"You are impressive. I can see why Tharan likes you."

I snatched the sapphire back into my palm.

"Will you take us to the Island now?"

His eyes flitted between Baylis and me.

"What about the monsters guarding the Island? Did you take care of those, too?"

"We don't have anything to worry about." A lie I hoped would come true.

Conrad cocked his head at me. "You got the queen of the Undersea to just… call off her monsters? After hundreds of years? How, pray tell, did you manage that?"

"Well, there is a tiny matter of me needing the song when you're done with it."

"Done with it? That's not our deal." He rose to his full height. Muscled shoulders, broad and thick from hundreds of years on a ship, rippled under his black linen shirt.

I sucked in a breath, praying he wouldn't see my nerves.

"Yes, well, we can discuss that after we are safely on shore."

He leaned down so that our faces nearly touched. I could smell the smoked salmon on his breath. A piece of unruly ebony hair fell over his good eye.

"If you try to cheat me out of the song, I will gut you like a fish. I don't care if you are Tharan's beloved. I will burn that bridge if I have to."

I swallowed the fear pooling in my stomach. The heat of a dagger burned beneath my chin.

"Have you ever wanted revenge so badly you could feel it in your bones? Every heartbeat was a testament to your survival, and every day was an opportunity to get one step closer to vindication?"

"What?" His brows arched with intrigue.

Conrad was trying to intimidate me, but I wouldn't allow men to scare me anymore. I had walked through fire, through death and pain, and come out the other side. I would not be frightened by this sea captain. I'd seen real monsters, and Conrad was not one of them. Nevertheless, I still had to convince him I was as confident as he was. Strength respected strength.

I moved the dagger closer to my chin so that the tip drew blood.

"I have dreamed of nothing but revenge for five years. I have envisioned killing my enemy in every way, shape, and form. I am fueled by bitterness and hate alone. Do you think I would jeopardize that over something as trivial as a song?"

"You surprise me again, Mind Breaker. There is more to you than meets the eye." His smile was as handsome as it was twisted.

"If you want to shake on it. I will."

"I will not risk my life or my magic. I have been burned by a bargain before." Conrad sighed, rolling up his sleeve to reveal the black veins of a bargain breaker.

"Which party broke their end of the bargain?" I said, touching my arm where my own brand had been.

"Not me. It's why I need the siren's song. I, too, have a vendetta to fulfill."

"How are you not dead?"

Conrad pointed to vials of potions on his nightstand.

"A concoction of tinctures slows the spell. Doesn't stop it but slows it for a time."

A whisper of sympathy nudged my heart, but I dared not show it.

"Then we understand one another."

"Let me gather my crew. Meet me by my ship, *The Salty Bitch* —the one with the black cherry hull in the harbor and the big-breasted woman on the front."

"Charming," I said.

Not daring to turn my back on him, I slowly backed toward the door.

"I hope you brought weapons."

I stared at him in disbelief, pulling my cloak to the side, revealing a sword and my dagger.

"We'll need more than that."

"Do you not have weapons on your ship?"

He arched a brow. "Well, that'll cost extra."

My mouth fell agape.

"I already killed the siren queen to get you your song."

"Yeah, well, *I* don't have it yet."

I *could* break into his mind. I could *make* him help me for free. No, no, I couldn't slip back into the mercenary. I had to stay the diplomat. It wasn't just about me now. Although there was a part of me that yearned to show anyone who tried to take advantage of me just how powerful I really was.

"Fine," I huffed, digging into my pocket for gold. "How much?"

"More than you have in your pocket. I'd say 10,000 pieces of gold will do. I can at least buy a new ship if the monsters destroy this one."

My mouth flattened into a straight line. I needed him, and he knew it.

"Fine," I hissed through gritted teeth.

"Meet me at the docks with the coin in two hours," Conrad said, returning to his work.

Baylis and I left the decrepit bar and headed up the steps to the bustling harbor.

"We'll need to get you a bow."

"Excellent," Baylis said with a gleam in her eye.

We walked through the busy streets to the bank, where satyrs and halflings counted large stacks of gold and jewels behind solid iron bars.

I filled out a deposit slip before handing it to the teller.

The halfling with a mop of blond curls looked between me

and the slip multiple times. "This is quite a large withdrawal, Lady Springborn."

"Yes, I know. Is there a problem?"

"No, no, ma'am, not at all." He hopped off his stool and hurried to the back. He returned with a velvet sack filled with gold coins. "Just sign here, and you will be all set." He slid a piece of parchment through the opening in the bars, and I quickly signed my name in big swooping letters. "Here you go, my Lady. Have a good day and thank you for choosing Free Cities Bank."

I smiled, grabbed the velvet sack, and tucked it into my cloak. Baylis and I headed for the blacksmith, where Tiernan, the giant with a bright orange beard, greeted us warmly. "Aelia! You haven't been to see me in quite some time. How have you been?"

"Uh, well, that's a loaded question," I chuckled. "I'm fine but busy as usual."

"Well, as long as business is good." He pounded a hammer down on a burning blade. "Be right with you."

Baylis examined the bows hung on the wall.

"These are all excellent. But that's the one I want." She pointed to a bow made of pearlescent metal.

"Aethril, an excellent choice," Tiernan said, pulling the weapon down. "I'm happy to string it for you. What are you thinking? I have Arachne silk as well as chimera tendon."

Baylis tapped her finger on her lip, mulling over her options.

"Let's do Arachne silk. It'll last longer."

Tiernan nodded.

"Very good. Let me string this right quick, and I'll be back shortly." He slipped into a doorway I thought would surely be too small for him.

Baylis and I perused the selection of fine weapons hanging on the walls of the shop. The smell of molten metal filled the air. Tiernan was known all over the continent for his fine craftsmanship, and he showed it off proudly.

"I'll feel better with a bow in my hand," Baylis said.

"Me too. Who knows what the guards on the island will be like." I ran my hand over the tip of a battle axe.

"They haven't been used in hundreds of years. They might be useless."

"Doubtful, but I like the optimism."

Tiernan returned, holding the strung bow.

"Give her a try," he said, pointing to a target at the far end of the shop. He handed the bow and an arrow to Baylis, and she promptly nocked it.

"Too easy." Turning, she fired an arrow out the open double doors, hitting a pigeon perched on the roof of the neighboring building. The creature toppled over, rolling off the roof onto the nearby butcher's stand. The man with a long mustache gasped but, upon seeing the bird was fresh, pulled the arrow from its neck and began to pluck the feathers out.

"It'll do," Baylis said, turning to Tiernan and giving him a friendly smile.

He nodded, and I handed him a stack of gold coins.

"Come back any time, ladies."

"We know where to find you."

We left Tiernan's shop and returned to the harbor, where we easily found Conrad's ship. With its black hull and voluptuous maiden spearheading it, quite hard to miss.

I stood by the ramp leading to the ship. Conrad approached, followed by twenty of the roughest-looking sailors I'd ever seen. Everyone looked like they had been in multiple fights the night before. Blood stained their shirts. Whether it was theirs or someone else's, I couldn't decipher. Some of the men stumbled as they walked.

"Lovely day for a sail," Conrad said, reveling in the breeze coming off the bay. He wore a long black coat with red accents and a large-brimmed hat with an exotic red feather.

Baylis and I smiled politely at him.

"Yes," I said, examining the sky for ominous clouds, but saw none, only the blue of a crisp winter day. Across the bay, the Island of Fate sat still and menacing, unnerving me.

Baylis and I boarded the ship, and the crew prepared to sail. The smell of seawater wafted up over the bow of the ship. I hoped Ursula had delivered my message, and that Calliope would not enact her revenge too swiftly.

We took our places behind Conrad and pushed off from the dock. Rocks piled in my stomach the farther away we got from shore and the closer we got to my mother and the monsters waiting for us.

"The sea is calm today," Conrad called out, looking through his spyglass. "Even around the Island. Your plan must have worked."

"How can you tell?" I yelled over the blustering wind making my hair a tangle of knots.

Conrad pointed a finger toward the Island.

"Usually, a dark ring of water encircles the Island and never calms, no matter how tranquil the water is. That ring is gone."

I allowed myself a moment of triumph. My plan had worked, at least for now.

"Settle in, ladies. It will take us a few hours to reach the Island."

Baylis did her best to keep her composure. The sea did not agree with her, and her skin turned a greenish hue.

"Why don't you sit down?" I ushered her onto a bench.

Even on a calm day, waves rocked the ship violently. I borrowed a bucket from one of the crew members in case Baylis's breakfast decided to reappear. Anticipation made my blood run quicker as we approached the Island. I tried not to be nervous—tried to think about getting the information and leaving as fast as we could.

"Everyone, hold on! We're reaching the outer ring!" Conrad called to his crew.

I held my breath.

Nothing.

I scanned the water for any sign of monsters.

Still nothing.

The boat glided through the water; sails unfurled.

I let out the breath I'd been holding in.

"Pull in the sails. We're going to dock!"

Baylis and I gripped the polished wood of the boat as it glided in beside the dock weighed down by encroaching flora.

Conrad lowered the anchor, and the men set about their duties.

"Welcome to the Island of Fate," Conrad said.

I looked out at the vast, overgrown island. Birds called to one another, and the smell of pine carried on the wind. I swallowed my fear.

"I wish Tharan was here to tame this growth."

"I don't think you need to worry about it." Conrad pointed to where the thick bush rustled. Two eternal soldiers emerged dressed in pearlescent aethril armor. They stopped when their feet touched the wood of the dock. Placing the tips of their swords in the soft soil, they awaited our arrival.

I took Baylis's hand in mine.

"Let's go."

26 AELIA

Conrad and his crew watched us as we descended the ramp onto the dock—only the sound of the gulls squawking filled the air. A gray overcast of clouds replaced a once-sunny sky.

The Eternal Guards did not move as we approached.

Baylis and I exchanged knowing glances. Were they really going to let us just walk in?

Any hope of an easy entrance was dashed when the guards gracefully crossed their swords upon our approach.

"We are here to see our mother, Morta," I said, trying my best to hide the tremble in my voice.

The knight stuck out his armored hand. A needle shot out of his palm.

"Prove your lineage, and we shall let you pass."

Wearily, Baylis and I each pricked our fingers.

The guards lowered their swords.

"You may pass. Follow the lights, and do not stray from the path."

We did as we were told, walking through an ominous forest to the looming tower. Lights filled with fire sprites were strung between massive pines. An eerie stillness lingered in the air. The only sound was our feet on the earthen path. My hand drifted to my sword, not quite touching it—I didn't want to alarm whatever lurked in the woods.

The woods gave way to a garden with expertly crafted topiaries covered with snow. My stomach twisted with every step. What would I say to her? What would she say to me?

"This must be quite something in the summer when all these plants are in bloom. I wonder who cares for them?" Baylis ran her hand over the bare branches of a rose bush.

I eyed my sister. How could she be so calm at this moment? We hadn't seen our mother for half a decade and all she could focus on was the flowers?

"Magic, probably," I said.

Two more sets of guards stood in front of the entrance, their faces covered by helmets with no openings.

"How are they breathing?" Baylis asked out loud.

I studied the ancient figures.

"Perhaps they are not."

"Well, that's disconcerting." Baylis lifted a finger to touch the soldier, but I caught her hand before she could make contact.

"Best not."

She scowled at me, though it quickly faded from her face. "You're right. I don't know what came over me."

"This palace is teaming with magic. It only makes sense we'd be attracted to it." The hairs on the back of my neck stood on end, and a metallic taste fizzled on my tongue as we approached the entrance.

The two massive wooden doors creaked open before we could touch them, revealing a hooded figure dressed in fine muslin robes. I tried to see his face, but only darkness met my gaze. "Welcome, daughters of Morta. We have been waiting a long time for your arrival," an ancient voice echoed from under the hood.

A cold dampness lingered in the dark tower. Only a few low-burning candles lit the ancient hallways. A layer of dust coated everything, and treasure lay strewn about—fine pieces of artwork, jewels, and gold all collected cobwebs in large piles. This place had once been a testament to the Fate's power, but now only the ghosts of grandeur remained.

"This way," the figure said, grasping the railing of a massive circular staircase with a decrepit hand covered in paper-thin skin. Whatever this creature was, it had died a long time ago.

A beam of silver light cascaded in from the glass ceiling above. Dust floated like snowflakes as we climbed higher and higher into the tower.

"The sisters reside at the top," the wraith said.

Rocks piled in my stomach. Each step brought me closer to our mother. I didn't know what I would say to her. Anger, love, resentment, and guilt all swirled around my head. I wanted to turn around and run the other way, but that wasn't an option. I had to be brave now. I had to fix my past mistakes. I would not run any longer. I was better than that.

I looked at my sister whose eyes were on the floor. A sullen look etched across her pale face.

My breath hitched in my throat when we reached the precipice. Two bronze doors inscribed with a depiction of the Trinity endowing the Fates with their power were the only thing standing between me and my mother.

"Through the doors," the wraith said. I wondered how long they had been trapped here. Not dead, but not fully alive, lingering in the in between.

Hesitating, I straightened my leather cuirass, trying to work up the nerve to push the door open.

"Go on. The sisters do not like to be kept waiting."

I turned the golden handle, pushing the heavy door open. Inside, an ecosystem unto its own awaited us. Trees grew from stone, their leaves splayed out in vibrant yellows and oranges.

The smell of honeysuckle and lavender filled the air, and exotic birds flew from branch to branch. A small waterfall flowed into a river that snaked through the floor.

Three golden thrones sat in the center of the room, each occupied by a Fate. My eyes raked over each one. Clotho: elven with sharp features, pale skin, blue eyes, and hair as white as snow. She wore a traditional elven top, white with blue accents and buttons to her chin. Decuma: sylph, tawny skinned, voluptuous, with lush lips and long dark lashes. Thick black curls cascaded over her bare shoulders. She wore a beautiful linen dress that hugged her curves in all the right places, and her fingers were adorned with jeweled rings. My eyes fell upon my mother. Hair as black as night twisted into tight braids and woven into intricate patterns led to her angular face where freckles like mine dotted her nose. Piercing green eyes peered back at me from beneath lowered lashes. She wore her signature purple satin ballgown with gold accents.

"Welcome," Decuma said in a voice like rich molasse. "Morta has told us about you. We were wondering when you'd grace us with your presence."

"Mother!" Baylis said from behind me, running to our mother's open arms.

A pang of jealousy ran through me at how easy it was for Baylis to forgive our mother—to love her unconditionally. I guess I too was the recipient of Baylis's grace. I too had betrayed her, and she'd forgiven me.

"Baylis. You're alright," she said, kissing my sister on the head. "I thought you were dead."

"Couldn't you ask one of these two whether she was alive?" I snipped, pointing at Clotho and Decuma. One of them has the power to see the present.

"We don't work for each other," Decuma hissed. "That has always been our way. All or nothing. Past, present, and future."

"For being sisters, you sure are cold to one another." They had been gods once, but I never worshiped them, and I didn't want them to think they had any power over me.

"You have no idea what we have been through in the past ten thousand years. We have predicted the rise and fall of nations. Seen gods tremble. Watched dragons fall from the sky. And still, we remained loyal to one another until Morta left." She gave my mother a sneering look.

"I heard a different story."

"Whatever you heard is nothing but petty gossip," Clotho said, holding her head high.

Squashing my annoyance, I plucked an apple from one of the trees, slicing into it with my knife. These women wanted me to bow before them like the kings of old. But those days were over, and the Fates lost their way long ago. I bit into the tart flesh of the fruit. A flavor unlike anything I had tasted before bloomed in my mouth, but I would not give them the satisfaction of seeing me enjoy their fruit.

Spitting it on the floor, I tossed the apple to the side. Too long had they held the fates of men in their greedy hands without recourse. They were nothing but myths now… ghosts of an era long passed, and I would treat them as such. Not all gods deserved to live forever.

"Aelia, come here. Let me see you," my mother begged, arms outstretched.

I wanted to be mad at her, I wanted to scream at her and shake her until she told me everything she knew of my fate. Did you see what my future held? Was this all apart of some grand plan the Trinity had, or did you just not care? Rage boiled in my veins. But seeing the desperation in her verdant eyes made my heart crack a little. I missed her. She'd been as lost as I was. Perhaps she did what she thought was best for me… for us.

Sheathing my dagger, I wrapped my arms around her, inhaling

the scent of rosewater she loved to bathe in. I let my body relax in her embrace.

"I've missed you," she said, running her hands through my hair.

"I've missed you too," I said through the growing lump in my throat. Tears welled behind my eyes, hot and heavy, but like the fruit, I would not give these women the satisfaction of seeing me cry. I had shed enough tears for a lifetime, and I would not shed anymore for people who didn't deserve to see them... even myself.

"Touching," Decuma said, tossing her curls over her shoulder. "But I'm sure you came here to ask something, not just for a reunion."

"You are the Fate of the present. Shouldn't you know?" I snapped at her.

"Not how it works, deary," she smirked.

I wiped my tears from my eyes and straightened my cuirass again.

"We need to know about the Trinity Wells. Where they are, what they do. What would happen if someone found one or all of them."

All three women exchanged knowing glances.

"The Trinity Wells are a myth," Clotho blurted out.

I squinted at her.

"I don't have to be a Fate to know you're lying."

"Like we would tell you if we did know anything about them," Decuma hissed. "If they exist. They are meant to be hidden so only the Trinity can find them."

"That's right, you worked with Erissa to imprison my mother. You're probably working with them right now. Probably told Erissa where to look. What is she giving you in exchange? Did she offer you a chance to regain your power?"

Decuma's amber eyes widened, and she leaned forward on her throne.

"Erissa came to us saying she'd found Morta. We need all three of us together for our powers to work correctly. If one is gone, the others cannot see."

"So you say. But I'm sure your power doesn't just fizzle and die."

"That is the way the Trinity made us, unfortunately." Decuma crossed her legs. "If we didn't need Morta, we wouldn't have gone looking for her."

I wasn't sure if I believed her. These women wanted power. They had been worshiped once, and they wanted to be worshiped again for the gods they were. Power corrupts. I needed to find a way they couldn't refuse me.

"Fine then. Tell me what you see for my future."

"No!" my mother yelled. "Don't do this, Aelia." She grabbed my arm.

"Why? I've already walked through hell. It cannot be worse than living in a prison of your making."

"Morta is the one who sees the future. Are you sure you want to make your mother do this?"

My mother squirmed uneasily in her chair. "Don't make me do this, Aelia. You will not like what I see. The Trinity will make it so."

I set my jaw, collecting myself before answering. "You held your visions from me once before. I think I am owed at least an ounce of truth this time."

My mother's mouth fell open, but no sound escaped her lips.

Decuma and Clotho looked at me like wolves waiting to devour a lamb.

"Fine. Show me the present as well. I don't need to relive my past."

"You're no fun," Clotho said, crossing her arms like a petulant child.

A wide smile cut Decuma's beautiful face in two. "Let's spin, sisters."

All three rose, hands outstretched. Threads of luminescent magic twisted together from their fingertips, weaving my fate—their eyes rolled a placid white. Baylis grabbed my hand, and I swallowed a rising dread.

Energy danced through the air, filled with magic. Copper fizzled on my tongue. This sight had not been seen for hundreds of years. Heads tilted to the heavens; the sisters hummed a foreign melody.

"What's happening?" I asked Baylis.

"How should I know? I have no control over my powers."

"Just thought Mother might have told you."

The humming reached an unbearable pitch. Letting go of Baylis's hand, we covered our ears.

A wind blew in from an unseeable source, rattling leaves on their branches, and darkness blanketed the once-sunny room.

I sunk to my knees, clutching Baylis tightly and shutting my eyes. Adrenaline coursed through my veins.

The sisters quieted, the room stilled, and light filled the atrium.

They took their seats on their thrones.

"We are ready, Aelia Springborn," Decuma said, in a voice deep and ancient.

I stood and prepared to hear my fate.

"Go ahead."

Clotho began, "In the desert, a man in black wanders. Searching for something. A power hidden in a tomb." Her eyes glazed over. "Hands laid upon a bare back. Tears falling from joyous eyes. He has returned to lead us. HE HAS RETURNED

TO LEAD US." She jolted backward, hitting her head on her throne. "Oh no. It can't be."

My blood boiled in my veins.

"Is it Crom? There's no way it's him, right?" my mother asked.

"You saw what I saw," Clotho breathed out.

I tapped my pack of cigarettes on my palm before taking one out and lighting it on a nearby candle.

"It's not him," I said, letting smoke billow out of my mouth.

"How do you know? We are the all-seeing eyes of the world. You think you know better than us?" Decuma's nostrils flared in annoyance.

I took another drag off my cigarette.

"I know visions can be wrong. If Crom was back from the dead, I would have known."

"And how is that? Are you psychic, too?" Clotho sneered at me.

A crack in their armor. I wanted to play with them a little more.

"Would it surprise you if I was? I am a daughter of a Fate."

More nervous glances between the sisters. I had them rattled. I savored the taste of their unease.

"You know one of us has the gift, don't you?"

Neither of the sisters said a word.

I looked at my mother, and her eyes fell to the floor.

Baylis stepped forward. "Did you think I wouldn't find out? Or did you do something to stop me from knowing?"

"Everything I have ever done has been to protect you," our mother said, taking my sister's dainty hand in hers.

"So, you knew I had the gift and kept it from me?" Baylis's eyes filled with tears.

"I never wanted to hurt you. You have to believe me. It was

for your own good. I am a servant to fate. But fate can be changed."

"Enough," I said. "We can discuss this later. What did you see in my future?"

Baylis crossed her arms over her chest with a little pout.

My mother narrowed her eyes on me.

"Two loves. One a storm of turmoil. One the giver of life. Your heart is tied to both, but you will have to choose between them."

A dull horror settled over me. I had already chosen Tharan. Caiden didn't even remember me anymore. That twisted knot in my chest tightened that much more. What was she playing at? There had to be more to this vision than just a choice. Hiding my horror, I blew out the smoke from my lungs.

"Great. Anything else?"

"Someone close to you will betray you before your journey is over. Not everyone is who they say they are."

"I thought you were the Fate of the Future? I've already been betrayed by someone I trusted."

She looked at Clotho, who shrugged.

"Sometimes our threads get crossed. We have not woven a fate in some time."

I shook my head. "Anything else?"

My mother closed her eyes.

"I see a quest in your future. From the Court of Screams to the Bog of Eternal Suffering to the Great White North. Through the Rasa Desert… and even into the world beyond."

"Do I kill Gideon?"

"That part is hazy," my mother replied, her voice faint and far away.

"So, you never see a full scene, or is this a new development?"

Decuma chimed in, "We see what the Trinity wants us to see.

Nothing more, nothing less. They are the Divine Fate. They decide the past, present, and future, you see."

I nodded as if I understood. The Morrigan's words echoed through my mind: *They twist fate to suit their needs.*

I breathed deeply.

"You have been incredibly helpful."

Decuma cleared her throat. "We don't work for free."

Rolling my eyes, I reached into my cloak pocket.

"Like you have anything to spend it on. You can't even leave this island."

She held up her hand.

"Do not give it to us here. Put it in the offering bowls in temples across the continent. If people think others believe they will come back."

Were their visions spottier because of a lack of belief? Had the magic died before my mother left, and that's how she was able to escape? So many questions swirled through my head. It was hard to keep them from slipping out of my mouth. I didn't want to say too much in front of the sisters. My mother could probably keep a secret. She fled all those years ago for a reason. She knew what these women were. They were beautiful on the outside but rotten to the core.

The sky darkened above, shading the once-bright room.

"It is time for you to leave. Weaving is tiresome work, and we have not done it for an age," Decuma said, hiding a yawn.

"Please, let them stay for dinner. I haven't seen them in years, and I would love to spend some time with them," my mother said.

Guilt clawed at my heart. I wanted to spend time with my mother, but I didn't know how long Calliope would keep the sea monsters at bay.

"I, um, I don't know how long we have. If I'm being honest."

A wicked gleam sparkled in Clotho's blue eyes.

"Yes, the monsters. How ever did you get past them?"

I swallowed hard. "I made a deal with Calliope, queen of the Undersea."

"You're either incredibly smart or incredibly stupid," Decuma scoffed. "Calliope has never made such a deal before. What did you give her in return?"

"Her sister's head on a platter," I spat out. I wanted them to know even goddesses could die.

All three of the sisters' eyes widened.

"Calypso?" Decuma asked, looking at me with a mixture of astonishment and respect.

I kept my face stoic, loving the surprise on their faces.

"As far as I know, that's her only sister."

My mother ran a tired hand down her elegant face.

"What have you done? She will come for you."

A mixture of shame and fear washed over me. Even as an adult I didn't want to disappoint my mother, but the truth was, life puts us in positions we'd never thought we'd be in, and we have to do the best we can to survive. There was nothing I could do now other than accept my fate.

"Let her come," I said, blowing out another plume of smoke.

"You are trifling with forces beyond your comprehension. You have upset the natural balance of things." Decuma gripped the arm of her throne so tightly her knuckles turned white.

I narrowed my eyes at the ancient goddess.

"You have no idea what I know. You call yourself a Fate, but you are nothing more than a fortune teller. No wonder people stopped believing."

I turned and grabbed my sister's hand.

"Come on, Baylis. We're leaving. They cannot help us."

"Wait!" our mother cried, running after us to envelope us in her arms once more. I held on tight, not wanting to let go. I didn't want this to be goodbye, but we all had a role to play in this game.

"Remember what I told you. Great white north, bog, desert, screams. That is where you will find what you are looking for. That is how you will save this continent," she whispered in my ear while running her hands through my hair the way only a mother can.

I kept my face as stoic as possible. I did not want the other sisters to be more suspicious of me than they already were.

"I love you, Mother. I will find a way to free you," I whispered, using her long thick hair to hide my lips.

"I love you both," she said.

Baylis's body shook with tears.

We held on to our mother for as long as we could before the wraith ushered us out through the bronze doors.

Stars twinkled in the night sky above as we exited the tower. I did not dare look back. I didn't want to see them looking down at us. I just wanted to get off this island.

"We can discuss what she saw when we get back. Do not mention anything on the ship," I said to Baylis who nodded, wiping tears from her eyes.

The forest glowed an eerie green as we headed to the docks. Guards lined the borders of the earthen path. The sounds of rustling leaves could be heard in the distance. What was going on here? What was hiding in these woods?

The lights from the ship appeared at the end of the lane and my muscles relaxed a little. We just had to make it to the ship, then cross the bay, and we would be fine. Everything was going to be alright.

My feet couldn't get me to the dock fast enough. A rustling ripped through the forest and a large vine descended upon me, knocking me backward. Stars dotted my vision, and my body ached from the impact. The unruly tendril snaked its way around my waist, tightening its grip.

"Aelia!" Baylis shrieked.

A guard quickly sliced the vine from where it wrapped itself around me.

"It's okay, I'm fine. Go ahead, get on the ship."

She took a step toward me but one of the guards stopped her.

"You cannot go back."

"It's fine go," I repeated.

Baylis turned and headed for the ship.

The guard offered me a hand and pulled me from the ground. When I looked up, Clotho stood before me.

I blinked at her in disbelief.

Her blue eyes flitted around the forest.

"We do not have much time, so listen closely, daughter of Morta. I know you did not want to hear of your past, but there is a message I need you to hear. Be careful of who you keep close, someone has already betrayed you."

"Who?"

"The Trinity will not let me say more." She tapped her temple.

I bit the inside of my cheek. Unsure if I could bear what I was about to see. I didn't want to break minds anymore, but this seemed important. Letting out a breath, I focused my energy on the Fate.

A door of pure ice awaited me. Hesitantly, I knocked. Cracks formed around the outside of the door, and slowly, it opened.

Clotho sat on a throne of intricately carved ice. Her blue eyes trained on me.

"Listen to me, child. I may look young, but I have seen everything since the dawn of time. What I'm about to show you will be confusing at first, but it is the only way I can show you what you need to see without alerting the Trinity or my sisters to my treachery."

I nodded, swallowing the dread blooming in my gut.

Images of Baylis and Gideon in compromising positions flashed before my eyes. Kisses shared in the comfort of his bed.

Words of love, whispered in the dark. Baylis and Gideon together in his study. He ran a loving hand down her dainty neck, brushing her hair behind her shoulder.

My blood boiled and my stomach turned.

"You know what you must do," his deep voice said.

Baylis nodded. Her gray eyes obedient as if she were looking at a god incarnate.

"Yes, my love."

Bile rose in the back of my throat.

"That's enough," I shouted.

Clotho spit me out of her mind.

"Why?" I said, my voice more of a cry than I intended.

"I cannot answer that question. I can only show you what you need to see."

I went to speak but she vanished into nothing. Brushing the dirt from my butt, I hurried to the ship. Clotho's visions rattled in my head. The grit of sand made my mouth dry. Baylis was a traitor. I already knew that from before. But was she really one now? I'd seen the creature lurking in her head. Did Gideon put it there? Did she?

I would have to confront her. Smacking my pack of smokes on my palm, I lit a cigarette. My hand shook as I held it to my lips. *Get your head on straight, Aelia. Don't be a fool like before. Trust your gut.*

I couldn't look at my sister as I boarded the ship. She stared out at the water. A hood covering her blonde hair. She looked so innocent. Could she really be the architect of my demise?

Taking a seat next to her, I tried to put it out of my mind for now.

The moon painted the sea with silver light, and I could see the waves were already rougher than when we arrived. *Wind is natural, Aelia, you have nothing to worry about. Waves happen.*

"Took you long enough," Conrad said, taking a drag off a long, curved pipe.

"Fate doesn't run on your schedule."

Conrad smirked. "Maybe it should."

I rolled my eyes. "Let's just get off this island before our luck runs out."

"As soon as you give me the siren's song we'll leave."

I ground my jaw. Of course, I wouldn't get out of this that easily. The crew drew their swords on us.

Conrad grinned.

"A deal's a deal, sweetie."

Reluctantly I reached into my pocket and handed him the sapphire.

"This really brings out my eyes, don't you think?" he said, fastening the jewel around his neck.

"Let's just get out of here."

"As you wish." He stalked up to the helm and spun it hard to the right. "Let's go, boys!"

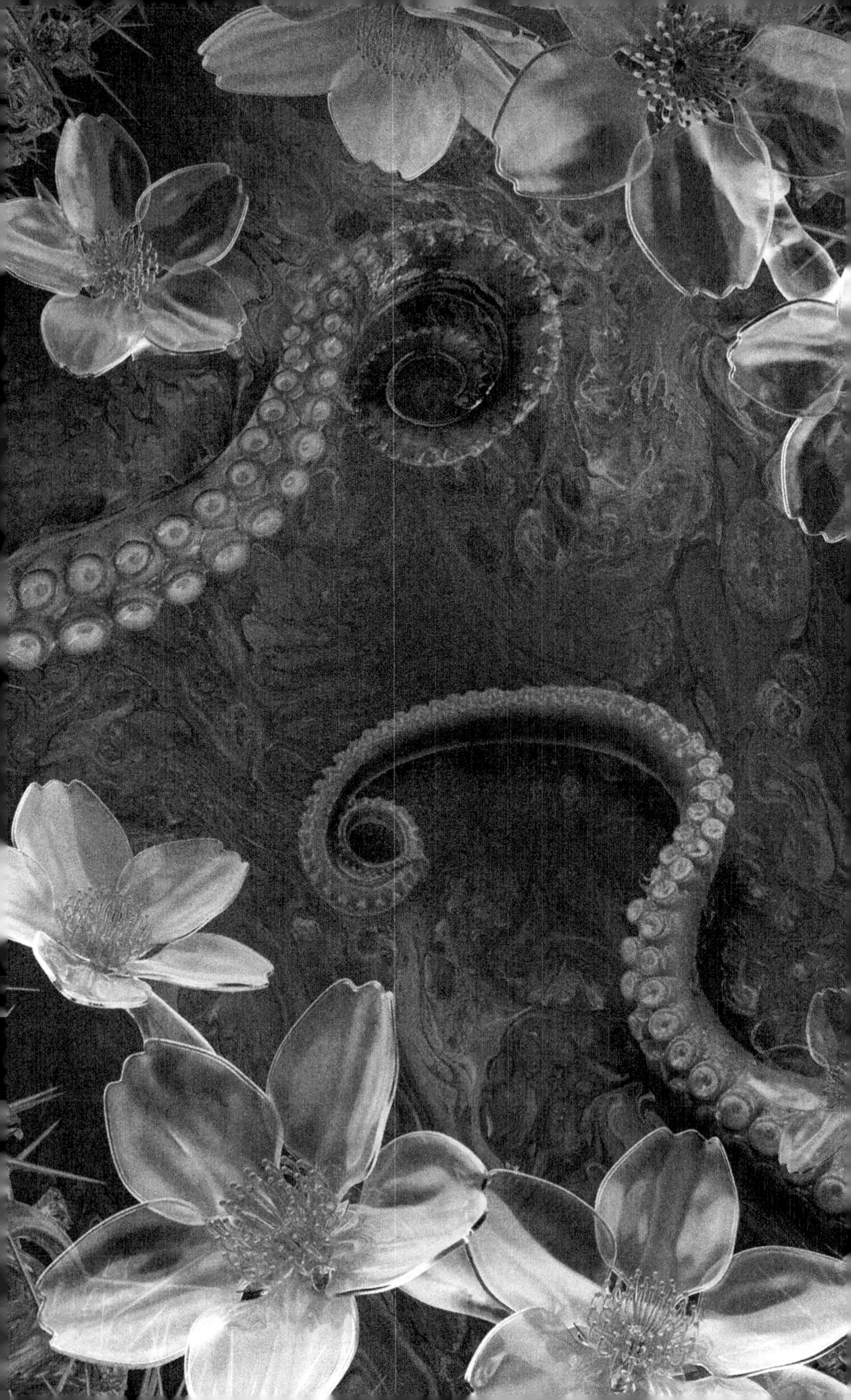

27 AELIA

THE WAVES SLOSHED AGAINST THE HULL OF THE MASSIVE SHIP, rocking us back and forth. My stomach turned at the violent movements. Across the Atruskan Bay, the lighthouse shone like a heavenly beacon, guiding us home.

"The sea is angry tonight. I wonder…" Conrad's words were cut short by the back of a massive sea snake cresting through the water ahead. Its green scales shone in the moonlight.

"Hydralisk!" Conrad called to his men. "Ready your bows! Ready the Ballista!"

The men got to their stations, loading the massive crossbows while others grabbed their bows. The creature encircled the boat. Bigger than anything I had ever encountered; its head was the size of a hay cart on market day.

My breath hitched in my throat. I was powerless to stop it, never having been good at using a bow, nor had I ever tried to infiltrate an animal's mind.

"Looks like Calliope got your message," Conrad said, turning the ship violently.

The snake broke through the surface, sending a wave of water over the bow, knocking many of the men down. I held onto the railing of the boat. The last time I had seen a snake even close to this size was when Gideon and Erissa attacked the Court of Sorrows. The hydralisk made that snake look tiny in comparison.

The snake hissed, turning a few unlucky men to stone. Frozen, fighting for their lives for an eternity. "Don't meet its gaze!" Conrad called his men. "Try to aim for the body. A hit is a hit!"

The men fired at the great sea creature. But only the mighty bolts of the ballista could penetrate the serpent's thick scales.

"Get down and out of sight," Baylis said, taking aim at the creature. I watched as her arrow soared through the air—hitting the hydralisk dead in the eye.

The creature reared back his mighty head in pain, letting out a cry that shook the boat. Men fell to their knees, clasping their hands over their ears.

"Make it stop!"

I hunkered under the ship's railing. Water soaked me through, chilling me to the bone. I tried to keep my teeth from chattering, but even my best attempt was feeble.

Baylis nocked another arrow. Pulling the string back, I noticed her mouth something to herself.

"Can't turn anyone to stone if you're blind." Another arrow whizzed through the air, blinding the snake fully.

In a fit of rage, the creature violently swung its head back and forth while the crew continued to unleash their arrows. Even in the dark, blood stained the water, turning the once clear water red.

"We're beating her back! C'mon, men, give 'er all you've got!" Conrad yelled. More bolts buzzed through the air, finding a home in the snake's hard flesh. Reluctantly, the creature retreated into the water.

A cry of joy ripped through the crew. They shook their fists at the sea.

"Nice try, Calliope! But you know I don't die easily!" Conrad pulled a bottle of rum from a chest near the helm. Tilting his head back, he took a celebratory swig before handing the bottle to Baylis. "Nice shooting," he said.

"Thanks," Baylis said, drinking back some of the amber liquid.

"Good work, men! The sea witch has yet to take us down!"

The men cheered in return, taking swigs of their own bottles of ale.

I let out a long sigh and slumped onto the deck. All these men had risked their lives for me. I almost got them killed and did get a fair number turned to stone.

"Will you be able to fix them?" I asked Conrad, trying not to throw the contents of my lunch overboard.

"The men?" He arched his brow. "Yeah, I've got a witch who raises basilisks to harvest their venom for a remedy."

"Sounds like dangerous work." I took a long pull off the bottle of rum. The alcohol burned away the queasiness still lingering in my stomach.

"She's blind, so it works out well for her."

"We all play to our strengths."

"That's all we can do."

A silent understanding passed between us. We survived the hydralisk. Surely nothing else could be worse, and we were almost out of the ring Conrad pointed out earlier. I let my body relax a little. We just needed to make it out of the danger zone, and it would be fine. Just a little farther, and we would be safe.

The sound of rustling waves behind us made the hairs on the back of my neck stand on end. By the time I turned around, it was already too late. The hydralisk bared its giant fangs before diving headfirst at the boat.

"Abandon ship!" Conrad cried out.

The massive snake split the ship like a toothpick, sending men and pieces of debris flying into the shadowy water. Grabbing Baylis's hand, I stepped onto the ledge of the hull. "Jump!"

We plunged into the icy water just as the serpent's tail decimated the remainder of the ship. Debris flew into the air in a thousand different directions.

Heart pounding, we sank farther and farther into the icy depths—so deep, the light of the moon barely trickled through the water. Still, I did not let my sister's hand go. I saved her from Gideon. Calliope would not take her from me. I kicked my feet hard toward the surface, pulling Baylis the entire way. I could not look back. I would not look back. My lungs begged for air, burning like a hot fire as they squeezed tighter.

Breaking through the water's surface, I gasped, savoring the feeling of my lungs contracting and expanding. Grateful for another few moments of life. Baylis popped up behind me, taking in a large breath of air as well.

"It's so cold, Aelia. We'll never make it," she said through chattering teeth.

All around us, bodies and debris floated in the water. Some men clung to crates and barrels, while others floated lifelessly. A pang of guilt stung my heart. They would be alive if it weren't for me.

My self-pity was cut short by the screams coming from the men closer to the ship. I whipped my head around to get a better look, but all I saw was bodies being dragged under the water. One by one, they disappeared beneath the waves. Their cries muffled by water filling their lungs.

Adrenaline coursed through my veins. We needed to get out of here.

"This way, follow me."

"They're almost to us, Aelia!" Baylis screamed.

The flame of the Ruska lighthouse blazed ahead of us.

"We are the children of fate. If we were going to die tonight, Mother would have told us. Now swim!"

Fighting the current, we swam toward the light. My muscles

burned, and my body fought me with every stroke. I tried to focus on anything but the pain. I was stronger than this.

Waves battered us at every turn, filling our lungs with water. We coughed and spat the liquid back up but did not stop. The sound of bodies being towed beneath the waves continued to echo behind us.

"Don't look back! Just swim!" I cried. My fingers were numb from the cold. Any feeling in my lower half had gone a long time ago, but still, I kicked, and Baylis did the same.

The screams faded. We were out of the ring guarding the island. I slowed my pace, trying to conserve my energy.

"We still... have... so far... to go..." Baylis said, trying to keep her head above water.

I prayed to Ammena the Harbor Master saw the attack and sent help. I failed my sister once. I would not let her die here in the icy waters of the Atruskan Bay.

"Just keep going, Baylis. We can do it."

"I'm so tired, Aelia." Her pace slowed, and fear bit at my heart.

Looping one hand around her waist, I did my best to support her.

"C'mon, just a little farther, I'll help you. It won't be long."

"Okay, Aelia, I trust you." Her voice faded.

"You have to stay awake, Baylis. You have to keep swimming."

Her pale skin was utterly colorless, and her lips were the color of ripe blueberries. She wouldn't last long. This tender creature couldn't be a traitor. Was Clotho trying to sabotage me? I pushed the questions from my mind. If Baylis died, none of this would matter.

Out of the corner of my eye, I caught a rescue ship's blue-and-white sails.

"Here! We're here!" I called out in the loudest voice I could manage. Waving my free arm frantically, hoping they saw me.

"Please! We're here!" My heart raced in my chest.

A sailor onboard pointed in my direction, and slowly, the ship began to turn.

"They're almost here, Baylis. We're going to get you warm." Her body convulsed in my arms.

The ship approached. A sylph from the Court of Light shined a beam in our direction, and I squinted from the brightness.

"Two survivors! Get the gurney!"

I let out a sigh of relief. The cold crept in. I had been so worried about Baylis's wellbeing I had forgotten about my own. A chill wrapped itself around me like a snake. My lungs seized, and I gasped for air.

"Hold on! We're coming for you!" The crew lowered a sailor down on a gurney, and I helped heave Baylis on. Her breaths were so shallow I wasn't sure if she was actually breathing or if I was hallucinating.

"You too, miss," the man said, pointing to Baylis's feet.

I climbed on, and the men hoisted us up. The bitter wind bit at my wet body, making me shake uncontrollably.

Once onboard, the crew rushed Baylis below deck, where a healer waited. They handed me a thick black wool cloak lined with wolf's fur. My skin welted red as though I had been burned, and it felt the same. All I could do was sit and shake.

A witch with gray hair and eyes approached, wearing the white and blue of the healers' guild of the free cities.

"I need to examine you. Here's a heating potion for the cold." She handed me a glass vial filled with red liquid. I slugged it back. The taste of cinnamon tingled on my tongue.

"You've got hypothermia," the witch said, taking off my boot and examining my toes. "But it looks like you'll keep all your extremities. Are you a magus? A human would have died long ago in these waters."

I tapped my pointed incisor. "Half-breed, as they say."

The witch frowned at me.

"On my ship, everyone is equal."

"My sister—is she alright? Did anyone else survive?"

"I'm having my two best healers work on her. She's in bad shape. May even lose a finger or two, but she'll live."

A breath slipped between my lips, turning to vapor in the cold night air.

The witch continued, "As for any other survivors. We've only found one. He was floating on a barrel, half-dead."

She didn't have to say who it was. Conrad was the only person aboard stubborn enough to survive.

"Black bargain mark snaking up his arm?" I asked.

"Yes." The witch nodded.

"Figures." I leaned back against the railing of the ship. The heating potion worked its way through my body, making my skin tingle in some places and burn in others.

"It has to fight the cold," the healer said, seeing the grimace plastered across my face.

"When can I see my sister?"

"When you're well, and we're back on dry land. I can't have you in the way while we work on her. I promise I will come and get you as soon as possible." The witch turned and walked away. The tails of her coat flapped in the wind.

I needed to talk to Tharan and didn't care if anyone saw. Twisting the whisper stone, I waited for the sound of his voice.

"Aelia?"

"Tharan? Thank the Trinty. You have no idea how much I needed to hear your voice."

"What's going on? Are you alright? Did you see your mother?" Concern filled his voice, and I pictured his brow furrowed.

I took a deep breath, trying to collect my thoughts. "Yes, we saw her. She's fine, and there's a lot of stuff I need to tell you, but that can wait. As we were leaving the island, a sea serpent destroyed Conrad's ship. He survived, but none of his crew did."

"Oh Aelia… I… I'm so glad you're alright. I don't know what I'd do if something happened to you."

A tear streaked its way down my cheek. I had no words. No one had cared for me this way in a long time. Not since Caiden, and he didn't know who I was anymore. The realization washed over me. My nerves were frazzled. I cried harder.

"Don't cry, Aelia. You're alive, that's all that matters."

A lump grew in my throat. I tried to speak, but the words came out mumbled and wrong, "I know where they are."

"What? Aelia, I can't talk about this right now. But are you saying you've found what we were looking for?"

"Yes."

There was a long pause.

"Come home, Aelia. I love you."

I went to tell him I loved him, but the line went dead.

"Tharan? Tharan!" I frantically twisted the earring, but he was gone.

"Hot cider, miss?" A sailor handed me a warm cup, and I settled in for the ride back to the harbor, gazing at the wreckage of *The Salty Bitch* in the distance. The night concealed most of the carnage, and the waters surrounding the island had turned tumultuous again.

A skeletal hand grasped at my heart. Was that the last time I would ever see my mother? Was my sister really a traitor or were the Fates playing tricks on me? No, I couldn't think like that. Pushing the thought out of my head, I turned to brighter thoughts. We had the information we needed. All we needed to do was get back to the Woodlands.

One step at a time, Aelia. One step at a time.

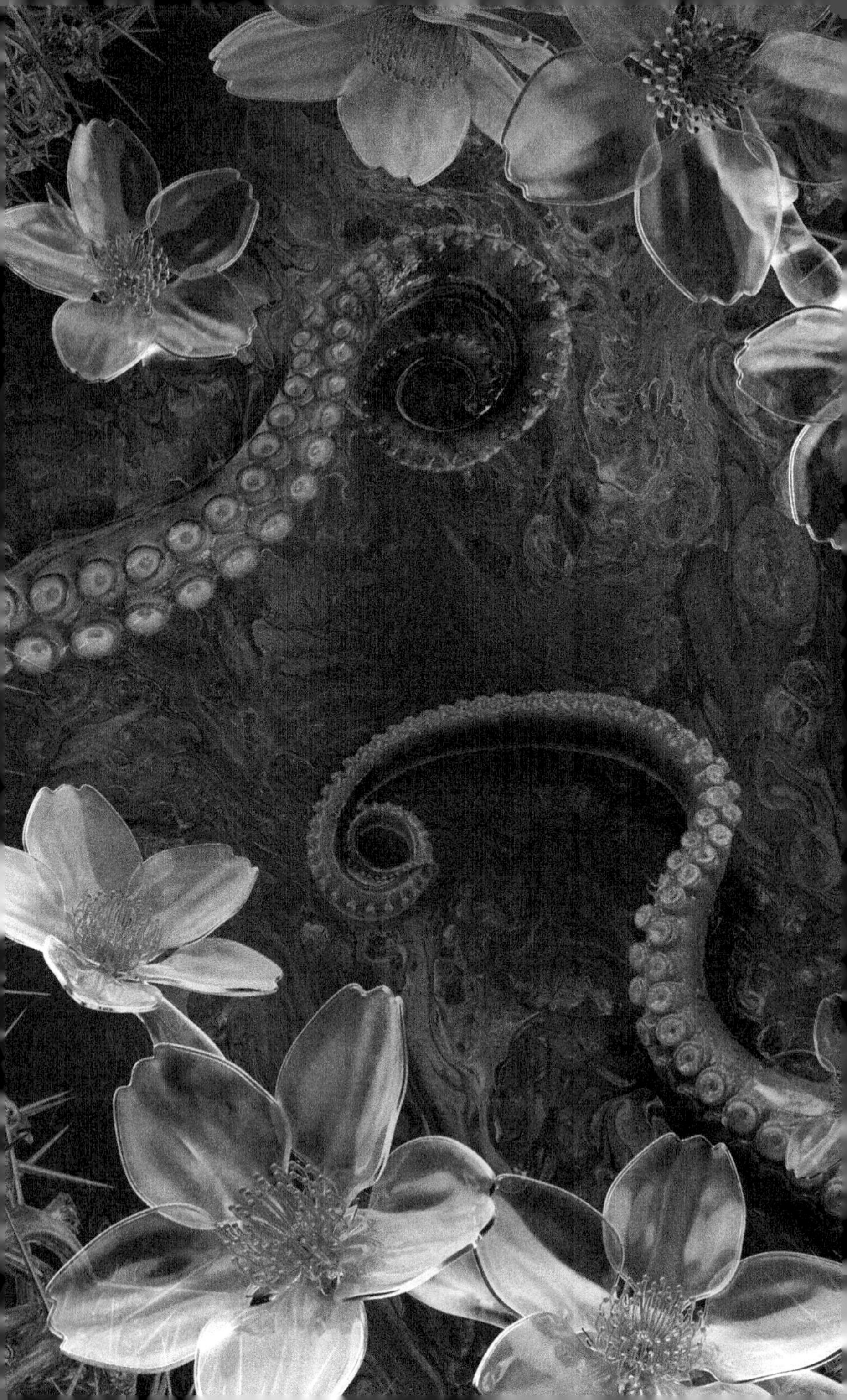

28 AELIA

"We need to take your sister to the infirmary so we can watch her for the next day. She is resting comfortably, but we did have to amputate her right pinky and ring fingers.

I grimaced.

"Oh, Trinity."

"There was nothing we could do. The cold got to her. They would have rotted and possibly killed her."

The whole of me shuddered at the thought of them hacking off pieces of my sister. All I could do was nod.

The witch touched my shoulder gently.

"Why don't you go home for the night? We put your sister in a deep slumber. She won't wake until tomorrow."

"And what of Conrad?"

She shook her head.

"That bargain brand didn't help him, but he'll make it."

"Thank you," I said, wrapping the blanket tighter around myself.

"Bring that back tomorrow, will you?" she said reassuringly.

"I will." I headed into the cold night.

The first blush of dawn was just beginning to peek over the

horizon when I reached the Alder Townhome. Finneas flinched when he opened the door for me. "Lady Aelia, what happened?"

"So much," I said, collapsing on the plush couch in the parlor. Finneas pulled off my boots and laid another blanket over me before shutting the blinds and closing the doors.

When I awoke, the room was still dark. I blinked, letting my eyes adjust. My muscles ached from use. I lay there staring at the ceiling for a moment. The memories of last night came flooding in.

Baylis!

I jumped to my feet and hurried to the study, where I found Amolie poring over books on ancient magic and necromancy. Two lamps burned on a large wooden desk, and bookshelves stretched from floor to ceiling. The room smelled of old parchment and pine. Her face brightened when she saw me.

"Aelia! You're awake." She sprung from her seat, pulling me in for a hug. "You smell awful," she said, gripping me tighter. "I love it."

"Baylis is in the infirmary."

"What happened? I feared the worst when you returned without her, but I didn't want to wake you."

I rubbed the bridge of my nose, deciding where to begin.

"I need some coffee first."

Amolie rang the servant's bell, and a halfling woman appeared in the doorway.

"How may I assist you ladies?"

"Coffee and some sugary confections if you have them," Amolie said.

"Some bacon, too, please," I added. The woman nodded and

left the room. I leaned back in the plush armchair, listening to the crackling fire and reveling in its heat.

Amolie took a seat in the one across from me.

"So? What happened?"

I sighed.

"Well, we saw our mother."

"And?" She leaned forward, elbows on her knees.

"And she said I'd have to choose between Tharan and Caiden."

"Well, it seems to me like you already made your choice."

"But what if that choice was wrong?" I had been wrong before. What if I was wrong again? What if I was doomed to pick bad men? What if I pushed the good ones away? My heart couldn't take much more of this. I loved Tharan, except… what if we could never be together? What if I was wasting my time loving someone only to have the world rip them from my hands again?

Amolie moved closer and placed a reassuring hand on mine.

"For once, I don't think you are. I think you should trust your gut."

I nodded.

"You're right. I'm being foolish, and she could be playing games with me."

"Trust your intuition, Aelia," Amolie said.

I told her at length about our misadventure, finishing with Conrad's near miss with death just as a servant entered the room.

"Excuse me, Lady Aelia, but we just received word that your sister has woken and is asking for you."

With those words, I breathed a little easier. "Wonderful. Prepare a carriage for us."

The infirmary was housed in one of the old god's temples, built long before the Trinity came to dominate the continent. Light streamed in through stained-glass windows, painting the room with color. Below the arched windows, beds lined the ancient shrine. Baylis was located at the far end. Healers rushed from patient to patient, checking on them, wearing their signature blue-and-white coats that buttoned to their chin. The Healers Guild of the Free Cities accepted all skilled practitioners into their ranks. Elves, sylph, witches, and all manner of magus mixed together freely.

A sense of relief flooded over me, seeing more sailors had survived. Even Conrad was awake and flirting with the healers.

Amolie and I pulled up chairs beside Baylis's bed. She still looked so fragile, with her skin-tinged blue and shadows beneath her eyes. She couldn't be a conniving backstabber. That wasn't in her nature. Even as I thought the words, something in the back of my mind told me not to trust her. She had seen so much already. If she wanted to, she could destroy me. It's something I would have done to get the information I needed.

"How are you feeling?" I asked.

"As well as can be expected." She held up her hand with the two missing fingers wrapped in a bandage.

"Makes you look fierce." I mustered the best smile I could. "You'll have to think of a good story for it."

"Because a giant sea serpent destroyed the ship I was on isn't good enough?"

I chuckled, pulling her in for a hug. "I guess that is a pretty good story."

"Not too tight," she gasped. The briny, earthy smell of the Bay still lingered on her skin.

"I can't help it. I thought I'd lost you again."

"You should know by now... Springborns are hard to kill."

A lump formed in my throat, and I nodded into my sister's long, blonde hair.

"Save some for the rest of us," Amolie said. "She's not going anywhere."

Wiping the tears from my eyes, I sat back in my chair. When did I get so emotional? *Get it together, Aelia.*

The healer from the ship approached us. Her silver hair was braided in a tight bun behind her sloped ears. The creases around her eyes marked her as an elder, but I couldn't say how old she really was.

"Your sister is doing quite well for almost having died last night." She grinned at Baylis. "You can take her home today. I've had the attendants gather some clothes, and you'll have to keep the wound wrapped for at least the next week."

"I'm going to have to learn how to shoot again," Baylis said, pretending to shoot a bow and arrow.

"I'm sure you'll be fine. Let's get you dressed and back home to rest." I pulled a curtain surrounding Baylis's bed, and Amolie and I helped her change into a loose-fitting wool dress.

Conrad waved us over as we made our way down the rows of beds.

"Aelia! Baylis! You made it." Somehow, he managed to keep his hat through the ordeal.

"You're looking well, Conrad. I'm sorry about your crew."

"They were good men," he said, a sullen look on his face. "But there is no better death for a sailor than a death at sea. So, in that way, we honored them."

I didn't know what to say. The blood of his men was on my hands, and I would not be able to shake the guilt of that for some time. Maybe ever.

"I'm still sorry."

"Death is a part of life. We will all meet our makers someday." He leaned back on his bed. "But the sea has not claimed me yet. Although she did get my left hand this time." He held up a stump wrapped in bandages.

I grimaced.

"Oh, Conrad, I'm so sorry."

His eyes brightened, and a charming smile crossed his handsome face.

"Don't be. I'm having Tiernan fashion me a hook."

"Well, that's something." My eyes flitted around the room, looking for any wandering gazes, but all I saw were healers tending to the sick and injured. "Do you still have the…" I scratched my chest where a necklace would hang.

"I do. And you're not getting it back."

"I guess the point is moot now. Queen Calliope already sent her sea snake after us. She will not stop until she has her justice."

"You should be ready for her to attack at any time. I have sailed her seas for hundreds of years. She is as smart as she is wicked—a creature of the blood and the water. Be ready for a fight."

"I have been fighting my whole life, Conrad."

He smirked.

"Tharan said as much, Mind Breaker."

"We are both fighters." I turned to leave, knowing this wouldn't be the last I'd see of Conrad. "Enjoy your new ship."

"Oh, I will," he said.

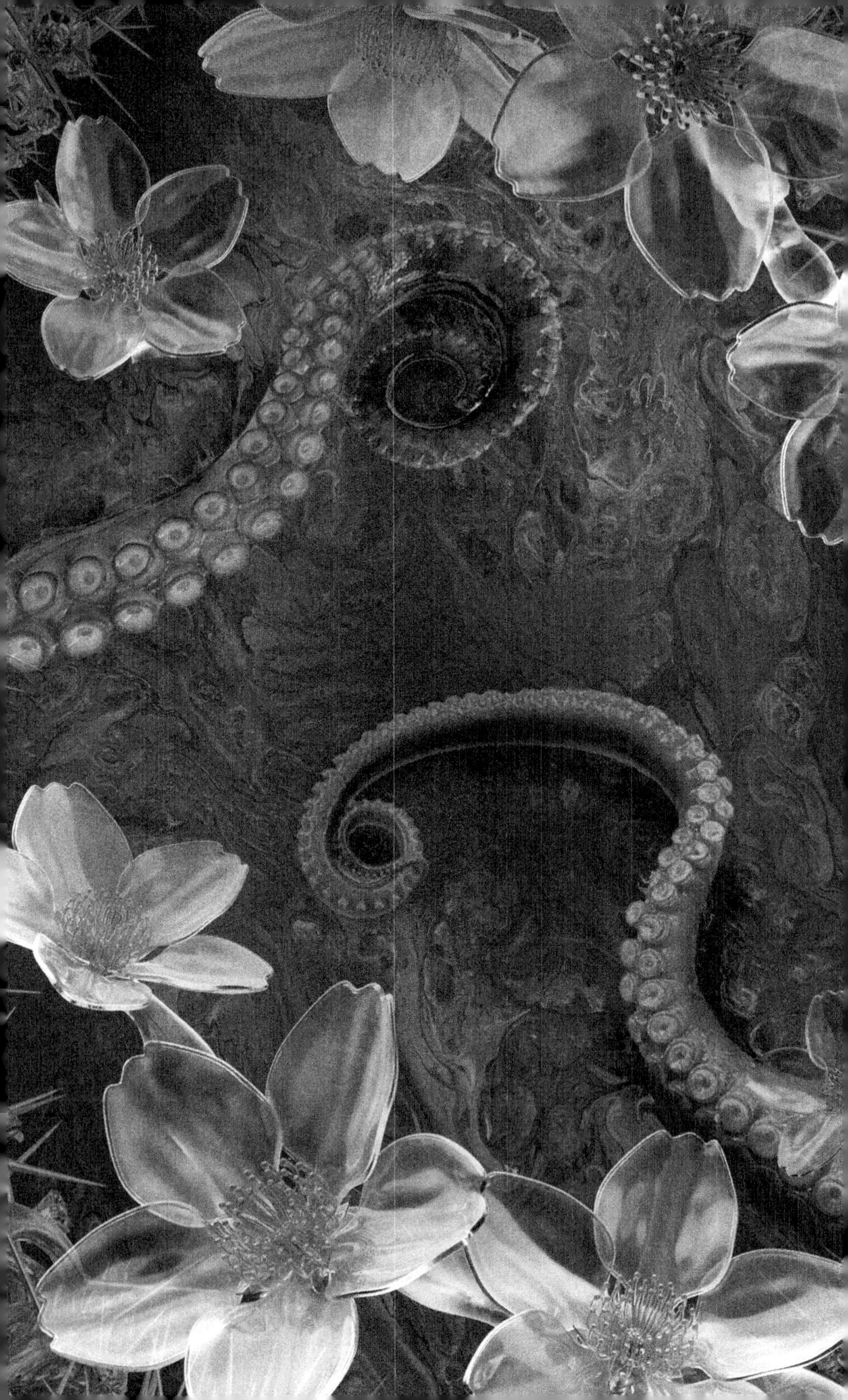

29 CAIDEN

Caiden paced around his mother's parlor, chewing on a piece of willow bark.

"You're going to wear a hole in my fine rug," Tempestia said, looking at her son through lowered lashes as she knit a sweater for her future grandchild. Caiden's older brother, Aaryn, was expecting a child with his wife, a half sylph from the Court of Ashes.

"I just can't believe it."

"Believe what?" Tonin entered the parlor followed by Ora, joining Roderick and Tempesta around the fire.

"We think we located one of the Wells in the Court of Screams."

Tonin flinched, shutting his eyes tightly. The Court of Screams was known for its brutality. Even among the sylphs who were made for battle, they were considered extreme. "The Trinity would choose a place like that. Even the elves dared not tread on their land, and when the courts split between Wild and Council, they took no side."

"Have you been there before?" Caiden asked.

"They are wild—wilder than any court. Anyone who dares to

tread there would be risking their life. They worship pain, thinking it makes you stronger. The more pain one can endure, the closer to the Trinity they become." He took a seat next to his wife on the leather sofa. "I'd say it's barbaric, but that would be an insult to barbarians."

Caiden swallowed hard and shot a knowing glance at Roderick, who said out loud what Caiden was thinking, "We need Lucius and his Shadow Hunters."

"I'll send a raven to the Court of Myst tomorrow, but there's no telling if he'll get it. He probably hasn't even arrived yet. It's on the other side of the continent, after all."

"True." Roderick thumbed the still healing gash on his palm where the binding scar would soon form.

"I will have a chat with the representatives from the Court of Honey and the Court of Ash tomorrow," Tonin said. "Perhaps they know something."

"I can do some research at the library," Ora added.

"Well, then, it seems we have a plan for the interim," Tonin said, leaning back on the sofa. "Now, there are some horse races tonight I'm obligated to attend if anyone is interested."

"I should get back to the library." Ora rose, dusting off her robes. The firelight illuminated the beautiful angles of her face, and Caiden could not look away.

"Please, accompany us," Caiden said, grabbing her hand and immediately letting it go. "I… uh… I mean, you've done so much for me. It only seems right we reward you. Let me take you out for a night. As thanks." Caiden's pulse raced, and he could feel everyone's eyes on him. The air was suddenly much warmer. "If you're allowed, that is."

Ora let out a shoulder-shaking laugh.

"We're not prisoners. We are allowed to have fun now and again."

Caiden could've sworn the scholars who weren't grandmasters had to be in by a certain hour, but perhaps he was mistaken.

"So that's a yes?"

"Yes." Ora's entire face lit up when she smiled, and Caiden's chest lightened a little at the thought of being near her the entire night.

"Well, then, we better get going," Tonin said, rising from his chair and extending a hand to his wife. "I like to get there early and meet the horses beforehand. I'm better at picking a winner then."

"Sure, you are, my dear," Tempestia said, kissing her husband on the cheek.

"Shall we?" Caiden said, extending his arm to Ora, who hooked hers through.

The amphitheater in the center of Vantris buzzed with the energy of ten thousand sylphs, all eagerly anticipating the start of the races. In Vantris, horse racing was a regular event, even in the dead of winter.

Being a member of the Sylph Council, Tonin was afforded a luxurious suite at the top of the amphitheater, complete with staff who kept them plied with ale and delicious morsels while they cheered on their favorite horses.

Caiden, Roderick, and Ora took their seats while Tempestia and Tonin went to survey the horses before the race began.

"Nothing like a good night of sporting to get the blood pumping," Roderick said, taking a pint of ale from one of the servers.

Usually, Caiden loved the races. As children, he and his brother had raced their ponies around the Stormlands estates, pretending to be their favorite riders.

Caiden remembered the first time his father brought him to the amphitheater to see a race. He had been six, and the world seemed huge then. The statues of champion riders outside of the amphitheater were like gods to Caiden. Each court brought a bevy of riders to the capitol, and it was common for people to hang their favorite riders' colors outside their houses.

But tonight, Caiden couldn't relax. Knots tied themselves in his stomach, and he couldn't tell if that was because of Ora or because he knew he'd eventually have to travel to the infamous Court of Screams. He let out a breath. *Just enjoy this moment here with the people you care about. You can worry about everything else tomorrow.*

"Who are you betting on tonight, Roderick?"

"Stormlands, always," Roderick said, taking a swig of ale. "Greysong is a winner, and I know it. She just hasn't hit her stride yet. The jockey isn't giving her enough rein around the backend turn."

"Did Amolie tell you that?"

"No… yes…" he said with a sheepish grin.

"She knows her horses. Perhaps I should make a bet on her, too." Caiden hastily filled out one of the betting sheets before handing it to an attendant.

"I've never been to the races before, although I did enjoy riding from time to time when my studies permitted," Ora said, staring down at the track of hard-packed snow that would soon be filled with jockeys and their mounts. Tension and excitement hung heavy in the air, making the stadium pulse with a buzz only a race could conjure.

"You should have said something," Caiden said, "I would've taken you down to the stables to see the horses."

"It's alright." Ora's cheeks flushed pink.

"At intermission, I'll take you down. It's really something to see how it all works."

Her long face brightened. "That would be lovely."

Caiden's chest warmed, and he hoped his face wouldn't give away his excitement at the thought of spending time alone with her.

Tonin and Tempestia entered the suite, glowing as they always did, even after centuries of marriage. "I've picked a winner this time. I felt it when I passed by his stall," Tonin proclaimed to everyone in the room.

"Oh? Which one did you bet on? Greysong?" Roderick asked.

"Winterwinds," Tonin replied.

"You didn't bet on a horse from your own court?" Roderick arched a brow at the lord.

"Of course, I put a little money on all the Stormland horses. But, I think Winterwinds can go all the way this year. I see the Trinity Crown in his future."

"I'll bet on that—fifty gold coins," Roderick held out his hand.

"A bargain easily kept." Tonin shook the half-giant's hand, binding them to their words.

Tempestia rolled her green eyes. Her tight ringlet curls bounced as she shook her head at her husband.

"What?" Tonin said, giving his wife a coy smile.

"Nothing, my dear." She kissed him on the cheek, making the old king blush.

Horns sounded, signaling the start of the races. Traditionally, there were three races, with an hour break between the second and third race for the horses to recover. The horse with the most wins won it all. Fans often got heated over their favorites and how they performed.

"Let's get closer," Caiden said, offering Ora his hand. Together, they walked to the edge of the suite, where they had a view of the entire course. Jockeys and their mounts lined up behind a row of flags. The horses danced in anticipation of the race under their rider's steady seats.

Caiden held his breath as he always did at the start of the race.

A horn sounded, and the first horse leapt over the barrier before the flags could even fall. The rest followed suit.

"How are they not slipping on the snow?" Ora asked.

"Special shoes made to grip the ice," Caiden answered. It was well known that the Court of Wailing Winds produced some of the finest racers on the continent. Surely, she'd understand how they raced on the snow. He brushed his apprehension to the side. Perhaps her family wasn't into racing—she'd never been, after all.

The horses rounded the first bend. Caiden could see the blanket of the Stormlands on the head horse.

"C'mon, Greysong!" Roderick cheered, clenching his fists tight as the horse took the lead. "Give her her head!" he called to the jockey as if he could hear him.

The horses rounded the second turn, and the dark gray stallion pulled ahead of the Stormlands mare. "That's it, Winterwinds! Give it all you've got!" Tonin called.

The two horses were neck and neck until, out of nowhere, a horse black as night rounded the final curve, catching up with the competing grays.

"Who's that?" Ora asked no one in particular.

Roderick looked down at his roster. "Looks like it's Tallon's Delight from the Court of Wailing Winds."

"Oh, that's my home! Go, Tallon!" Ora shouted.

The three horses crossed the finish line together. The crowd held their breath while the officials decided who won. After what seemed like an eternity, the round official, wearing a deep blue vest covered with embroidered hoof prints, announced Tallon's Delight as the Winner. A mixture of cheers and disappointed sighs rippled through the crowd.

The next set of horses lined up while men frantically smoothed the track again.

"The horse from my court won!" Ora said, clapping her hands together in delight. "Can I see him during intermission?"

Caiden smiled. Seeing her happy lit something inside him he hadn't felt in a long time. "Of course."

They cheered on the next two races, of which a mare named Cherry and Greysong each won a round.

"Let's go down and see your winner," Caiden said to Ora, who nodded enthusiastically.

"Oh, this is so exciting," she said as they made their way down to the stables.

The smell of oats, hay, and manure all mixed together in the bustling stables.

Horses snorted and whinnied to one another.

"Oh, this is lovely," she said.

Something gnawed at Caiden's mind, like an itch he couldn't scratch. Someone else he knew loved horses. Amolie was a royal trainer once, but that's not who he was thinking of. His thoughts were interrupted by the sound of a horse neighing.

"This is him! Look how beautiful he is," Ora cooed over the stallion, who munched on hay happily.

"Yes, he is gorgeous," Caiden said, admiring the horse.

"Thank you for bringing me to see him." Ora held out her hand flat, and the horse gently nudged it, looking for a treat. "I don't get out of the library much."

Caiden swallowed hard. "I'd like to see you again, if that's alright with you."

Her face brightened, and her eyes darted to where the horse nuzzled her.

Caiden wanted to say something, but it had been some time since he'd courted a woman, and his tongue refused to untie. "We could go somewhere right now if you'd like."

"I…" She hesitated, digging her toe into the dirt of the stable floor. "I'd like that."

A wave of relief washed over him. "Great, there's a little pub not far from here that I haunted as an up-and-coming commander."

"Sounds lovely," she said.

He extended a hand and clasped hers. Together, they walked through the sparkling night. The lights of Vantris twinkled like little stars all around them, hands laced tightly together.

"I've not done this before," Ora said.

"Done what? Hold hands? Surely you had suitors in school?"

She shrugged. "Not really. It's been my dream to be a Master Scholar since I can remember. I'm not very good with my powers. Books and knowledge made more sense to me."

"And what exactly is your specialty?"

She cleared her throat. "Ancient elixirs, potions, and the gods of the old world."

Caiden arched a brow. "That's a lot."

"I never get bored."

Caiden nodded. "Quite right."

"Hey, I've got an idea. Let's grab a bottle of wine and head down to the river." She gave him puppy-dog eyes.

"You won't get too cold?" Caiden asked.

"If I do, you can keep me warm."

Caiden tried hard to fight the smile growing on his face. Scholars were often known to take a vow of celibacy until they reached the Grand Master Level, but maybe Ora did not believe in such things. "Of course. It would be the gentlemanly thing to do."

They stopped outside a lively tavern where the sound of boisterous laughter and song spilled into the street. Caiden hastily bought a bottle of wine, and the two headed to the river walk where lovers were known to have their first kiss.

Only a few people lingered on the boardwalk.

They sat on a secluded bench overlooking the river. Caiden sipped the wine, hoping it would calm his nerves.

"Thank you for this," Ora said, taking the bottle from his

hand. "I haven't been out in ages. Sometimes, I forget what it's like to be out here in the real world."

"Plenty of scholars have families."

"Yes, but plenty don't." She sighed. "I fear I may be the latter. Bound to the work."

"Are your parents scholars too?"

She snorted. "No, they are wild wailers. They help ships cross the Black Sea. Dangerous work, but very lucrative."

"And you didn't want to go into the family business?'

"You saw my gift. I'm an extinguisher and not a very good one."

"Yeah, I guess you're right." Caiden scooted closer to her. "How long have you been here in the capitol?"

"Oh, nearly thirty years."

"Nearly?" Caiden cocked his head. "You have three bars on your hood. If I'm not mistaken, that's thirty years of training."

Her cheeks flushed. "Oh, yes, where has the time gone? Being cooped up in that library, you lose track of time."

"Maybe you need to get out more?" He prepared himself for the next question. His palms sweated, and he rubbed them on his trousers. "Are you interested in accompanying me to the Woodland Realm for an Ostara festival? I'm supposed to meet some friends there to discuss what we've found. We could use someone with your expertise." His heart beat faster.

"I'll have to ask my elder," she said, shivering slightly.

Caiden wrapped an arm around her, and she rested her head in the crook of his neck.

"I promise to be a gentleman the entire time."

Ora chuckled. "I have no worries about you, Lord of Lightning."

"Hey, what does that mean?"

"Oh, I uh, just mean you're known for being a respectable man."

343

"I try to be," he replied.

"Those are hard to come by these days, I hear."

The hair on Caiden's arms stood on end. He wanted to kiss Ora, but he didn't know if she wanted that.

"Caiden…" Ora whispered.

He swallowed hard. "Yes?"

"Can I ask you something?"

"Anything."

"I'm almost one hundred years old and I've never been kissed. And since the world may be ending soon, and you seem like a good enough… well, not that you're some second-place prize…"

He cut her words short, pressing his lips to hers.

Ora leaned into Caiden, letting her hand wander into his thick hair. Her mouth tasted like blackberries and the mulled wine they had been drinking.

Arousal boiled in Caiden's core, and he slipped his tongue between her lips.

She let out a little moan, but didn't pull away. Instead, her hand went to his belt.

Caiden pulled away. "It's okay, we don't have to."

"Excuse me. I didn't mean to be too forward." A heat flushed her cheeks.

"I just don't want to do anything you're not comfortable with." Caiden grabbed the wine bottle and took another swig. When the wine hit his lips, he knew something was off. He looked at Ora.

"What's wrong, my Lord? Feeling sleepy?" A wicked smile cut her beautiful face in two.

"What did you do? Who are you… really?" His words slurred as they left his lips.

Ora's face transformed before him into something sharper,

with bloodred hair, deep tanned skin, and a hooked nose. "Oh, prince, that's not for you to worry about."

"But…" His eyes grew heavier with each passing moment. Heaving himself to his feet, he tried to run, but his legs were clumsy, and he toppled into the snow.

The stranger clicked her tongue, and she stood over Caiden. "You men are all the same. All it takes is a bat of an eye and you forget your own names."

Caiden tried to speak, but his whole body was numb. All he could do was blink as the cold of the snow seeped into his bones. The world went dark.

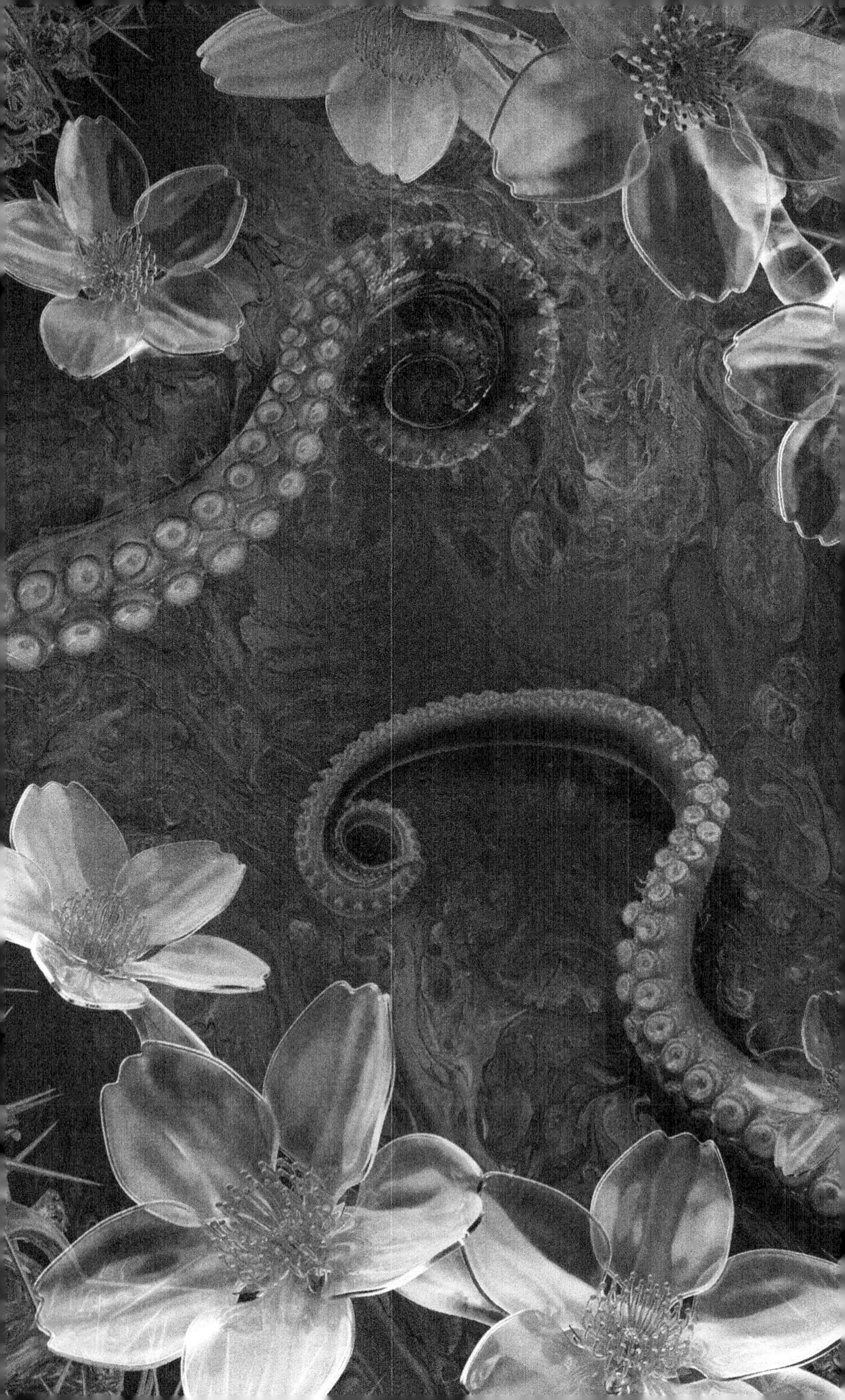

30 AELIA

Upon returning to the Alder Townhome, I tucked Baylis into bed before heading to the parlor to instruct the servants on what to pack for our trip back to the Woodlands.

Finneas was waiting with Amolie when I arrived, his goat-like face twisted with concern.

"What?" I asked, handing my coat to another servant.

"The mermaid was here again."

My eyes widened and my stomach twisted.

"Here? What did she say?"

Finneas held out a folded piece of parchment.

"She told me to give this to you."

Cautiously, I took the note and unfolded it. Ursula's swooping script read: *She will not stop until you are dead. You have been marked.*

I swallowed the fear bubbling in my stomach.

"What does it say?" Amolie asked, tilting the paper in my hand to get a better look. "Oh no."

Fear threatened to drown me.

"Say something, Aelia."

"The Court of the Alder King will not be intimidated by the

queen of the Undersea. If she wants me so badly, she can come to the surface and get me." I ripped the parchment in two and tossed it into the fire.

"Aelia," Amolie touched my elbow. "I know you are tough, but you are not immortal."

My mouth flattened into a straight line.

"I control an army that does not need to eat, sleep, or breathe. Let her come."

Amolie's expression softened.

"You don't have to be so tough all the time. It's okay to be scared. I'm scared. I'm scared every day."

"I have bigger things to worry about than Calliope and Ursula." Pulling the Scepter from the box where it lay, I gripped it tightly. "Morrigan, we need you."

A white smoke poured through the mouth of the bird, and the goddess took shape. "Hello, ladies," she said, stretching her long arms high into the air. Her golden hair fell in soft waves over her signature plated armor.

"Morrigan, we need to know if Crom is still in the world beyond the veil."

She shifted her weight to one hip. "You think I wouldn't alert you if he'd found a way back into this world?"

I shot her an incredulous look.

"Well, you come back and forth."

"Crom has wards around his grave that keep his soul bound to the other side. It would take the Trinity themselves to revive him."

"That's what we're trying to avoid, Morrigan."

"I think you'd know if a Well had been found," she said. "Everyone on this continent is desperate for power in one form or another. If Erissa and Gideon had found a Well, you'd know. Their allies would be lining up to get their hands on that kind of magic. Wars would break out over the Wells. That's why the Trinity hid them."

"I thought you said they were a myth?"

She scowled at me.

"Look, I don't know where the Trinity Wells are. And those goddesses never trusted anyone. Not even their own Fates. So they wouldn't have told me. But if I were them, I'd put the Wells in places no human or magus would find hospitable."

"Like a bog?" I arched a brow at her.

"Yes."

"And a desert?"

"Possibly." She shifted her weight to her other hip.

"The Great White North?"

She huffed. "Are you just going to quiz me on all the awful places on this continent?"

"Go back to the underworld, Morrigan. See if your men know if Crom is still there."

"What's this all about?" She raked her blue eyes over me. "What do you know that you're not telling me?"

I sighed, taking out my cigarettes from my pocket.

"Decuma saw a vision of a man in black being worshiped like a god in the desert."

"No, it can't be."

I took a drag. "She thought it was, but I'm not convinced. That's why we need your help."

"I'll send word to my scouts." Her face was awash with worry.

"Thank you," I said, blowing smoke into the air. "I don't think it's him, but better to know for sure than to assume."

She nodded before disappearing into a cloud of smoke.

I sank into the plush velvet couch. "I can't wait to get back to the Woodlands." My heart skipped a beat thinking about seeing Tharan again.

"Me too," Amolie said, wiping her hands on her skirt. "Roderick sent word… they have news."

I arched a brow. "Do you think they found something?"

"I hope so."

I didn't dare to hope we'd all found something useful. Life didn't work out that way for me.

"I want to give Baylis one more day to rest. We'll leave in the morning. Amolie, are you coming with us or going to Vantris first?"

"I had planned to go with you."

"Great. Did your research turn up anything useful on necromancy?"

"Yes. It seems there was a sect of witches who used sacrifices to bring someone back. Blood for blood, they called it. But you had to sacrifice someone of equal or greater power to the person you were bringing back."

"Hmmm," I scrunched my nose at her.

"There's more," she said. "Apparently, the elven mages found a way to replace the soul of one with another."

"Like possession?"

"Perhaps. The book was a thousand years old, and the mage order no longer exists."

"Blink of an eye for an elf. Maybe they went into hiding."

"Or maybe Arendir killed them as he was known to do to orders who displeased him."

I grimaced. "The elves are brutal."

"It is easy to become numb to mortality when you will never have to face it."

"I don't want to think about that. Let's focus on what we *can* do. Once we're all back together, it will be easier to plan."

Amolie sipped her tea.

"You're right."

I gazed out the window. The sun disappeared over the horizon and swathes of pink and orange mixed with the dark of night. Days were so short in winter, but that was fine with me. I preferred the darkness. I was safe in the darkness. It is the light I feared. True evil revels in the light.

With my sister slumbering upstairs, the Hunt guarding the door, and Amolie entrenched in a book, my eyes became heavy, and my body relaxed. Sleep claimed me.

The slamming of a door woke me. "Lady Baylis!" Finneas's frantic voice echoed through the empty townhome. How long had I been asleep? Someone placed a blanket over me, and the fire turned to embers. Trying to orient myself, I looked out the window where a full moon cast the city in a silver light. It must have been well past midnight.

Throwing off my blanket, I moved to the foyer, where a worried Finneas paced back and forth. His goat eyes widened when he saw me. "Lady Aelia, I was doing my night checks, and when I went to check on Baylis, her bed was empty." His brows knitted with concern. "I don't know how she could have gotten out. There are guards posted at every door."

The fog of sleep still clouded my mind. What was Baylis up to? An inkling in the back of mind warned me it wasn't good. Either she had been taken or she was up to something, and my gut told me it was the latter.

"I'll go after her." Grabbing my cloak, I headed out into the night. The chill of dread crept down my spine. Clotho's words echoed through my head. "*Someone close to you will betray you.*" But was this a betrayal, or was this some kind of retribution from the queen of the Undersea? A sister for a sister. That would make sense. The sylph loved to enact revenge they saw as "fair." Killing my sister would be fitting.

Bile rose in the back of my throat. What if she had Baylis? What if she was going to behead her just like I did to Calypso?

Two of the Hunt followed me. Their armor nearly silent as we moved cautiously through the city.

"Where did Baylis go the other day when she left?" I asked one of the soldiers.

"To the temple of Ammena, my Lady. To pray."

"Did she speak to anyone?" The sounds of our boots on the cobblestones echoed through the silent night.

"Just one of the priestesses and one of the other parishioners."

"What did they look like, the parishioner?"

"It looked to be a Barbarian. He was sobbing to himself in the last pew. Baylis chatted with him briefly before one of the priestesses came to help him.

"Hmm... how tall was he?"

"Very tall. I'd sworn he was a giant if not for the signature tattoos of his clan."

Could it have been Gideon in a glamour? No. Even the best glamours couldn't change a man's size, and Gideon was lean. I bit the inside of my cheek nervously. Was Baylis a traitor?

Fuck. I should have kept a closer eye on her. I should have known. But her memories... they were all so fragmented I couldn't make sense of them.

We approached the deserted temple. It was customary for them to stay open all night for those seeking the goddess's guidance and for those down on their luck to take refuge. But something was off. The hair on the back of my arms pricked, and my senses heightened.

The two soldiers must have sensed it, too. They silently drew their swords from their sheaths.

"Do not hurt Baylis," I said, touching the door. "And be careful."

Both the soldiers nodded.

Holding my breath, I pushed open the door, preparing to strike, but only darkness met my gaze. In the center of the room stood a giant statue of Ammena holding the apple she used to make the humans, bathed in moonlight. My eyes raked over the curvaceous goddess from her long braids down to her feet, where my eyes beheld a sleeping figure.

"Baylis," I gasped, a little louder than I intended.

Weapons clanged in the distance, and the sound of racing footsteps followed.

"Go, see what that's about. I'll get my sister."

The Hunt headed off toward the sound of footsteps.

Slowly, I approached Baylis so as not to frighten her. She looked so fragile, crumpled at the feet of a goddess who had never once answered her prayers.

"Baylis," I whispered. "What are you doing here?"

"Waiting for you," a deep voice echoed through the darkness, but still my sister slumbered.

"Who's there?" I grabbed my sword, preparing to strike.

From the shadows, a hulking man emerged. His dark curls tied back, revealing the sloped ears of an elf. The rune tattoo on his earlobe marked him as a Barbarian, but from which clan I did not know. He must have been a half-breed. Even through his thick wool tunic, I could make out the markings of a body honed by heavy weightlifting. Was this one of the sea queen's mercenaries or... My mind spun with possibilities.

"They call me Alwin." A devilish smile cut his scarred face in two.

"What do you want?" I asked, gripping my sword tightly.

"You." A hand clasped around my mouth from behind while the tip of a knife—cold-pressed iron—seared into my lower back. I sucked in a breath as the assailant buried the knife deeper.

Using what power I had; I launched into the captor's mind. A patchwork of shoddy traps awaited me—each one old and rusted.

This man had been trained to keep telepaths out but never used any of what he'd learned. I kicked over a beartrap covered in cobwebs. His mind was an old storeroom with a cot in the corner and a little stove burning hot. Upon a tiny shelf were paintings—cherished memories. Some of him as a child, hugging his mother. His first kiss. It was a shame I'd have to wipe all of these.

One by one I lit the pictures on fire.

Lots of mercs liked the comfort of places like this—hidden away where no one could find them. The man with a hefty frame and wide-set eyes sat trembling in the corner.

"Pl… please… miss… don't hurt me. They said you could break minds, and I didn't believe them."

Rage rattled my bones. This fucker stabbed an iron knife into my back and now he wanted mercy?

I leaned down in front of him, so our eyes met.

"You know I was a merc like you once?"

He nodded.

I ran a hand down his wide jaw.

"I know the struggles mercs face. Never truly able to call any place home. I would never hurt one of my own."

His beady eyes brightened.

I was playing with him now. He didn't get to threaten me and live. Whatever was happening on the outside, they wouldn't dare risk killing him by attacking me.

"Don't worry, I won't make one of my own suffer."

"Oh, thank you, miss."

A clever smile tugged at the corner of my lips.

I snapped my fingers and the fire in the stove tipped over, consuming the room.

The merc scrambled to his feet.

"Wha—"

I snapped my fingers and the man froze. In the real world he would easily overpower me, but I was the master of this domain and could control every muscle in his body. Of course, I gave him the ability to turn his head and open his mouth, but that's as much mercy as he would get from me. Blowing out a breath, I fanned the flames before leaving his mind.

The sound of shrieking pounded in my ears. When I opened my eyes the merc lay in a crumpled pile on the floor. The horrible sound was coming from the other, larger, man.

"Shut up, you blathering idiot," Baylis said, standing tall, arrow nocked at me.

The pieces of the puzzle slid into place.

My heart sank.

Clotho had been right. Baylis was working with Gideon. This was no scheme of Calliope's. My sister had engineered this very moment from the day she woke in the Woodlands; even before that. A bitter taste filled my mouth.

"Why, Baylis? Why are you doing this?"

She pulled her bow string tighter.

"You thought he loved you, but he never did. He told me. You were nothing to him. Just a means to get the Midlands. You couldn't even produce an heir."

"Baylis... listen to yourself. I'm your sister." My words stuck in my throat. "We are close. We've walked through hell together. Don't let this monster come between us."

She pulled the bow string tighter.

"You're the monster."

I sighed.

"You're right, I am." I launched into her mind. Running for the library of her thoughts as fast as I could. She wanted to eject me, but she couldn't, she wasn't fast enough. The walls closed in on me, tighter and tighter until I could barely move, barely breathe. My hand touched the brass knob of the library. With my last ounce of strength, I pulled the door open, using it as a shield. The big cat pounced but hit the closing corridor and knocked himself unconscious. I ran into the library, shutting the door behind me.

Baylis appeared in a cornflower blue silk dress. She clapped her elegant hands together slowly.

"Very clever, sister. I didn't think you had it in you."

Rage boiled in my blood. My own sister had betrayed me. Had this been her plan all along? How could she love Gideon after everything he'd done to me? How could he be good to her when he wasn't good to me? Was I so undeserving of love?

Chest heaving, I tried to still my breath and organize my thoughts.

"You... you did this?" I pointed to the library, which was now intact, every book where it should be.

She gazed up at the shelves of books then back to where the feline had lingered.

"I had help, of course... but yes, this was my idea." A wicked smile crossed her delicate face. The ghost of the girl I used to know stared back at me. This was not my sister. This was one of Erissa's creations. A monster posing as a lamb.

"Why? He destroyed our home..." My voice cracked just like my heart.

"*You* destroyed our home," she snapped at me.

"You can't possibly believe that." Tears streamed down my cheeks. I truly had no one left. Everyone I loved was gone. Caiden was a stranger, my mother was locked in a tower, and my sister hated me. My knees buckled beneath me. I was alone—a ghost with no past.

Her eyes narrowed at me.

"You were the one who told him where the weaknesses were. You were the one who told him to attack. He showed me." She tapped her temple.

Ice ran through my veins. He'd changed the memory. His own

memory to suit his needs—to get Baylis to hate me. Bile lapped at the back of my throat. She'd never trust me again.

"That's not what happened. You have to believe me."

"I have all the proof I need." The room filled with smoke, clogging my lungs. I coughed, and she pushed me out of her mind.

The same smoke filled the temple. Choking, I reached for my sister, but the smoke didn't affect her.

"See, I can play games too," she said.

The world went dark.

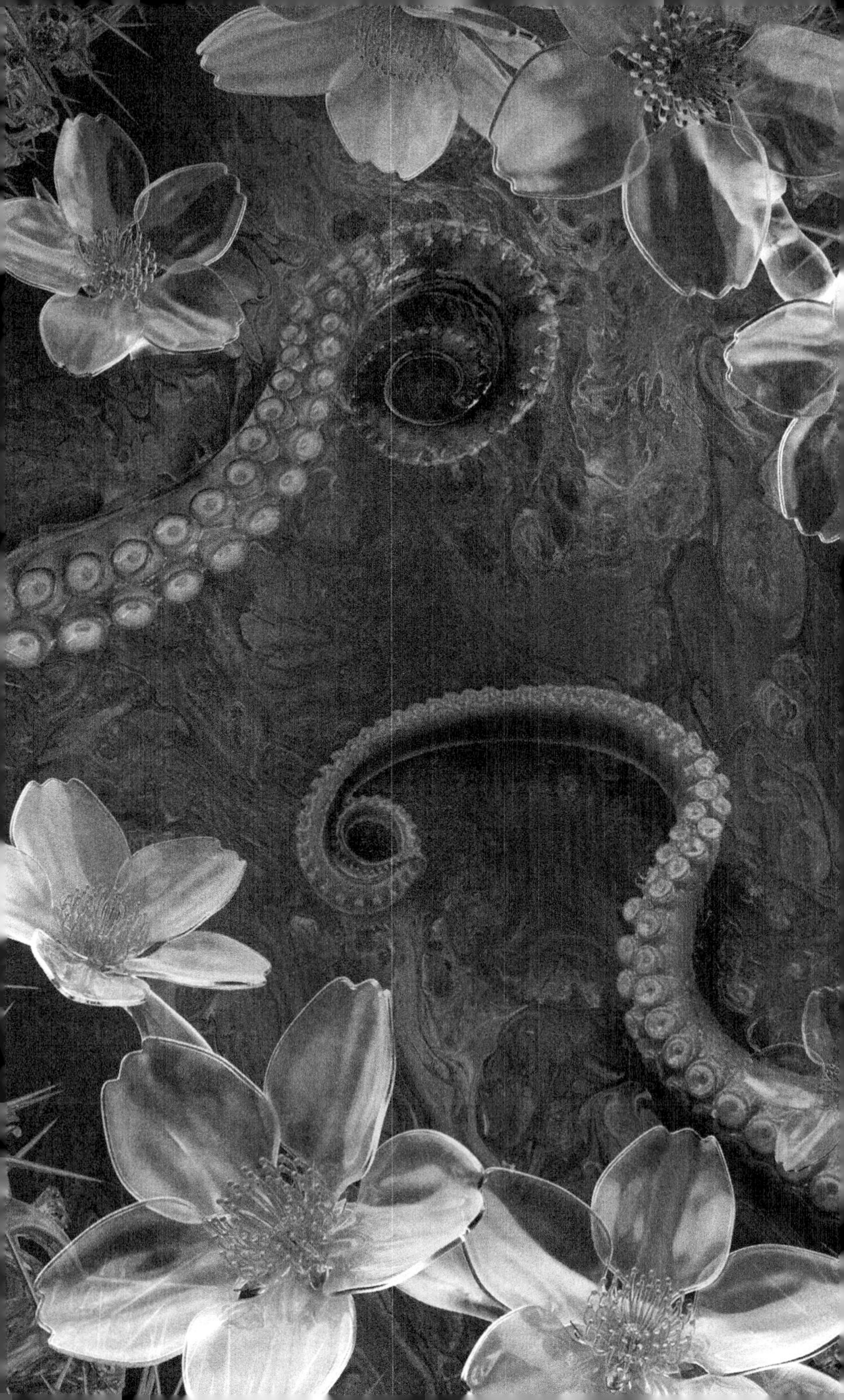

31 THARAN

THARAN TRIED TO SLEEP, BUT HIS MIND WAS A MESS OF TANGLED thoughts. The escape from Elohim left them all scarred. He twisted the whisper stone, not caring if anyone saw him talking on it. He needed to hear Aelia's voice, but nothing came through the line. Worry tugged at his heart, but he pushed it to the side, he had other things to worry about. Aelia could take care of herself.

Driving the horses as fast as they could go, they raced through the elven Kingdom of Eden toward the Woodland Realm. If they were lucky, they could find a portal along the way, but Tharan knew word of their treachery would spread quickly, and a sylph traveling with six elven maidens and four dire wolves would look suspicious on an average day.

When the horses needed a rest, they stopped beside a babbling brook. The women flung themselves out of the carriage, running down to the stream.

Tharan threw up a silencing shield.

"What are we going to do with them?" Hopper asked, hands on his hips.

Tharan brushed his auburn locks out of his eyes.

"We're going to give them a home in the Woodlands if that's

what they choose. Otherwise, they are free to live wherever they like."

"You think our kingdom is just going to accept them? And what about the kingdoms they came from? Won't they be wanting their women back?" Hopper paced back and forth in the pale moonlight, rubbing his sharp jaw. "This is a mess. We could have six different elven kingdoms knocking at our door, and for what? They will hunt these girls down if need be. I will not let sylphs die for these women. Figure out something to do with them, Tharan."

"Okay, well, I can't really send them back."

"You can, and you will."

"We'll discuss it once we're back in the Woodlands." Tharan didn't want to send the women away, but Hopper was right. Their kingdoms would want them back.

Sumac cleared her throat. "Why don't we just leave them here?"

Hopper looked at the women sitting on the shore of the brook. "I mean, we could. They're elvish. A town will accept them."

"And we can ride on the back of wolves with the Hunt. They're faster than a carriage, and we will be home in no time."

Tharan bit the inside of his cheek. The cool night air sent a chill up his spine. He wanted to help the women, but he also had to think about his kingdom. He had done them a favor and gotten them out of the Elohim.

Sighing, he said, "Alright, let's go. Leave them the carriage. Tell the driver to take them anywhere they want." His stomach turned at the thought of betraying the women, but he couldn't take them with him.

Sumac whistled, and the Hunt sauntered over on the backs of their massive wolves. Their silken fur shone in the pale moonlight. Tharan patted one on the head. The fierce beast whined like a puppy for more.

"She never even does that for me," the rider said.

"I have a way with creatures." Tharan mounted the wolf, hooking his arm around the soldier's waist.

Sumac and Hopper did the same.

"Hold on, my Lord. Once I let her go. There'll be no stopping her."

Tharan took one last look at the women chatting by the river and swallowed the guilt gnawing at his heart.

He tried the whisper stone one more time. Nothing.

"Sir? Are you ready?"

The hairs on the back of his neck stood on end, but he pushed the ill feeling away to focus on the immediate worries.

"Let's go."

The riders clicked their tongues, and the wolves sprinted off into the night. Tharan didn't dare look back.

They rode until the sun crested over the horizon. Far from home but closer than they had been, they took shelter in a copse of pines.

"We'll let the wolves rest during the day. It's safer for us to travel at night," Sumac said, dismounting.

"How far are we from the Court of Malts? At least they'll be friendly and likely have a portal."

Sumac looked at the sky, squinting to make out the fading stars. "I'd say we're at least two days' ride away."

He rested his head against the trunk of a tree. The night's events took a toll on him, and his body begged for sleep. Twisting the whisper stone, he hoped the sound of Aelia's voice would calm him.

He waited for the sound of her high-pitched voice, but she

didn't answer. Was she mad at him? They'd quarreled over the proposed marriage, but he thought they'd moved past it.

A sinking feeling in his stomach told him what he'd always feared. Something had happened to Aelia, and he hadn't been there to protect her. Once again he'd failed the one he loved.

"You okay?" Hopper asked, taking a seat next to Tharan.

Not wanting to alarm his friend, he buried the feeling deep down. He had to be strong for his kingdom. He had to get them to safety, then he could worry about Aelia.

"As well as can be expected." Tharan rested his hands on his chest. "I knew it wouldn't be easy to persuade Arendir to help us. I just didn't think it would be this hard." He rubbed the bridge of his perfectly straight nose. "And those women… we just left them."

Hopper let out a long sigh.

"You have always wanted to save everyone, Tharan. You are king now, and it's high time you learned that not everyone can or wants to be saved."

"I know," Tharan said, shutting his eyes. "But I hate that I can't."

"That's just something you must learn to live with."

"I suppose you're right."

Tharan awoke just as the sun was setting. A feeling of dread sat like a pile of rocks in his stomach. Something wasn't right. Hopper still slumbered beside him, and Sumac prepared the wolves for another ride, her short hair pulled back behind her ears. Was it his guilt from leaving the women eating him up inside, was it Aelia, or was it something else?

"Ready to go?" Sumac said, tightening the girth of one of the massive wolves.

"I guess so," Tharan replied. "Sumac?"

She arched a brow at her friend.

"Does something feel... off?"

She scoffed.

"Something has felt off since the moment we entered the elven kingdom. You'll have to be more specific."

Tharan got to his feet, wiping the snow from his behind. "I have a terrible sense of dread."

"You're the one with the intuitive powers. You'd know better than me."

"I don't trust myself after what happened back there."

Sumac placed a hand on her friend's shoulder. "Don't beat yourself about it. Anyone would have been disoriented in that situation."

Tharan swallowed the hot taste of embarrassment.

"A king should know better."

"You have only been king for a short while. No one expects you to be your father right away."

Tharan sighed.

"I know, but he was so beloved. I don't want to dishonor his memory."

"Your father was beloved, that is true, but he never got to be with this true love, Elowen. You honor him by doing what he could not. You honor him by trying to save the forest he loved so dearly," Sumac said, her normally stoic demeanor softening.

"Thanks."

"We better get going," Hopper said, rubbing sleep from his eyes. "If we ride through the night, we can hopefully make it to the Court of Malts by tomorrow."

They rode silently and swiftly as shadows through the vast lands of the elven Kingdom of Eden, so named because it was considered heaven to the elves. With its rolling hills and fertile soil, it provided everything the immortals needed to survive.

The stillness of the forest unnerved Tharan. In the Woodlands, he could control the magic, but here, the magic was different. Older, wilder. Arendir said he knew everything that happened on this continent. Why hadn't he alerted his outposts the women were missing? Was he lying or…

As if summoned by Tharan's thoughts, an arrow whizzed past his head.

"Archers! In the trees!" Sumac called. Her rider pulled their wolf to the left. Arrows rained down upon them, striking the wolves but not harming them. Dire wolves were bred to have thick hides.

"Split up!" Tharan called. The four wolves and their riders divided. He hoped they would all make it to the next court alive. His heart raced as they moved swiftly through the trees.

The elves wanted him alive; they wouldn't kill him, but they would do whatever it took to stop him.

The elves' breath turned to vapor in the cool night air, giving away their hiding places. Tharan summoned his power. A fire lit beneath his skin, and he fired poisonous darts into the trees where the mist lingered.

The sound of an elf falling to his death and landing in the snow echoed through the silent forest. How many were there? How did they find them?

"Hold on," the soldier guiding his wolf said, turning the creature violently and flinging Tharan to the ground.

The cold snow bit into his skin, and a rogue stick ripped a gash in his cheek.

"Got you now," a voice said through the darkness.

Tharan tried to shake the stars blurring his vision. He stumbled to his feet, calling more spikes to his hands.

"Stay back."

Five elven soldiers emerged through the darkness, tall and

sleek, their armor shining in the moonlight. Tharan gripped his sword.

"Come with us, Lord, and no one will get hurt."

A dire wolf growled behind him.

"Leave now, or I will have my wolf tear you to bits. You will not take me back to Elohim."

"Are you really foolish enough to attack an elf on our own land?" The elf smirked, and tiny creases formed around his eyes.

Tharan's palms wetted with sweat, his rapid breath turning to vapor in the cool night air, casting a halo around the ethereal figures. A smile tugged at the corners of his mouth.

"What are you smiling at, half-breed?"

"You forget, oh wise and ancient ones... this may be your territory, but I am king of the Alders in all domains." The sound of creaking wood echoed through the forest. The elves looked around, trying to find the source of the sound, but it was too late for them.

Spikes jutted from the forest floor, skewering two of the men before they had time to scream. Their bodies dangled limply on the wooden spires.

This far from the Woodlands, Tharan's power was not as strong as he hoped. He tried to call for more, but something was blocking his magic.

The lead elf let out a cackle.

"Something wrong, Lord?" He tapped a purple jewel on his headdress. "It's a violet diamond pulled from the deepest depths of the Cheyne Mountains. Blocks magic." He circled Tharan, looking down his long nose at him. "But yours must be particularly strong to have any of it work." He snapped his fingers, and Tharan felt the power drain from his limbs. He'd seen a stone like this once before.

"Fucking elves," he whispered under his breath.

"Yes, you recognize this stone, don't you?" Twigs crunched beneath his feet. "It's similar to the one my sister, Lysandra, had."

Tharan swallowed hard. Lysandra had a brother. This must be him. He'd been waiting five hundred years for this moment. "Cassius."

"Yes, I'm surprised you remembered after so long." His sunken eyes raked over Tharan. Tall and slim, he resembled his sister with his high cheekbones and sharp-cut chin. "Kneel," he said in a voice as soft as tanned leather.

Magic swirled around Tharan like a snake around a mouse. His eyes darted to the wolf behind his back, and the two elves flanking him with their bows nocked.

"Don't even think about it," Cassius said smugly.

"Don't hurt the wolf."

"Come with us, and I won't have to."

"You'll have to kill me."

Cassius clicked his tongue.

"Now, now, you can't do that." He removed his gloves before sending his fist flying into Tharan's jaw.

Tharan's teeth came down hard on his tongue at the impact, filling his mouth with blood. He knew better than to let them see his pain. He'd been in plenty of fights with elves.

"Is that the best you've got? You're growing weak in your old age." He spit blood into the snow.

Another ringed fist hit his cheek, slicing his skin. He sucked in a breath, trying to dull the pain.

"A scar to match the one my sister gave you."

"I loved your sister, Cassius. She betrayed me. It was war."

Cassius crouched so his eyes met Tharan's.

"Even in war, they send the bodies of the dead home. My parents had no ashes to cast into the wind. Do you know what that was like for them?"

Tharan clenched his jaw.

"She knew the risks when she decided to play both sides."

The crack of Tharan's nose breaking echoed through the forest, and he fought back tears welling in his eyes, kneeling in the frigid snow.

The dire wolf snapped at Cassius, but he dodged its powerful jaws.

"Watch your dog, or I'll wear his hide as a pelt."

Tharan held a hand to the wolf, who backed away, bowing to his king.

"Good," Cassius said, malice gleamed his blue eyes. "Get up."

Tharan did as he commanded, just as two long swords skewered the two elves before him.

Blood trickled from their stunned mouths.

"Wha—" the wolf pounced on Cassius before he could finish his sentence, shaking him violently and flinging him into the nearest trees.

A flash of green light lit up the forest. Cassius could portal.

Sumac and the other soldier sliced the heads off the two remaining elves.

"Try coming back from that," Sumac said, pulling the teeth from the man's mouth.

"Good work," Tharan said, wiping the snow from his pants.

"It was nothing. My teeth collection was looking a bit thin." She held up an incisor to the moonlight. "These will do nicely."

"Let's get out of here before Cassius comes back with reinforcements." A thousand pins and needles poked into Tharan's skin as his magic returned to its full strength, healing his broken nose.

Climbing onto their wolves, they sped off into the forest. Tharan let out a sigh of relief, but somehow, he knew he hadn't seen the last of Cassius.

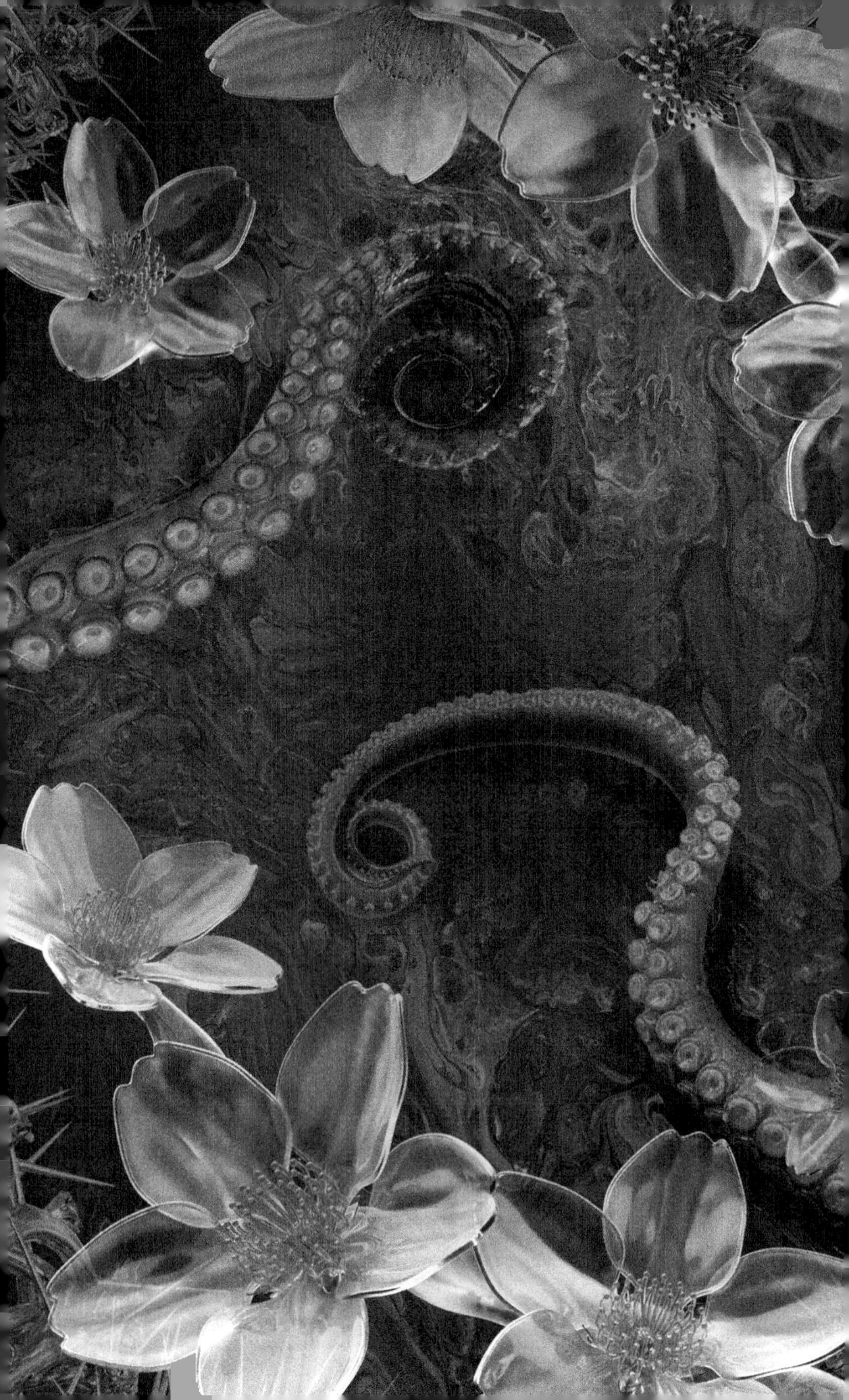

32 THARAN

THEY RODE THROUGH THE NIGHT, NOT BOTHERING TO STOP AND rest when the sun's first light crested over the horizon. Tharan held his breath for most of the trip, not daring to look back.

The Court of Malts was the smallest of the Wild Courts, inhabited mostly by halflings with a penchant for brewing the continent's finest ales. Tharan's muscles relaxed as they crossed the boundary. The aroma of barley and hops wafted through the air even in the dead of winter.

They stopped in the capital city of Dunhaven, a cheery little city where cottages lined the cobblestone streets. Old ale barrels, no longer fit for use, served as flowerpots and bar tables. The halflings went about their evening, carrying roast hams and other assorted goods home for dinner after their shifts at one of the many breweries ended. Situated between the elven territory of Eden and the Atruskan River, it was said that the fertile soil and clean water made the ale taste better.

They stopped at the Hoppy Toadstool for the night.

"Feels good to be back on sylph soil," Tharan said, stretching his arms wide.

"This was a free kingdom before the Sylph and Elven War.

Halflings aren't technically sylph. They're just magus," Hopper corrected his friend.

Tharan and Sumac both rolled their eyes.

Children came running from their houses to catch a glance of the dire wolves.

"Look! Look!" they cried, their jovial faces filled with awe.

"Careful," one mother said, holding her toddler's chubby arm.

"It's alright," Sumac said. "They're really just big puppies." She whistled, and one of the giant wolves lay down in the middle of the street so the children could pet him. His fluffy tail wagged relentlessly as the little ones patted his soft fur and kissed his wet nose.

Once the children had their fill of the beasts, Sumac let the wolves run free for the night in the nearby woods. Despite being domesticated, the canines still loved moonlit hunts.

"Let's get a pint and relax," Sumac said, dismissing the other riders to do as they pleased for the evening.

"I'm starving," Tharan said, trying to hide his growing concern for Aelia. Perhaps a full belly would help.

The Hoppy Toadstool was a lively, cozy place with plush armchairs, roaring fires, and a string band. The walls were lined with intricate wallpaper depicting forest creatures.

The trio sat at the old oak bar, where a halfling with curly brown hair and hazel eyes greeted them warmly.

"Lord Greenblade," he said with a smile that lit his entire face. "To what do we owe the honor of such a distinguished guest? Surely, you'd rather stay in the Brewer's Palace."

Tharan's cheeks reddened, and he waved the barkeep off.

"No, no, I am a man of the people. The Hoppy Toadstool is just fine for me."

"If you say so, sir." He shrugged his little shoulders. "What'll it be?"

"I'd quite like a hot cider with rum if you have it," Tharan replied.

"Course, my Lord, anything for you. And for your companions?"

"Two blonde ales, please," Hopper spoke for both himself and Sumac.

The barkeep nodded, pouring the pints before getting the hot cider for Tharan.

"It's on the house, my Lord. The brewmaster would never forgive me if I charged you."

Tharan went to object but knew it was pointless. Instead, he smiled and raised his mug to the halfling. "Thank you."

"What a day," Hopper said, sipping his ale.

"It's been over a month since we left the Woodland Realm. It'll be Ostara before we know it." Tharan took a long drink of his cider, letting the hot beverage warm his cold bones.

"Can't come soon enough. I'm tired of winter," Sumac added.

"To making it out alive." Tharan held up his mug, and the three cheered. He wanted to put on a good face for his friends. They didn't need to be burdened with his growing suspicions that Aelia was in danger. They'd nearly escaped death earlier. It wasn't right to add to their load. As king, it was his job to lighten it.

They drank and ate until late into the night, but despite their celebration, Tharan still couldn't shake the feeling of trepidation lingering over him. Maybe he was just tired. When the candles burned low, and most of the other patrons had gone home for the night, the three friends went to their rooms.

Tharan sank into the squeaky bed. He didn't care that it was made for someone half his size. He was grateful for a soft place to land for the night. His head felt light from the spiced cider, and he wished Aelia was beside him. He twisted the whisper stone in his ear and waited for her voice at the other end.

Nothing.

He tried it again.

Still nothing.

A chill crept down his spine, and he swallowed the bile rising in his throat. Something happened to Aelia.

They had to act fast if they were going to save her. He should have left the moment she didn't answer the whisper stone. He should have trusted his gut. Now she was in danger, and he was ten steps behind.

He flung the blankets off his bed and crept down the hall to Hopper's room.

"Trinty, can a man get any rest these days?" He answered the door, half naked, running his hand through his thick green hair.

"No, apparently not. We need to go. Something has happened to Aelia." Tharan burst through the door, throwing his friend a shirt.

"What? Hold on. What's going on? What happened?" Hopper asked.

"I don't know. I just have a feeling something terrible has happened to her."

Hopper stood with his hands on his chiseled hips.

"So, you want to run out of here on a feeling?"

Tharan nodded.

"And to where exactly? The Alder Palace? Ruska?"

"I…" Tharan bit his pouty lower lip. "I don't know exactly. Ruska, I guess."

Hopper sighed, tapping his foot on the floor.

"Fine, get your things together. We'll get them to open the portal to Ruska. Leave the wolves here."

Tharan nodded and said, "I'll get Sumac."

"She's not going to be happy."

"She's been my best friend since I was six. She'll be fine."

Hopper made a face that said *it's your funeral.*

"Just get the portal open," Tharan said, disappearing into the dark hallway.

"Anything for my king. Even in the middle of the night. When I am exhausted," Hopper mumbled under his breath.

"I heard that!" Tharan called down the hall. He went to knock on Sumac's door, but she opened it before he could land the first wrap.

"I heard everything you two said. These walls are paper-thin." Her dark hair fell in a crisp bob to her collarbone, and her white tunic popped against her dark skin. "I took the liberty of getting ready."

"You're always one step ahead of me, Sumac."

"As it should be." Sumac donned her wool cloak. "Now, let's go save your girl."

They hurried out of the Hoppy Toadstool into the snowy streets of Dunhaven, where dawn had yet to rise.

"The portal house is this way." Hopper ushered them to a tiny stone cottage with two red and white toadstools out front. "I woke the master, and the portal should be ready." He turned the brass knob, and the door creaked open.

A swirling portal of green light awaited them. Next to it, a small halfling with curly gray hair and spectacles waited in his pajamas. Dark circles ringed his eyes.

"Thank you," Tharan said.

The man nodded. "Anything for my king."

Tharan slipped through the portal, followed by Sumac and Hopper.

The portal spat them out in the center of Ruska. The city still slumbered, but the first light of dawn was just beginning to crest over the horizon.

They hailed a petty cab outside the portal and sped through the quiet streets to the Alder Townhome. Tharan fiddled with his rings nervously, wishing the cab could go faster. The hairs on the back of his neck pricked.

"If you pulled me out of bed for nothing, you're going to owe me one," Hopper said as the carriage jostled him around.

"I hope you are right, and I am being ridiculous." Tharan gazed out the window. The city sped by, blurry in the morning haze.

The Alder Townhome sat silent on a hill. Tharan didn't bother to pay the cab driver before he burst from the carriage and through the carved double doors.

"Lord Greenblade," Finneas said, startled at the sight of his master. "We… we weren't expecting you."

"Is she here?" He paced frantically through the parlor and then up the stairs. "Is Aelia here?"

"No, my Lord, she went after her sister last night, and they have not returned."

Tharan's eyes glowed a verdant green, full of power and malice. "Where did she go, Finneas?"

"I didn't see, your Highness," the satyr bowed low, trying to hide his trembling voice.

Tharan did his best to keep his temper at bay. There was no use raging at his servant. That was not who he was. Taking a deep breath, he flattened the wrinkles on his vest.

"Did the Hunt go with her?"

"Yes, my Lord, but they have not returned either."

Tharan paced around the foyer, running his hand through his auburn locks. He needed a cigarette.

Amolie appeared at the top of the stairs.

"Tharan? How did you know to come?" She rushed down the stairs, her curls bouncing in her wake. "I wanted to tell you, but I didn't know how to get a message to you, and you know how

Aelia can be. She always comes back." She flung herself into his open arms. Her tears stained his cloak.

"I'll find her, Amolie. Don't you worry." He patted her head reassuringly.

Amolie wiped the tears from her hazel eyes.

"Calliope, the sea queen, is after her. I'm afraid she may have laid a trap for her."

Tharan bit the inside of his cheek nervously; he had to be strong now, for all of them.

Turning to Hopper he said, "Call a meeting with the sea queen. Here. In Ruska."

Hopper nodded and quickly drew up a royal invitation, his mouth twisted as he concentrated.

"I need your signature, my Lord."

Taking a deep breath Tharan calmed his nerves before signing the invitation with big, swooping letters, and sealing it with the sigil of the Alder King in hot wax.

"I expect you to deliver this to Ursula by hand."

Hopper took the parchment and headed out the door.

Tharan pulled his long hair back and tied it with a leather strap—anything to distract himself from the panic bubbling in his gut.

"Sumac?"

She stepped into the study, having already changed into her Wild Hunt Armor.

"Yes, my Lord?"

"Let's see if we can retrace Aelia's steps. Where's Amolie?"

"I'm right here." The witch donned a pair of wool slacks and a cape. "I think we should go see Conrad. He has the siren's song. The queen will want that if she's going to give Aelia back."

"Smart."

"He's probably still at the infirmary. They might not let us in this early."

"They'll let me in." Tharan turned to Sumac. "See if you can track Aelia. Amolie and I will go to see Conrad."

The three parted ways.

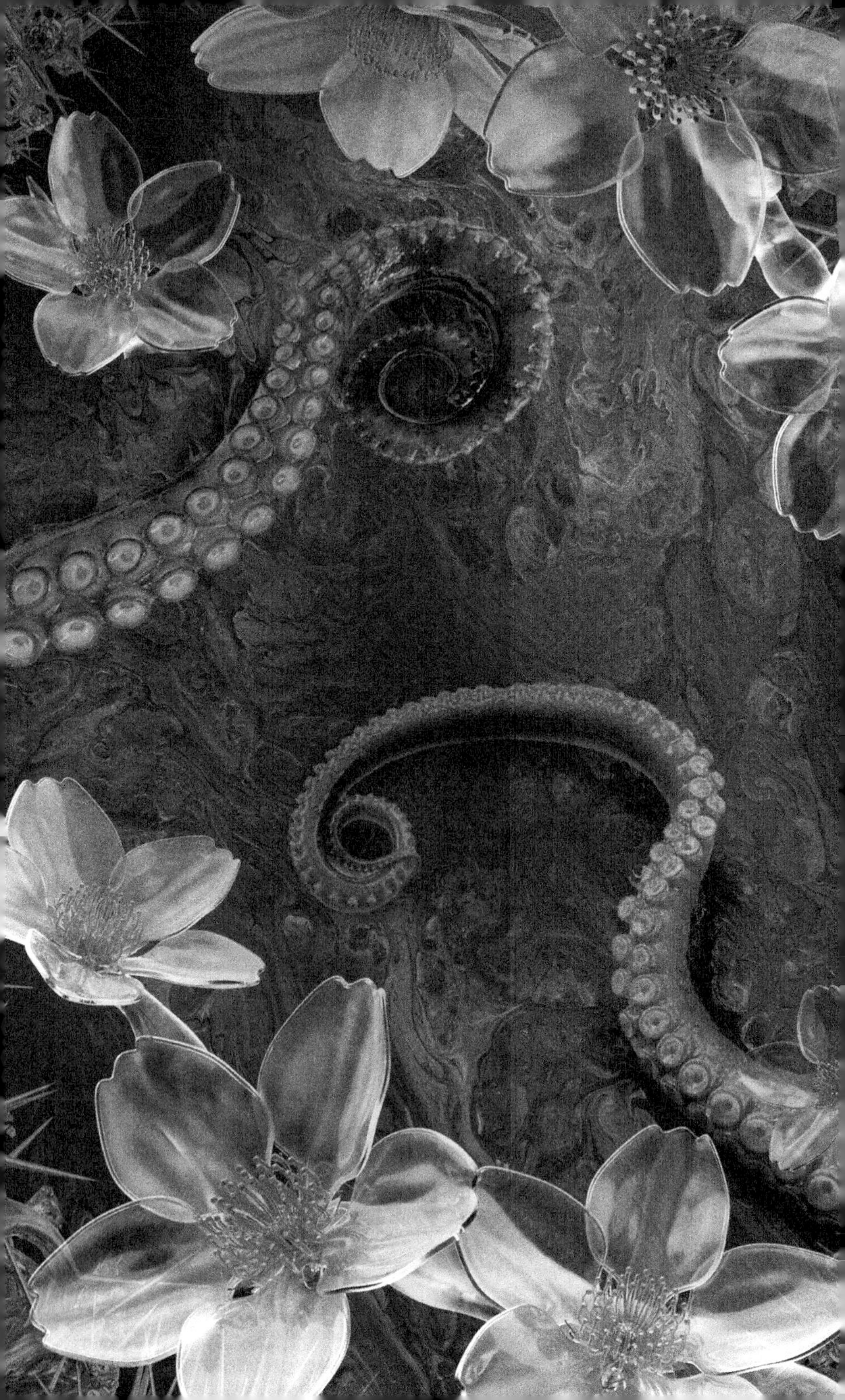

33   THARAN

The first rays of dawn's light streamed in through the infirmary's stained-glass windows. The staff took one look at the flames burning in Tharan's eyes and didn't bother to stop him when he burst through the double doors.

"Conrad?"

A stunned healer pointed to the back. "Last bed on the right."

A gush of wind followed behind Tharan. Magic sparked in the air, and copper fizzled on his tongue.

The patients slept soundly in their beds as he tore through the great room, but Conrad's lay empty.

"Where is he?" Tharan growled. Rage built in his chest with each breath he took. His acute hearing caught the faint sound of muffled moans of pleasure. Tharan stalked to the nearest closet, yanking the door open. Inside, Conrad had one of the healers on his lap, her face twisted in a mixture of pain and pleasure. His hand covered her mouth in a desperate attempt to quiet her moans.

"Get out," Tharan said.

A shit-eating grin crossed Conrad's long face.

"Tharan! It has been too long."

"I need the song, Conrad."

The woman, still sitting on Conrad's lap, flitted her eyes between the two.

Conrad's expression darkened, and he ran his hand through his dark hair flippantly.

"It's mine. I got it fair and square from your paramour. In fact, I'd say I got the short end of the deal. Lost my entire ship."

Tharan gripped the collar of Conrad's shirt, lifting him to meet his gaze. The woman on his lap slid off, making a quick exit.

"Calliope has her, and I need it to get her back."

Conrad's eyes widened.

"I'm sorry, Tharan, I can't. I need it."

"For what? So you can control the seas? You're already a revered pirate. What else could you need?"

Conrad held up his arm with the bargain snaking its way through his veins like ink.

"I need my magic back. Without the song, I can't get past her guards to kill her."

"What did you do?"

"I made a bargain with the serpent queen. She said she'd grant me the ability to breathe underwater if I brought her the Cursed Coin of Coronado, but when I delivered the coin, she cast me out without fulfilling her end of the bargain."

Tharan released his friend.

"How are you not dead."

"With a concoction of potions that may kill me before the bargain does."

Tharan clicked his tongue.

"How could you be so foolish as to make a deal with the serpent queen?"

"I thought I was smarter than her."

"Ha! She has been haunting men for a millennium."

A look of resignation washed over Conrad's face.

"I need my magic back, and the only way to do that is to use the siren's song to control her guards."

Tharan was torn between wanting to save his love and helping his friend.

"You know what Aelia is, right?"

Conrad raised a brow. "Yes, I know of her powers."

"Then give me the necklace, and when I have freed her, we will use her power to break the guards' minds."

Conrad's brows now knitted as he considered his friend's offer.

"Would she be able to do something like that?"

"There is a well of untapped power stored within her. There's no telling what she can do."

Conrad sighed.

"Fine. Take it." He unclasped the necklace and handed it to Tharan. The warm stone lay heavy in his hand. "You know I'm a romantic, Tharan."

A smile tugged at the corners of Tharan's lips.

"I know you are a good man under all those layers of stone."

"Get out of here before I change my mind." Conrad rolled his eyes at his friend.

Tharan looked at Amolie, who nodded to the pirate.

"Thanks again."

The two headed back to the Alder Townhome as fast as they could.

"I called for Roderick and Caiden. Hopefully, they can portal here quickly," Amolie said, taking a seat in the study. "I guess I should tell you. I think they found something."

Tharan stoked the fire, thinking of the torture Calliope could inflict upon Aelia. He barely heard Amolie.

"What? Oh? Really?"

"Yes."

Tharan let out a breath. "Well, that's good." Taking a seat across from Amolie, he lit a cigarette. "I don't know what I'll do if anything happens to her, Amolie."

Amolie let out a small chuckle.

"Aelia is good at getting out of shitty situations."

"I know, but this feels different." Tharan let out a plume of smoke.

"It *is* different when you love someone."

"I guess you're right. I was never this protective with…" His voice trailed off.

"It's different when you're young and in love," Amolie said. "You were both soldiers in the heat of battle. Everyone knew the risks. The fact that you worry about Aelia means you care. Trinity, I worry about her, and I've known her for years. Although, half the time, she gets herself into messes. I'm extra worried about Baylis. If Calliope knows they're sisters, she'll likely take her head as payback."

Tharan took another drag from his cigarette.

"That's what I don't understand. Why were they out late together?"

Amolie shrugged.

"Finneas said Baylis disappeared sometime in the middle of the night. Slipped right out under our noses."

"Hmm… that's curious. Has she ever done something like that before?"

"I've only known her for a short while. I cannot say what she would and would not do."

Tharan stared into the fire. What was Aelia going through right now? Was she hurt? Afraid? Dead? He shook his head. He couldn't think like that. He needed to believe she was alive, and he would save her.

"Amolie, did Aelia tell you what she saw in Baylis's mind?"

"Yes, she thought she saw Baylis with Gideon." Her eyes went wide. "No... you don't think."

A little voice in his head *did* think Baylis was behind this, but for Aelia's sake, he didn't want to believe it. If Baylis was a traitor, it would break her.

"I don't know, Amolie. Calliope seems like the obvious answer. She has every reason to kidnap both Baylis and Aelia."

"But how would she get Baylis out of the house unseen? For Trinity's sake, the Wild Hunt is guarding the place. Would she really be that daring?"

Tharan took another drag from his cigarette.

"She's cunning, that's for sure. But what if..."

Amolie finished his sentence.

"What if Baylis left on her own accord?" She tapped her bottom lip. "What if she was sleepwalking and just happened to slip past the guards? Calliope could've had Ursula watching for just such an occasion."

"Could she have slipped something to one of the servants? Had them drop a potion into Baylis's drink?" He rang a bell, and Finneas came running.

"Yes, my Lord?"

"Who was on duty the night Aelia disappeared?"

"This is a small staff, my Lord. We all work every day there are house guests."

Tharan ashed his cigarette.

"When Sumac gets back, I want them all interviewed. We need to know if they saw anything."

"Yes, my Lord." He bowed and left the room.

"I should have paid better attention to my senses. I should have known she was in trouble," he said, pinching the bridge of his nose.

"Don't beat yourself up about it. I'm sure you were busy with the elves."

Tharan sighed.

"You've got that right. Found out my mother was alive shortly before I discovered she's been sharing a bed with my grandfather for a century."

Amolie's mouth fell open, and her hazel eyes went wide. "I don't even know how to respond to that. Why?"

"I had the same reaction." Tharan took a drag off his cigarette. "The elves' magic is fading. I think some of them are even dying. They are desperate to get their magic back. So desperate they are essentially breeding their most fertile women to their own families."

"I always thought they used humans for that."

"Humans are a conduit for magic, but they are not inherently magical. I think all the mixing with the humans bred the Breath out of the elves. And if they are no longer immortal… they are no longer the supreme race of the continent." Tharan ashed his cigarette and rang for a servant.

"So, this is a way for them to stay in power, even if they damage the gene pool in the making." Amolie asked.

Tharan cocked his head, looking at the posh library around him.

"Power is a drug no one wants to quit."

Amolie nodded. "I think that's why the witches didn't take a side in the war. I think they thought they were powerful enough to withstand any conflict."

"Foolish of them," Tharan replied.

Finneas entered the study again.

"Yes, my Lord?" He bowed low.

"Would you bring us some wine and a bite to eat? Perhaps croissants with cheese?"

"Yes, my Lord." He backed out of the room.

"You're going to eat the food and drink the wine when you think someone may have poisoned Baylis?"

Tharan shrugged, repositioning himself in the seat. The fire cast a golden hue on his ethereal features.

"Oh, I'm sure word has spread throughout the house by now that I am suspicious of the staff. No one would dare to poison me now."

Finneas returned carrying a tray with a hand-blown carafe of wine and an assortment of pastries, which he set on a little table between Tharan and Amolie.

Hopper came stalking into the study, pulling his hood back to reveal his distinguished face. "It is done. Ursula is delivering the letter."

"Thank you. Did she seem like she knew anything?" Tharan asked, pouring himself a glass of wine.

Hopper shook his head.

"You never can tell with the mer. Slippery folk, even when on dry land." He helped himself to a pastry topped with melted cheese before taking a seat at the large oak desk in the back of the room.

Tharan thrummed his fingers on the arm of the chair. A mixture of guilt and anger swirled in his mind.

"I shouldn't have left her. I should have been here. If I were here…"

"Don't blame yourself. You both had a job to do," Hopper said.

On the outside, Tharan remained calm and collected as any king should… While on the inside, he was raging against himself. Who else *was* to blame? He should have been here.

"How can I be king if I cannot keep the ones I love safe?" He took a drink of his wine.

"You are a king, not a god."

Tharan twisted a stray lock of hair around his finger. "Technically…"

Hopper scoffed at his friend, and Tharan rolled his eyes. He needed to focus on the upcoming meeting. It wouldn't do anyone any good if he was unprepared and unfocused. Reluctantly, he pushed his guilt deep inside himself.

"What should we know about Calliope?"

"Well, she's incredibly smart and incredibly conniving, vindictive…" Hopper trailed off.

"Oh, so just like every sylph, elf, and human on this continent."

"Except all of them don't control every creature living underwater. Calliope is more powerful than Arendir and could crush him if she wanted to. The only reason she doesn't is because she knows they would come after the Wild Courts, of which she is one. She likes to keep to her own business, and I much prefer it that way as well."

Amolie chimed in, "So, were the mer enslaved by the elves too?"

"No," Hopper answered. "Calliope slipped into the river before her throat could be slit. She and Eoghan… er, the Alder King, worked together to fight back against the elves, which is how she became a member of his court."

"The mer aren't technically sylph, although I guess you could consider their ability to breathe underwater and walk on land a 'gift.' They worship both Illya and Manannán mac Lir."

"Like the witches are and aren't human," Amolie said.

"Yes," Tharan said, leaning back in his chair. "If I had to guess, I'd say witches are the result of humans and sylph mating and then the offspring of two half-breeds and so on and so forth, until witches appeared to be human but still retained a bit of magic."

Amolie chuckled.

"That makes much more sense than what they tell us."

Hopper arched a brow, but Tharan's mind was a million miles

away. To wherever Aelia was. How could he sit and enjoy his friends while his love was out there suffering?

Sumac waltzed into the room with the grace only afforded to those of the Hunt. "I've found something."

Tharan sat up straight in his chair. He didn't dare to hope for good news.

Sumac continued, "The snow covered most of their tracks since they left, but what I could make out seemed to point toward the temple of Ammena."

Now that was intriguing... "Go on..."

"The trail went cold after that, but I did find one of my men half alive, huddled in a closet in the temple."

"Is he going to be alright?" Tharan asked, concern flaring. There were few who could take down a member of the Hunt. Either they were ambushed or outnumbered.

"He'll live. The healers took him to the infirmary. I could not find my other man who went with them." Her face knitted with concern.

"Only someone both powerful and well trained could take down two riders of the Hunt." Tharan ran his thumb over his bottom lip as he gazed into the fire. "Could Calliope's mer have done this?"

Sumac cocked her head.

"Perhaps. They are certainly known to be ruthless. But usually, they devour their victims."

Amolie's already pale face whitened at the thought.

Tharan's stomach churned. First Aelia, now two of his Hunt. He could feel his authority slipping away and a heat rising in his veins.

"Perhaps that is what happened to the other soldier," Tharan said, trying his best to keep his voice calm.

Sumac nodded.

"We will question him when he wakes. He was so bloodied I didn't bother to ask him any questions."

"Did you find anything else?"

"The priestesses said there looked to be signs of a struggle in the temple, but they cleaned it up so no parishioners would see."

"Of course they did," Hopper chimed in.

"So, we have three missing people and no leads. Perfect." Tharan took a long drag from his cigarette.

"I guess we'll have some answers in a few days," Hopper said.

"In a few days, both Aelia and Baylis could be dead." Tharan slammed his fist on the arm of his chair. "I wish there was more we could do besides wait."

"Do not be rash, my King," Hopper said. "I know you want to save your beloved but acting out of emotion and not thinking things through could get her killed."

Tharan took a deep breath and sat back in his chair.

"You're right. There's no use getting worked up."

"I need you to keep your head on straight. Calliope is a slippery fish, and if you're upset, she will rub salt into the wound."

"Alright, alright." Tharan threw up his hands in surrender.

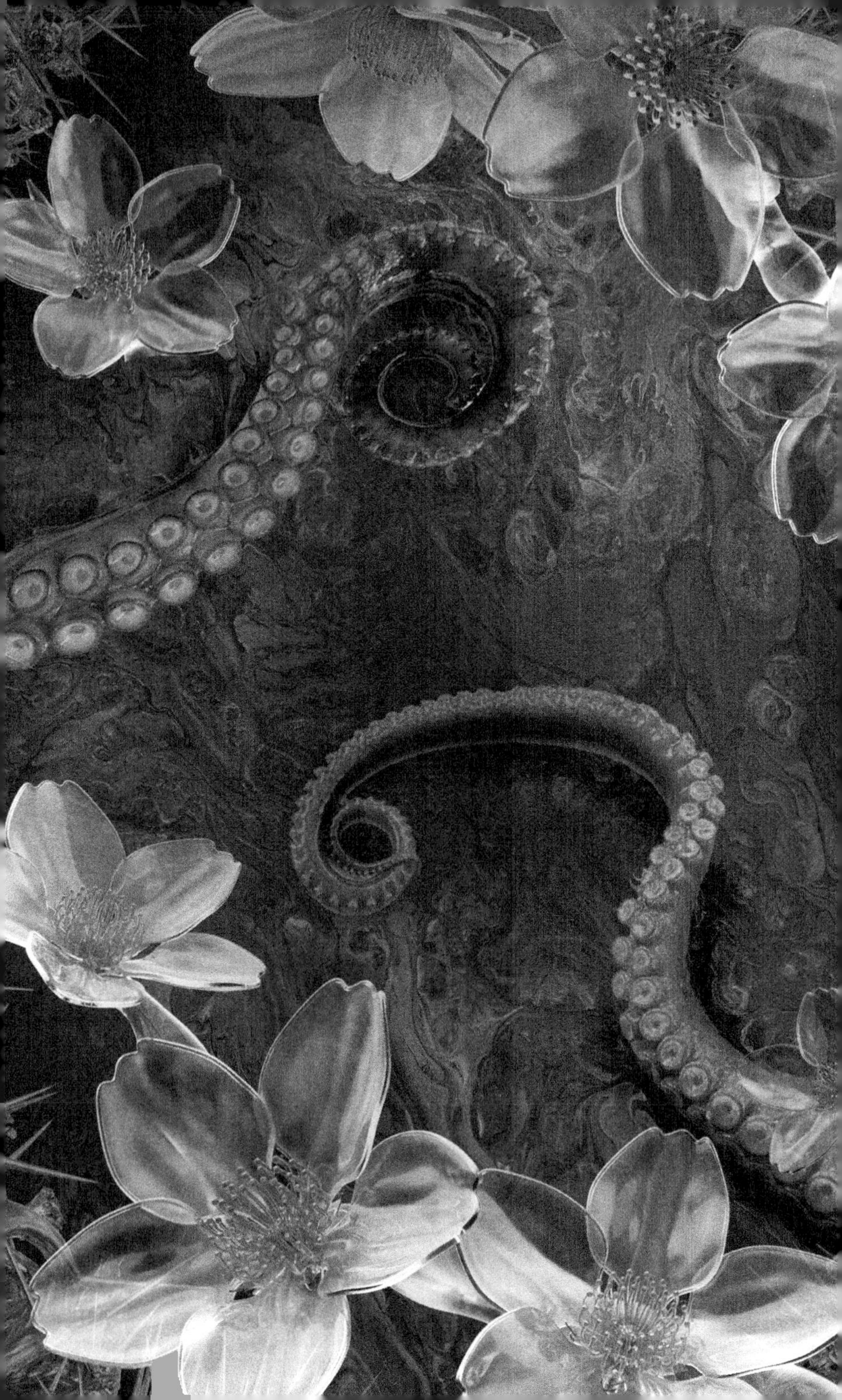

34 THARAN

Tharan's fingers shook as he buttoned his expertly crafted pourpoint to the top of his chin, his mind a mix of anger and worry.

He brushed his long auburn hair before placing the golden antler crown atop his head. Kohl ringed his eyes, making them pop.

"Well, you look fierce," Hopper said, leaning against the doorframe. His hair was tied back in a tight knot, and he wore his traditional emissary outfit of finely milled black wool with the golden seal of the Woodlands on the breast depicting the Alder Palace.

"That's what I'm going for. This is my first meeting with Calliope, and I need to make a lasting impression."

"You always make a lasting impression, my King."

Tharan shook his head at his friend.

"You don't have to blow smoke up my ass all the time."

"Just some of the time." Hopper adjusted the crown on his head and wiped any stray hairs from his coat.

"Where are we meeting Calliope?"

"At the docks. In a warehouse. She won't venture far from water."

Tharan rolled his eyes.

"Of course. Do we think she'll bring Aelia and Baylis?"

"If she's smart, she'll have them nearby," Hopper replied.

Tharan took a deep breath, trying to conceal his nerves, and headed down to the foyer where Amolie, Sumac, and four members of the Hunt waited.

Pausing at the top of the stairs, he cleared his throat.

"Hopper, Sumac, Amolie, and I will go into the warehouse alone. The Hunt will watch for trouble from the land."

The stoic crew nodded.

Sumac twirled a knife between her fingers before sheathing it.

"Alright, let's go. The queen of the Undersea is dangerous and cunning. Do not underestimate her," Tharan said.

The party headed out into the night.

Tharan fiddled with his rings as he stared out the carriage's window. The snow was melting, and the first inklings of spring were beginning to sprout. Ostara would be upon them soon enough. He would be expected to preside over the Woodlands festival and provide blessings to newlywed couples. Ostara meant new beginnings. Perhaps if he got Aelia back, they would have a binding ceremony of their own. He shook off the thought. It was foolish to think that way when she clearly had hesitations about marrying him.

The carriage came to a halt in front of an unremarkable warehouse. With its peeling paint and warped boards, it was hardly a place for a meeting of two royal houses, but neither was stupid enough to meet the other on their turf.

The smell of old fish wafted through the air, turning Tharan's stomach. The Hunt took up a position at the front and sides while Amolie stood behind Tharan and the others, covered in shadow.

Sumac, Tharan, and Hopper walked to where the water lapped at the dock once used to unload goods meant for the Fates. In the distance, the Isle of Fate stood ominously bathed in moonlight. Tharan swallowed hard and touched the sword at his side, if only to remind himself it was there. A briny wind blew in through the open door, making him shiver.

Three creatures crawled from the water, their muscled arms hauling up their transforming bodies. Covered in darkness, their monstrous bodies shifted from tentacles and fins to long, sensual legs.

Tharan's pulse quickened at the sight of the sea queen. With skin the color of mint, long, white hair, and eyes as white and ancient as Tharan had ever seen, the woman towered over them—a force to be reckoned with. From the shape of her hourglass body, Tharan wondered how many men or women found themselves lured into her bed. She did not seem abashed at her nakedness but instead reveled in it. She snapped her fingers, and Ursula appeared from the shadows, wrapping a silken robe around her queen while another attendant placed a crown of shark's teeth atop her head.

Behind her, two of her attendants, a male and a female, slipped on robes of their own.

Calliope narrowed her pupilless eyes on Tharan.

"So this is the new Alder King?" She placed her hands on her hips. "I see you have inherited your father's strong jaw and height... and his penchant for troublesome women."

Tharan's blood boiled.

"Cut the shit, Calliope; I know you have Aelia and Baylis. Now tell me what you want to return them to me."

The queen of the Undersea wagged one long finger at him in disapproval.

"Now, now, that's no way to talk to a lady. Especially one you want something from."

Tharan took a deep breath, remembering Hopper's warning. He needed to keep his head on straight if he wanted Aelia back.

"Excuse my outburst," he apologized.

"I'll forgive it this once. Men in love are known to be hot-headed. If I listen closely enough, I can hear your heart racing in your chest." She tilted her head at Tharan like the predator she was. "You want to kill me, don't you, Lord of Nothing?"

Tharan squared his shoulders. She was goading him, and he knew it. He would not step into her trap. Everyone in the room held their breath as the two rulers sized each other up.

Hopper cleared his throat.

"We are here for a reason."

"Yes, we are. You want your little princess back." Calliope snapped her head at the diplomat.

"I have what you seek." Tharan pulled out the sapphire containing the siren's song. Strung between his fingers, the jewel sparkled in the faint moonlight.

Calliope sucked in a breath.

"You insult me, King. I want my sister back, and unless you know a necromancer. I don't think that's going to happen."

Tharan did his best to calm his racing pulse. He didn't want Calliope to think he was up to something, but at the same time, he wanted to call her bluff.

"I do know a necromancer, actually."

"Bullshit."

Turning to the darkness he called, "Amolie! Come out here."

The witch emerged. Her hood covered her face, but Tharan knew she was cursing him underneath. He hoped his little plan would work. Some witch covens dabbled in necromancy, but sea sylph were known to be suspicious of any land dwellers and notoriously bigoted toward witches.

Calliope growled at Tharan.

"A witch? Witches can't be trusted. Everyone knows that."

He laid a reassuring hand on Amolie's shoulder.

"This one can, and she will do her best to bring your sister back if you hand over Aelia, Baylis, and my soldier."

"There is no bringing my sister back. The siren guppies devoured her body," the sea queen hissed, her fangs on full display. "All I have left is her head."

Tharan knew this could go sideways quickly. If the queen felt threatened, she wouldn't hesitate to attack. He wanted to touch his sword, but neither did he want to alarm her further.

"Perhaps Amolie could deliver a message from the other side. Witches are known for their ability to speak with the dead."

"They are?" Ursula blurted out.

Calliope crossed her arms over her chest, eyeing the two with suspicion.

"Yes, I've never heard this about witches. Then again, I've not spent much time on land or in their presence."

Taking a deep breath, he collected his thoughts, trying his best to keep his pulse steady. He had to commit to this lie.

"Yes, they are. And Amolie here is one of the finest."

Amolie pulled back her hood.

"My king is too generous with his praise."

Calliope's mouth twisted with concern.

"I should take your beloved's head for what she did to my sister."

Tharan's heart clenched in his chest.

Calliope held out a hand for the siren's song, and he gently placed it in her palm.

Running her webbed fingers over the smooth stone, she whispered something under her breath.

Tharan and Hopper exchanged knowing glances, hoping this would be enough to quell the sea queen's rage.

Suddenly, Calliope's head snapped up.

"This is enough for now."

Tharan's shoulders relaxed.

"So you'll give me Aelia and Baylis back?"

A devious smile cut her macabre face in two.

"Oh, precious king, you have so much to learn."

Tharan's heart sank.

"You're not going to give her back, are you?"

An evil cackle echoed through the old wooden building. Calliope moved closer to Tharan. The scent of the sea lingered on her skin. Leaning in, she whispered in his ear, "I never had her, but if I find her before you do. I will skewer her and her sister's head on a pike in my throne room."

Before he knew what he was doing, Tharan clasped his hand around the queen's slippery neck.

"You lie."

Her eyes went wide as she struggled for air.

Power rippled through Tharan like lightning in his veins. Ursula and the queen's guards drew their blades, but the Hunt blocked their paths.

Tharan lifted the queen into the air. A green flame flickered in his eyes. He could end her here. He could take control of her kingdom and install a proxy of his choosing.

"Where is she?" he said in a preternatural voice drawn from the depths of his magic.

Calliope grasped violently at her neck.

"I swear I don't have her."

The fear in her eyes told Tharan she was telling the truth.

"The song. Give it back then, and I will spare your life."

"No."

He squeezed her neck tighter. The muscles tightened beneath his fingers as they worked harder to get air in.

"Are you sure?" he asked through gritted teeth.

"It's true." Ursula stepped forward; her eyes filled with tears. "She doesn't have them. I swear it!"

Tharan held out his hand.

"I'll take the necklace back then."

Reluctantly with a shaking arm, Calliope handed the sapphire to him.

A dark part of him wanted to end her and be done with it. That would start a war he didn't know if he could win. Would the Undersea bow to him? Would it matter? Calliope would never bow to him again. He glanced at Ursula, who could not be trusted but was loyal to her queen. She would be livid if he killed her queen, but zealots need a god, and he could be her savior if he installed her as acting regent.

Shaking the dark thought from his mind, he released Calliope.

Ursula ran to her queen, helping her up.

"How dare you treat my queen this way!"

"Careful, little mermaid," Tharan warned. "We've seen how fish fare on land."

She bared her sharp teeth at him and pulled Calliope back into the water. The queen's guards followed behind her. The splashing of their tails echoed through the empty warehouse.

Tharan let out a heavy breath.

"What was that?" Hopper hit his friend on the shoulder. "Do you want to start a war with the Undersea?"

He didn't want to admit the dark thoughts flying through his mind, but there was a part of him regretting letting Calliope go.

"Honestly? I considered it."

Hopper clicked his tongue at his friend.

"Your magic is wild. You need to learn how to contain it before you hurt someone, whether you mean to or not."

"It won't happen again." Tharan pinched the bridge of his nose. "But if she doesn't have Aelia and Baylis, then who does?"

Amolie stepped forward.

"There is only one other person who would want them."

"Gideon and Erissa?" Tharan said, his voice was no more than a whisper. "But how?"

Amolie shrugged.

"We all knew this was a possibility."

Tharan shut his eyes.

"Is someone going to tell us what's going on?" Sumac said, sheathing her sword. "We almost just killed a queen."

A fire rose in Tharan's blood.

"I would do anything to get Aelia back. Even if it meant war."

"I think it will." Amolie turned to Hopper and Sumac. "I believe Baylis was acting as a kind of double agent. Perhaps she does not know what she is doing. Perhaps she does. All we can do is try to get Aelia back."

"That backstabbing bitch," Sumac spit the words out as though they were poison in her mouth.

Tharan rubbed his face. His heart sank with the weight of his guilt.

"I told her she was being overly sensitive. I feel so guilty. I should have believed her."

Amolie sighed. "There was no way for you to know. For any of us to know for sure."

"Let's get back to the house and figure out a plan." He kicked at the old wooden floor aimlessly.

They rode through the sleeping city up to the hill, where the Alder Townhome stood silent as the grave—no candles burned in the windows. Two of the Hunt stood like statues at the gate.

"Someone is here to see the king," one of them said.

A chill crept up Tharan's spine.

"Who?" he asked.

"A knight from the Stormlands."

"Roderick?" Amolie chimed in. "Was his name Bonecleaver?"

"I believe so. Finneas let him in."

Amolie burst from the carriage, and into the house, before any of the others had a chance to take a breath.

Tharan and the others followed behind her to the parlor, where they found Roderick and Amolie wrapped in each other's arms.

Tharan cleared his throat.

"Sorry to interrupt, but I'm assuming you came here for a reason, Roderick."

Amolie and Roderick parted. Roderick bowed to Tharan. "There is, your grace." His face twisted with a mixture of fear and sadness. "It's Lord Caiden. He's gone."

"What do you mean, gone?" Amolie asked.

"We went to the races together, and he didn't return."

The hair on the back of Tharan's neck stood on end.

"What do you mean you went to the races together, and he didn't return?"

"He went to show Ora around the stables and never returned." He swallowed hard. "They found her body floating in the river the next morning."

The room sucked in a collective breath.

"They don't think Caiden…" Amolie couldn't finish her sentence.

"He hasn't been charged, but there are whispers rippling through the city—a council member's son. A lord, in his own right, goes missing, and the woman he was last seen with winds up dead in a river. It doesn't look good, that's for sure."

"But Caiden wouldn't. He's not like that," Amolie said.

"We know he's not, but you know how the city loves to gossip."

"What of Tonin and Tempestia? They must be devastated."

"They are distraught in so many ways, but the best way to help them is to find their son." He looked around the room at the faces, both new and known. "Where is Aelia?"

"She is gone too," Tharan said, stepping forward. "Disappeared a few nights ago with her sister. We thought the queen of the Undersea might have them, but alas, she did not."

"We think Baylis was working for Gideon the entire time. Our new working theory is she lured Aelia out and… well… I don't know," Amolie said.

Tharan ran his thumb over his bottom lip while he paced the room. "When did Caiden disappear?"

"Five days go."

"Same with Aelia. So Baylis must have been working with someone… likely Gideon, and Erissa must have been after Caiden. But why not come after me?"

. "They don't need to kidnap you. They know you will come for Aelia," Sumac said.

Tharan's heart skipped a beat. There, it was laid out before them, a twisted web made to ensnare him and the woman he loved. There would be no wedding on Ostara for them. The sky would turn dark, and the rivers would run red with the blood of those who thought they could play with their lives. Power coursed through his veins.

"I think I know where they're taking them… or at least where they will eventually end up," Roderick said.

"Go on…" Tharan said.

"You're not going to like it."

"Try me."

"The Court of Screams."

Tharan grimaced. "How do you know?"

Roderick sighed.

"It's a long story, but we found books from the original sylph families that led to a map pointing to the Court of Screams. The scholar… the one who they found in the river, helped us."

Tharan nodded slowly, mulling over the information. The Court of Screams was not a place any sylph wanted to trifle with, but if it meant getting Aelia back, he would go to the underworld and back.

"Erissa was severely burned at the battle of Ryft's Edge. She is powerful, and we know she's stopped aging." He tapped his finger on his lips. "Could she have used a glamour to make herself look like the scholar?"

"I knew Ora for years. Her voice was the same. Glamours don't change voices. Nothing seemed off about her in the library."

"Did you see her the night she disappeared?"

"Yes, she was in the suite with us at the races," Roderick said.

"And did she seem different?"

"I can't really say. I wasn't paying attention to her. I take the races very seriously."

Was Erissa behind this? Or had she hired someone to do her dirty work. He wouldn't put it past her to hire a look alike and then glamour them to do her bidding. If she had Caiden, then she would know the location of at least one of the Wells. His throat went dry at the thought.

"Hmm." Tharan rubbed his jaw. "Sumac, Hopper, find out if Caiden returned to the Woodlands."

They both nodded.

"What are you going to do if he did?" Amolie asked. "Are you going to turn him in?"

"He has not been accused of anything yet. We need to find out his side of the story before we do anything rash."

Amolie let out a sigh.

"Until he is charged, I will not consider turning him over, and the Council Courts are not likely to come looking for him in a Wild Court," Tharan assured.

"That's true," Roderick said. "There's another possibility."

"And that is?"

"He went to find the Well on his own."

"Well then, I guess the Court of Screams is our best bet. If he is not in the Woodlands, we shall have to make the journey," Tharan said.

Sumac interrupted, "You can't possibly be thinking about going there. It is suicide. They are a court as much as I am a butterfly. They worship pain. They think it brings them closer to the goddess. No one has entered that court for hundreds, maybe even thousands of years. Even the elves wouldn't touch it! I cannot allow you to risk your life. That is exactly what they want. They want you to come. They want you to fall on your sword for Aelia." She knelt before Tharan, tears in her eyes. "You have been my best friend since we were children. Please do not be this foolish. Let me or Hopper go. Let us take this arrow for you."

Tharan swallowed the dread bubbling in his stomach. "We will not sneak in."

Everyone gave him a puzzled look.

Looping his hands behind his back, Tharan paced the floor. "Just because they are uncivilized doesn't mean we have to be. Hopper?"

"Yes?"

"Ask them for a formal visit. Say we want to strengthen our alliances or something like that."

Hopper's mouth fell open.

"There is a possibility they could say no. We've been making a name for ourselves around the continent."

Tharan mulled over his friend's suggestion.

"Send a raven. If they say no, we'll think of something else."

"Yes, sir." Hopper turned to leave but stopped himself. "There's one more thing."

Tharan arched a brow.

"Get rid of the whisper stone. If they know you have it, they will use it against you."

Tharan nodded and pulled the stone from his ear. "Here, you keep it."

Hopper took the earring from Tharan before disappearing into the dark hallway.

Tharan turned to the rest of the group.

"I guess you should all prepare for a journey to the Court of Screams."

35 AELIA

My head throbbed, and my mouth tasted like dirt. A pair of cold-pressed iron manacles weighed heavy on my wrists, blocking my magic. I sucked in a breath and tried to push the searing pain of the stab wound out of my mind. My skin crawled. Getting out of these chains was my only hope of escape.

Shame and anger fought like rabid dogs in my chest. I should not have trusted my sister, and it weighed heavy on me. My sister was a traitor. My sister hated me. My family was destroyed.

A bare room met my foggy gaze. Wallpaper hung in tatters from the walls. The smell of burning wood wafted through the air. I tried to orient myself, but I was utterly lost with no window to see the sky. A chill sank into my bones.

Using the wall as a brace, I pushed myself to my feet. My knees cracked and stars blurred my vision, but I managed to stumble to the door. I pressed my ear to it, hoping to hear voices on the other side. Had Baylis been planning this the whole time? Bile burned in my gut, working its way up my throat and out of my mouth. How could I have been so foolish? I'd given her all the information she needed to destroy me and empower Gideon.

My brain burned for the calming smoke of a cigarette—or

better, a pinch of dust, but I wasn't that person anymore. I was stronger than that.

Voices echoed from the room beyond—a man's, deep and brooding, alongside Baylis's.

"Did you use the amulet to call Erissa?" Baylis asked.

"Yes," the man answered, his voice thick with annoyance.

"Well, we can't stay here long. They will come looking for her."

"That's the point. She's the carrot on the end of the stick."

"And what of your rival? You don't think she could have gotten one of them?"

"Kita is clever and cunning. I have no doubt she's been stalking the Lord of Lightning. Only time will tell if she gets to him before he discovers Aelia is missing."

My blood turned to ice in my veins. I was bait for Tharan and Caiden, but how would they know where to look? The heavy weight of dread settled on me. I looked down at my hands. All my fingers were still intact. They hadn't sent a ransom note yet. Reaching up to my ear, I felt the hole where the whisper stone had been. My stomach turned. They didn't need to send a finger. They could use my voice to lure Tharan out. Would Erissa be that foolish? We didn't have the exact locations of the Trinity Wells. Did she?

The sound of heavy footsteps scraped across the floor. I placed myself in the same position I had been in and closed my eyes.

The smell of salt stung my nose before the man entered the room.

"Alright, Mind Breaker. Time to wake up." The slap of his palm stung against my cheek, and I groaned.

"Who are you? What do you want with me?" I asked, playing dumb. If I could get him to identify me as a person and not a mark, perhaps I could work my way into his good graces.

"Name's Alwin and that's all you need to know, Mind Breaker."

I bit my lip. If Alwin was like any of the other barbarians I'd encountered before, he would underestimate me.

"What are you going to do with me?" I put on my best puppy-dog eyes.

He set a pitcher of water and a bucket down.

"Just sit tight."

This wasn't working, and with the iron searing into my skin and boiling my mind, I couldn't waste any more time.

"Where's my sister?"

His amber eyes flitted to the door.

"She's too much of a coward to face me? I can't break any minds with these iron shackles around my wrists." I shook the manacles behind my back, and the ball of power bound in my chest twitched. *It's never done that before.*

Alwin chuckled.

"I have nothing to say to you," Baylis's voice echoed from behind Alwin.

"Just tell me why?" My voice cracked with desperation.

"I told you why. You destroyed our kingdom. Our life. All for what? For the love of sylph, who you can never marry?" She chuckled, and I did not recognize her voice.

My heart sank. My sister was truly gone.

"And now you've shacked up with another one." She clicked her tongue. Alwin moved, and her slender frame came into view.

Gone were her gowns. Now, she wore the red armor of the Highlands. Her blonde hair was braided in a crown on top of her head—an iron widow made from the remnants of my sister. Gideon had torn her down and rebuilt her from the ground up, just like he had me. Only this time, he succeeded. I was his test subject. She was his success. Or should I say, Erissa's success?

"Gideon tricked me. Manipulated me. Just like he's doing to you now."

Malice flared in her gray eyes.

"Manipulated? He set me free. All my life I have been cleaning up your messes. Being the good little sister while you got to trollop around the continent playing dignitary."

An invisible dagger seared through my heart. This was not my sister.

Was I really that horrible to be around? I bit the inside of my cheek. Maybe I was.

I shook my head.

"What? No. It was never like that. We each had our duties. We knew what we had to do to keep our kingdom running."

"Yes, and you conveniently got the job where you got to leave. Do you know what it was like for me? To watch Father slip away day after day and never be able to escape?"

I didn't know what to say. Had Gideon wiped her mind entirely and rewritten the very fabric of who she was, or had she always harbored this resentment, and Gideon just found a way to release it?

"I… I'm sorry, Baylis."

"Save your fucking apology for someone who cares." She scoffed and left.

"I'm not getting paid enough for this shit," Alwin muttered under his breath, shutting the door behind him.

I sat in silence for a long time. My heart was heavy with a thousand emotions. Anger and guilt fighting a war inside my mind. I should have protected her, but what could I have done? I was fighting my own demons for years while Gideon was shaping her into the acolyte he always wanted. My breath turned to vapor in the cold air. With no window to the outside, I couldn't tell what time it was. They left me water but didn't realize I couldn't drink it with my hands tied behind my back. Was this intentional cruelty or just sheer stupidity?

I had to get out of here, but first, I had to remove these manacles. Twisting my wrists in the shackles, I tried to slip my thin wrists out, but they were tight. I gazed around the barren room. There was nothing here to help me. I would have to get out another way.

I pushed myself up against the wall again. The iron still burned my wrists. I listened at the door for their voices but could hear nothing. They could have put up a sound shield, though Baylis didn't have that kind of magic, and I didn't suspect Alwin did either.

I tried the knob, but it was locked. *Shit*. Okay, it's time for plan B. I kicked the door as hard as I could.

"Hello! I need to relieve myself!" I called to no one. "Hello! Did you hear me?"

Silence answered my call.

Examining the door, I noticed its age. The hinges surely hadn't been tightened in years. Could I risk making that much noise? No. Best to try and find another way out. A poker leaned against a fireplace on the side wall. If I could angle it just right, I could break the taut chain binding my hands. That's if I could get the poker to stand straight.

I blew out a breath, annoyed at my lack of options and even more annoyed I let myself get into this situation.

Using the fire poker as leverage, I hooked the ring of my manacles over the top then pulled as hard as possible against the metal spike, praying the base held. For a moment, I thought it would work. The metal bent against the strength of the poker, but it did not break.

Gritting my teeth, I pulled harder. "C'mon." They did not break. Exhausted and still sore from the wound in my back I slunk to the floor. I'd have to find another way out. I looked at the door once more. It was risky, but I could probably break it down.

I weighed my options: I could stay here and wait for them to call Gideon or Erissa or whoever, or I could try to make a break for it.

Fuck it.

Hurling myself at the door, I lowered my shoulder to take the brunt of the impact. The wood creaked and groaned as I slammed my body into it, but it did not break. Pain throbbed through my shoulder. I checked the hinges again. They were looser. Dare I try again?

I held my ear to the door. If anyone were on the other side, they would surely have heard me. I braced myself for Alwin to come bursting through, trying to think of an excuse. My blood pressure rose, and I winced.

Nothing.

No one.

Huh.

I backed up one more time and hurled myself at the door again. The wood cracked. The door fell open, and I along with it. Dust billowed in the air and clogged my lungs. I coughed, trying to clear it. My head buzzed.

I tempered the lightness in my chest. A small success, but Alwin and Baylis could be lurking around any corner.

Slowly, I got to my feet, using the wall for support. I looked around for a way out. Two low-burning candles lit a decrepit hallway. Just like in my room, wallpaper peeled from the wall, revealing exposed boards and old brick. The smell of dust and cobwebs filled the space. Moonlight trickled in through the boarded-up window. Were we still in Ruska or someplace else?

I tip-toed down the hall toward what I thought was a staircase, using the dim moonlight as my guide, listening for any sign of

Baylis or Alwin. The ancient floorboards creaked beneath my delicate steps. My heartbeat pounded in my ears. I wanted to cut and run, but I needed to be smart. Being flighty would not help me now.

I held my breath as I worked my way down the stairs. Each step brought me closer to freedom. A fire roared in the hearth. I could make out Alwin's silhouette slouched in a chair. His massive hand was still wrapped around a bottle of amber liquor. The sound of his snoring drowned out the crackling fire. Did he have the key to my shackles? Even as I thought it, I knew he didn't. Baylis wouldn't risk it. She was a hardened warrior now. A master of her domain, she wouldn't trust just anyone with the keys to my freedom.

My eyes flicked from the parlor to the door. Adrenaline coursed through my veins. Turning my back to the knob, I slowly turned the brass handle. Its engravings made dents in my skin. My hands fumbled to turn the knob. I scanned the stairwell, the parlor, and the blackened hallway for any sign of Baylis.

A winter wind whipped violently at the door.

Click. The door opened, and a chill swept through the foyer. My joy soured in my mouth.

Shit.

I didn't have time to think. Pushing the door open, I ran into the snowy night. Thin air filled my lungs. A forest of pines surrounded the cabin. The moon loomed overhead. Two horses dug in the snow. If only my hands were free, I could ride away from here.

I scanned the dense forest. Baylis was out here. I could feel it in my bones. But where? My breath turned to mist in the cold night air. I couldn't stay out here in the open for long. I needed to run. But where? Judging by the sky, we were east of Ruska. Likely Eryndor or Leighton. A human kingdom was better than an elven one, and Leighton was known to have dense forests.

I headed east into a thicket of pines. The snow hadn't melted here yet. Baylis would be able to track me easily. I just had to hope she was far away from wherever this was.

An arrow whizzed by my head, lodging itself in a tree. *Shit.*

I sunk into the snow, resting my back against a tree trunk.

"Don't worry, sister, I can't kill you," Baylis's high-pitched voice echoed through the forest, surrounding me. She was everywhere and nowhere at once. I needed to move.

I listened for the sound of her feet crunching through the snow, but I could not hear them over the crows cawing in the canopy.

The snow burned my skin. I had to run. My vapored breath would give me away if she came close. I scanned the trees. We were on a steep hill. This wouldn't be easy, but I didn't have another choice. I had to move forward.

My knees cracked as I braced myself against the tree. *Do it, Aelia, just run.* My pulse quickened, and my mouth dried. It was now or never. I started down the hill. Arrows whizzed by. She was trying to scare me. If she wanted to hit me, she would have.

"Don't make me hurt you!"

Birds took flight. The sounds of their flapping wings echoed through the silent forest. I could feel her behind me. I was a mouse running from a cat in a maze of her making. She'd let me run myself out. Let me think I was going to escape. Then she'd strike.

But I wouldn't give up that easily. If she wanted me so badly… I'd make her work for it.

Zigzagging my way down the hill took everything in me to keep upright. With my hands tied behind my back and my feet slipping in the snow, a fall was imminent—arrows whizzed by me.

"Stop, Aelia. There is nowhere for you to go."

I didn't answer. I wasn't trying to go anywhere, just trying to escape her.

"Aelia! This is your last chance."

She trained her bow on me.

I closed my eyes and threw myself down the hill. Sticks and rocks bruised my skin, and blood filled my mouth. Whether it was from my tongue or my nose, I couldn't tell. As I tumbled down the hill my foot caught on a root, twisting until I heard an audible *crack*. A hot scream ripped through my lungs, but still I kept rolling. Rocks battered my body. Pain radiated through me as I finally came to a halt at the bottom of the hill. Pushing myself up, blood poured from my face, staining the pristine snow below. I dragged my leg, trying to keep moving.

The cold tip of sharp steel ripped through my back, and my breath turned to a wheeze. I cried in pain.

The birds silenced.

I pulled in a ragged breath. My lungs filled with blood and the gash in my back ripped anew. Sinking to my knees, I prayed Ammena would take me, but I knew I wouldn't be that lucky.

My vision tunneled. The sweet, earthy scent of the river wafted in the air.

"I told you not to run," Baylis chided me.

Another heavier pair of footsteps approached.

"Pick her up. Erissa is not going to be happy," Baylis snapped.

"I'm still going to get my coin, right?" Alwin asked, scooping me up. My broken body lay limp in his massive arms.

I gasped for air.

"What happens if she dies?"

"She's not going to." Baylis released my manacles and magic rushed through my veins, healing my wounds. Tears trickled down my cheeks. I stared up at the sky, watching the birds flee the forest. I pictured Tharan's face. The smell of pine on his glowing skin. The taste of his mouth on mine. The way his eyes brightened when he laughed.

The tears came harder, mixing with the blood already on my face.

I shut my eyes.

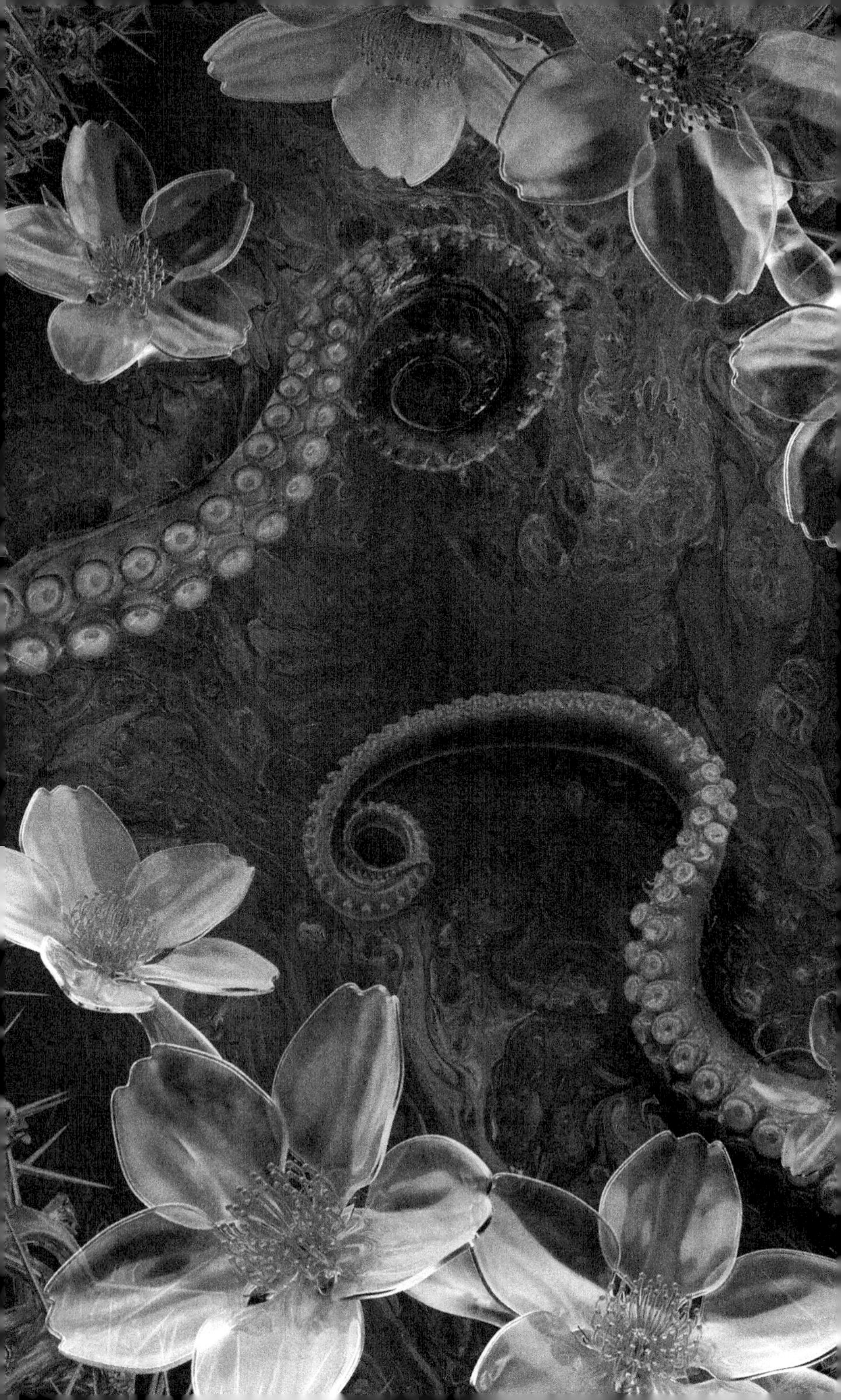

36 CAIDEN

"Open your eyes, prince." A voice like smooth caramel in milk surrounded Caiden's senses.

He blinked rapidly, trying to bring the world into focus.

"Who are you? What do you want?" he eked out. His throat begged for water, and his back ached from lying on hard stone. A cold dampness sunk into his bones. Nearby, a fire crackled. The woman who impersonated Ora stood before him. The fire gilded her sharp features. Long, red hair snaked its way down her back in round knots. A rigid nose and almond eyes marked her as hailing from the desert. Could she be a Rasa? What would they want with him?

"It's not best to exchange names with the product," she said, leaning down before him.

His hands and feet were bound in iron chains.

"What are you talking about?"

She held up a glass of what appeared to be water.

"Drink. We can't have you die before I get my payment."

Caiden pursed his lips.

"It's not poisoned. I swear. The contract holder specified they wanted you alive."

Caiden let her tip the glass to his lips. Cool water rushed into his mouth, and he gulped it down. His body begged for more.

"Easy, prince. Don't choke yourself," she said, pulling the cup back.

"What did you do with Ora?" His words caught in his throat. He already knew the answer but wanted to hear her say it.

"She went for a swim, you could say."

Caiden grimaced.

"I'm sure they've found her body by now," she continued.

"What is a Rasa doing out of the desert? Aren't you all a member of the same cult?"

A smirk tugged at her thin lips.

"Worry about yourself, prince."

"Well, you kidnapped me. I'd love to know why?"

"I don't ask those kinds of questions. I just deliver the target," she said matter-of-factly.

Caiden arched a brow. "And where are you delivering me, exactly?"

She leaned back on her palms, her expression unreadable.

"Great question." She squeezed an amulet in her palm. Its red jewel looked similar to the one Erissa used to ensnare Baylis. Could that be who hired her? "I'm to wait for the contract holder to arrive. I've been squeezing this stupid thing for hours."

A raven cawed in the distance, dropping something at the mouth of the cave. The mercenary grabbed it before unrolling the tiny parchment. Her mouth twisted with concern as she read it. Letting out a huff, she crumpled the paper into her pocket.

"My contractor?" Caiden asked.

"None of your business."

Caiden blew a blond lock of hair from his eyes.

"If someone has a contract out on me, I should be at least entitled to know who it is and how much they're offering you. My family is very rich. I could probably match it."

She ran her hand over the amulet.

"They promised me your weight in gold."

Caiden chuckled. "Is that it? I can match it. Have my father send it."

She mulled over Caiden's proposition, placing a piece of willow bark on her lower lip.

"Nah. You see, your contract is special. If I go back on it, my counterpart, Alwin, could just capture you again and claim he's a better merc than me." She slapped his cheek lightly. "And I can't have a rumor like that getting out."

"Your reputation is worth more than gold?"

She narrowed her amber eyes on him.

"My reputation is everything."

Caiden considered his words carefully. If her employer was Erissa or Gideon, their threat alone would not be worth his release.

He needed to get out of here, but with the chains binding his wrists and ankles, it would be nearly impossible. He needed to get her to release him. Everyone had a weakness; he just had to keep talking to her.

"What was in the note?"

"None of your business." She skinned a rabbit for her dinner.

Caiden scanned the cavern. A bow and a curved sword rested against a boulder. This woman was well trained. The Rasa were known to be fierce warriors but rarely left the desert. Had she been excommunicated from her people, or did she choose to leave on her own?

"Well, considering I'm in your care, I think it is."

"Marks don't get a say in how they're treated." She skewered the rabbit on a stick and stuck it into the fire. The smell of burning flesh filled the cave.

"Could you at least tell me where we are?"

"No. And if you don't shut up, I'll gag you."

Caiden closed his mouth. He knew when to push and when to pull back. She was a mercenary—a killer for hire. Her fuse was likely short.

He watched as she devoured the rabbit, pulling the flesh from its bones with her teeth like an animal. Her weapons were well made—mercenary work paid well. Was this a custom of the Rasa people, or had she become feral from being out in the wild for too long?

When she finished her dinner, she rose, pulling a sack of wine from her pack. She drank deeply, red liquid dripping from her mouth. She wiped it on her arm.

When she'd finished, she grabbed Caiden's arm, hauling him to his feet.

"What's going on?"

The mercenary bent down, unlocking the shackles binding his feet.

"We need to move out, and I released the horse." Their eyes locked. "If you try to run from me, prince, I will bring you within an inch of your life."

Caiden swallowed hard and nodded.

She buttoned a wool coat up and over her mouth. Then, she pulled a hood over her head so that only her eyes could be seen. She fastened a cloak around Caiden before pulling up his hood as well.

"Can't have anyone recognize those blond locks." She attached another chain to Caiden's shackles and the other end to her pack before equipping her sword, bow, and arrows. "Let's go," she said, dowsing the fire and tugging on his chains.

Caiden's stomach rumbled, but he didn't say anything. The mercenary wouldn't be sympathetic to his plea.

No stars blanketed the sky as they made their way through a thick wooded forest. The smell of snow and pine filled the air, and only the sound of their feet on the snow echoed through the forest. Caiden tried to orient himself, but it was nearly impossible without the stars. He'd have to wait until sunrise.

They walked and walked through the dense forest. Snow soaked Caiden's boots, sending a chill up his spine and through to his core. How was the merc navigating without a light? Could Rasa see in the dark?

Lost in thought, his foot caught on a root, sending him tumbling to the ground. The snow burned his face, and with his hands tied in front of him, he was utterly helpless.

The mercenary heaved him up.

"You are more trouble than you are worth, prince."

"Then set me free."

"Well, maybe not."

"Keep moving, prince!" the mercenary called back at him. "We'll be out of this soon enough."

The hairs on the back of Caiden's neck perked. They were not alone in this wilderness, but being attacked could be advantageous to him.

A stick cracked in the distance, and the merc's head snapped to the left.

Another snap to the right.

Something or someone was playing with them. Night Folk stalked the woods of the Court of Whispers. Is that where they were?

The mercenary drew her blade.

Caiden swallowed hard.

Darkness surrounded them, but Caiden surveyed the woods anyway. With the iron blocking his magic, he couldn't see anything, but he hoped he could at least make out the shape of a predator.

Something black raced across the snow in front of them. The merc stopped dead in her tracks.

"If you undo my shackles. I can help you fight."

She scoffed.

"And have you run off? Nice try…" Before she could finish, something yanked her into the forest. Caiden watched the chain attached to her pack go taut before his head hit the snow. He could only watch as the creature dragged him through the forest.

The rough snow scraped at his skin, and rocks and twigs bruised and bloodied his face. All the while, the mercenary screamed. He'd heard stories of the Night Folk before. Half men, half monsters who moved like shadows through the woods of the Court of Whispers, so named for the maddening whispers one heard while in their sacred forest. The sylph of this court regarded the forest with great reverence. Laying sacrificial lambs at the mouth of the forest to appease these ancient creatures. Now, he and the mercenary would be their next meal.

Caiden shut his eyes tightly, hoping to stave off some of the damage. With his hands bound, he couldn't protect his face. He tried to get a look at the creature dragging them farther and farther into the forest, but all he saw was darkness. He prayed that if Illya took him, it would be a swift death.

The mercenary's pack slipped free, and Caiden slowly came to a halt in the snow. He just lay there, chest heaving violent breaths. Rolling over on his back, he noticed the first rays of dawn trickle through the dense canopy of pines. Silence surrounded him. Not even the mercenary's screams could be heard. Caiden swallowed hard. He had to find the key to his shackles.

Using every ounce of will he had, he pulled his battered and bruised body out of the snow. His mouth tasted of metallic blood and dirt. With the iron blocking his magic, he could not heal quickly.

Caiden's broken fingers shook as he undid the latch to the satchel. "C'mon. Please let it be here," he whispered under his breath. His heart beat frantically with each second he failed to find the key. Pain radiated through him. He needed to find the key if he wanted to survive.

He emptied the contents of the backpack onto the snow.

"Fuck, fuck, fuck!" He cursed the Trinity for putting him in this situation. He'd have to rescue or, more likely, recover the mercenary if he wanted to be free. Dread churned in his stomach. His eyes followed the trail of blood deeper into the forest. The pack contained the mercenary's bow, quiver, and some basic rations—hard cheese and bread. Caiden scarfed them down before starting down the trail. The pack dragged in the snow behind him. Not an ideal situation if he wanted to be stealthy, but something told him the Night Folk did not like the light of day.

He followed the trail to the mouth of a cave. Vines crisscrossed their way over the entry, but Caiden easily pushed through them.

The smell of rotting flesh brought bile to the back of his throat. He lifted the pack and held it as he wandered deeper and deeper into the cave, trying his hardest to be as silent as he could.

The acrid smell grew stronger as he ventured deeper. Light streamed in through tiny holes in the ceiling, lighting his way. The caverns twisted and turned with no end in sight. Would he be able to get out?

The dim glow of a low-burning fire caught his attention. Crouching down, he moved closer, his steps dragging on the cold stone. In a darkened chamber, three creatures slept by a dying fire. Caiden's breath caught in his chest at the sight of them. Taut, black skin stretched over bone, and too-long extremities led to enlarged hands and feet capped with clawed nails. Their gaunt faces were stoic. Were they men or sylph once, or had they come before?

The merc was chained to a rock with a hook in the corner of the chamber. Slumped against the wall, her breaths were shallow, and her face looked worse than Caiden's.

He swallowed the fear bubbling in his stomach. Without his magic, he couldn't take on these monsters. How would he even get the key from her?

Taking a deep breath, he tip-toed into the cavern. The sounds of the creature's snoring reverberated off the walls, drowning out Caiden's steps.

The mercenary's chest barely rose and fell with shallow breaths. He held his ear close to her mouth just to make sure she wasn't dead.

He slapped her cheek lightly. Her head bobbed, but she did not wake.

Caiden's heart beat rapidly in his chest. *C'mon, c'mon. We need to get out of here.*

He slapped her harder in tight little intervals while trying to remain as quiet as possible.

Her eyes slowly flitted open, but upon seeing Caiden's face, they went wide, and she sat up straight, wincing in pain.

Caiden held a finger over his pursed lips.

The mercenary turned to see the sleeping demons. She pointed at her leg. Caiden grimaced at its unnatural bent. A bone protruded from her shin. *Shit.* He'd have to carry her out, but first, he had to remove the cuffs. He lifted his hands, and the mercenary pointed to her pocket. Caiden fetched the metal key, and together, they worked to free him. With the shackles removed, magic flowed through his veins once more. He clenched his jaw at the feeling of the magic returning, like pins and needles prickling his skin.

Using his lightning, he broke the mercenary free of her chains. She did her best not to scream in agony when he scooped her into his arms.

Caiden kept an eye on the creatures who slumbered deeply as he tried to maneuver quietly out of the cavern.

He barely breathed, and the merc buried her head in his chest.

Nearing the door, a crack sounded behind them. Caiden paused, not daring to breathe.

The pack had fallen over.

The mercenary peered over his shoulder. "Run," she whispered, panic dripping from that single word.

Caiden could feel the eyes of the creatures upon him. A low growl echoed through the air. Even at full strength, he couldn't outrun them.

"I'm going to set you down. Try to wedge yourself in between those two rocks." She nodded.

Setting her down, he turned to face the monsters at his back. Their eyes glowed red, and long fangs protruded from their lips. They towered over Caiden.

Calling his lightning to his hands, he backed toward the wall. "Stay back. I don't want to hurt you," he said, sparks flickering at his fingertips.

The creatures closed in on him, communicating with one another through a guttural *click*. A shiver ran down Caiden's spine. He mustered all the magic he could, creating a rope of lightning between his hands.

The clicking grew louder.

Caiden snapped the rope like a whip at the first monster, splitting him in two—the smell of burnt flesh filled the room.

In an instant, the other two monsters were upon him. Their sharp claws sank deep into his flesh. He cried out in pain. Was this it? Was this the end? He would be consumed by two Night Folk. Calling his lightning to his fingers again, he blasted one off of him. It's charred remains smoked in the corner.

Caiden pounded his fists into the second creature. His rings barely made a dent in its leather hide. Blood poured from his shoulder where the creature's sharp fangs sunk deep into his flesh. Only sparks flickered at his fingertips. The iron took most of his magic. He would need to eat to regain his strength.

The creature lunged, knocking him to the ground. Kicking it in the abdomen, he rolled away, only to feel the steel grip of the creature wrapped around his ankle. He needed a weapon, but there was none in sight. Frantically, he felt around for a rock… for anything he could use.

The monster dragged him closer. A look of delight flickered in its red eyes. Caiden kicked with all his might at the creature's macabre face, but he was no match for the giant, with his magic drained and his shoulder bleeding profusely.

The Night Folk rose to its full height and dragged Caiden toward the fire. Panic and adrenaline coursed through his veins. He would not let this creature beat him.

The Folk dropped him near the fire. Caiden's vision blurred. He tried to will his legs to move, but they felt leaden, and his eyes grew heavy. Caiden searched his mind for anything he could remember about the Night Folk. Were their bites venomous? He couldn't remember, and it didn't matter now.

The clanking of wood being thrown into the flames startled him, but his body did not flinch. Why was Illya's gift not protecting him? He should have run. He should not have tried to save the mercenary. Now, they'd both be a meal for this preternatural creature.

His breaths shallowed as his lungs filled with blood. He thought of his wife—of her golden hair and rosy cheeks. The reaper would appear any moment to take his soul. Or perhaps he would be punished to endure the cooking of his flesh.

The Folk appeared over the top of him, speaking to itself in the low clicking tone he'd heard before.

The creature cocked its head at him, and Caiden shut his eyes, hoping death would take him quickly.

The sound of metal crunching through bone, followed by a howl, echoed through the chamber. Blood sprayed onto Caiden's face. Through his blurry vision, he saw the end of the mercenary's curved sword sticking through the monster's gaunt abdomen. Shock radiated through its red eyes. It reached for the sword, but it was too late. The mercenary pulled the blade from the Folk only to ram it back through its chest with a feral wail.

The creature toppled over into the fire. Flames consumed its ancient body.

The mercenary dragged Caiden's body away from the gruesome scene. He couldn't move. His whole body was paralyzed.

"Don't worry, prince. No Night Folk is going to get in between me and my payment."

He wanted to nod, but he couldn't.

"Shit," the mercenary said, applying pressure to his wound. "Guess we'll have to find a healer."

37 THARAN

THARAN KNEELED BEFORE A SMALL STATUE OF ILLYA IN HIS study, *Trinity let her be alright. Let her be safe.* Tears welled behind his eyes. He should have protected her. Should have known they would come for her. His heart ached, and rage boiled in his veins. Whoever took her would pay dearly.

His ears perked and he cracked an eye.

"Do you have news, Hopper?"

Hopper's mouth flattened into a straight line.

"Yes," he sighed. "Caiden has not returned to the Woodlands."

Tharan got to his feet, wiping any dirt from his pants.

"I was really hoping it wouldn't come to this."

"As was I."

"Call the others in. Let's make a plan." He took a drag off his cigarette.

Hopper nodded and turned to leave.

"Oh, and Hopper?"

"Yes?"

"Fetch a scholar who is familiar with the Court of Screams."

Hopper bowed and excused himself.

Tharan flicked the butt of his cigarette out the window into the last remnants of snow before taking a seat at his desk.

Amolie and Roderick entered, holding three mugs of spiced cider.

"Thought you could use this," Amolie said, setting the copper mug down on Tharan's desk. The aroma of apples and cinnamon filled the room.

Tharan smelled the intoxicated elixir before taking a sip. The taste of brandy danced on his tongue. "Just what I needed."

He went to speak but Hopper entered with a scholar from the Ruskan Library and Sumac in tow.

Tharan stood, and the scholar bowed. "King Tharan, how may I be of service." The sylph man with dark hair and skin wore rounded spectacles and a brown robe with twenty bars on the hood—a sign he'd been studying for two hundred years.

"Thank you for coming, Grand Master…"

"Marcus, your grace. Grand Master Marcus, but just Marcus is fine." He clutched a tome in his hand.

"Very well, Marcus. I'm assuming my associate, Hopper, told you why we've invited you here?"

"He has, your grace. If I may…" He motioned to Tharan's desk and Tharan nodded for him to proceed. The tiny man laid the large, leather-bound book on the desk and cracked it open.

The smell of old parchment and dust tickled Tharan's nose and he sneezed.

"Excuse me, your Highness, this book is very old."

Tharan took a handkerchief from his pocket and wiped his nose.

The scholar continued.

"The Court of Screams is a court in name only. No one has entered from a Wild or Council Court since before the Sylph and Elven War and maybe even before that."

Tharan rubbed his jaw nervously.

"So, are they sylph? Elf? Something else?" Hopper asked.

Marcus sighed.

"They used to be sylphs. What they are now, I cannot say. They turned away from the Trinity a long time ago. They worship a god called Algea. In the old world before the Trinity, she was the goddess of pain and suffering. The Court of Screams takes that seriously, believing pain and suffering brings you closer to Algea."

"I'm surprised the Trinity let them live," Roderick chimed in.

"The Trinity did their best. A deal could have been struck. They could have strayed from the path of righteousness. We will never know."

Tharan's stomach hardened. Of course, the Trinity would hide their most valuable possession among the wildest of the courts.

"Hmmm..." Tharan said, his mouth twisted into a straight line.

"Yes, my King?" Marcus asked.

"It's nothing. How would one go about getting into the Court of Screams? Is there a leader of sorts?"

Marcus's brows knitted.

"My King, why would you want to go there? Only death could await you there. They are hostile to outsiders."

Because the love of my life is there, and I will set the entire court ablaze in order to get her back.

"It's a hypothetical."

"Ah yes, in that case... Anyone can enter the Court of Screams. Whether you get out is another thing entirely." He ran a nubbed finger over the page. "It says here the last person to make it out did say they had a king. But that was over five hundred years ago."

Tharan took a breath.

"Alright. Anything else we should know? What is the terrain?"

"It looks heavily wooded with some mountains, but who can say for sure."

Sumac stepped forward, examining the scholar's book. "What of weapons? If they're sylph, they'd have a gift from Illya."

"Primitive would be my best guess. I don't think they've got a contract with the Highlands or the gnomes of the Cheyne Mountains. But you could ask for their records."

Doubtful either would give him information.

"Thank you, Master Marcus, that will be all."

The scholar bowed. "Any time, your Highness."

After he'd gone, Hopper said, "We obviously can't let you go to the Court of Screams. You're much too valuable. And we don't even know that's where they're taking Aelia."

"I'm almost certain that's where they're taking her." Tharan took a swig of his cider, trying to still his nerves. He knew his friends would try to stop him, but there was no changing his mind. He would not fail Aelia again.

"Why would the Trinity hide one of their Wells in a place that doesn't even worship them?" Amolie wondered aloud.

"Sounds like the perfect place to hide one," Roderick said. "Think about it. They don't worship you, so they'd never go looking. And neither would anyone else because they'd be risking their life."

"So what are we going to do?" Amolie looked at Tharan.

"Hopper, send a raven to the *king*. See if he'll grant me an audience."

"I don't even know where to send the bird. There is no castle. No town that I know of."

"We could go to the border," Tharan suggested. "See if anyone knows anything. Surely, the Court of Honey or the Court of Whispers must trade with them. Even if it's off the books."

Roderick rose.

"I'm from the Court of Honey. It would be my pleasure to have you as my guest. I am friendly with their queen."

"Very well then, send a raven," Tharan said. "We'll leave as soon as we get word."

"If I may, your grace," Roderick said. "I think it would be better if I carried the news. Amolie and I can go ahead and ask in person. They have a portal here that we can use. It'll be faster than a raven. Amolie will portal back with news."

"Very well," Tharan said. "We eagerly await your return."

Amolie and Roderick said their goodbyes and went to prepare for their trip.

38 AELIA

Pain seared through every limb of my body. I didn't want to open my eyes, but I knew I had to. Vultures circled overhead. Their black bodies contrasted against a gray sky.

"Good, you're awake," Baylis's voice rang in my ears.

I didn't respond at first; the shaking of the rickety cart made my head hurt and my stomach turn.

"Where are we?" I said, my voice hoarse from disuse.

"We're on our way to the Court of Whispers."

"Why?" I eked out.

"We're meeting Erissa there."

My chest tightened, and I shut my eyes once more. I didn't want to think about what awaited me. The Court of Whispers was a poorer court whose mere existence depended upon sacrificing people to the Night Folk. Why would anyone want to live there? I had no idea. Pride, I guess.

I tried my best to sleep for most of the trip, but the shackles around my wrists and ankles made it difficult. They'd purposefully put the shackles on to inhibit my healing. Smart on their part, I'll give them that. The smell of hops and barley wafted through the air. We must be in the Court of Malts. Technically, a Wild Court, if I could get to a town, they would shelter me. That was a big *if*.

We pulled into some brush for the night.

"Don't go anywhere," Baylis said, fastening my shackles to an O-ring hook before hopping out of the back of the cart.

I rolled my eyes.

"Alwin, start a fire," she commanded the mercenary who was twice her size.

"You know, you don't hold my contract. The mage does. So, if I were you, I'd cool it with the orders," he said.

I peered out over the cart's edge just in time to see my sister nock her bow.

"I am betrothed to the king of the Highlands, Midlands, and soon to be…"

A ringing in my ears drowned out her next words, but I heard enough to know Gideon was on the move. He was up to something. But how would he conquer anyone without the full strength of his army?

My head ached, and I tightened my jaw to try and numb the pain. Had they given me something to knock me out, or was this just a side effect of being shot in the back by an iron arrow?

I laid back down in the bed of the cart. There was little else I could do with my arms and legs locked tight.

The wind howled overhead. I looked to the stars and thought of Tharan. Was he looking at the stars as well? Was he wondering where I was? Did he even know I was missing? Surely, Amolie had sent a raven or told Roderick by now. But would they know where to look? I had made so many enemies. Anyone could have taken me. Would they think of Gideon and Erissa first, or would they look to the sea queen? At least I had enough foresight not to bring the Scepter of the Dead with me.

My breath turned to vapor in the cool night air. I imagined Tharan's arms wrapped around me. Would I ever see him again? My heart sank. I should have told him how I felt. I should have told him how much I loved him. Why did I have to be so afraid of a good thing? Why couldn't I accept the love I knew I deserved?

None of these thoughts mattered now. Tharan would kill Baylis and this mercenary without another thought. I wasn't sure how I felt about that. My sister had betrayed me, but I hoped she was still in there somewhere.

I should have listened to my instincts and kept a better watch on her. The time for regrets was over. I had to move forward. She was Gideon's creature now, and I had to accept that. My thoughts drifted to my horse, Adion. I would likely never see him again—never feel his soft fur beneath my fingers—never feel the wind on my face as we raced through an open field. Would he wonder where I've gone? Would he think I've abandoned him? My heart clenched in my chest, and I smothered a sob.

From where I lay, I could see the golden hue of fire licking the trees. There would be no warmth for me.

Baylis returned.

"Here," she said. "Three rabbits. Cook them up, and I'll get some water for Aelia." My name sounded foreign on her tongue.

A few minutes later, she returned. The smell of roasting meat wafted through the air. Holding a sack of water in one hand and a roasted rabbit in another, she jumped into the back of the cart.

"Can't have you dying on us now. Erissa will be pissed, and we both know it's better to be on her good side."

She pulled me up into a sitting position. It took everything I had in me not to scream in pain. A heat radiated from where she'd shot me, bringing tears to my eyes.

With her delicate fingers, she stripped the meat from the bones. "Open up."

Despite my growling stomach, I shut my mouth tightly.

Her brows knitted.

"Now, Aelia, don't be stubborn. If you want to heal, you need to eat."

She was right. Without sustenance, it would take longer for me to heal, which meant more time in this sustained state of agony. Reluctantly, I opened my mouth, and she placed a piece of the rabbit on my tongue. I considered biting off another one of her fingers so she couldn't hold a bow but thought better of it. I needed to appeal to my old sister. The one I knew. Going tit-for-tat on who could inflict more pain on the other would get us both maimed or killed.

The meat tasted rough and gamey in my mouth, but I was starving, so I ate every bite.

"Good," Baylis said, uncorking the water sack and holding it to my lips. "Drink."

I did as I was told, guzzling down the water as if I had been wandering in the desert for ages.

"Get some rest. We're heading out in the morning."

I didn't say anything, just nodded. The perverse part of me wanted to know their plan—to see where this was all going.

Baylis covered me with my cloak before jumping out of the cart.

A voice in the darkness startled me awake. Only blackness surrounded me except for the dim glow of a lamp.

"Who goes there?" the voice called.

Was this my chance?

Neither Baylis nor Alwin answered. Either they were asleep or off hunting. The voice sounded again.

"Who goes there?"

"Help!" I cried out. "Help me!"

A small halfling with a wrinkled face came into view. Through the dim light, I could see his gray eyes widen.

"Miss, are you alright?"

"Do I look alright?" I whispered, desperately. "Help me get out of here."

The man looked around wearily.

"Hurry, please." My voice was barely a whisper.

Climbing into the cart, the man pulled away my cloak, gasping at my chains.

"I am Hand to the Alder King. I have been kidnapped. Please help me."

"Ma'am, I am but a halfling. I cannot carry you."

"Run to town and alert a magistrate. We are on the move. Tell them where you saw me last. King Tharan will know what to do."

The man nodded so frantically the hat he wore nearly fell off.

"Go, now."

The halfling fled into the woods.

An arrow whizzed through the darkness, but I did not hear it hit its mark.

I sat up. Through the red light of the dying fire, Baylis emerged. The shadows playing against her delicate features turned her into the monster she really was.

She scoffed, kicking the mercenary who'd passed out from drink hours ago. "Get up, fool. We need to get out of here."

The man continued to snore.

Scooping up a ball of snow, she threw it at Alwin, who jerked awake, running a giant hand through his dark, wavy hair. "Wha… What's going on?" His voice slurred with the clumsiness of a drunk.

"We need to go," Baylis said, throwing snow on the fire. The flames hissed as they died.

Alwin hooked the horse up while Baylis loaded the cart.

With a click of his tongue, the cart lurched forward, and with it, any hopes of my rescue. I said a silent prayer to Amenna that the halfling had made it. Baylis couldn't see in the dark. Her aim would've been off.

We rode through the night and into the next morning. The sun crested over the horizon, casting everything in a pale pink light. The first buds of spring peeked through the snow. From where I sat, I could see grape vines hanging from wooden braces. We were in elven territory now.

"Baylis, what are you doing? The elves don't take kindly to outsiders."

"It's fine. We have permission to pass."

"What? What do you mean?"

"Erissa made special arrangements for us."

"Erissa has been banished from these lands for thousands of years."

She scoffed.

"There are still some who are loyal to Crom Cruach and want to see him rise again."

"King Arendir?"

"I don't know who the bargain was made with."

The conversation ended.

A chill ran down my spine. Was Arendir working with Erissa? Sure, he was power-hungry, but I just hadn't realized the lengths he'd go to get what he wanted.

We rode through the day. Not one elf stopped us. Not even for a toll. My body slowly healed as we went along. I could feel my powers returning and my wounds mending. I faded in and out of consciousness. The sky overhead turned from faint pink to blue to orange and then to black. All the while, the horse never stopped. Or perhaps he did, and I did not notice.

A fever left my brow wet and clammy, and my breath rasped in my chest as the magic in my veins worked hard to heal the iron-infected wounds.

We stopped in front of a tiny shack that couldn't have been more than two rooms. The roof sagged, and the shutters barely hung from their hinges.

Alwin lifted me from the cart like I weighed nothing at all.

An ancient-looking elf with long pointed ears, a bulbous nose, and pock-marked skin answered the door.

"Come in quickly. We don't need anyone snooping around." The cottage smelled of mildew and old soil.

The elf led us to the back of the house, where a portal stood open—swirling colors of blue and green.

"And this will take us where we need to go?" Baylis asked.

"Yes, my Lady. Unlike the sanctioned portals, this will take you anywhere you want to go. I've already put in your coordinates."

Operating an unsanctioned portal carried a hefty price. They were outlawed ages ago during the Sylph and Elven Wars. I didn't even know any still existed. They must have paid this man a small fortune for him to risk his life like this.

"Very well, let's go." Baylis walked through the portal, and we followed, stepping into a dense wood steeped in fog with mountains at our backside. The portal promptly closed behind us.

Baylis scoffed. "That idiot sent us to the wrong place." She paced around the darkened wood. Her blonde hair glowed in the streaks of moonlight trickling through the thick canopy. The smell of damp earth and pine wafted through the forest. "Okay, let's go this way. We must be close. He can't actually be that bad at the one job he had." She started off into the forest.

Alwin followed, still carrying me. The smell of liquor on his breath mixed with the smell of sweat on his skin. I tried my best not to breathe.

Baylis used a machete to hack through thick brush blocking our path. Thorns scraped at our skin, snagging on our clothes.

"You know, if you undid my ankles I could walk."

"And risk you running again? I don't think so."

"Suit yourself," I said.

A faint clicking sound echoed in the distance. The hair on the back of my neck stood on end. We were not alone.

"Stay alert," Baylis said.

Alwin nodded.

"Do you know what hunts us?" I asked.

"Shh. Be quiet. We don't need to draw any more attention than we already have," Baylis said without even looking back at me.

I shut my mouth. If something attacked us, they could deal with it.

We walked through the black night until the faint light of a cabin came into view. A single candle burned in the dust-covered window. Where were we?

Smoke billowed from the chimney of the log cabin, dissipating into the night. I tried to see in the window as we approached, but the grime made that impossible.

Baylis knocked three times, paused, then knocked two more times.

We waited, silent as the grave. The forest moved around us. Hungry eyes raked over our bodies. Whatever was out there was preparing to strike. My pulse quickened. I didn't know which to fear more: whatever was in the cabin or the monsters lurking in the woods.

Baylis knocked again.

A rustling in the brush.

Alwin set me down on the damp ground before pulling his sword. "Try the knob, Baylis."

She jiggled the handle.

"It's locked."

Alwin gazed out at the forest, where dozens of glowing red eyes came into view.

"Break the window. We need to get in there now," he whispered out of the side of his mouth.

Baylis pounded frantically at the door.

"Hello, hello! Let us in!"

My eyes flitted between my sister and the eyes in the forest.

A latch scraped against its base, and the door opened.

"Quickly," the voice of my nightmares said.

A clicking echoed through the forest, and dread pooled in my stomach.

Alwin scooped me up and brought me inside as the sound bore into my brain.

Baylis shut the door, and the clicking stopped.

Inside, the cabin was shabby and old. The smell of mahogany lingered on its beams, but it had been ages since someone had inhabited it.

Erissa pulled back her white hood. The flame danced across her burned face. I grimaced at the sight of her mangled skin.

A coy smile pulled at the corners of her lips.

"Nice to see you, Aelia. You're looking… well, you've looked better." She turned to Baylis and Alwin, her brow knitted. "I thought I said she wasn't to be harmed."

Baylis shrugged.

"She ran. What was I supposed to do?"

"Not shoot her in the back." Erissa scolded. "Lay her down here. I'll fix her up."

Alwin set me down on a rickety cot. My blood boiled in my veins at the sight of the ancient mage.

Erissa sighed, resting her hands on her hips.

"Aelia, Aelia, Aelia. Always getting into trouble."

Alwin lit a fire in the hearth.

"Yeah, well, excuse me for wanting to escape. I've already experienced your hospitality once. I don't care to experience it again."

"Oh, but you'll want to see who else will be here soon."

My heart lurched into my throat. Tharan? Caiden?

A fist pounded at the door.

"Right on time," Erissa said, moving gracefully across the cabin, her white robes flowing behind her.

She opened the door, and a panting woman with dark red hair and angled features nearly fell through the door. Behind her led on a chain, was Caiden.

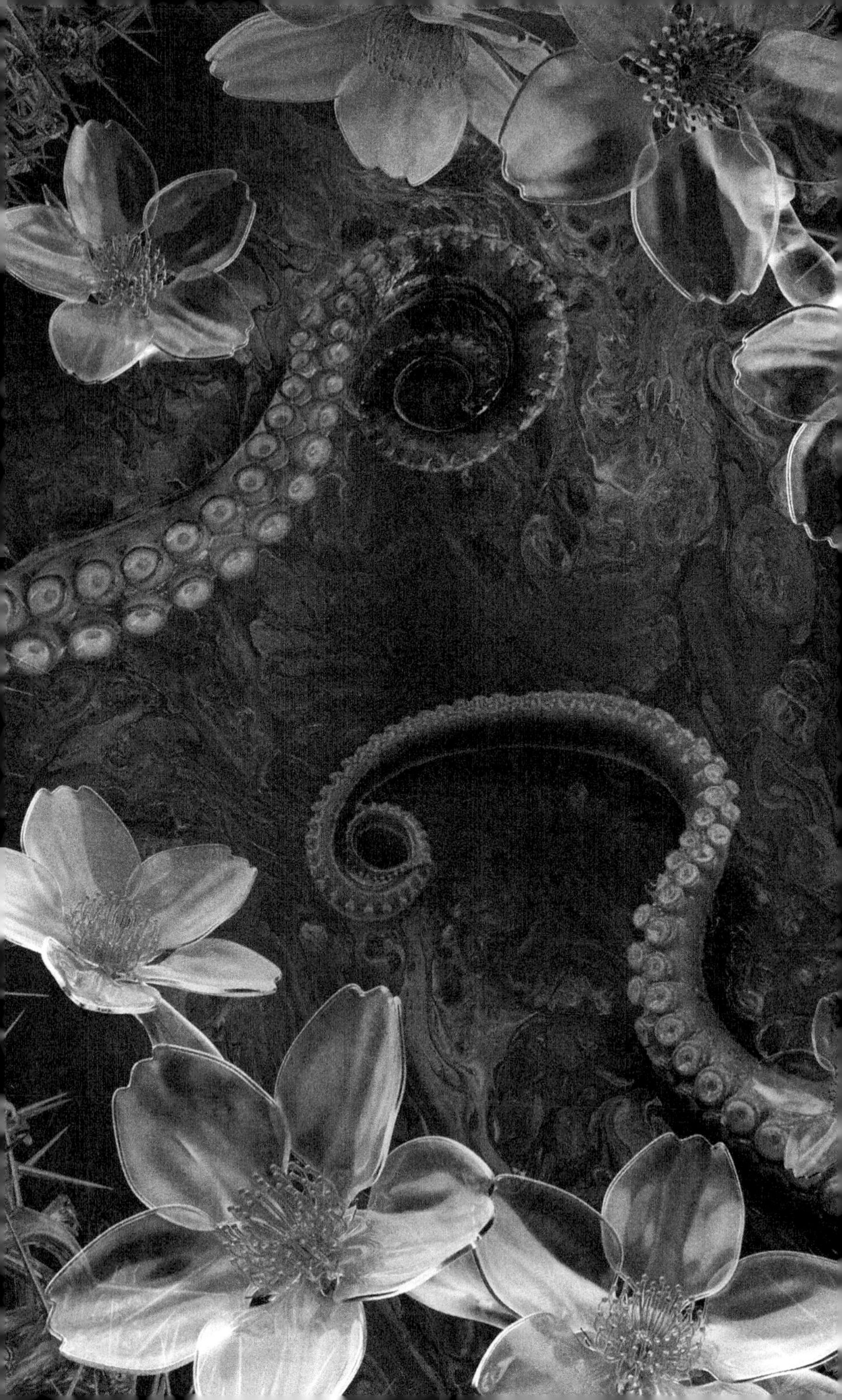

39 CAIDEN

CAIDEN'S HEART NEARLY STOPPED AT THE SIGHT OF AELIA LYING on a cot, arms and legs strapped in chains.

His shoulder ached from where the Folk had sunk its teeth into him, and his movements were slow and clumsy from the poison, but they'd found a healer on the road, and he was slowly healing.

Erissa, with Baylis next to her, had a smug look on her delicate face, her long, red hair braided over her shoulder. "Well, hello, prince."

"I should've known you were behind this." He ground his jaw as he narrowed his eyes on the mage.

A smile tugged at the corner of the good side of her mouth.

"You underestimate me, prince. I have been biding my time for thousands of years. One little setback was not going to stop me. Now, what in the Trinity happened to you?" She scowled at the two mercenaries. "You two had one job. Bring me them… alive."

Caiden's eyes flitted between the mage and the mercs. What was her endgame here? Bleed them dry and use their blood to access the Wells? Would that work? He bit on the inside of his cheek nervously.

"You didn't say unharmed," the female mercenary said under her breath. Her sharp features were covered in blood.

Erissa slapped the woman, sending her stumbling backward into Caiden.

"Insolent fool," she exclaimed. "You are standing in the presence of greatness. I have walked the earth for ten thousand years. Respect your elders."

The mercenary rubbed her face where Erissa's hand landed.

"Take your prize, where's my pay?"

Erissa tapped her thin lips. "Yes, there's the matter of the third."

"He is the Alder King. Did you really expect us to take on the Wild Hunt?"

"For what I offered, I expected you to at least try," Erissa scoffed, throwing her braid over her shoulder. "But that's over now. He'll come to us now that we have her." She pointed at Aelia.

"You'll regret that," Aelia spat at the mage.

"That's enough out of you." With a snap of Erissa's fingers, Aelia's mouth disappeared from her face. Her lips dissolved into a thin flap of skin. She screamed, but the sound barely came out.

Caiden swallowed the fear growing inside him.

Baylis's eyes went wide, and she backed into the wall of the cabin.

"Have a seat, prince." Erissa pointed to a chair next to Aelia's cot, and Caiden sluggishly made his way to it.

"Now, I cannot have you two in this kind of condition. We have a long road ahead of us, and I need you two to be in fighting shape."

Caiden couldn't look at Aelia. His heart hurt for her, but there was nothing he could do. His body was bruised and broken, and his magic was depleted by the iron manacles around his wrists.

Erissa turned to the mercenaries. "You look a little worse for wear. Let me fix you up before I send you on your way."

The mercenaries exchanged questioning glances.

"I promise you; your reward is here." She gracefully glided to a large chest in the far corner of the cabin. Caiden swore it hadn't been there before. She kicked the chest engraved with the seal of the Highlands, a hawk carrying a snake in its talons. The top sprung open, and a pile of gold and jewels sparkled inside. "My word is good. Now, let me mend you." She held out her long, elegant hand. The mercenaries' eyes glimmered with a lust for gold. Without hesitation, they both held out their hands for Erissa to administer whatever potion she'd brewed.

The hairs on the back of Caiden's neck stood on end. Something was off... well, more off than things already were.

Erissa attended to the woman first.

"Kita, is it?"

The female mercenary nodded.

"Here, drink this. I need you relaxed if I am going to heal your wounds."

She handed them both a vile of valerian root, and they slugged it back. Instantly, they swayed before falling to the floor with a *thud*.

"Idiots," Erissa said under her breath. Slamming the chest shut, she crossed the room to a hutch with a wooden latch, where she pulled a jar of worms. The slimy creatures slithered around in the putrid water.

Caiden and Aelia exchanged worried glances.

"What are you doing?" Baylis asked.

"You'll see." Using a long pair of tongues, Erissa gently pulled one of the wriggling creatures from the jar before setting it on one of the gashes on Kita's face.

Caiden could only look on in horror as the creature wriggled its way into the wound, disappearing beneath the skin.

The mercenary shot up, gasping for air. "What did you do to me?"

"It's a control worm. I traveled to the Land of Myst to get them and bred them with my blood. Only I can control them, and therefore you." She placed another worm near Alwin's eye, and the worm slithered in.

Caiden spat bile onto the floor.

"Oh, Prince. Don't be so dramatic," Erissa said.

"Do… do I have one of those things in me?" Baylis examined her skin, looking for any sign of the worm.

"No, I didn't need any magic to control you. Just a handsome king."

Alwin's eyes flung open. "What in the Trinity is this?"

"It's a parasite. Designed to make you obedient. Normally, I would've just glamoured you, but glamours don't work as well on magus, and I wanted to test these out." She set the empty jar back on the shelf. "You'll be under my control now."

Both mercenaries' mouths fell open in shock. Their wounds healed.

"Rise," Erissa commanded.

The mercenaries' eyes glazed over, and they did as she instructed. They stood like soldiers, straight and stiff. No emotion graced their faces.

Caiden couldn't believe his eyes. These mercs were completely under her control. Was this part of her master plan? How many of these did she have? He only saw two, but there could be more. The Land of Myst was known for coming up with horrible creatures. They created the wraiths, after all. His skin tingled with fear, but there was nowhere for him to go. His body was too battered and his magic depleted.

"Excellent." She turned to Caiden. "Now for you, Prince."

She paced the room. "I have been thinking about how I was going to repay you for this." She waved a hand over the mutilated side of her face. "Sure, I could cover it with a glamour, but I want people to know what you did to me. For centuries, people have underestimated me because of how I look. Sweet, innocent, Erissa. No one knew my power. No one saw my potential. Except for Crom." She stared off into the darkness, looking but not seeing. "He saw me when I was broken. When I was nothing, he lifted me up from the gutter and turned me into this. Crom made me more powerful than I could ever have imagined." Sparks sputtered at the ends of her fingertips.

Caiden didn't know what to say. He wasn't sorry for what he did. She deserved every bit of retribution she got, but there was something sad about her.

Erissa continued, "I couldn't save him. Those last moments replay in my head over and over and over on a continual loop. I have watched him die every night in my dreams for a thousand years. Each time, I think I can save him. But I can't." She bit her lip. "It is a punishment from the Trinity, I know, but it does not make it hurt any less."

"I, too, lost someone," Caiden's voice cracked. "Someone very dear to me. I know what it is like to lose the one you love. The pain never really goes away. You just notice it less as time goes on."

"Yes, dear prince, but you're forgetting one very important thing… or should I say person?" Her green eyes flicked to Aelia, who didn't move, her mouth still missing.

Caiden cocked his head to the side.

"Aelia?"

A muted scream echoed from the patch where her mouth had once been. Desperation flickered in her hazel eyes.

"Yes, prince. Aelia."

"I don't understand."

"You will." She crossed the room to where Aelia was strapped to the cot. Placing a long, spindled finger on Aelia's sweaty temple, she pressed hard, muttering some ancient words under her breath.

Aelia screamed, writhing in pain. Erissa twisted her finger, her words becoming louder and quicker with each passing moment. Erissa's eyes darted underneath closed lids. Aelia gritted her jaw. Her breath came fast and shallow.

"I can't watch this." Baylis disappeared up the stairs.

Slowly, Erissa pulled a long glowing string from Aelia's mind, wrapping around her hand as she went. Aelia's screams ripped through the silent cabin despite her lack of a mouth.

"Stop, stop, whatever you are doing to her. Just stop it!" he yelled.

"All done," Erissa said. Pulling the string tight between her fingers. "Hold him down," she commanded the two mercenaries.

Strong hands held Caiden in place.

"What are you doing?" His throat thickened, and he could barely get the words out.

"As I said, I've been thinking of how to punish you for my face. At first, I thought about returning the favor in kind. But then, I thought that might give you some sympathy points. So I thought of something better." She threaded the string through a sharp needle. "You got to forget your first love. But I never did. I replay our fondest moments together as a way to both keep him alive and punish myself for not saving him."

Caiden scoffed.

"There is nothing you can do to me that I do not already do to myself. You don't think I replay my wife's death every day in my mind?"

She scoffed. "Oh, prince, I'm giving you something much worse. A love you don't even remember."

She jabbed the needle into his temple.

A scream scraped its way from Caiden's gut up through his throat and out of his mouth. He tried to wriggle free, but the mercenaries held him firmly in place. A searing pain ripped through his temple as Erissa sewed the thread into his forehead.

A rush of memories came flooding into his consciousness, overwhelming his senses. Every touch, every kiss, every painful moment fit into jagged empty spaces in his mind. His breath caught in his throat.

"Is it all coming back, prince? The hurt? The lust? The love? You thought you could have your Mind Breaker take it all away, and you'd just waltz off into the sunset?" Erissa's voice faded into nothing.

A flood of emotions overwhelmed Caiden as each memory found its home. His heart rose and fell with each moment he'd shared with Aelia. They'd been in love—really, truly in love. They had known each other for years—before he met his wife. It all made sense now why he felt the insatiable scratching at the back of his mind. These pieces were missing. Aelia erased them. And worse… he'd asked her to.

"There we go. All done."

The pain subsided, and the thread disappeared into Caiden's skin.

He looked at Aelia, who stared at him with tears in her eyes. An invisible dagger sliced its way through his heart. So many memories. So much hurt, but also so much joy. They had shared something special, and he'd asked her to erase it.

He turned to Erissa. "Give Aelia her mouth back."

An evil smile creased her macabre face. "If I can't escape my past… neither should you." She snapped her fingers, and Aelia's mouth reappeared.

"Caiden… I don't know what to say. I'm sorry. I'm so, so, so sorry." Tears snaked their way down freckled cheeks.

"You have nothing to apologize for, Aelia. We loved each

other once. I knew what I was doing when I asked you to take those memories." He turned away from her. Pain bloomed in his chest like a rare flower, familiar and foreign all at the same time.

"And now you'll feel the pain doubly. For the love you couldn't save and love you let slip away," Erissa said. "Now." She clapped her hands together with delight. "You two get reacquainted, and I'll see you in the morning. We have a long journey ahead of us, and I need my beauty rest." Erissa began to climb the stairs. "Mercs, guard the door."

The mercenaries did as she commanded, taking positions near the door, arms crossed over their chests.

Erissa climbed the creaking stairs into the darkness, leaving Caiden and Aelia alone.

"Caiden?" Aelia's voice trembled.

"Yes?" Caiden said, unsure of how he should feel about the woman next to him. She was both a stranger and an old friend, and his mind couldn't reconcile both. A pang of shame rippled through his heart. *He* had asked her for this—no *begged* her to erase his memories. No wonder he felt something when he saw her in the Woodlands after the battle of Ryft's Edge. His heart remembered what his mind could not. A bitter taste filled his mouth, and he couldn't decide whether he was grateful to have the memories back or if he would've preferred to live in ignorance for the remainder of his existence.

"Say something, anything. Tell me you're alright, at least."

"There is nothing to say, Aelia. I need to process what just happened." His heart ached for her.

One memory in particular stood out to him. They were lying in the glass-roofed house in Elyria. Her head rested on his bare chest as he gently stroked her back. She was crying, but he didn't know why. The memory wasn't whole yet. Perhaps it never would be. Erissa yanked all the most pertinent memories from Aelia's mind and gave them to him, but these weren't really his. They were all Aelia's: her feelings, her hopes, her dreams for them. Bile rose in his throat again, and this time, he couldn't hold it in. Leaning over, he hurled acidic spit onto the grimy floor.

"Oh, Caiden," she said, sobs clotted her words.

Stilling himself, he turned back to her.

"You really loved me."

"Always," she whispered.

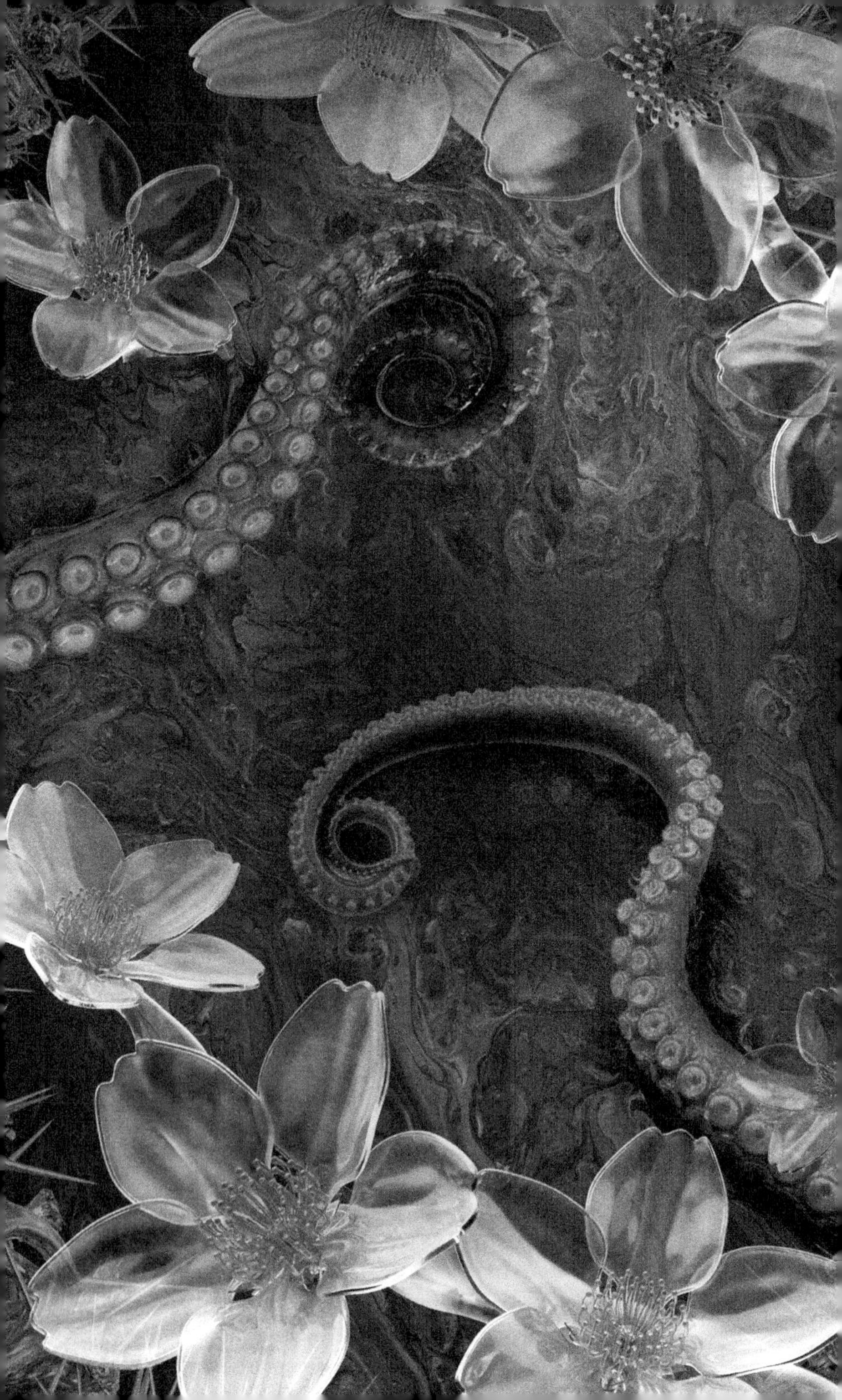

40 THARAN

Tharan kneeled in front of Queen Rhyhinia, or as her people called her, the Queen Bee, the name for the ruler of the Court of Honey. Built inside a massive beehive, the smell of fresh honey wafted through the air. Bees buzzed about, unbothered by the sylphs living inside their home.

The queen sat atop a carved wooden throne. Live flowers were embroidered into her massive white dress, bursting against her umber skin. Her hair was braided into long pleats, and she wore a crown of sunflowers. Next to her, her husband, Melkar, sat strong and silent, radiating power, with a square jaw and broad shoulders. His toned physique was visible through his silk shirt. Since hives had no king, he was referred to by name only.

"Rise, Alder King." the Queen's voice was smooth and deep like the honey they coveted. "You are a friend here. Roderick has told me of your plea."

Tharan rose. His wine-colored hair sparkled in the amber light. He could only stare in awe at the massive combs rising like mountains behind the queen. "Yes, your grace. We have come seeking help with the Court of Screams. We believe there is something our enemies want there. Any information you can give us would be helpful."

She mulled over Tharan's words. "Let us speak in private. Follow me."

She rose, cradling her heavily pregnant belly, grasping her husband's hand. He escorted her off the dais into an antechamber off the throne room. Tharan, Sumac, Hopper, Amolie, and Roderick followed.

Gold covered every inch of the meeting room's walls, and the table was made from an old hive encased in glass. Light flooded in from a giant window, where Tharan could see the first flowers of spring beginning to bloom in the fields.

Queen Rhyhinia took her seat at the head of the table. Tharan took a seat at the other end, and their advisors filled the space in between. His stomach hardened with trepidation, but he tried to remain optimistic.

"So, you want to know about the Court of Screams?"

"Yes, your Highness," Tharan said, sitting back in his chair, he commanded the attention of everyone in the room.

She drummed her ringed fingers on her taut belly. "They have a leader. You could call him a king, but he's more like a cult leader in my opinion."

"What do you mean?"

"They believe he is the son of Algea or he is Algea or he's Algea's representative. I still haven't fully figured it out myself. I've never met with him, but my scouts have heard screams coming from the woods."

Tharan mulled over the queen's words. The old gods were brutal, and anyone who worshiped them would likely be the same.

"Do they have a palace?"

"I have no idea. I assume they do. Could be ruins for all I know. They rarely leave their own borders. Some of the townsfolk believe the Trinity cursed them long ago for not worshiping them.

Others believe they were like us once, but when the War of Three Faces came, they sealed themselves off from the rest of the world, and all that time in isolation made them mad."

"Is there a way in?"

Her amber eyes flitted to her husband's then to her advisors.

"There are some at our farthest borders who trade with them. It would be a crime to enter their domain, but I'm sure some do. You may walk this land freely, on one condition."

Tharan leaned forward in his chair.

"And what's that?"

"You bring some of my hives to your Woodlands. Let them feed and grow for a season and then I will collect them."

"That's it?"

"That's it," she said.

Hopper leaned into Tharan, whispering into his ear, "They think the bees will absorb the magic of the realm and deposit it into the honey. It's a risk, but one we might need to take."

Tharan cleared his throat.

"Very well. I will send word to my groundskeepers."

"Excellent." She smiled with a mouth full of blinding white teeth. "I thought you'd agree, so I took the liberty of drawing up this." She snapped her manicured fingers, and a servant approached carrying a royal decree on a platter. With a white gloved hand, he gently placed it in front of Tharan. "You may travel freely within the Court of Honey, your Majesty. I hope you find what you are looking for… for all our sakes."

"Thank you, your Highness. Consider us allies." He gazed at the letter written in big swooping letters.

"Do not say things you do not mean, King."

"I never do."

"Very well." She rose, cradling her stomach once again. "I must depart for my afternoon rest. I hope you'll try some of our court's delicacies. The honeyed ham is one of my favorites."

The rest of the table stood and bowed to the queen as she departed.

A servant opened a door behind them and ushered them out.

The capital of the Court of Honey was Hiveton, a quaint village with thatched-roof cottages, cobblestone streets, and, of course, a beehive in front of every house and business.

"It's so cozy here," Amolie said as they walked through the flower-lined streets. The smell of honey and lilac wafted in the air and a trio of flutists played in the town square.

"A far cry from Elohim, that's for sure," Sumac said.

The people of Hiveton seemed not to notice them. They went about their daily business, saying hello to their neighbors, and haggling with shop merchants, much like the bees they cared for. They dressed in bright colors and most of the women wore flowers in their hair.

"This must have been a nice place to grow up, Roderick," Amolie said.

"It was. But Vantris and the Court of Storms are my homes now."

"Anywhere we are together is my home," Amolie said, kissing her husband on the cheek.

His face reddened.

"Everyone, enjoy your night. We'll meet up in the morning and head north," Tharan said.

Three days of travel through the lush lands of the Court of Honey had their bellies round with all sorts of honied treats and confections. Tharan gazed out the window of the carriage as they trotted through rolling hills of budding flowers and fruit trees.

"This is quite something," he said to Roderick.

"Yes, this court is blessed with an abundance of resources. It is why they are so desperate to preserve it. You'll see when we get to Honeyville what a stark contrast the Court of Screams is."

"Lovely," Tharan said with a sigh. His mind was elsewhere, churning over every terrible thing Erissa and Gideon could be doing to Aelia. He fiddled with the rings on his fingers to distract himself.

"We'll get her back," Amolie said.

Tharan mustered the best smile he could. Leaning back in his seat, he tried to remember her smell, the way her hair felt as it slid through his fingers, the way her face lit up when she laughed, and what he wouldn't give to kiss her lips.

The carriage turned into the small town of Honeyville. It was a quaint place with a crystal-clear river snaking its way through the village. A wall of twenty-foot-high honeycombs guarded its inhabitants.

"I've never seen anything like this before," Sumac said, mouth agape at the tiny village.

"Honeyville is an apt name," Hopper added.

They stopped at an inn in the center of town and unloaded their things. As much as Tharan wanted to throw himself into the plush bed, he had bigger concerns.

"I've arranged for a meeting with the mayor," Roderick said. "We should go as soon as we are able."

"Lead on, but I'll be needing some of that honeyed cider afterwards," Tharan said.

"I think we all will." Roderick patted Tharan's back, and together they walked through the bustling town to the mayor's home with Sumac and Hopper in tow. Amolie stayed behind to set up her potions.

One of the mayor's advisors met them at the door. A short, plump, sylph man with a mop of curly hair and a button nose. He had to be part halfling. Sylph were naturally tall and muscular, built for battle.

"Roderick and Lord Tharan, I presume," he said.

"Yes. We have a meeting with Mayor Thistlebottom."

The man looked at his parchment and nodded. "Right this way."

They walked through the quaint halls of the mayor's residence, much like the Hive of the Queen Bee, the walls grew hundreds of varieties of flowers. All in bloom. Bees flitted from one to another gathering their pollen to bring back to their hive. The floral scent of honeysuckle filled the air.

"Right through these doors," the attendant motioned. "The mayor is waiting for you."

"Thank you," Roderick said, pushing the doors open.

The mayor, a sylph woman with dark skin and white hair braided into two buns on the top of her head, stood at a large oak desk, examining some documents. Her brown eyes lit up when she saw Roderick.

"It has been too long, my friend," she said, smiling brightly.

Roderick embraced the woman in his massive arms.

"It is good to see you, Lydia. Or should I call you Mayor."

"Lydia is fine." She slapped him playfully.

Tharan and Sumac exchanged knowing glances.

"Very well, Lydia, these are my friends, Lord Tharan Greenblade, Sumac, and Hopper, of the Woodland Realm."

"It is very nice to meet you," Lydia said, rounding her desk and taking a seat at a long cherry table in the center of the room. "Please, take a seat, and I will tell you what I know of the Court of Screams."

They each took a seat in a plush, velvet chair. An assortment of honey cakes and pastries adorned the table, and a silver mug sat before each of them. Lydia rang a bell, and two servants carrying teapots filled their mugs.

"Now that we have refreshments, where to begin?" she said, taking a sip of tea. "Roderick told me you want to get into our neighbors to the north. If that's true, I'll say you'll have no trouble doing so. It's getting out that's the issue."

"Have you seen their leader?" Tharan asked, leaning forward in his chair. "Should we seek him out?"

"Their leader is called Cyrus, and you will want to avoid him at all costs. He will not take kindly to you trespassing in his domain. But the good news is there aren't many of them, so they should be easy to avoid. Roderick mentioned something about a well…"

Tharan shot Roderick look that said, "*You better not have.*"

Roderick averted his eyes.

"Yes, we're looking for something old. Older than the sylph."

Lydia nodded.

"So, something ancient, like a shrine?"

"Yes," Tharan said.

Lydia sucked in a breath. "There is a place where the Court of Screams performs their sacrifices. They call it 'The Well of Blood' and it was there long before they were. I'm wondering if this is what you're searching for."

"How do you know all of this?" Tharan asked.

She gave a little chuckle.

"You don't think we'd live next to a cult that worships pain without at least sending some scouts in once in a while, lest they come knocking at our door."

Tharan nodded.

"Very well. Then we shall make our way into the forest tomorrow."

"Best to go at night, when they are sleeping or doing their rituals. That way you can get close in the day when they hunt."

Tharan let out a breath.

"Fine, we'll rest and head out tomorrow night. Do you have any spies or even hunters who know their way around the forest?"

"I will call upon my men and see if someone will take you. I will have them meet you at the inn tomorrow night when the last rays of light have hidden behind the horizon."

"Thank you." Tharan nodded to the mayor.

"Do not make me regret this, King."

"I won't."

They rose and said their goodbyes and headed to the local tavern, where a string band played, and people danced and sang. Meanwhile, knots tied themselves in Tharan's chest. They would have to blindly walk into another hostile court. He prayed to Illya that they weren't too late to rescue Aelia.

"I don't have a good feeling about this," he said to Sumac, who was downing a pint of honeyed ale.

"Oh, most definitely. No good can come of this. We don't even know if Aelia is there. What if we get all the way into their little temple and she's not there? What are we going to do?"

"I… I don't know. I know we need to find and harness the power of the Wells, but right now my priority is getting Aelia back."

"We will." She patted his back.

"Don't worry, you've got one of the finest soldiers in Moriana on your side," Roderick said.

"Hey…" Sumac chided.

"Well, two of the finest, I should say."

Tharan smiled, but out of the corner of his eye, he caught sight of a cloaked figure lingering in the back of the tavern. Something about the man set his nerves on edge.

Sumac's smile dimmed and her brows knitted "What is it?"

Tharan took a swig of his ale, letting the alcohol calm his nerves. "We have an admirer."

"Do you want me to say something?" Sumac whispered.

"No," Tharan replied.

"What are we whispering about?" Roderick and Hopper leaned in.

"Make it more obvious," Tharan scoffed. They broke from their huddle to find the hooded figure standing next to them. Tharan's heart leapt in his chest.

The man pulled back his hood revealing a long, elegant face.

"Trinity be, Lucius. What are you doing sneaking up on us like that?" Roderick said.

"You need to leave, now. Blood Riders are coming. I saw them hunting on my way here."

"Blood Riders? But I thought we killed them at Ryft's Edge."

Lucius cracked his neck.

"They made more."

"How did you get here so quickly, Lucius?" Roderick asked.

"That's my secret to keep. Now let's get to the inn and I'll tell you of what I know."

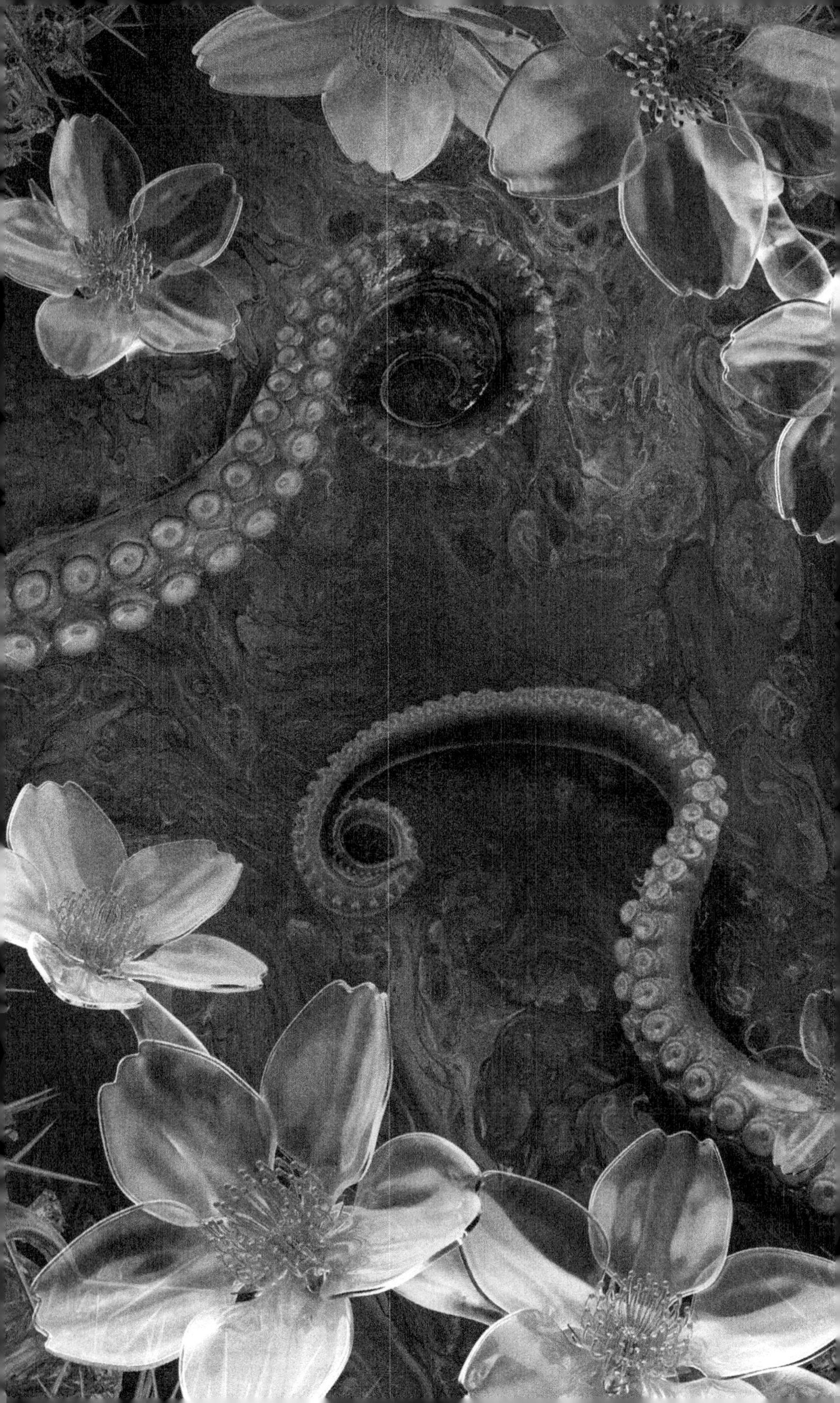

41 AELIA

MY HEART TWISTED INSIDE MY CHEST. CAIDEN HAD HIS MEMORIES back and there was nothing either of us could do about it. I lay awake all night thinking of something to say to him, but nothing seemed right. This was not how it was supposed to be. I was supposed to let him go. We were not meant for one another. My stomach threatened to empty itself. I would have to hurt him again. Was this what the Fates meant when they said I'd have to choose? Would I have to erase his memories again? Had I picked the wrong man? Was Tharan not my destiny? Had I been hesitant to reveal my feelings to Tharan because deep down I knew Caiden would come back?

"Aelia?" Caiden whispered, just as dawn's first light dribbled through the dirty windows of the cabin.

"Yes?" I said, trying to hide the shaking in my voice.

"We shared so much, and yet I only have your memories, not my own. They feel foreign inside of my head."

"So you have *my* memories, *my* emotions, *my* feelings, but not your reactions?"

"Yes."

I bit my lip. This was much worse. He would know every

terrible thing I ever thought of him. Every moment of lust… of love. There was so much he wouldn't understand. He'd know my ire, my disappointment, but not the reasons behind them. There was so much I wanted to say… to explain, but words evaded me. Where would I start?

"Oh Trinity. I'm so sorry, Caiden."

"Yes, oh Trinity is right. It's like I have only half of the story. What was I like? What did I feel?"

"I don't know if I can help you with that, Caiden. I can only rewrite memories that are already there, not bring back ones I erased."

"I don't know if I want you to, Aelia," he said in a voice that was barely a whisper. "At this point, I'm more worried about…" his eyes flitted upstairs, "than these memories."

"You're right. With these injuries and the iron blocking our magic we'll never be able to get out of here."

"If they're taking us to the Court of Screams… I can only imagine what kinds of horrors await us there."

I nodded but could not say more. With Erissa controlling the two mercenaries, I couldn't be sure she wasn't listening in on us through them. All I could do was shut my eyes and wait for Erissa to decide her next move.

Caiden's head went limp on his neck as he faded into sleep, his body finally giving into exhaustion.

I lay still, listening for the creatures on the outside of the cabin. Were we already in the Court of Screams? Or somewhere else? I had never ventured this far north. I wouldn't know what either looked like. Thorns grew in my throat. Caiden and I had been free of each other. We'd both moved on and now we were right back where we started. Both hurt and unable to do anything about it. Would I be able to pull those memories again?

Letting out a breath, I closed my eyes and tried to sleep.

"Open your eyes, Aelia." My mother stood before me,

surrounded by white light. Her black hair whipped in an invisible wind. "I don't have much time, so listen closely. You will have to choose, and you may not even know you're making the choice."

"What?" I stammered.

"Things that were set in motion thousands of years ago will come to fruition soon. You must trust your instincts. The magic that lives inside you was never meant to be discovered. I thought if I could hide it somewhere no one would look, and it would be safe, but that is not how things worked out." *Her nostrils flared and she clasped her hands around my face.* "You must be strong now. Stronger than you've ever been. Everything will work out as it should. Believe in the Trinity, Aelia. Let them guide you." *She faded into nothing.*

I opened my eyes to find Alwin standing over me.

"Time to go," he said. His brown eyes were glassy, and his brow was damp with sweat. He hadn't drank last night and soon the shakes would set in. I could use this to my advantage.

"He can't carry me. He's going through withdrawal," I said loud enough so Erissa would hear me.

She crossed the room and took the giant man's face in her slim fingers.

"Ugh. You can't travel like this, and we can't wait. Not when we're so close." She turned to Baylis. "Undo her ankle shackles."

Baylis did as she was told, and the lock sprang open.

"Now for these wounds." Erissa opened the cupboard where she had pulled the parasites and grabbed a jar of red salve. "I need you two at your full strength for the ritual, so I'm going to heal you."

Caiden and I exchanged skeptical glances.

Erissa took the paste into her hands and slowly spread it over Caiden's wounds. The gashes healed and closed, like they had never been there at all.

"There we are, right as rain." She turned to Baylis. "Fetch them some water, and hunt for our breakfast."

Baylis huffed but did as commanded.

"Alwin, go with her. Make sure she is safe." The glassy-eyed man followed Baylis out the door and into the morning mist.

"Now for you, Aelia."

I gritted my teeth and winced, preparing for the burn of the salve, but instead a calming sensation flooded over my body.

"Why not use this for your face?" I asked, trying to look for a glimmer of any emotion on her face. Was she upset about her wounds? Could I connect with her this way?

"The wounds have to be rather fresh for this to work."

"Why heal us at all?"

"The task ahead of us is dangerous and fraught with peril. I cannot have two injured captives slowing us down. And I'm sure you don't know, but long ago, I was a healer. Perhaps there is still some of that in me."

A rare moment of kindness in an otherwise cold existence. I pushed for more.

"Where is Gideon?" I asked.

"He is on an important mission. One that will change the fate of this world."

Gideon was her favorite subject besides Crom Cruach. I hoped she'd get overzealous and spill more.

"Why him?" Maybe it was delirium or maybe I just didn't care anymore making me so bold, either way I wanted answers.

The mage sighed.

"I served the Ironhearts for generations. They took me in after Crom, when no one else would. I hatched my plan then and waited... waited for a son to be born under the right set of stars, with just the right temperament to be what I needed him to be." She rolled me over and rubbed the salve over where the arrow had pierced my back. "Of course, I planted the seeds to make sure each generation was crueler and more power-hungry than the rest."

I sucked in a breath at the touch of her cold hands. The salve burned as it regrew my skin. I gritted my teeth, fighting to keep control of my thoughts.

"All for what? So you could reclaim some lost glory? Bring your lover back from the dead? Why let men control you like this?'

"Control me? No one controls me." Power flared behind her green eyes. "I would be nothing without Crom. I owe my life to him. I will honor him in death as I did in life."

"Let the dead stay dead, Erissa. No good can come of this."

A smile curled on her lips.

"Says the woman who controls the army of the dead, but not for long."

I arched a brow.

"What do you mean?"

"You didn't think I'd bring you all the way here and not have Baylis grab that little scepter of yours?"

Power surged through my body. My chest tightened with fear and anxiety. Did she know how to delink my blood from the scepter or was she just hoping she did? I pursed my lips. She would not get any more information from me.

She pulled the scepter from Baylis's pack. Running her fingers over it, she closed her eyes as if reading a language only she could see.

"Hmm…" Her eyes flitted open and she shoved the bone into my hand. "Call the Morrigan." She handed me the scepter.

"With my hands bound my magic doesn't work." A lie, but one I hoped she believed.

"Nice try," she smirked. "Just call her."

I sighed. "Morrigan, show yourself." The magic of the scepter tugged at a knot in my chest, making me wince, but it subsided. *That's never happened before.*

Smoke plumed from the mouth of the crow, taking the shape of the goddess.

"Ye—" Her blue eyes widened at the sight of Erissa. "You…" She crossed her arms over her chest. Her eyes flitted between me and the mage, fitting the pieces of the puzzle together. "I will never allow you to control my army," she spat at the mage. Two ancient creatures locked in a heated game of tug-o-war.

"Oh, I don't think you have much say in the matter. As soon as I prick my finger and lay the first drop of blood, you will be mine for eternity."

"Try it." The Morrigan shot me an uneasy glance.

Erissa pulled a long needle from her robe and pricked her pointer finger.

"Who do you think designed the spell that imprisoned you all those years ago?"

"You…" Morrigan said through gritted teeth.

A smirk tugged at the corners of Erissa's lips.

"Yes, me. So, I think I would know how to use it." She pressed her finger into the carved bone.

Both the Morrigan and I winced, but nothing happened.

The smile disappeared from Erissa's elegant face.

"No, it can't be."

"Looks like you're out of practice, Mage."

Erissa leaned in close so that their noses were practically touching.

"I will find a way to control your army. The Wells will give me the power."

"My army will never fight for you. I'll make sure of it." She disappeared into the scepter once more.

Baylis and Alwin returned, rabbits in one hand, a bucket of water in the other.

"Cook those up quick and make sure these two get water," Erissa said.

Baylis set to work skinning the creatures while Alwin and Kita poured us some water.

I sat up for the first time in nearly a day. The blood rushed to my head, blurring my vision.

Kita held the glass to my lips. I hadn't realized how thirsty I was until the cool water touched my lips. Taking greedy gulps, I drank deeply. "More," I said, my words clotted in my throat.

Baylis brought over some roasted rabbit, and Caiden and I hungrily tore into them. My stomach groaned, and my mouth salivated at the taste of the roasted flesh.

After the rest of them ate, they packed up the little cabin.

Erissa sighed. "Time to go. We have a very important meeting."

My chest tightened at the thought.

She linked Caiden's chain to mine with a snap of her fingers and handed one end to Kita. "Alwin, take up the rear with Baylis. Shoot anything that moves."

"Why not just portal us? I know you have the power."

She did not look back at me. "I can't portal all of us. It would deplete my power."

42 AELIA

We walked for ages through the silent forest, not stopping for food or water. My back ached, and my muscles cried out for rest, but still, we kept walking. A tugging pulled at the knot in my chest. Was it calling to something? To the Well?

I tried to focus on my steps and not on Caiden behind me or Tharan somewhere far off, or the magical knot I had no way of controlling. We would have to stop eventually, and with Caiden and I tied together, we might be able to make a break for it. I scanned the forest floor for any herb I could use to poison them.

Alwin hurled the contents of his stomach up every so often. He would need a drink soon if he wanted to avoid the worst parts of withdrawal. He would be the easiest target. I just had to avoid Baylis seeing. She knew her herbs. She'd know if I slipped him something, but taking on Alwin would be our best bet. He was Erissa's muscle. I could probably take Kita, even without my magic. Erissa and Baylis would be a different story. I wish Amolie were here to help me with a potion. I wish I were better at herbology. I wish my magic weren't blocked so I could crush each and every one of these asshole's heads.

When darkness fell, the forest came alive. Creatures called to one another in a preternatural language I could not identify—guttural clicks and clacks. The hair on the back of my neck stood on end. We were in Night Folk territory. Why weren't they attacking?

"I don't like this," Alwin said. "We're not supposed to be here."

"These creatures will not harm you as long as you are with me," Erissa said, tapping her staff with the green stone on the end. A light lit within the rock

"And why is that?" Baylis asked boldly.

Erissa turned toward my sister. "Because they know their time will come when Crom rises again." A feral look flickered in her eyes and her nostrils flared. "You would be wise to remember that."

Baylis only nodded in response.

With darkness covering everything, I could barely make out the plants at my feet. Out of the corner of my eye, I thought I caught a streak of red. Rhubarb. Although put into many delicious pies, the leaves could leave one with a nasty case of food poisoning. And what luck, growing next to it: the purple-leafed valerian root. Feigning a trip, I tumbled to the ground, pulling Caiden with me. I started to cough and quickly grabbed some leaves and stashed them in my pants.

"Clumsy fool," Erissa said. "Get her up."

Alwin took the opportunity to hurl more bile into the nearest bush. The smell overwhelmed me, and I, too, heaved the contents of my stomach onto the forest floor. Acid burned my throat, and tears welled in my eyes.

"I need to relieve myself," Kita said.

Erissa huffed. "Worthless… go."

Baylis nocked her bow at us.

"Don't try anything, you two. I could kill both of you before you made it to the next tree. That is, if the Night Folk don't get you first."

"Shut up, Baylis. I need them in one piece. I just healed them. I don't have the ingredients to make another salve." Erissa blew out a long breath. "Fine, we'll camp here for the night."

My gaze shifted between Erissa and Baylis. Was Erissa jealous of my sister or more annoyed she had another woman to deal with? Hmm... how could I exploit this?

"Are you going to let her talk to you like that?" I asked Baylis. "You're basically the queen now."

Baylis's brows knitted as she considered my question.

"You're right. I am the Queen in Waiting now. You should show me more respect. I doubt Gideon would be happy to hear of you treating me this way.

Erissa scoffed, pointing a long, elegant finger at Baylis.

"I made you, girl. Don't forget that. I'll take orders from you when dragons roam the sky again."

Baylis stomped her foot into the damp soil but did not retaliate. She needed Erissa to get through the wilds. Still, the seed of discord had been planted between the two.

Alwin stood, wiping his mouth on his cloak.

"Go fetch us some wood for a fire," Erissa ordered.

Kita returned, chest heaving. "They're just watching us out there."

"Yes, idiot, the Night Folk are always watching. This is their land, and we are being granted the privilege of walking on it. Now, tie these two to a tree and get some rest. We're moving out first thing in the morning."

Alwin tied us to a tree a short distance from their camp. Before he turned to leave, I whispered, "I have something for your stomach."

"What?"

"Yarrow leaves to help with your stomach. They're in my pocket."

Alwin eyed me suspiciously.

"Why are you helping this oaf?" Caiden asked. "He should suffer for what he did to us."

"He's still a person, Caiden. I know what withdrawal feels like." I nodded toward my pocket. "Go ahead, take it."

Reluctantly, Alwin reached into my pocket, pulled out the rhubarb leaves he thought were yarrow and sauntered back to camp.

"Thanks for that," I whispered.

"What's the plan? I know those weren't yarrow."

"My hope is he gets violently ill, and then we can take out the other two."

"And how do you propose that? We're tied to a tree and have iron blocking our magic."

"I'm working on it, but if I know anything about addicts, and I do, they do things half-assed to get back to whatever high they want. Alwin is a drunk and going through withdrawal. He will do anything to stop the hurt. I bet he didn't even tie our ropes correctly." I tugged on the ropes binding us a bit. They weren't tight, and if we both moved in opposite directions, the knot would likely come undone.

"How do you know that?"

It's what I would've done if I were going through withdrawal.

"Because his head is probably killing him. You've had a hangover before. Now, just imagine it being ten times worse. Your vision is blurry, and your movements are shaky. We've been walking all day. He doesn't have Illya's gift and he probably just wanted to rest."

"That still doesn't solve our problem with the other three. And these chains."

I looked at Baylis and Erissa, their rigid movements and cold words led me to believe they were both stewing on the earlier exchange. I hoped I'd done enough to build the pressure between them.

"Alwin will hurl, and I'm hoping Baylis and Erissa's hostility boils over into a full-blown fight."

"And what about the Night Folk? I've seen what they can do." He motioned to his shoulder.

"We're healed now, and we can run. This forest can't last forever, and they go underground at dawn. We just need to pick the right time. They can't touch the light."

"This is a ridiculous idea. Your sister could kill us with one arrow."

Yes, it was a ridiculous idea, but it was the only one I had. They wouldn't risk undoing my shackles, and night was the only time we would be left alone.

"Erissa won't let that happen. She needs us alive. But I won't go on her terms. We need to get to that Well before she does. We need to claim it for our own."

Caiden sighed and I could picture his mouth scrunching as he thought about the plan.

"Alright, what do we have to lose, really?"

"Possibly our lives… but that's just a normal day for me."

"Fine." I could hear the smirk in his voice.

I let out a breath that turned to vapor in the cool night air. "Alright, let's wait until they fall asleep."

Kita took the first watch, bringing us water and something to eat. Caiden and I greedily scarfed down the minuscule meal of what I could only guess was a crow.

My body begged for sleep. "Caiden, do you want to take the first watch?"

"Yes, that's fine. I'll wake you if I see anything." His hand slid over to rest on top of mine.

I swallowed hard. Emotions I thought I buried rose to the surface. Reluctantly, I shut my eyes.

Caiden nudged me awake, and I let out an audible gasp. The fire burned low, and I could make out the sleeping bodies of Erissa, Baylis, and Kita.

"It's happening," Caiden whispered. "Alwin ran into the forest."

Adrenaline coursed through my veins. "Okay, on the count of three, we try to stand, and the ropes should loosen."

"This better work."

"One, two… three." We both stood, and the ropes loosened. "Pull…"

We heaved against our restraints, pulling as hard as we could. My heart beat faster with each passing moment. The rope tightened around us. For a moment, I thought it wasn't going to work. Then the tension eased, and the hastily tied knot came undone.

"Thank the Trinity, that worked," Caiden said.

"How long was I asleep?"

"Kita and Alwin changed posts about two hours ago. I'd say dawn is not far off."

"Do you think we should run now or wait a little longer?" I asked.

The sound of Alwin's cries of pain echoed through the forest.

"I say we run for it while we can," Caiden said.

I debated the merits of each. If we stayed, we would be protected from the Night Folk, but if we didn't leave soon, the rest of the party would likely wake. "Where do you think we are?"

Caiden squinted at the sky through the darkness.

"If my training serves me right, the stars are saying north is that way." He pointed into a particularly dark part of the forest.

The hairs on the back of my neck prickled, and my dinner sat like stones in my stomach.

"Alright, let's go. But as softly as you can."

Caiden nodded, and we headed into the darkness, stepping as softly and as quickly as we could. Nothing moved around us. I looked for the red eyes that hunted us earlier but saw none. Perhaps they went back underground. Perhaps they were waiting to strike. Maybe Erissa's bargain still protected us. If I thought too much about it, I would jinx us. So I just kept moving.

Twigs and branches snapped underneath even our lightest footsteps. I cringed at each one.

We ran for as long as we could until the cold burned deep in our lungs. I lagged behind Caiden, but he kept moving.

"We can't stop. Not until dawn."

"I know," I said through heaving breaths. "I need a moment." My footsteps stumbled over the managed roots in my path.

Resting my palms on my knees, I hurled the contents of my stomach onto the forest floor.

"Aelia," Caiden whispered.

"I know, I know, I'm ready."

"It's not that," Caiden said, his body rigid with fear.

A low guttural clicking echoed through the forest around us, sending a chill down my spine.

"We have to run… now." He held out his hand, and I took it.

Within seconds, we were running again.

The massive creatures followed. Their claws dug into the frozen earth as they raced after us. The smell of rotting flesh wafted through the air. Silhouettes slipped through the trees.

My blood froze in my veins at the thought of their claws ripping through my flesh. A scream built in my chest, but a didn't dare set it free. I wasn't sure I could stop once I started.

"Don't look back," Caiden said. "Dawn will be upon us soon. We… just… have to… keep… going."

The clicking grew louder. And the creatures split apart, flanking us on either side. I didn't dare to look. The creatures ran on all fours like dogs, but there was something distinctly human about them.

The sky lightened with the haze of dawn, and I breathed a little easier. They couldn't stay on the surface much longer. But I couldn't keep running at this pace either. We were lambs to slaughter if they caught us. With no weapons and no magic, we would make for a tasty treat.

Our feet pounded on the hard soil, matching the pace of our fast breath. Each gasp burned deep in my lungs. My mother mentioned a quest. If I was going to die, it would not be here.

The snapping of Caiden's ankle brought me back to reality. He tumbled to the ground, dragging me down with him. Together, we rolled into the wet carpet of leaves and branches until we came to a stop underneath a pine. Our eyes locked, and electricity shot through my veins. The tension pulled taut between us but quickly faded when the sound of panicked clicking echoed through the forest.

Caiden's blue eyes widened, and he blinked rapidly.

The pink hues of dawn streaked through the forest. From our position underneath the tree, I could see the clawed hands and feet of the creatures searching for us.

"I don't think they can see in the light," Caiden whispered.

The creature stopped in its tracks.

I held my breath, afraid to move. All we had to do was hide here until the sun fully rose.

The Night Folk scratched at the ground in frustration. The stench of their breath wafted through the cold air to where we hid, bringing bile to the back of my throat.

Caiden scowled at me with a look that said: *You better not.*

A preternatural scream echoed through the forest, ringing in my ears. I gritted my teeth, burying my face into Caiden's neck. The smell of leather and bergamot still lingered on his skin, buried beneath a layer of sweat. Memories flashed through my mind of a time when I would have given anything to be this close to him.

The Night Folk scattered into the forest, leaving giant gashes in the frozen earth.

I let out the breath I had been holding in, and I could sense Caiden's skin twitch underneath me. We hadn't been this close in a long time. Perhaps it was the adrenaline coursing through my veins after nearly being torn apart, or maybe it was the realization I'd never truly let him go, but I had the urge to kiss him.

Our breath mixed in the cool morning air. Chests heaving just like they had that night in the glass house by the river all those years ago.

"Uh, Aelia?" Caiden asked.

My throat went dry.

"Yes?"

"You can get up now."

Heat flushed my cheeks.

"Oh, sorry." I stood, my hands still bound to his.

"A little help?" He held out his hand, and I helped pull him to his feet.

"How's the ankle?"

"Sprained, if not broken."

I let out a breath.

"Let's make a splint for it. You can lean on me. We have to be close to getting out of here." I found some sticks and used them to brace his ankle before wrapping some old vines around it to hold them in place.

The faint smell of lavender and honey wafted in on the breeze.

"We must be close to the Court of Honey!" Caiden exclaimed. "They're friendly. C'mon, let's go."

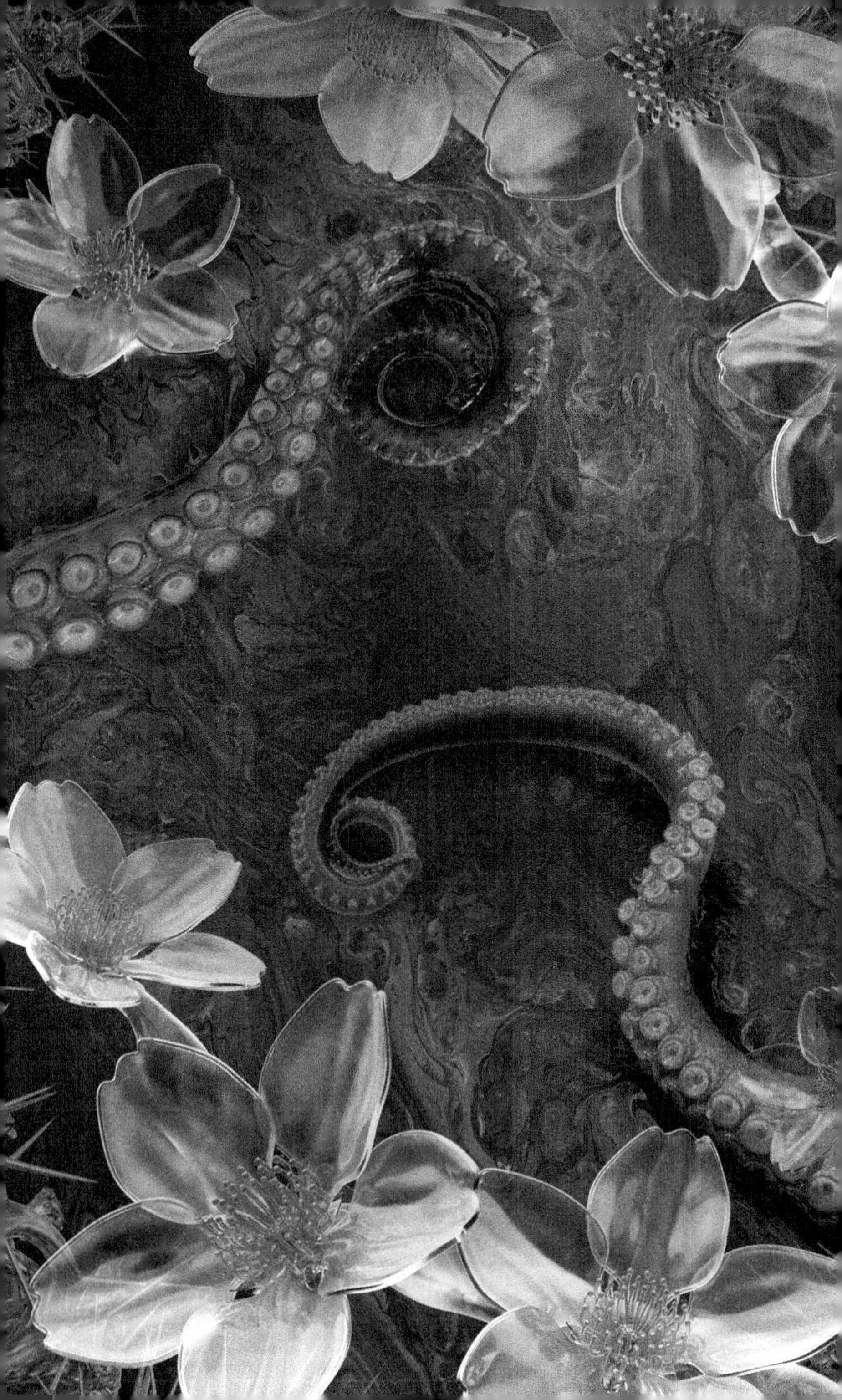

43 THARAN

"How did you know where to find us?" Tharan asked, shutting the curtains in his room.

Lucius picked at his nails.

"I wouldn't be a very good spy if I didn't know how to uncover secrets."

"I sent him a raven," Roderick chimed in.

"And that."

"Well, tell me what you know."

"I know that Caiden is missing and accused of murder and judging by the Blood Riders I saw on the way here, Erissa and Gideon are behind it. I'm also guessing you think a Trinity Well is in the Court of Screams."

"Correct," Tharan said. "Aelia is missing too. We think they were both taken by Erissa."

"Seems right. Likely, they're setting a trap for you as well."

"They are the trap. There is an ancient ritual site in the Court of Screams. We think that's where the Well is. We need to get there before Erissa and Gideon do."

"I've got my Shadow Hunters scouting in the Court of Screams as we speak. If they are there, my men will find them."

"Very good. We have a guide who will take us tomorrow night."

"We don't need him. I will take us tonight."

"When did you travel to the Court of Screams?" Roderick asked.

Lucius arched a brow.

"I've been keeping an eye on them for a while. The rest of the council liked to think they were content worshiping their false god, but I think they underestimated them. I think Erissa has had her claws in them for a long time."

"What makes you think that?" Tharan asked.

"It's her signature. She likes to make gods out of men she can control. She did it with Gideon and I bet she did it with the leader of the Court of Screams. Although, it could have been one of her sisters from her time in Crom's inner circle."

A chill ran down Tharan's spine. Erissa had tried to seduce him once. Could she have been grooming him to be one of her "gods"? He didn't want to think about how his life would have turned out had he succumbed to her advances.

"I hadn't thought about there being more of them…" Tharan rubbed his chin with his palm nervously.

Lucius scoffed. "You know better than I Crom had thousands of followers. He was charming and handsome, and I'm sure Erissa wasn't the only woman he made a zealot of."

"True." Tharan pulled back the honey-colored curtain, scanning the quaint town for any sign of the Blood Riders. He sighed. "I guess we better get going. Everyone, prepare. Meet me downstairs in an hour."

Everyone agreed before heading to get ready.

"I'm going to warn the mayor," Roderick said.

Tharan gave him a curt nod.

Hopper and Sumac lingered in Tharan's room after the others left.

"I don't want to hear it. I know you don't want me to go, but I have to. I have original blood. I have to be the one who opens the Well. I have to be the one to save Aelia. I couldn't live with myself if I just stayed here and let all of you go off and do my dirty work for me."

"We won't stop you," Sumac said, tying back her short, black hair. "But if it comes to it, we will both gladly lay down our lives to protect you."

An ache ripped through Tharan's heart.

"I will not try to convince you otherwise. I know you both too well."

"Then we are in agreement," Hopper said, turning on his heel.

An unspoken knowing passed between Tharan and Sumac. They'd fought beside each other in battle and watched their comrades die together, but this was different somehow. A heaviness hung in the air, and without saying a word, Sumac turned and left.

Tharan took a deep breath as he donned his armor—the armor his father wore in battles for millennia. Thousands of tungsten laurel leaves woven together in a mail as hard as dragon scales. He braided his hair back in the traditional military fashion, one woven knot from forehead to back before twisting the bottom. Taking a razor, he shaved the stubble from his face and applied kohl around his eyes. A fearsome warrior stared back at him from the mirror—one he had not seen in a very long time.

The anticipation of a fight sent adrenaline coursing through his veins. Taking his curved sword from its sheath, he ran a damp cloth over its blade until it shone in the candlelight.

"Well, old friend, looks like we'll be fighting again," he whispered to the weapon he'd carried into battle hundreds of times. The thought of spilling blood never got easier. His stomach churned with a mixture of dread and anticipation.

Sheathing his sword again, he adjusted his armor one last time before heading down to the foyer of the inn where the others waited, each dressed in their respective armor. Even Amolie wore a boiled leather cuirass.

Lucius held a lantern in one hand.

"We better get going."

Tharan nodded, and the group followed the wraith into the silent night.

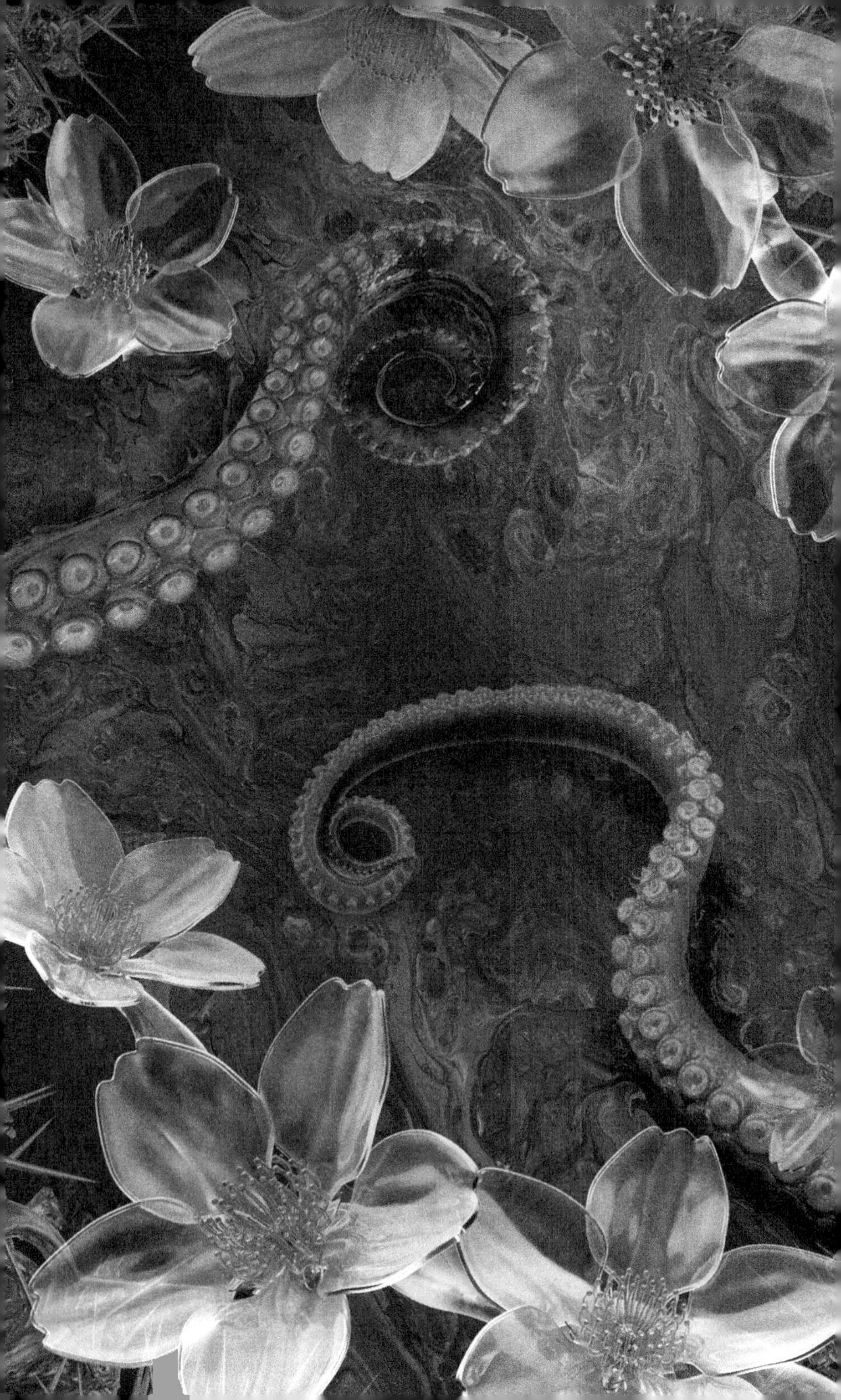

44   CAIDEN

Caiden's breath turned to vapor in the cool morning air as they trudged through the forest. Pain shot through his ankle, and he leaned on Aelia for support. Even through the dirt and the grime, the scent of jasmine lingered on her skin. A scent he remembered. Not from her memories but from his own. Were *his* memories coming back, too?

"The smell is getting stronger. We must be getting closer to the Court of Honey," Aelia said.

A memory rose to the surface of Caiden's mind.

"Aelia?"

"Yeah?"

"Do you remember the last time we were in the Court of Honey together?"

Her cheeks flushed.

"Yes. That was a very long time ago."

Butterflies flitted in his stomach. Back then, they'd used their secret sign to sneak out to the town proper. They'd danced and drank with the townsfolk. She'd fallen asleep in his arms on a cool summer night in a bed of wildflowers. To her, life couldn't get better. The night sparkled with fireflies.

Caiden tapped his nose—the signal they used to give one another when they needed to escape an awkward conversation.

"We were so young," he said.

"*I* was so young. You were like seventy."

A smile tugged at the corners of his lips, and he averted his eyes. This was how they used to be together. Flirtatious.

"Young for a sylph."

She chuckled.

"But, yes, I remember. I remember dancing the night away and then falling asleep in your arms."

"You thought life couldn't get much better."

"It didn't for a long time."

A skeletal hand clenched Caiden's heart. He hadn't meant to bring up such painful memories.

"I'm glad I could be a port in the storm that was your life." His heart ached for her.

"You saved me more than you know," she whispered.

Caiden's throat thickened.

"And now we are strangers. I have your memories, but it's like someone telling me a story about us… except I wasn't there."

He wished he had his memories—wished he knew how he felt during these precious moments.

"I'm sorry she did that to you," Aelia said. "I'd hope we could just move on."

"I've seen the way you look at Tharan. You used to look at me that way." The words stuck in his throat. "But he looks at you the same way I looked at my wife. He really loves you Aelia. I wouldn't dare to stand in the way of your happiness." It wasn't what he wanted to say

A tear trickled down her cheek. Caiden wanted to reach out and catch it before it fell off her chin.

"I didn't want to let you go; you know. If there was a way I could have saved us, I would have. You were my first love."

"First loves rarely last, Aelia." Memories flashed through his mind of fights and screaming, of her longing for him to come and save her. Shame clutched his heart.

"I didn't want to hurt you," she sniffled.

And he never meant to hurt her, but he had. She'd loved him. Had given herself to him in so many ways, and he failed her when she needed him the most. A vision of her fingers slipping through his flashed through his mind. She didn't want to leave him, but duty called them both in different directions.

Another memory bubbled to the surface. He had come for her in the dungeons of Ryft's Edge, but it had been too late. She was broken, in both mind and body, laying there in a pile of hay, starved and frozen. He'd scooped her up and carried her out of the palace. Aelia clung to his scent, hoping it was real and not just some cruel joke.

A mixture of shame and guilt rippled through his heart. If only he had taken her away before she went to Ryft's Edge. It would have been hard, but they'd have been together.

"I know," he said. "I can feel every emotion you had."

"That's awkward," she said through a half-hearted laugh.

"No, it's not. We loved each other once. The world pulled us apart. I have been a thorn in your side at times, but the love we shared was real. You couldn't wait forever for me to save you, and by the time I did it was too late. I wish we'd run away when we had the chance, but we can't go back now."

"I was really angry at you for a long time," she sniffled.

Caiden swallowed hard.

"You had every right to be. I failed you when you needed me the most."

"I should've known I'd always have to save myself. White knights only exist in bedtime stories."

Caiden went to speak, but an arrow whizzed past them.

"Shit," Aelia said. "We have to move faster."

Caiden did his best to keep up with her, but his foot dragged in the frozen mud.

"Just a little farther. They won't touch us across the border," Aelia said through panted breaths.

"You don't know that. They stole me from Vantris."

"True, just wishful thinking, really."

Another arrow whizzed past them. Caiden didn't dare look backward. Their only chance of surviving was if they could make it to the Hive in the Court of Honey. They had a large army and would be safe there.

The sun shone on the frost-covered grass, casting everything in a gilded light. Caiden squinted to see ahead.

"We're not going to be able to make it, Aelia." Caiden's throat thickened.

"They're not going to take us again." Her eyes narrowed on the path ahead of them. She looked back. "I don't see them. Baylis must be shooting blindly."

The sound of pounding hooves echoed through the quiet morning, reverberating through the hard earth. Caiden's stomach sank. Over the horizon, the silhouettes of five Blood Riders appeared, running full speed at them.

"Fuck," Aelia said. "What are we going to do?"

Caiden looked down at the chain linking them, and an idea formed in his head.

"Let them get close. We're going to use our chain to trip the horse."

"Are you insane? That's never going to work."

"At worst the chain breaks and we're free."

"They could trample us, break our arms, we could die."

"They're going to kill us anyway. Better to go down fighting."

Aelia looked toward the riders. They were so close they could see the drool coming from the water horses' sharp fangs. The riders smiled a mouth full of lip-less rotten teeth. Their bloodred eyes thirsty for a kill.

"Wait until they get close and then we pull apart. The horses won't be able to stop."

"But I feel bad about the horse."

"That horse will eat you if given the chance."

The rumbling grew more violent.

"You're right," Aelia said.

Caiden could see the horses' breath in the cold morning light.

"On my cue."

The pocked faces of the riders became clearer. The stench of rotting flesh hung heavy in the air.

"Wait," Caiden said as calmly as he could.

The lead rider kicked his steed, and they shot ahead of the rest.

The rider held up his sword ready to lop off Caiden's head.

Caiden held his breath, saying a silent prayer to Illya to let them live. He watched as the horses' hooves grew closer and closer, throwing mud in their wake.

"Caiden…" Aelia whispered.

The horse was nearly upon them. The rider lowered his sword.

"Now!"

They broke apart and fell to their knees, pulling their chain tight.

Caiden's wrists twisted against his manacles but did not break. He let out a guttural cry as the chain buckled under the weight of the horse. With a *snap*, the chain broke.

The rider's eyes widened. He tried to stop his horse, but it was too late. The animal's leg hit the trip chain, sending the horse tumbling headfirst into the brush.

The riders called to each other in wicked screams sending a shiver down Caiden's spine.

Aelia picked herself up. The chains linking her manacles fell to the ground. Caiden's did the same. They were free. Aelia's face brightened and darkened in an instant.

The other riders closed ranks around them. Caiden and Aelia stood back-to-back.

"If you have another plan, now would be the time to implement it," Aelia said.

Caiden's chest tightened, and adrenaline coursed through his veins, but he had no plan. There were too many for him and Aelia to take on; his ankle was broken, and neither of them had magic.

"Uh, well, if you pray to the Trinity, now might be a good time to put in a cry for help."

The Blood Riders licked their bare teeth. The smell of their acrid breath wafted through the air. Closer and closer, they moved until Caiden and Aelia were within inches of the horse's long fangs.

"Don't harm them. The lady wants them whole," one of the riders called to the others, raising his fist in a sign to hold. "We are to keep them here until she arrives."

Dread coiled like a snake in Caiden's gut. This was it; they were done for. Erissa would take them back and probably give them parasites like the others. He reached for Aelia's hand, intertwining their fingers.

"I'm sorry, Caiden," she whispered. "For everything."

"You have nothing to apologize for. We're going to get out of this. We didn't escape and face the Night Folk, just to be captured again."

"Alright, well, any actionable steps we could take would be great."

An arrow soared through the air, hitting a Blood Rider between the eyes. The man didn't even have time to blink before he was on the ground. His water horse ripped into his lifeless body with its massive fangs.

The knot in Caiden's chest unraveled. Baylis wouldn't kill a

Blood Rider. It could only be a friendly court coming to rescue them, but who? Court of Honey? The Woodlands? The Stormlands? Strangers looking to hunt Blood Riders?

The other men looked around to see the source of the arrow. Caiden swore he could see a flicker of fear in their cold dead eyes. In an instant, the other three were on the ground.

He blinked stupidly at the lifeless bodies. The sound of crunching bones echoed in his chest as the water horses devoured their riders, a reminder every triumph balances on the edge of a knife.

"Run," Aelia said.

Caiden looked at his twisted ankle, and dread pooled in his stomach. He couldn't outrun a water horse even with a good leg.

"I can't."

"Lean on me. They'll hunt us down when they're finished. They've had a taste of blood now, and they'll want more."

With his arm looped over her shoulder, he rested his weight on her, trying his best to help her as much as he could. He couldn't help but see the woman she was. The one from long ago who tamed horses and charmed dignitaries. The one he knew in a different lifetime. The one he let slip through his fingers.

Dark hooded figures emerged from the forest.

Caiden sucked in a breath. He and Aelia paused in their tracks. They couldn't go back. Not with the water horses behind them.

One of the figures pulled his hood off, and Caiden recognized him as one of Lucius's Shadow Hunters. He breathed a sigh of relief at the sight.

"Lord Caiden, we've been searching for you. Master Lucius has instructed us to bring you back home, but seeing as you're injured, we will take you to the Court of Honey."

Two tall and lanky Shadow Hunters looped their arms around Caiden, lifting him from Aelia's grip.

He reached back for her, but their fingers slipped through one another.

They walked for hours until they reached the Hive, where the Queen Bee awaited them.

Exhausted, bloodied, and bruised, Caiden fell to his knees before her.

"Your Majesty, I am sorry to come to you like this, but I am in great need of aid."

"I can see that," she said. Bees buzzed around her flower crown. "You are a Council Court. Of course, I will shelter you." She waved to her attendants. "Remove their shackles and take them to the infirmary so a healer can tend to their injuries."

Attendants rushed to Caiden and Aelia's side, lifting them onto gurneys. Caiden let his body relax for the first time in weeks. He was safe. Aelia was safe. That's all that mattered now.

They took them both to the infirmary where healers tended to their wounds and locksmiths came to break their manacles open.

A rush of magic seeped into Caiden's blood, roaring like a fire through his veins. He winced as the pain consumed him.

A healer came over to administer elixir of poppy to help with the pain. His eyes felt heavy, and his head wobbled on a rubbery neck.

"Alright, all healed," Aelia said, sitting up in her bed next to his. She twisted her hands around her wrists where the manacles had been.

"Not so fast," said the lead healer, a tall, lanky man with gray hair and a short, trimmed beard. "You need your rest. I'm having the cooks add some magical herbs to your dinners to aid in rejuvenating your magic. You were wearing those manacles for a long time. Your magic must have been nearly gone.

Aelia huffed but lay back down on the bed.

"Fine."

The healer turned his attention to Caiden.

"We're going to have to regrow the bones in your ankle. I've got a tonic, but it will take at least a day."

Caiden groaned but agreed.

The healer nodded and went to mix the tincture.

Aelia fiddled with her fingers. "I hate laying here. We need to act."

"Yeah? You don't even know what you're looking for."

"A magical well should be easy to find."

"Let's ask the queen. Hopefully, she can point us in the right direction. We will take my Shadow Hunters with us as reinforcements."

"I suppose you're right. Old habits die hard." She shut her eyes.

A memory flashed through Caiden's mind. Their bodies entwined in red silk sheets. His fingers trailed the curve of her back. Her long, brown hair in a mess of curls. His heart swelled and cracked. Shaking his head, he tried to focus on something else… anything else but her.

A flurry of movement proved a worthy distraction. The queen entered in a sweeping gown the color of sunflowers in full bloom, her round belly on full display. Bees buzzed around her tight curls.

"Are you two feeling better?" she said in her deep feminine voice.

Both nodded as they sat up in their beds.

"Very well, I've got two pieces of information I think you will find helpful. The first is your Captain Roderick was here yesterday. They were asking about the Court of Screams. I sent them to Honeyville. I assume you'd want to know."

"Yes, thank you," Caiden nodded.

She clicked her tongue.

"What?" Caiden asked.

"I didn't know the Court of Storms had allied with the Woodland Realm."

Aelia twisted her hair into a knot. "Was the Alder King with them?"

"Indeed. He is looking for something in the Court of Screams."

She turned to him, eyes wide and wild.

"We have to go. Tonight, Caiden."

"He needs to heal," the healer chimed in. His brows furrowed. "And so do you. You can leave in the morning."

Caiden couldn't help but feel like he missed her already. She loved someone else now, and he would have to accept that.

"I know you want to help Tharan and find the Wells… I want that too. Please, do not leave without me. Besides, we don't know if we need all our blood to unlock the Well."

Her gaze softened on him and her face contorted with indecision. Was she feeling something long forgotten too?

Moments of silence passed until finally, she said, "Fine. We'll leave in the morning. Is there a portal or are we hoofing it?"

The queen sighed, and her eyes shot to the ceiling.

"I do have a portal for my own personal use. I suppose you could use it. Since it's for a good cause."

Caiden smirked.

"You don't do anything out of the goodness of your heart, Queen. What do you want in return?"

"Well, there is something the Court of Storms could help me with."

Caiden shook his head.

"Of course there is."

"We are expecting a drought this year. Our bees depend on

flowers. I'd like you to send some of your citizens with the gift of rain to help if that is the case."

"It is done."

A blinding white smile cut her face in two.

"Excellent. You may use my portal in the morning." The queen turned on her heel and promptly exited the infirmary, followed by her attendants and a buzzing of bees.

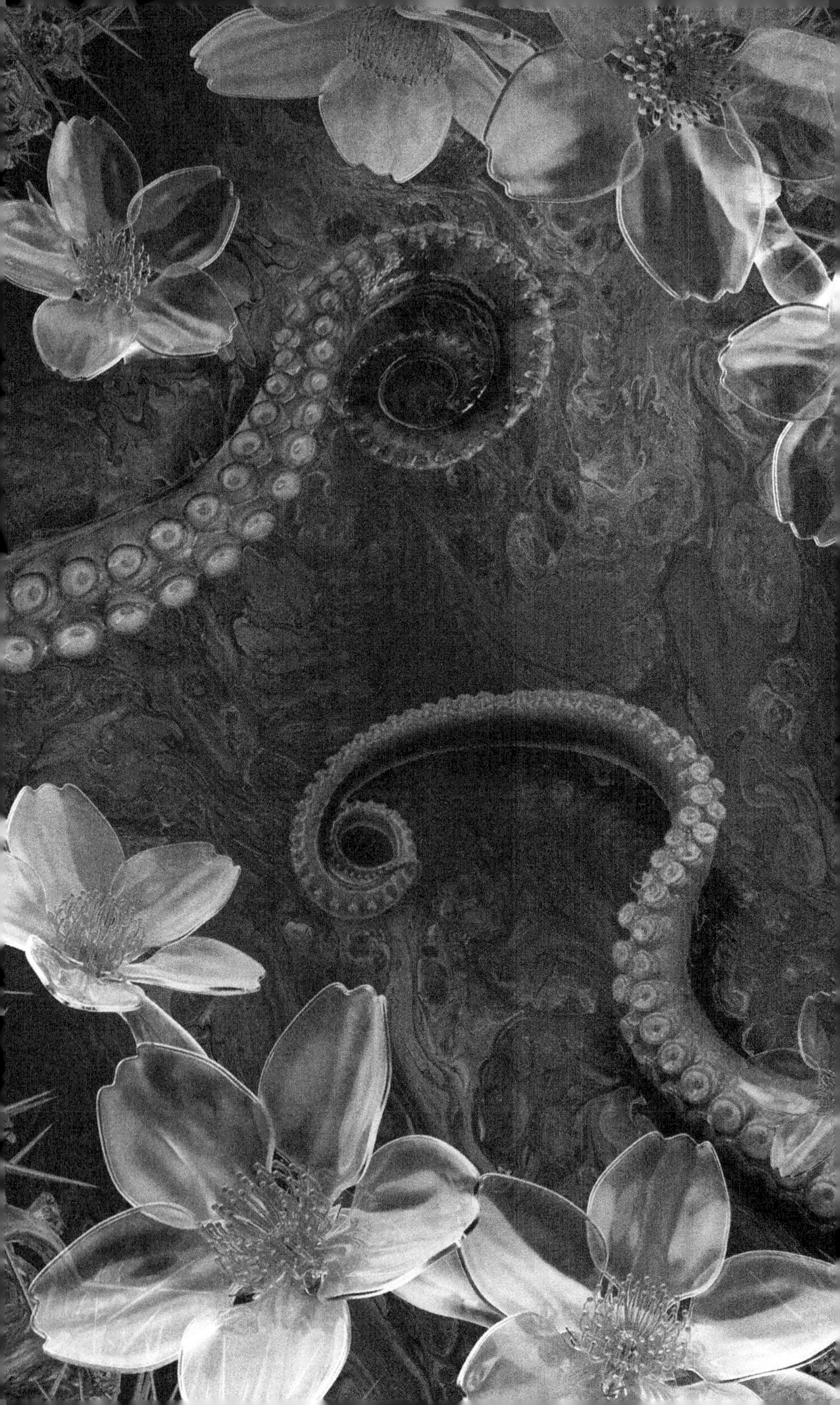

45 AELIA

I tossed and turned all night thinking about seeing Tharan. He had come for me, just like I hoped he would. Worry settled like a blanket over me. What if he had already left for the Court of Screams?

As soon as dawn broke, I jumped from my bed and flung the blankets off Caiden. Seeing his toned body wrapped in bandages made my breath catch in my throat. I had put my feelings aside for Caiden when I erased his memories, but now that he had mine, I somehow felt closer to him. Everything I'd ever thought about him laid bare. There was something oddly freeing about it.

"How's the ankle?" I asked. It was the only thing I could think of to say.

He rubbed his eyes.

"We've been traveling for days, we're battered and bruised, and I'm regrowing bones, let me sleep, woman."

He was right, but we needed to catch up to Tharan if we had any hope of succeeding.

"You can sleep once we've harnessed the power of the Well and defeated Gideon and Erissa."

Caiden pulled the pillow over his head.

"Fine, I guess you're right, but I'm not happy about it."

We quickly bathed and donned new clothing. The queen was nice enough to provide us with leather armor. Complete with a hive embossed on the breastplate.

Caiden came in while I tightened my bootstraps. He leaned against the doorway in a way I hadn't seen since we were young. The golden light of morning highlighted his square jaw and blue eyes. My gut tightened with a lust I thought I'd erased along with his memories, but I pushed it away. Although I would be lying if I said Tharan's proposal didn't run through my mind. *Get it together, Aelia. You can think about sex later.*

"Ready?" he asked with the coy smile I'd fallen for all those years ago.

"As I'll ever be."

He extended his hand and pulled me from where I sat.

Together we walked to the portal room flanked by Shadow Hunters. Tall, dark, and silent—just like Lucius. Only these were pure sylph. Though they looked thin, they were nothing but lean muscle underneath their cloaks.

The heels of our boots clicked on the polished wood floors of the Hive. An ominous feeling hung in the air. I swallowed my thickening throat, hoping we weren't too late to catch Tharan, Roderick, and the others.

The honey-colored portal opened, and I held my breath before stepping through to a wood paneled library where a sylph woman with white hair and umber skin waited, leaning against a solid, oak desk.

"Aelia?" she said, arching a brow. I noted her leather armor, complete with spiked shoulders.

"Yes," I said.

"Lydia." She held out her hand in a sign of peace and friendship as Caiden and the Shadow Hunters shot through the portal. "I'm the mayor of Honeyville."

I shook her hand and Caiden did the same.

"Roderick and Tharan were here earlier. I was going to have a hunter show them the safest route into the Court of Screams, but when my hunter showed up at the inn, he said they had already gone."

Rocks sank in my stomach.

"We were so close and yet so far apart," I said.

"Can your hunter take us into the Court of Screams?" Caiden asked.

"She can. Best to wait until sundown though. They hunt during the day and my clout will only carry you so far. You are welcome to explore our town or rest at the inn until sundown."

Knots twisted in my chest. I wanted to leave now. Every second counted when lives were on the line.

"I understand you have your customs, but our friends are out there. We need to go now. Evil is coming and daylight will not stop them from getting what they want. We need to beat them to it."

The mayor tapped her fingers on the desk indecisively.

"I suppose you're right. I will send for the hunter."

I let out a breath.

"Thank you."

The mayor rang a bell, and an attendant entered. She whispered something into his ear, he nodded and left.

"I've arranged for some provisions for you to be wrapped up as well. The hunter will meet you outside. Good luck on your journey. For all our sakes."

Caiden and I nodded curtly and went to wait for the hunter.

The scent of honey and lavender carried on the cool spring air. All around us flowers were beginning to bloom. Birds sang their springtime songs and the anticipation that comes with new beginnings hung in the air. In just a few weeks Ostara would be upon us. I looked at Caiden who was testing his lightning—little sparks flew from his fingertips.

Long ago we'd danced the night away at the Ostara balls. On our last night together he'd worn a white tailcoat embroidered with golden flowers. The same flowers were embroidered on my dress. I was supposed to spend the night dancing with many suitors, but once Caiden and I locked hands, I knew I never wanted to dance with anyone else ever again. My heart was so full I thought it would burst, but our happiness would not last. I should have treasured those moments more. If only I'd known what I'd had then. If only I'd known how dark my life would become.

I popped into a shop to grab some cigarettes. Through all this stress, I hadn't thought about using dust once. That must be growth. The shopkeeper handed me the pack wrapped in parchment, and I slid a gold coin across the stand. Before I left, I made sure to light one on the nearest candle. Taking the smoke deep into my lungs, I let it calm my senses.

Tug, tug-tug the knot in my chest reminded me it wanted to return home. I waited for the sensation to stop before leaving the store.

When I returned, the hunter, a short sylph woman with tan skin and dark hair, was waiting to take us into the forest. She wore a long leather jacket over a beige tunic and trousers, with knee-high boots. Her face looked like that of a teen, but knowing the sylph she was probably much older.

"Alright," she said in a heavy northern accent. "We're goin' inta the Court of Screams. You must keep yer wits about ya. Do you hear me?"

We all nodded.

"The forest has a mind of its own. It'll play tricks on ya. Follow me and dunnot stray from the path." She chewed on a piece of willow bark as she spoke. "Now, I'm takin' ya to the ruins, am I?"

"Yes," Caiden said.

"Very good. I dunno what ya think yer gonna find there, but I'll get ya there."

"Thank you," I said.

"Don't thank me yet. We still have ta make it out alive."

Fear coiled in my stomach, but I had made it this far—past the siren and the sea serpent, escaped Erissa, and the clutches of the Blood Riders. If Ammena existed, she must have been looking out for me. "Let's go."

The hunter nodded. "See where the tree line becomes black and dead?"

We all turned to the forest. A murder of crows took flight from the ominous trees.

"That's where we're going."

I didn't dare look back as we crossed the barren field toward the trees. I couldn't focus on what was behind me, only on what lay ahead of me. The sky seemed to grey as we drew nearer, as if the light was being sucked from the sky.

The hunter didn't hesitate before entering the forest. Just went right in as if it was the most normal thing in the world.

"We have ta be quiet as spirits now," she whispered, holding her pointer finger up to her mouth.

The Shadow Hunters, who were with us, rolled their eyes. Silence was their domain.

The forest still wore its winter bareness. The black-bark trees grew together in a mess of mangled limbs and vines. The stench of sulfur hung in the air.

"Sulfur wells," the hunter said. "That's what makes the smell."

"Wonderful," I said under my breath.

We walked for hours through the dead wood. Not one creature stirred, and no birds called to one another. I focused on my feet as we walked. Even the soil was black here. Had the Trinity cursed this place for a reason?

A light rain fell, coating us in a fine mist.

My thoughts drifted to what lay before us. Erissa had my scepter but couldn't use it and neither could I. If I could get my hands on it, we would be in control. We could destroy anyone who stood in our way. My blood boiled as I thought about it more. Perhaps she knew all along it would not bind to her blood. If Erissa created it, she had to know the limitations.

At midday we stopped by a stream to eat our rations and drink from the cool water.

"Keep a lookout," the hunter said. "You neva know what lurks here."

Caiden and I quickly downed the cheese and hard salami that had been packed for us before switching with the Shadow Hunters so they could eat.

"What do you think the Well will look like?" Caiden asked.

"To be honest, I haven't thought much about it. I just kind of picture the fairy wells from the stories we heard as kids. But since there's blood involved, I'm sure it's something much darker."

"It has to be if it's in this place," Caiden replied. "If I had to guess, I bet the people of this court perform their rituals right over the Well and have no idea what they're doing."

"I mean, they'd have original blood, wouldn't that open the Well?"

"They'd have to have all three... allegedly."

"Perhaps they've already opened it, and this pain god thing is just an act to keep people out." I arched my brow, and Caiden gave me a smirk. His dimples indenting on his cheeks made butterflies flit in my stomach, just as they had ten years ago.

"Only time will tell I guess."

A whistle echoed through the woods and the hunter appeared. "It's time to go."

46 THARAN

BRANCHES SCRATCHED THARAN'S FACE AS HE FOLLOWED LUCIUS deeper and deeper into the Court of Screams. The sound of pounding drums echoed through the silent forest, matching pace with his heartbeat. An ominous tension pulled taut in the air.

A light rain began to fall *drip*, *drip*, *drip* until it was a steady stream, soaking them.

"Keep up! Not much farther!" Lucius called over the sound of the rain hitting their armor. Their breath turned to mist in the cold spring air as their feet avoided mangled roots marring their path.

They'd been walking for hours and still not seen another soul, but now the drums pounded heavy, reverberating in Tharan's chest.

Lucius ducked low just as something flashed before them.

"What was that?" Roderick whispered.

"Ancient creatures lurk in these woods. Follow the path and they will not bother us."

Tharan swallowed past his thickening throat.

They moved swiftly and silently through the ominous woods toward the sound of the drums. The flicker of a massive fire painted the night sky with oranges and reds. The smell of burning wood and an incense Tharan couldn't quite place wafted through the forest.

"What is that smell?" Tharan whispered.

"It's part of their ritual. What you smell is what happens when a fresh heart is burned."

"Trinity…" Tharan's mouth went dry. "What are we walking into?"

"Nothing you've likely seen before." Lucius ducked low and Tharan noticed they were standing in front of an ancient stone structure. "This way," Lucius said, ushering them through a crack in the wall.

Tharan climbed in and the others followed behind him.

Through cobwebs and dust, he crawled toward the flickering light of the fire. With each step he took, his heart beat faster. The drums grew louder and the sound of voices chanting in unison echoed through the ancient structure.

They exited onto a balcony overlooking a massive fire. People danced around the flame chanting something Tharan couldn't quite make out.

They were in what appeared to be the remnants of an ancient temple, but time and the elements had worn away at its once-pristine marble and granite leaving only the bones of something sacred.

Tharan's eyes fell to the carving around the fire, ancient runes of a language long since dead, stained with what he could only assume was blood. Tharan's eyes flitted to where six bodies were strewn up on poles. Naked and covered in blood, he gasped when he discovered half of their chests had gaping holes where their hearts had once been.

"Amolie, don't look," Tharan warned, but it was too late. Her hazel eyes widened, and she covered her mouth. Roderick put his arms around her, pulling her close.

A tall, sylph man wearing black robes stood at the center of the circle. Tattoos wrapped themselves up his exposed hands. Atop his head he wore the skull of a bull, disguising his face.

"That's their leader, Cyrus," Lucius whispered to Tharan. "They call him the Blood Shepard. It's an honor to be one of the chosen to have your heart cut out and sacrificed to the ancient flame."

Cyrus walked around, holding a heart in his hand. Blood dripped down his forearm onto the white granite, pooling in the carved stone.

Beyond him people stood together, hands linked, heads to the heavens.

"My friends, we honor these six souls who have graciously given their lives to honor Algea. They put their bodies through rigorous torture so that they may be closer to her. Tonight, we honor them by giving their hearts."

Tharan noticed their gaunt faces barely resembled the muscular sylph they used to be. No, these creatures had become a part of the forest. With their pale white skin and dark eyes, it had been a long time since they'd been creatures of the blood.

The crowd cheered and chanted. "Blood for blood. Blood for blood."

Cyrus held the heart high in the air, squeezing it so that blood shot from the ventricles. The crowd's chanting grew louder.

"Blood for blood. Blood for blood."

Cyrus tossed the heart into the fire and the flame turned bloodred. A sulfuric and sweet aroma wafted through the air.

"We should go," Lucius said. "It will do us no good to linger. I know a cave we can camp out in for the night and decide what to do in the morning."

As they turned to leave, a flash of white caught Tharan's eye and he turned to see the crowd parting for none other than Erissa.

Cyrus bowed and the crowd silenced.

"Mistress Erissa, to what do we owe this visit?"

The crowd kneeled in front of the ancient mage.

"I am sorry to interrupt your ceremony, but I have a task for you."

Whispers ripped through the crowd.

"For many years I have come here with messages from beyond. I was the one who knew Cyrus was the living embodiment of Algea. And now I have another task for you."

Hushed questions abounded.

"Tomorrow we will go on a hunt. But not for lamb or boar, but for something much more sacred. Three originals lurk in these woods. We will find them and bring them here where I will perform the sacred ritual that will open the vaults to the Well of Power below. You will be given back the magic that was taken from you long ago."

The crowd cheered, raising their fists in the air.

Lucius and Tharan exchanged knowing glances. Tharan's stomach hardened. They would hunt them down. Lucius had been right—Erissa had her claws in more than just Gideon. She was sowing seeds all over the continent. He let out a long breath, hoping no one would see the vapor. If she was hunting for three originals, then she didn't have Aelia anymore. His heart lightened a bit, and he prayed to Illya Aelia would not come looking for him here, though he knew she would. She was hardheaded and her thirst for revenge would not be quenched easily.

"If she's here, where are Caiden and Aelia?" Lucius whispered.

"They must be here somewhere. We must go now. We have to find them before she does." A primal urge rushed through Tharan's veins. He was so close to saving Aelia. So close to finding the Well. If they could just survive long enough.

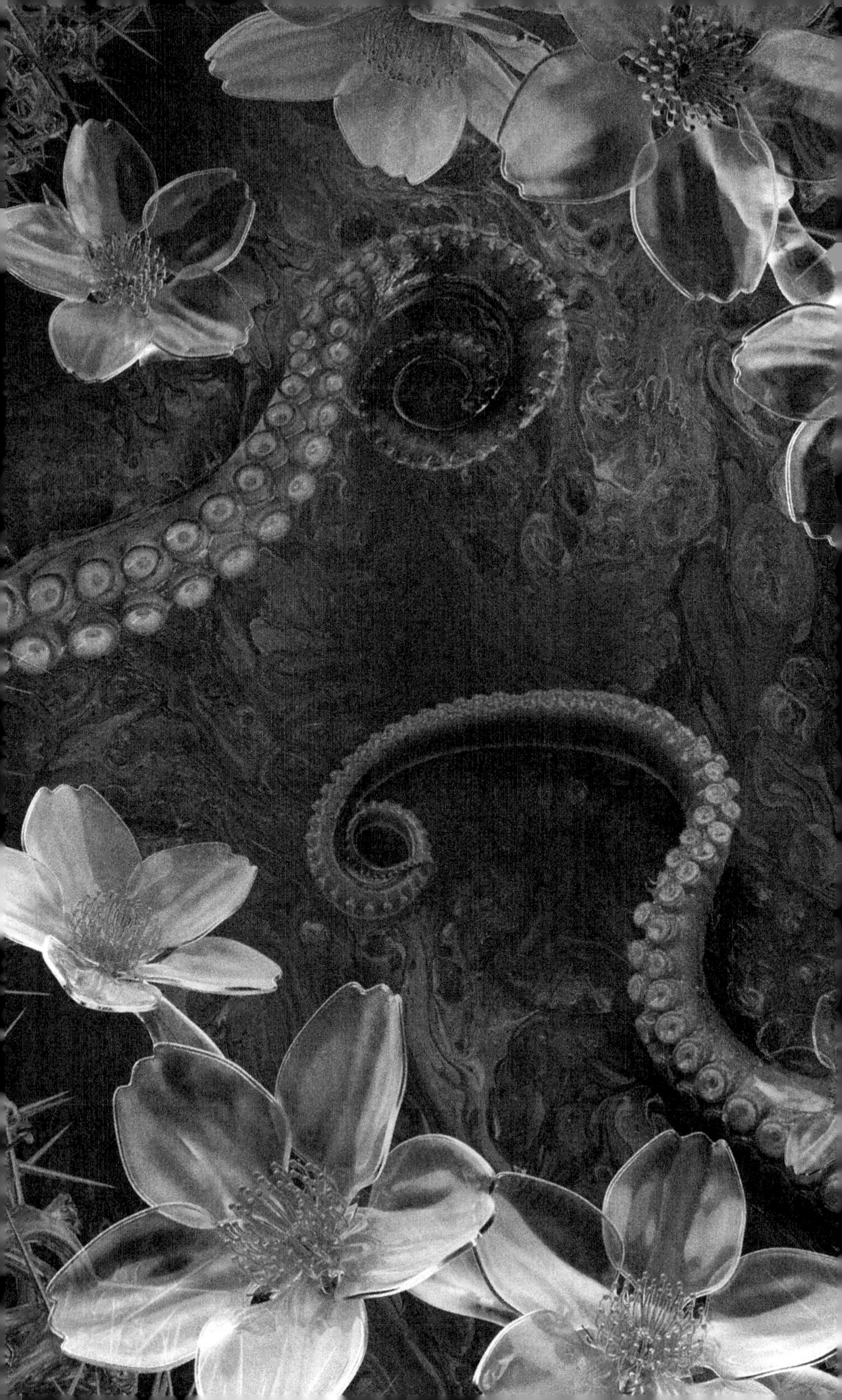

47 AELIA

Something pulled at the knot in my chest, drawing me deeper into the forest. Darkness surrounded us, save for the light of the hunter's lantern. With each step I took my throat grew thicker. Something ominous awaited me in these woods. Something called to the knot in my chest. I tried not to think about it and instead focused on finding Tharan.

The distant smell of a bonfire wafted through the silent forest. Caiden walked behind me followed by the Shadow Hunters. I scanned the trees for any sign of a threat.

A loud cry echoed, sending a chill down my spine. I looked back at Caiden, the moonlight cut a path across his chiseled face. Only Tharan knew about the weaver's magic resting in my chest and I couldn't put that on Caiden. A bitter taste filled my mouth. My mother had once again saddled me with a burden I did not wish to have. I never wanted magic. I was content being a human. And now I had this *thing* inside me that could go off at any moment and I had absolutely no control over, besides a cryptic message from my mother asking me to trust in it.

I let out a breath. My fingers itched to light a cigarette, but I fought the urge.

A wind whipped through the trees, carrying cheering voices with it.

"We are close to their sacred ritual ground," the hunter said, sinking low. Before her lay the ruins of an ancient temple. Time and the elements wore most of the granite away. Tall, twisted columns rose high into the sky.

I swallowed the dread pooling in my stomach.

The hunter extinguished her lantern. "Do not linger here. We need ta find a place ta rest for the night. Then tamorra I will take ya inside."

We nodded and followed the hunter around the back of the ruins.

The unruly knot burned, and I fell to my knees grabbing at my chest.

"What's going on?" Caiden asked.

"It's my chest... there's something woven into me. Ancient magic. It's never acted like this before." I gritted my teeth, trying to fight through the searing pain.

Caiden scooped me up into his muscular arms.

"We need to get her somewhere safe, now."

The hunter nodded. "There's a cave... this way."

She ushered us along. I shut my eyes, unable to bear the pain. The knot twirled in my chest calling to something in the ancient temple.

We walked for what seemed like ages to me but could have only been minutes.

"Hold on, Aelia," Caiden whispered in the darkness.

I did my best not to cry out, but every breath was agony. Sweat wetted my brow, and heat radiated from my skin.

The hunter pulled aside some vines, and we stepped into a damp cave. Lighting her lantern once again, the hunter motioned for us to follow her.

Through a tunnel of limestone, we traveled until we reached a cavern where a small stream cut through.

"We should be safe this far in," the hunter said.

Caiden lay me down on the cool stone and I sucked in a breath. The pain dissipated but not entirely. "I wish there was something I could do, but I'm no healer."

"The knot…" I winced in pain. "It's calling to whatever is in that ruin."

The scraping of boots on rock set us all on edge. A quiet swept over the chamber. I held my breath, and the Shadow Hunters pulled their swords silently from their sheaths.

More footsteps echoed through the massive chamber.

Caiden stepped in front of me, but did not call his lightning to his fingertips. We couldn't risk being found out.

Two of the Shadow Hunters laid themselves flat against the opening of the cave.

More footsteps. How many of them were there?

My pulse raced through my veins. I called my dagger to my hand. I would not go down without a fight.

Through the darkness a shadowy figure appeared.

My heart leapt into my throat and I let out a gasp at Lucius.

"My Lord," Lucius said, rushing to Caiden.

Behind him Tharan, Roderick, Amolie, Sumac, and Hopper filed into the cavern.

"Aelia!" Tharan said, rushing to where I lay. "Are you hurt?" He held my face in his warm hands, and I let out a sigh of relief.

"I'm alright."

He pulled me in for a kiss and I could taste blackberries on his tongue. How I'd missed him. I wanted to pull him close and never let him go.

"How did you get here?" He asked.

"The hunter brought us." I nodded to our guide and Tharan gave her an appreciative nod.

"I was so worried. I thought Erissa had you."

"She did. She had me and Caiden, but we broke free, luckily. Oh, and as I'm sure you've discovered... Baylis is a traitor."

"Oh, we're aware," Roderick chimed in.

Amolie rushed over, wrapping her arms around me.

"I'm so glad you're safe."

"Me too. I'm glad you're all safe as well." I took in the scent of nutmeg and honey still lingering on her skin. My heart soared and sank. We still had to get to the Wells before Erissa knew we were here. A chill crept down my spine. I didn't want to ask them to do more than they already had.

"We thought Queen Calliope had taken you at first," Amolie said.

"Oh no," I whispered.

"Yeah, Tharan had it out with Calliope and sent her crawling back into the sea."

I swallowed the dread pooling in the back of my throat. I had put the ones I love in danger again.

"I'll likely regret that later, but at least I still have the song." Tharan shrugged.

I rubbed the bridge of my nose. I had to tell them about Erissa and the scepter, but I couldn't bear to see the looks on their faces.

"That reminds me... Erissa has the Scepter of the Dead."

A hush fell over the room, and I sucked in a breath. I couldn't look anyone in the eyes. My love for my sister blinded me and now we'd all pay the price. More than that—the continent would pay the price.

"She can't use it, though. She's already tried. It won't bind to another's blood until I'm dead, and she can't kill me yet. She needs me for the Wells."

Tharan sighed, running a hand through his silken locks.

"Well, she has some hold over these people. She's sending them out to hunt for us tomorrow night. She promised them the power that had been stolen from them. Whatever that means."

I shuddered at the thought.

"Nothing good."

"So, what are we going to do?" Caiden asked, ringing his hands.

Everyone looked around at one another.

"Well, I'll tell ya what I'm doin'. I'm gettin' outta 'ere," the hunter said. She took her lantern and left.

"Alright, so what are *we* going to do?" Caiden asked.

Tharan thumbed his lip.

"I think we should try to open the Well tonight."

"Tonight?" Sumac's eyes went wide.

"They've gone to bed after their ceremony and won't be back until dawn. We should go now when they'll least expect it."

"Tharan, there's something I need to tell you." My voice was little more than a squeak.

"What is it?"

I took a ragged breath.

"The knot in my chest. It calls to the Well. To the magic within. It's like it's unraveling the closer we get. I don't know if I can bear the pain."

Tharan clasped his hand around mine.

"It's okay, Aelia. I will help you."

"You're going to have to carry me. I don't think I can walk."

"Of course, my darling." Even through the darkness I could see the beginnings of a smile on his lips, making my heart skip a beat. It had been a long time since I trusted someone so completely.

"Alright. Let's go."

We crept through the forest on silent feet. Amolie gave me a piece of willow bark to numb the pain, but it barely touched the fire in my chest. I kept looking down, expecting to see a glowing hole, but none surfaced.

I lay my head against Tharan's chest, focusing on the sound of his heart, reveling in his warmth.

"You're burning up, Aelia," he said.

A chill crept through my body, and I began to shake uncontrollably.

"I feel cold," I whispered as my teeth chattered together.

Tharan paused, laying me against a tree. An invisible hole bore into my chest. Squeezing my eyes tight, I tried to focus on anything but the pain. Tharan brushed the sweat-soaked hair sticking to my damp brow behind my ear. When had I started sweating?

"I won't take you a step further if you don't want me to. I will not risk your life for this." Removing his cloak, he placed it over mine.

"No," I said, fighting through the agony. "We have to do this. It's the only way to stop them."

"If you want to stop, just tell me. I can't lose you, Aelia."

Tears formed behind my eyes.

"You won't. I promise." A lie. I didn't know how this would end. Would the fire in my chest consume me completely?

"Don't make promises you can't keep, King Killer."

I smiled through the pain.

Lucius and his Shadow Hunters went ahead to scout for any adversaries while the rest stayed behind and waited for the *all-clear* signal. A fresh layer of frost coated everything in silver crystals, reminding us winter wasn't fully gone yet.

"What are we going to do, once we get in there?" Caiden asked.

"We'll need to look closely at the runes. They're ancient, and I don't know if I can read them," Tharan said.

"Roderick can read ancient sylph. Hopefully he can interpret."

Roderick nodded; his pale green eyes glowed in the darkness.

The cawing of a starling signaled the *all clear*.

We snuck around the opening of the ruins where heartless naked bodies still hung. Their lifeless heads tilted downward.

I gasped at the gruesome sight, some of their eyes were missing and their bodies were covered in whip lashings. Not dissimilar to my own.

"Oh Trinity, protect these souls."

"I don't think the Trinity has been in this place in a very long time," Tharan said.

Roderick stood on the balcony of the ancient temple, spectacles balanced on the bridge of his nose, hand over his mouth, as he tried to decipher the ancient runes carved into the granite.

In the center of the platform an empty bowl made of copper on a pedestal sat filled with the remnants of the fire. Two indentations ran from the bowl into the maze of runes engraved below.

Roderick sighed.

"You can all guess what you have to do."

"Spill our blood into the giant basin that runs into the maze?" Caiden called back.

"You got it. It says: Here three goddesses formed an alliance, each one granting gifts to their loyal subjects. Only those with sacred blood may enter their domain."

The knot in my chest burned and I swallowed back the agony. "Let's get this over with. Whatever is in there we need to get it before Erissa returns."

My heart pounded and I gripped my dagger tight before running it over the palm of my left hand. I winced as I held my fist over the copper bowl. *Drip, drip, drip,* the blood fell onto the ashen basin.

Caiden and Tharan cut their palms too, holding their hands next to mine. The blood spilled into the channels before seeping into the runes.

"This better work," I said through gritted teeth. Both my chest and my palm ached but I couldn't stop. Not now, not when we were so close.

As the blood filled the runes the ground began to shake.

"Oh Trinity. What's happening?" I asked, taking Tharan's hand in mine.

"It's a stairway!" Roderick called. "The blood opened a stairway."

Despite the pain in my chest, a mixture of relief and fear washed over me. We'd done it. We'd found the Well before Erissa. Now all we had to do was take the magic.

I looked down to see the bricks of granite transform into a circular staircase leading to a dark abyss. The hairs on the back of my neck stood on end, whatever lay at the bottom of the stairs would come easily. I looked around at my friends. Each one of them risked their life to be here. We were so close to succeeding, I couldn't let my fears get the better of me now.

"Amolie, come with us. The rest of you keep guard. Don't let anyone in," Tharan said before scooping me back into his powerful arms once again. The knot in my chest began to pulse like a second heart. I took shallow, shaky breaths, not wanting to breathe too deep and have the knot unravel.

Caiden led the way using his lightning to light an old torch, Amolie followed behind. The stairs wound round and round deep into the earth. Caiden used his torch to light a fire which burned around the edges of the staircase, lighting our way. Pictures of the Trinity culling the land lined the walls. A gruesome site I had never truly pictured before.

We descended into the first chamber where a golden book sat upon a stone pedestal. In front of it sat a stained-glass window depicting the Trinity gifting the Fates their power. It seemed to be lit from behind, but surely no light could reach this deep.

Caiden stepped up to the book. "Three trials for three

goddesses. Only those who truly believe shall pass." He swallowed hard.

"Great, just what I was looking forward to," I said.

"There's more," Caiden said. "One for the wise elves, keeper of the eternal knowledge; one for the warrior sylph, protector of the realm; and one for the mortal human, to whom all things are more beautiful because they are fleeting."

"That can't be good," Tharan said.

The pain in my chest beat faster.

The sound of clashing swords echoed from above.

"Shit. They're here," I said. "We need to go. Erissa will be here soon. What does it say we have to do?"

Caiden ran his hand over the golden pages. "Prick your finger and touch it to the book." He took a dagger from his bandelier and pricked his thumb, pressing it to the page. The parchment absorbed the blood like a sponge.

Without another thought we all did the same.

The sounds of fighting grew nearer.

Blood raced through my veins. If we didn't get through this door now, we'd be trapped like rats.

"C'mon, c'mon, please open."

Scraping footsteps echoed from above.

Ammena, hear my prayer. We are your faithful servants. Please open this door.

Tharan squeezed my hand tight as the clanging of steel against steel grew louder.

Please, please, please.

Beside us, a wall descended, revealing a chamber surrounded by flames.

Before the door could fully open Tharan pushed me through, followed by Amolie, and then Caiden. As soon as his feet hit the dais, the wall sprang up trapping us in.

48 THARAN

FLAMES FLICKERED AROUND THE WALLS OF THE CHAMBER. The smell of dampened earth mixed with the distinct smell of myrrh. Tattered tapestries of ancient battles hung on the walls. A narrow stone pathway surrounded by dark water led to another pedestal where another golden book sat. Only this one was empty. Beyond the pillars two barred doors stood ominously. Overhead, a painting of the goddess Eris giving the gift of the breath to Arendir.

Tharan swallowed hard.

"Aelia, are you alright if I set you down? I think this one is for me, as I am the only elf here."

"Yes, the pain is better now that we're down here."

He set her gently on her feet before kissing her forehead.

"Be careful," she mouthed.

"I always am." He gave her a wink, then approached the pedestal.

The book sat blank on its stone stand. He turned back at Amolie, Aelia, and Caiden who stared at him with eyes full of hope and dread. "What do you think I should do to trigger it?"

"Press your bloody thumb to the book," Caiden said. "That triggered the last one."

Tharan did as Caiden suggested. The paper absorbed his fingerprint like it had before. Moments later, a message appeared: *Hello, Lord of Nothing.*

Tharan swallowed hard. The book knew his shame. What did it have in store for him?

The book continued, *I have been waiting for you.*

He tried not to think of the thousands of questions the book could throw at him. It knew he was a half-breed. Would it use that against him? Punish him for being only half an original?

"Perfect," Tharan said under his breath.

"Did it work?" Aelia called from behind.

"Yes, it knows who I am," he replied. "…Or at least who I used to be."

More writing appeared: *Answer my three questions and prove you are worthy to hold the power of Moriana in your hands.*

A quill and ink appeared next to the book. "It's going to ask me three questions."

No one said anything.

Question one: Name the three originals who received the Trinity's blessings.

Tharan thought for a moment. He knew the elven original, obviously, and his father was the sylph, but who was the original human? He'd never even bothered to ask. A pit grew in his stomach. He tried to think of his elementary lessons from hundreds of years ago.

"Anyone know the name of the original human who received Ammena's gift?"

Amolie and Aelia exchanged glances before saying in unison, "Alaric Rathmusson."

"Thank you." Tharan scrolled the names onto the paper.

Very good, fair king. You are smarter than they say.

Tharan rolled his eyes and tried to calm his nerves.

Question two: Where did the War of Three Faces begin?

Tharan chuckled to himself. Everyone on the continent knew where the War of Three Faces began, it was drilled into them from birth. He went to scribble the Winter Kingdom but stopped himself. It was called something else long ago. What was the name?

He thought back to his history lessons. His teacher, Lady Olinna, stood in front of him and Briar. Her silver hair tied into a knot on the top of her head. She wore a black dress buttoned to the chin, and the creases on the side of her eyes marked her as the oldest person Tharan knew at such a young age. Now if he could just remember what the name of the region was called before it was the Winter Kingdom.

"Think, Tharan. Remember your lessons." He shut his eyes, envisioning his lessons room. A map with the old boundaries of Moriana hung on the wall. He racked his memory trying to bring the map into focus, but where a name should have been there was only a blank space.

Again, he turned to his friends, ashamed he did not know the answer.

"Does anyone know what the Winter Kingdom used to be called?" he asked sheepishly.

Aelia cocked her head.

"You're the oldest one here. You should know."

"It's been a long time since I was in lessons," he said, trying to focus.

"Hylinia," Caiden said, matter-of-factly.

Tharan's chest tightened.

"Are you sure?"

Caiden nodded.

Tharan scrawled the words across the page, and they disappeared almost instantly.

Very good.

Tharan let out a sigh of relief.

Question Three: What was the name of the last dragon to fall from the sky?

Tharan gave a little chuckle at how easy the question was.

"You can't be serious."

I am.

Tharan scribbled the name *Borwin the Black*.

The words disappeared into the page and Tharan waited.

Correct, fair king, you may pass.

Tharan let out a sigh of relief, twisting one of his earrings nervously. His ears and cheeks felt hot. He'd only gotten one of the questions correct on his own. Some king he was.

The bars on the door sank into the ground. Aelia looped her hand through his.

"Good thing we were here, my Lord." She gave him a coy wink.

Tharan swallowed his embarrassment.

"Well, I can't be this devilishly handsome and erudite. It just wouldn't be fair to the world."

Aelia squeezed his hand, and they filed through to the next chamber.

49 CAIDEN

They entered a darkened chamber where, yet another pedestal stood bathed in light while darkness flooded the rest of the room. Fog billowed around their feet. Engraved on the wall overhead was a depiction of Illya slitting her wrists to give the sylph the gift of the blood.

Caiden took a deep breath. This would be his challenge. Tension pulled taut in the air as he stepped forward while the others stayed behind.

Pricking his finger, he laid a drop of blood on the golden page.

Hello, Lord of Lightning.

His stomach hardened. What did the Trinity have in store for him? Sylph were warriors. He'd definitely have to fight something or someone. But who would the Trinity keep trapped down here for an eternity?

"Uh, hello," Caiden whispered.

Are you ready for your trial?

No, but he didn't really have a choice. An electricity ran through his body, making the hairs on the back of his arms stand on end.

"Yes."

Very well. The sylph were created to protect the land from those who seek to destroy it. No other creature is more fierce or brutal. Therefore, only those who can defeat themselves may pass into the Divine Well.

"What?" Caiden said. A chill ran down his spine.

Good luck. The words disappeared in an instant.

The world around him went silent. He could feel a presence next to him and when he looked up, a copy of him stared back at him. Only this Caiden was more of a shadow than a full flesh and blood man.

Caiden cocked his head, and Shadow Caiden did the same.

Fear coiled in his gut. He would have to fight himself.

He looked to where his friends were but only darkness met his gaze. Could they see him? Did they know what was happening?

Shadow Caiden lashed out with his fist sending him flying across the room.

Shaking the stars from his vision he called his lightning to his hand, but so did his shadow. He gritted his jaw and struck out with a bolt, only for it to be met with a shadow bolt. Electricity crackled in the air. Whatever force Caiden put behind his lightning, Shadow Caiden met it with an equal force of his own.

He cut his lightning and got to his feet. Both he and the shadow stared at each other. Equally matched in every way. Caiden's chest heaved with ragged breaths. He would have to do this without magic. Gripping his sword, he pulled the weapon from its sheath. He'd forgotten how he'd missed the feeling of the steel in his hand and the Court of Honey had given him a fine light blade, perfect for quick moves.

The shadow pulled a sword of his own. Long and lean, just like the one Caiden held.

They danced around one another, taking cautious steps. Their boots clacked against the stone floor.

Caiden would have to plan his move perfectly. The shadow

would copy him, and he needed to make sure he could land the blow swiftly.

He ducked right. The shadow did the same. Then left, then right again. The shadow followed his movements. They came within an inch of each other and Caiden's blade sliced into the shadow figure's side, but as his sword found a home, so too, did the shadow's. A searing pain ripped across his abdomen, and he stumbled.

The shadow caught him where his armor was weak, just as he had caught the shadow. Was this how it would have to be? A cut for a cut until one of them died.

He let out a sigh of relief as Illya's healing magic sealed up the cut. Would it do the same for the shadow?

He tried to see if the shadow was healed, but darkness clouded his vision.

Gripping his sword tight, he waited for the shadow to attack. His heartbeat echoed in his ears. The Trinity had designed this trial to bring him to within an inch of his life. Only the strongest and most worthy would survive.

Out of the corner of his eye he could see something move. The hair on his arms stood on end. Instinctively he raised his sword just as the shadow's fell upon him. The weapons clanged against one another. Caiden grit his teeth, pushing with all his might against the shadow, only to be met with equal force.

Their faces nearly touched as their swords braced one another.

Caiden stared into the shadow's eyes... his eyes, before tearing his sword away. The shadow did the same.

Chests heaving, they circled each other again.

Caiden ran through his old training in his mind, trying to remember the moves he'd learned half a century ago. But how could he outsmart this creature?

The shadow lunged, and he quickly sidestepped the attack. There had to be a pattern. For the most part, the shadow mimicked his attack, while other times it attacked on its own. What was the cadence of these attacks? Was it when he was distracted?

He decided to test his hypothesis.

The shadow looked at him, blinking every time he did.

He took a deep breath and turned his head toward where he thought he'd entered. Sure enough, the shadow lashed out with his sword, but Caiden jumped back, running his own weapon through its shoulder, bringing him to his knees.

"Got you," he said, just as the shadow ran a dagger through his side. A hot pain radiated through him. He stepped backward, pulling his sword from the shadow.

An evil smile cut the creature's face in two, but where Caiden had square teeth, this creature had a mouth of sharp fangs.

He got to his feet.

Blood poured from Caiden's side. Why wasn't Illya's gift clotting the blood? He desperately tried to cover the wound. His heart pounded in his chest.

"What magic is this?" he wondered out loud.

The shadow did not answer. He only moved closer. Caiden stumbled back. He had to end this, now.

The shadow raised his sword to strike again, and Caiden blocked it. The sound of steel on steel echoed through the chamber. His body screamed in agony, but he couldn't let the shadow win. Too much depended on this.

He sucked in a breath, before kicking the shadow in the gut, sending him flying across the room.

Caiden mustered every ounce of power in his veins and lashed out at the shadow before he had time to think, sending two massive bolts of lightning hurtling into the shadow. The creature's body convulsed as energy radiated through it. Caiden could feel his magic dwindling but still he summoned more, pouring every ounce of frustration, of hate and anger into the being that was a shadow of himself. He couldn't save his wife. He'd lost Aelia. He would not let this specter best him. The creature shook uncontrollably, until finally Caiden stopped his lightning.

The smell of chard flesh filled the air. A macabre feeling washed over him. He'd killed himself. And part of him was glad. Perhaps this was the part that loved Aelia. Perhaps this was the part of him that had caused her so much pain. He could move on now and be a better person. Be the person she hoped he was.

Smoke smoldered from the charred body of his shadow self. He stared at it, taking in this version of himself—charred and crisp. A pit opened in his stomach, and he hurled its contents onto the floor.

"Caiden!" The sound of Aelia's voice echoed through the chamber. "Caiden, are you alright?"

She came running at him—a look of concern etched across her beautiful face. His chest lightened. She still cared for him.

"You're hurt," she said upon seeing his blood-stained hands.

Caiden's eyes flitted to Tharan, who stood stoically behind her, arms crossed over his chest. He did not want to get between the Alder King and his love, but he couldn't help but be pleased she'd been worried about him.

"It's just a scratch."

"Bullshit," Amolie chimed in. "Let me see."

Caiden moved his hand to let Amolie have a look at the wound.

"Take off your armor. I'll have to sew it up," she said, already reaching for a needle and thread in one of her dress's many pockets.

"Here?"

"Do you have a better option?"

He muttered a curse under his breath before removing his armor.

"Lucky, I have this." Amolie quickly threaded a needle and began to weave it through his skin.

Caiden set his jaw, trying to distract himself from the pain.

Aelia squeezed his hand.

"Amolie will have you fixed up in a moment."

Caiden savored the feeling of her hand in his, but didn't dare show it on his face. Tharan's jaw tightened at the sight of Aelia comforting Caiden, but he did not say anything. Instead, he moved to the book.

"What does it say?" he asked through gritted teeth.

"It says: Well done, Lord of Lightning, you may pass."

The room rumbled and a stone wall opened before them, revealing a darkened passage.

Amolie tied her thread in a knot, closing Caiden's gash.

"It will hold until I figure out what magic is blocking your healing. But don't do anything too crazy."

Caiden gave her a knowing look.

"Tharan, can you help him up?" Amolie asked.

Looping his arms underneath Caiden's, Tharan pulled him to his feet. Caiden winced in pain.

"Let's go, Lord of Lightning," he said.

Aelia gave him a small smile.

"I'm glad you're okay."

He smiled back.

"Me too."

Together, they walked into the next chamber.

50 AELIA

Flames flickered around the circular room. In the center, another golden book sat. I swallowed hard, exchanging a knowing glance with Amolie. Walking up to the pedestal, I pricked my thumb and lay a bloody print on the pristine golden parchment. The blood disappeared and a message took its place.

Hello, Traitorous Queen. Although you are not fully human… not anymore, I will accept your offering.

"Great," I said under my breath.

The humans were created to care for the land and so their bodies nourish the soil once they have passed. Their mortality was a gift from the Goddess Ammena in hopes they would treasure the small things in life.

You have faced many trials, Queen of the Dead, but this one will take you closer to death than you've ever been before.

A chill ran down my spine.

Before you lay six vials. Five are deadly, one is benign. Choose wisely.

The script disappeared.

I looked up to see a table spread with six vials of brightly colored liquid.

"Amolie, do you know any of these?"

"Uh, it's hard to say without smelling them."

I stepped forward and a wall of flames rose behind me, stopping Amolie in her tracks. I called out to her, but she did not respond—I was on my own in this.

Taking a deep breath, I tried to calm my nerves.

You've dealt with toxins before. You can handle this.

The knot in my chest whirled like a cyclone.

"Not now," I said. "I need to focus."

I picked up the first vial filled with a lavender colored liquid and smelled it. The scent of rotten eggs overwhelmed me, bringing bile to the back of my throat.

Absolutely not. There's no way this can be it. Anything that smells this awful will surely kill me.

I set the vial back in its holder and moved on to a bright blue one. The scent of salt and sea tickled my nose.

What in the water could kill me? Possibly anything really. Everyone knows the sea is filled with poisonous creatures. There was a story about how the soldiers of the Midlands would cap the end of their arrows with sea anemone poison. Could that be it?

The third was a verdant green and smelled of pine and sap.

Hmm... there are hundreds of deadly trees, but is there a specific pine that is more poisonous than others? Yew tree, balsam, juniper? Which one was it? The witches were said to use Ponderosa pine needles to get rid of unwanted pregnancies... but would that kill the mother too?

I capped the lid. This would take longer than I thought. Any of these vials could kill me.

The fourth was the color of sunflowers in late summer and smelled of sweet grass.

Surely sweet grass couldn't be deadly. I'd played in it all my life. But had I ever ingested it?

How was I supposed to know which one of these was poison

and which was benign? They all smelled of familiar things and nothing like any potion I'd smelled before.

Blowing out a breath I picked up the next vile. A bright orange liquid swirled within. The smell of pumpkin and fall spices burst into my nose reminding me of the harvest festival the Midlands hosted. I replaced the cork and moved on to the next one. A fiery red, the color of cherry wine. It smelled of cinnamon and winter snow berries.

How was I supposed to know which one of these was safe to drink?

I ran through the options in my head. Each of these trials had been tailored to us, so this one must be no different.

Starting with the violet vile, I sniffed it again. There was no way I could stomach drinking it, so I set it back down.

Running my fingers over the smooth glass, I tried to conjure a memory from each. What could the Trinity want to tell me?

My eyes kept going back to the red vial at the end of the table. The one that smelled of the Yuletide season. The memory of my family—my mother, Baylis, and Caiden, huddled around a roaring fire, exchanging gifts and playing games filled my heart with a longing for simpler days. I had yearned for freedom then—to shed the chains of my past and forge a new path with Caiden by my side. A breath slipped between my lips. Oh, if I'd only known what awaited me.

But holly berries are poisonous.

My eyes fell to the orange vial and smelled the sweet and savory scent of pumpkin and nutmeg. A memory of the harvest festival surfaced in my mind. During the harvest, everyone pitched in—rich, poor, or royal, it did not matter, everyone did their part to bring in the year's crops, and when all the grain had been stored, the vegetables dried or canned, and the herbs hung from the rafters, we danced and sang under the harvest moon to honor the Goddess Ammena for giving us such fertile and bountiful lands.

Baylis always judged the pie contest, where women from all over the kingdom would present their most inventive pies and hope to win the coveted title of "Best Pie in the Kingdom."

A tear streaked down my cheek. In my youth, I thought the harvest festival simple in comparison to the grand balls and festivals of the sylph, but now I yearned for its comfort—for the belonging I felt in the company of my own people. I sniffled and set the vial back down.

The Reaper carries a harvest scythe.

I pushed the violet and blue vials aside; they invoked no memory and therefore could not be the correct choice. That narrowed it down to four. The pine scent had to represent Tharan and the Woodlands, but what did the golden vile mean? A memory of Baylis and I laying on our backs on the bank of the river during hot summer days as children passed through my mind. Our mother would watch from the shore as we splashed and played all day until the sun set behind the clouds and our skin turned a deep tan. A simpler time, when we were free to be children, and our family was intact.

My chest lightened. This is what the Trinity wanted. They wanted me to smell the scents of my past… of my life and appreciate the beauty in it.

I picked up the blue vile again and breathed in the salty air. Nothing. Our kingdom had a sea border, but we rarely went there; only when we needed to take a ship to one of the northern kingdoms. Although… a memory rose to the surface of my mind. Something long buried. The feeling of the wind against my rosy cheeks mixed with the scent of salt water. The sound of waves crashing against the shore echoed in my ears. I was five, holding my father's hand as we gazed out over the ocean.

"What sort of monsters do you think are in there?" I asked.

"They say giant sea serpents hunt in the water. That's why it's so difficult to cross."

My little heart twisted in my chest.

"But you'll never cross the ocean, right Father?"

He squeezed my hand, peering down at me with his sparkling gray eyes. He looked so young, so happy, with his dark hair and square jawline. A far cry from the man I watched lowered into the ground. "Of course not, princess." He kissed me on the forehead before scooping me up into his arms. "I'm never going to leave you, and you can count on that."

I wrapped my arms around his neck, and he pulled me in for a hug.

The memory faded. A tear trickled down my cheek. Was I becoming soft? Setting the vial aside, I picked up the violet potion once more. A rotten stench leached into the air and up into my nostrils. This had to be it. All the other ones would kill me. This was the only vial without a memory, and a hasty person would immediately assume this was the poisoned vial and disregard it immediately, favoring one of the potions that brought back a happy memory, but that wasn't right.

Ammena protect me.

Tipping my head back, I opened my mouth and downed the purple liquid.

The taste of moldy eggs overpowered my taste buds and bile burned in my gut, but I kept drinking, forcing the disgusting liquid down my throat. It settled in my stomach like a rock, but I did not feel faint nor ill.

I waited, fully expecting the toxin to take effect, but nothing happened. My shoulders relaxed and I let out a sigh of relief.

The fire behind me dulled and died. Tharan, Caiden, and Amolie came running through.

"You did it!" Amolie shouted, throwing her hands around my neck. "How did you know which one to pick?"

"I picked the one without a memory," I said, only now noticing the whirling in my chest again.

"Good work," Tharan said, kissing my forehead. A heat flooded my cheeks.

"All in a day's work," I replied, relieved I had passed the test.

Behind us, another stone door slid into the wall revealing the final chamber.

We all stood silently, staring at our destiny… or our doom.

My heart beat wildly in my chest.

Taking Tharan's hand in mine, I took the first step into the next chamber.

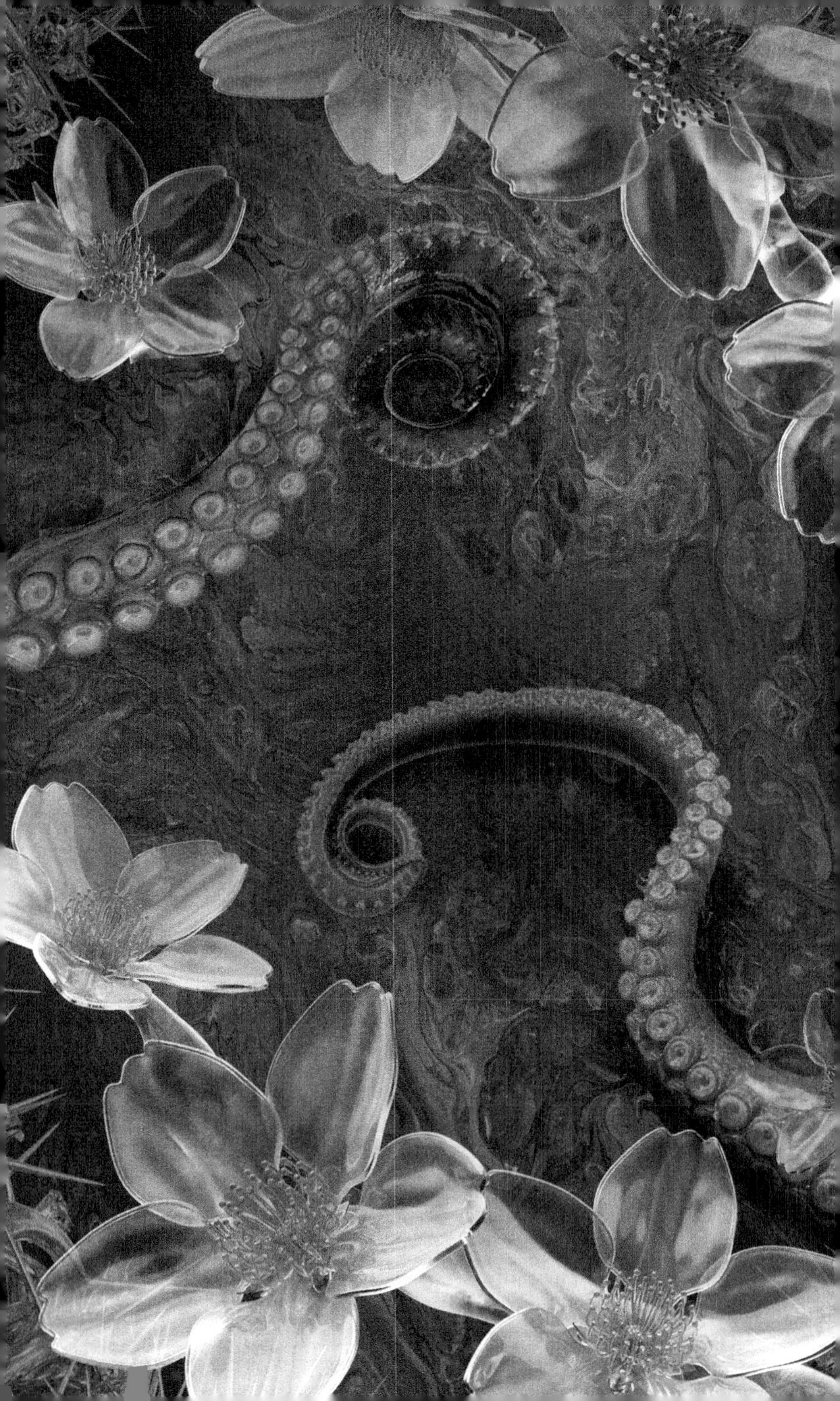

51 AELIA

Light poured in through an unknown source high above, flooding the chamber with an ethereal white glow. In the center of the room sat three giant statues of the goddesses of the Trinity leaning over a single flowing well, their eyes fixed on the waters below.

Another golden book sat open in front of the well.

Caiden, Tharan, and I exchanged knowing looks before reluctantly pulling our daggers from their sheaths and pricking our fingers, each laying a bloody print on the page.

Just as it had before, the blood absorbed into the paper.

We waited with baited breath for the script to appear. The whirling in my chest intensified.

Well done. You have passed my trials and proved yourselves worthy of the magic of the Trinity, but only one of you may reap the reward. Reach into the basin and claim your piece of the Trinity Stone.

"So, there's no actual well?" I asked, confused.

"No," a voice said from behind me, turning my blood cold.

I didn't want to turn around. I didn't want to see her monstrous face, but it couldn't be avoided.

Slowly, I turned on my heels.

"What are you doing here?" My words caught in my throat.

Erissa smirked.

"You thought your little band of warriors could stop me?"

Behind her, Baylis, Kita, and Alwin stood with their arms crossed over their chests. Their eyes narrowed on me, and I instinctively reached for Tharan's hand. I had moments to think of something. I jumped into Amolie's mind.

When we attack, run for the Trinity Stone.

'Got it.'

Ejecting myself from her mind, I squeezed Tharan's hand before letting go.

"If you value your life, you will leave now Erissa."

She huffed, tapping her foot on the stone floor impatiently.

"I've been dreaming of this day since they took Crom from me. Do you think I would really give up that easily?"

Rage boiled in my veins.

"You want to watch the world burn, for what? A man who didn't even care enough about you to ensure your safety? Did he love you in return, Erissa, or is this some fucked up way of getting him to?"

Her brows knitted.

"He loved me in his own way. Now, step aside."

"No," I said through gritted teeth.

She shrugged. "Fine, have it your way."

Tension pulled taut in the air. Baylis nocked and released her bow, letting it fly in Caiden's direction, but his senses were back, and he caught the arrow in midair, cracking it in two in his powerful hands.

Baylis swallowed hard.

"Now!" I yelled.

Caiden released a bolt of lightning while Tharan sprayed the group with poisonous spores.

Erissa threw up a shield, blocking our attacks.

The knot in my chest whirled faster, making a heat rise inside of me, like a burning kiln. Pain radiated through every limb. My breaths were short and ragged.

Amolie ran for the stone, but Baylis fired another arrow high into the chamber. I could only look on in horror as it found a home in her ankle.

Amolie tumbled to the floor, crying out in agony.

I narrowed my eyes on the ancient mage. My heart beat like a drum. It was always going to come to this. Just her and I. She made me this monster and I would repay the favor.

I launched into her mind.

There was no door marring my way. No set of traps to ensnare me, only a sea of stars met my gaze.

"I wondered if you'd have the guts to come here."

I whirled around to see Erissa as she had been before the potions destroyed her face. She wore her traditional white silken robes. Her long, red hair flowed in a wave over her shoulders. Her hips shifted from side to side as she approached me.

A chill ran down my spine.

"Did you orchestrate this whole thing to get me here, alone?"

She chuckled.

"No, this was just a happy coincidence. I knew you would show me to the Well." We circled one another. "I just didn't realize what was in your chest."

I narrowed my eyes. "You know about the knot?"

"I could sense it as soon as I entered the chamber. Morta was smart to hide something so powerful in plain sight. No one would've looked twice at a normal, human girl." She tapped her lush lips with her index finger. "But what I can't figure out is how she got it in you without killing you or setting it off."

"So, what is it?"

"You could call it a weapon of sorts."

"Of sorts..."

She waved me off.

"I can't be sure without examining you, but there were always rumors the Fates possessed the power to reset the world if they needed to."

"It can't be." Thorns grew in my throat at the words.

"It's whirling right now, isn't it?"

I nodded.

"Hmm... It must have something to do with the Trinity Well. The magic is loosening the knot."

I sucked in a shaky breath.

"I know what you're doing, Erissa, and I will not let you leave here with the Trinity Stone."

She clicked her tongue as we continued to circle one another.

"Oh, but I don't think you'll have a choice." Erissa pooled power between her hands before sending a ball of white light my way.

On the outside I had no real magic, but in here, I was the master.

Holding up my palm I blocked her attack, sending it flying back at her.

The bolt of magic lit up the dark space, hitting her in the gut and sending her flying backwards. Slamming into a wall, she slumped to the ground.

"You forgot I have power here," I said, carefully approaching her.

She dug her long fingernails into the stone floor, before pushing herself up the wall. A grimace graced her macabre face.

"This is my mind, child. You have no power here."

Erissa's body twisted and contorted in an unnatural way. Thousands of insect legs appeared from beneath her satin robe, and she grew in height. The linen fell away, revealing her bottom half to be that of a centipede. Her eyes glowed an eerie green and her teeth elongated into fangs.

I swallowed the fear rising in my gut. Two could play this game.

An evil cackled reverberated throughout the chamber.

Between my hands I molded the Scepter of the Dead and called upon the Morrigan.

Smoke molded into the body of the goddess. She wore her sacred armor with a raven engraved on the breastplate and her hair was woven into a long braid that snaked down her back.

"What the...?" She didn't have time to finish her sentence before Erissa was on top of her.

"You," Erissa hissed.

Despite being held down by the mage, a wicked smile twisted on the Morrigan's lips.

"I've been waiting for this for a very long time." Pushing Erissa off her, she rolled out from underneath the monster. Two long blades appeared in the Morrigan's hands. "You thought you could capture me and make me your war slave for an eternity, but our story ends here."

Out of nowhere, hundreds of ravens swooped in, attacking Erissa.

She thrashed back and forth swiping at anything she could.

Determination flashed in the Morrigan's blue eyes. She crouched low before bounding into the air, swords held high, releasing her wrath upon the mage.

The swarm of ravens clouded my vision, but the blood seeping onto the floor had to be coming from somewhere. The Morrigan was technically dead, could she die again?

Suddenly the birds scattered and the Morrigan went flying across the room, slamming into a wall and crumpling into a heap on the floor.

"No!" I cried out.

I turned to run to the Morrigan, but Erissa pounced upon me, clasping her hand around my neck. Blood streaked down her horrific face. Half monster, half mage, she used every ounce of her power to stay upright.

I gasped for the air I knew I wasn't breathing. Her arm trembled as her claws dug into my flesh.

"I wonder what happens when a Mind Breaker dies in a mind?" A fire burned in her green eyes.

"You need me for the other two Wells," I eked out, unsure if she even cared about them anymore or if her need for revenge would overpower her logic.

She gritted her teeth, hissing at me.

"I have your sister now. Surely, she got some of your mother's blood… although… whatever is in your chest could be useful to me." She pressed her finger into my sternum through my armor. "Yes, I can feel it. The magic wants to be set free."

I gritted my teeth. Pain ripped through me, hot and unrelenting. A blindingly white light blurred my vision. I had to make it stop. The magic would tear me in two.

"Get off of me!" I kicked her with all my might, sending her flying and releasing me.

She lay on the floor, hacking up blood, body fighting to stay alive.

A sense of relief washed over me. I had her—the architect of my demise. She'd tortured me for her own gain—watched as I endured psychological warfare from my husband, and used her goons to test my healing abilities. I'd wanted to snap her neck for five years, and now I had the chance.

Reaching out my hand, I used my power to pull her into the air above me.

A bloody smile crossed her face.

"What are you smiling at?"

"Oh, you'll see."

A chill washed over me. Something was wrong on the outside. No, I couldn't stop now. Not when I was so close to getting what I wanted. I squeezed my hand and Erissa clawed at her neck.

"You lie."

"I... guess... you'll... have to let me go and see..."

"Morrigan?" I called out, not taking my eyes off Erissa.

"Yes?" she said in a voice that was barely a whisper.

"If you're in here, where is your army?"

She coughed.

"They shouldn't have been able to come through without your orders."

A pit opened in my stomach. As much as I wanted to finish what I'd started here. I knew I had to leave.

I ejected myself from her mind. The chamber came into focus. The Scepter of the Dead lay in my right hand and the pit in my stomach filled with lead.

The bodies of my friends were strewn across the sanctuary floor.

Baylis, Kita, and Alwin were nowhere to be found.

A cough echoed through the chamber. I ran to Amolie.

"What happened?"

Deep down, I knew. Erissa touched the knot in my chest, and it unraveled. Not all the way, but enough to kill the two people I loved most. She knew my weaknesses and her ancient magic was enough to loosen the knot.

Tears welled in my eyes.

This was my curse: bound to be alone. Bound to kill the ones I loved. I was the Queen of the Damned, including myself.

"I don't know," Amolie said through a whisper. "Your eyes started glowing and then the next thing I knew light came shooting out from your fingertips. The others fled with Erissa's body, but..."

I looked at Caiden and Tharan lying still on the hard marble floor. My words caught in my throat.

"Amolie, what have I done?"

This was my fate. Why had my mother not warned me? Was she protecting me? Would I have to choose who to save?

"I don't think you meant to do it," she said, lifting herself up off the floor.

I went to Tharan. His radiant green eyes flitted up at me trying to make sense of who I was.

"Hey, beautiful," he said, blood gushed from his mouth.

I had done this. No one else. Only me.

"No, no, no, you can't leave me." Tears marred my words. "I don't know what to do without you. You're my rock. My life. My—"

The figure of a man dressed in all white muslin robes appeared before me.

"Aelia, let me take him."

"No," I said, pulling him tight to my chest. "You can't have him."

My attempts to save him were futile. His breath was shallow, and his eyes were shut. Soon his soul would be gone and there was nothing I could do about it. But I didn't want to let him go. I didn't want the only good thing left in my life to be gone. I'd lost everything, and this time, it was of my own making.

Hadron blinked slowly at me.

"You and I both know I must take him, as well as Caiden. I will give you time to say goodbye, but then I must take them."

My heart wrenched in my chest. How could I say goodbye to these men I loved so fiercely? I took Tharan's face in my hands.

"This isn't goodbye. I will bring you back."

He mustered the best smirk he could.

"Don't worry about me, my darling. I love you more than anything in this world or the next."

"I will bring you back," I whispered, my heart heavy in my chest. Tears trickled down my face. "I love you."

"I know." He shut his eyes, and his body went limp in my arms.

I laid a kiss on his forehead. My entire body shook with a mixture of anger and grief.

Hadron reached into his chest and plucked a ball of light that was his soul, before placing it in his satchel.

He was gone. The man I loved was gone.

Laying one last kiss on his lips, I set Tharan down and moved to Caiden, where Amolie was doing her best to keep him awake.

"Aelia?" he said. His whole body trembled.

Trinity, what had I done? I swallowed the dread rising in the back of my throat.

"I'm here, Caiden." I took his hand in mine, remembering all the times he'd been my port in the storm. Now I would be his.

"I'm not ready." His eyes welled with tears.

Neither was I. Not ready to let him go. Not ready to say goodbye. We'd hurt each other in the past, but none of that mattered now. Caiden loved me even when I didn't love myself. He'd forgotten and remembered me—found me at the edge of the world, and I would do the same for him.

"I will find you. Just as you found me." I gripped his hand tighter. "Hadron will take your soul, but I swear on the Trinity, I will find you and bring you back."

He nodded through his labored breaths.

"Aelia?" His blue eyes flickered with one last ounce of hope.

"Yes?" My chest twisted with an unbearable ache.

"If I don't make it back. It was a privilege to love you. You'll always be my princess."

Hot tears poured down my cheeks. My heart broke all over again.

"You were always too good for me." I tapped my nose in the

signal we'd given each other all those years ago. "I have always loved you. Even when I hated you."

"Aelia…" Hadron said, with a heavy warning in his voice.

"I'm not ready to let him go," I said, shakily. "Please don't take him from me too."

Hadron did as he had with Tharan and lifted the life from his chest. The light faded from his bright blue eyes.

"Aelia," Hadron said.

"Yes?" I sniffled.

"I know you won't listen to me, but do not go after them."

A fire burned in my veins.

"Trinity has no fury like what I will rain down upon anyone who dares to try and stop me from saving the men I love."

Rage burned in my chest.

He nodded and disappeared.

"I'm sorry," Amolie said, gently touching my hand. "But I have good news. I still have the Trinity Stone."

"I will get them back," I said through gritted teeth.

Gripping the scepter tight in my hand, I called upon the Morrigan.

The goddess took shape. Her wounds healed.

"Oh, what happened here?"

"I accidentally killed the two men I love, and I need to cross over and bring them back."

She stared at me blankly.

"You… want… to… die?"

"Yes." I couldn't believe the words coming out of my mouth. I had wanted to die so many times before, but this time was different. This time it wasn't out of self-hatred or pain. I wanted the men I loved back, and I would bring the underworld to its knees if that's what I had to do.

She let out a long breath.

"And how do you plan on getting back?"

"I control the Scepter of the Dead. There has to be way for me to come back through it. And if not, Amolie will bring us back."

I looked at my friend.

She bit her lip. Her normally jovial face awash with concern.

"I mean, I'm not an expert but, I think I could."

She'd have to. There was no stopping me now. I couldn't think about this any longer or else I'd back out of it.

"Great. That's all settled. Amolie will bring me back and I'll bring Caiden and Tharan with me."

"This is madness," the Morrigan said, her blue eyes going wide. "I've never seen someone bring two souls back with them."

Ice ran through my veins, but I pushed it aside.

"Then I guess there's a first time for everything."

The Morrigan shrugged.

"I will meet you on the other side, Commander." She disappeared back into the scepter.

Amolie and I stared at each other. There was so much left unsaid between us. We'd been best friends for five years. She'd seen me at my worst, and at my best, and now she would watch me die.

Bile rose in my stomach, but I swallowed it. Fear did not have a home here.

"How do you want to do it?" she asked. Her eyes downcast to the floor.

I could only think of one painless way to go.

"Got any poison on you?"

She nodded, pulling a vial of bright yellow liquid from her pocket. Hands shaking.

"The Kiss of Death from Pinky's."

I sighed.

"That will certainly get the job done."

"You don't have to do this, Aelia. I can find a way to bring them back." She grabbed my hands, shaking them, hoping she could hold onto someone who was already gone.

"No, you told me once, to bring someone back, you had to give up some of your life. I won't let you sacrifice yourself for us. Just do your best to bring me back, and I will do the rest."

She nodded, tears welling in her eyes.

"I love you, Amolie." I pulled her in close for one last hug, savoring the scent of honeysuckle on her skin. Memories of our time together flashed before my eyes. The lump in my throat grew thicker. A wail demanded to be released, but if I gave into it, I would surely not take the poison.

With one final squeeze, I downed the yellow liquid.

"I love you too." Amolie's voice faded into nothing.

The world went black.

**The Mind Breaker will continue in Book Three
A Queen of Death and Despair**

Want to discuss our books with other readers and even the authors?

JOIN THE AETHON DISCORD!

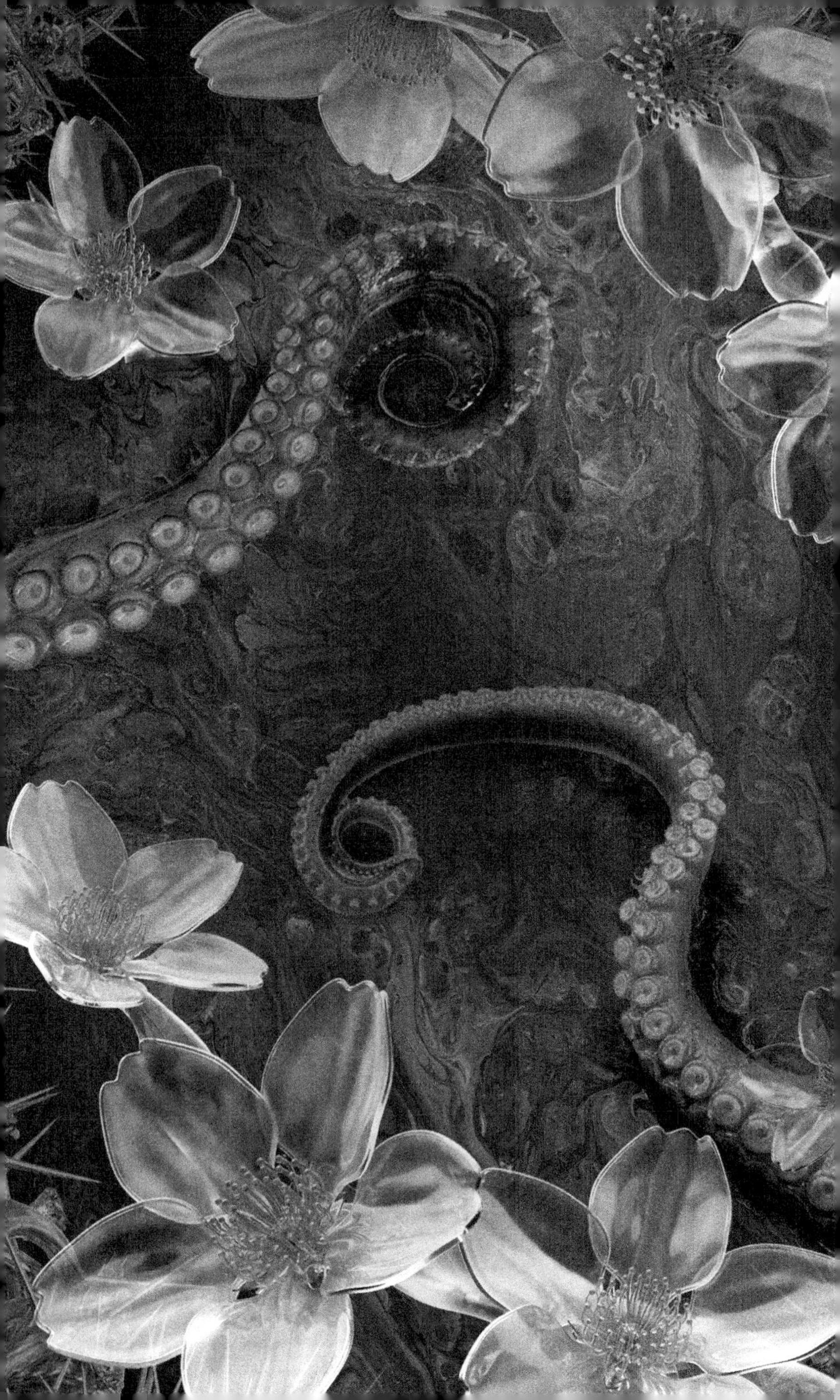

THANK YOU FOR READING A VOW OF WRATH AND RUIN

We hope you enjoyed it as much as we enjoyed bringing it to you. We just wanted to take a moment to encourage you to review the book. Follow this link: A Vow of Wrath and Ruin to be directed to the book's Amazon product page to leave your review.

Every review helps further the author's reach and, ultimately, helps them continue writing fantastic books for us all to enjoy.

Also in series:
A Curse of Breath and Blood
A Vow of Wrath and Ruin

Want to discuss our books with other readers and even the authors?

JOIN THE AETHON DISCORD!

You can also join our non-spam mailing list by visiting www.subscribepage.com/AethonReadersGroup and never miss out on future releases. You'll also receive three full books completely Free as our thanks to you.

Don't forget to follow us on socials to never miss a new release!
Facebook | Instagram | Twitter | Website

Looking for more great Romantasy?

A Fairy Hunter's Guide for the Recently (Un)Dead

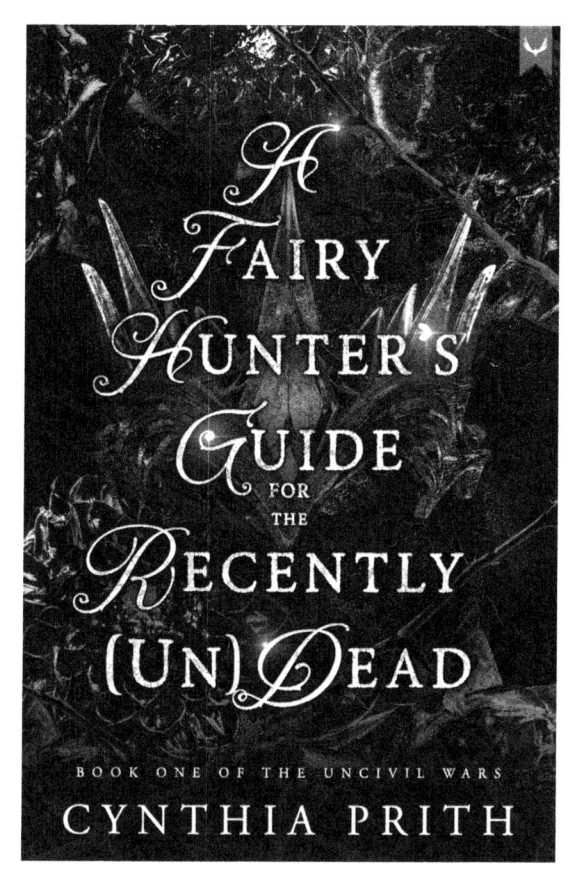

BOOK ONE OF THE UNCIVIL WARS
CYNTHIA PRITH

A fairy hunter desperate to save herself. A blighted knight hunting for his freedom. A looming war. Unexpectedly resurrected, Gwendolyn finds herself kidnapped by her mortal enemy: the fae. A distressing prospect considering her monster-hunting mother trained her to eradicate them. Worse, a bargain has been struck with the fairy lord on her behalf, and Gwendolyn knows too well that such deals always come with a terrible price. Trapped in the fairy lord's glittering court each night and banished back to her own world upon waking, Gwendolyn must find the terms of her bargain quickly if she hopes to survive and outsmart him. Yet, despite her inherited hatred of fae, the fairy lord is not without his charms. Gwendolyn struggles to resist his allure when every time they meet, he offers her anything she could ever wish—a bargain that would no doubt cost her entire soul in trade. She soon discovers the only creature in this twisted realm she can truly trust is a man as trapped as herself; a blighted knight made from the pieces of a hundred failed heroes. Cursed down to his literal bones, he cannot help but hunt her on his master's orders. Despite this, Gwendolyn's heart aches for him, his situation so very like her own. She knows, despite his insistence that she cannot trust him, that if she were to break his curse, they might actually stand a chance of fighting their way out together...

Don't miss this Romantasy debut where the monster hunting vibes of *VAN HELSING* meet the glamorous ballrooms of *BRIDGERTON*, in the Victorian style of Emily Wilde's *ENCYCLOPAEDIA OF FAIRIES*. Perfect for fans of *The Labyrinth*, *A Court of Mist and Fury*, and *Queen of Roses*.

Get A Fairy Hunter's Guide For The Recently [Un]Dead Now!

High stakes, gladiator battles, and second-chance romance collide in this steamy new adult fantasy romance perfect for fans of Heartless Hunter,

Bloodguard, and Gladiator. Four deadly trials will reunite them. One secret will tear them apart. **When a mission goes wrong and ends with her best friend dead, Drusilla Valerius is rescued by someone she never expected to see again: Marcus Scaevola. The only man she's ever cared for—the man who spurned her feelings six years ago.** Marcus should've known Dru wouldn't be the same woman he left all those years ago, and is he's unprepared for her distrust of him – and her uncanny ability to kill. But he has a purpose for seeking her out. Bound by loyalty, he convinces her to train King Cato of Anziano, one of the last countries yet to fall to the tyrannical Imperium, in the Valorem Blood Trials. Unlike years' past, the Imperium has a heavy hand in it, hiding beneath the guise of peace and unity between their two countries. When both Dru and Marcus find themselves joining the competition – Dru to take the place of an innocent and Marcus to protect the king – they're forced to trust one another with their lives. Now inescapably entrenched in the gory, duplicitous world of the blood trials, feelings long-buried surface, blurring the lines between duty and honor, love and loyalty. But Marcus carries a devastating secret—one that could destroy the foundations of Dru's world... **Don't miss this adult romantasy debut combining the second-chance romance ofHeartless Hunter by Kristen Ciccarelli with the deadly trials of Gladiator. With their lives and their hearts on the line, will love be enough to thwart the might of the Imperium?**

Get Trial of Bronze and Blood Now!

For all our Romantasy books, visit our website.

ACKNOWLEDGMENTS

As always, thank you to my husband who is my own version of Prince Charming. I could not have written this book without your love and support.

Thank you to my family who continues to support me even if my fairy smut embarrasses them.

Thank you to my writing group: Nicole, Crystal, and Arzu who helped me form what was a lump of clay into a sculpture. Especially Crystal, who manages to turn my vision into something amazing every time.

A Big shout out to my Street Team who made A Curse of Breath and Blood a success. I could not have done it without you. Thank you for loving my books.

And finally to all the ARC readers who took time out of their busy schedules to read and review my books. You are the real MVPs. Thank you!

ABOUT THE AUTHOR

K.W. Foster is the author of deliciously haunting and spicy fantasy romances featuring morally grey women and the men (and women) who love them. Originally from the Midwest, she now resides in the Mid-Atlantic with her husband and two big fluffy dogs. Follow her on Instagram @authorkwfoster, and on TikTok @kwfosterwrites

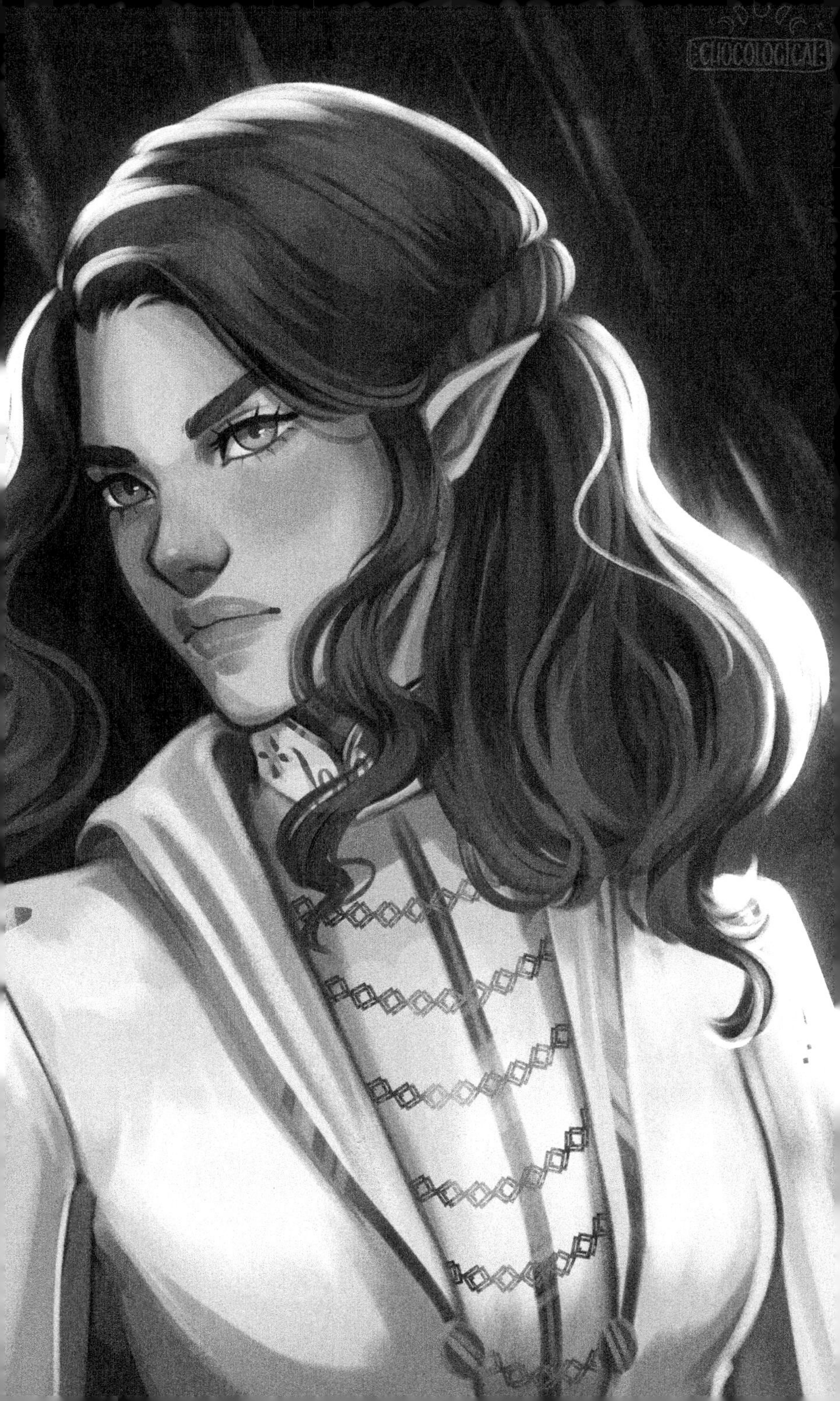
CHOCOLOGICAL

Printed in Great Britain
by Amazon